DARKNESS

By John Saul

·

JOHN SAUL

DARKNESS

BANTAM BOOKS
NEW YORK • TORONTO • LONDON • SYDNEY • AUCKLAND

DARKNESS
A Bantam Book / July 1991

Library of Congress Cataloging-in-Publication Data
Saul, John.
Darkness / John Saul.
p.   cm.
ISBN 0-553-07373-7
I. Title.
PS3569.A787D37   1991   90-25842
813'.54—dc20   CIP

DESIGN: Stanley S. Drate/Folio Graphics Co. Inc.

ISBN 0-553-07373-7

Published simultaneously in the United States and Canada

Bantam Books are published by Bantam Books, a division of Bantam Doubleday
Dell Publishing Group, Inc. Its trademark, consisting of the words "Bantam Books"
and the portrayal of a rooster, is Registered in U.S. Patent and Trademark Office
and in other countries. Marca Registrada. Bantam Books, 666 Fifth Avenue, New
York, New York, 10103.

PRINTED IN THE UNITED STATES OF AMERICA

BVG   0 9 8 7 6 5 4 3 2 1

For Tina, Brian, and Donna—
With Love

DARKNESS

PROLOGUE

Darkness wrapped around Amelie Coulton like a funeral shroud, and only the sound of her own heartbeat told her that she was still alive.

She shouldn't have come here—she knew that now, knew it with a certainty that filled her soul with dread. She should have stayed at home, stayed alone in the tiny shack that crouched only a few feet above the dark waters of the swamp. There, at least, she would have been safe.

She would have been safe, and so would the baby that now stirred restlessly within her body, his feet kicking her so hard she winced with pain.

But Amelie hadn't stayed at home. Now, huddled silently in the darkness, she could feel danger all around her, danger she knew her baby could feel, too.

Eyes were watching her, but not the eyes she was used to, the eyes of the animals that roamed the swamp at night, searching for food among the reeds and mangroves, creeping through the darkness, ever vigilant for other creatures even hungrier than themselves.

Amelie was used to those eyes. Ever since she'd been a child, the creatures of the swamp had been her friends, and when she was growing up, she'd loved to sit in the darkness of her mother's house, staring out through the glassless window frame, watching their bright eyes glimmer in the moonlight.

Often she'd wished she could slip out into the night with the possums and raccoons, joining them in their wanderings through the wetlands. But she never had, for always she had known that it wasn't only the animals who hunted the swamp at night.

The children of the Dark Man lurked in the shadows.

Amelie had never been sure who they were, but she'd known they were there, for her mother had told her about them, cautioned her to stay away.

"Dead—that's what they be," her mother had warned her. "An' if'n you git too close, they be takin' you, too, an' givin' you to the Dark Man."

So Amelie had always stayed in at night, never venturing outside, where unspeakable terrors waited in the darkness.

Until tonight, when her husband had silently left the house. She'd asked George where he was going, but he'd said nothing, only staring at her with his flat blue eyes—eyes that sometimes frightened her, sending shivers down her spine the same way it did when someone walked across your grave.

She had waited until he was gone, then turned the lantern down low and slipped down the ladder into her canoe.

Amelie had known how to follow him, for his boat left a stream of ripples over the still waters of the swamp, and her ears had picked up the sound of his squeaking oarlocks above the soft droning of the frogs and insects.

She hadn't known how far she'd gone before she saw the light of a fire in the distance, but when its flickering glow had first pierced the darkness, her instincts made her turn the canoe toward the shore, to creep silently forward in the deep shadows of the trees that overhung the water's edge.

Other boats had come, and she'd seen the people in them, though they had not seen her.

They were the Dark Man's children, prowling silently in the night.

They hadn't seen her, for as they passed her they'd looked

straight ahead, their eyes fixed on the fire that had sent her into the shelter of the trees.

But after they'd passed, and she'd seen their boats pulling up to the shore of the island on which the fire burned, she'd crept forward again, and now she could see them clearly.

They stood in a semicircle around the fire, black silhouettes against an orange glow, unmoving, as if the flames themselves held them in thrall.

She tried to tell herself that she was wrong, that her husband was not standing among this silent group, but then her stomach tightened as she recognized a shock of unkempt hair that hung almost to the shoulders of one of the thin figures.

Hair that she'd promised to cut tomorrow.

No!

It wasn't true. If George Coulton was one of the Dark Man's children, she would have known.

But how?

How would she have known him from any of the other children of the swamp?

The figure at which she stared, transfixed, turned slightly. Orange fire-glow illuminated his face.

His eyes seemed to reach out into the darkness, searching for her as if he knew she were there, concealed just beyond the wavering light.

She shuddered, shrinking low in the boat, holding her breath, afraid her own body might betray her.

The baby, as if sensing her fear, struggled within her, and she lay her hands on her distended belly, stroking the infant until he finally relaxed.

Her eyes remained fastened on the circle of shadows around the fire until another figure appeared out of the darkness, nearly invisible at first as it emerged from the trees and moved across the clearing.

A match was lit, and the figure held it to a candle, and then another and another. The flames of the tapers glowed brightly, and at last the figure turned, and a new wave of terror gripped Amelie.

The Dark Man stood silently in front of an altar ablaze with candles, his tall figure shrouded in black, his face veiled.

At last he spoke, his deep voice carrying clearly across the still waters. "Give me what is mine!"

A man and a woman stepped forward. As the light of the altar candles revealed their faces, Amelie gasped, instantly clamping her hand over her own mouth to prevent any sound from betraying her presence. She knew these two people, had known them all her life.

Quint and Tammy-Jo Millard, who'd gotten married a few months ago. Amelie had been with Tammy-Jo the night before Quint came for her, just the way Tammy-Jo had sat with Amelie the last night before she'd been claimed by George.

And yesterday Tammy-Jo had had her baby. Amelie was with her then, too, going in her canoe to the shack a mile from the one she shared with George, holding Tammy-Jo's hand and mopping her brow with a wet rag while Tammy-Jo screamed with the pain of her labor.

The pain Tammy-Jo endured had scared Amelie, but not half so much as the sight now of Tammy-Jo standing next to Quint Millard in front of the Dark Man, her baby cradled in her arms, its mouth fastened to Tammy-Jo's naked breast.

As Amelie watched, the Dark Man held out his arms.

"Give me what is mine!" His voice boomed across the water, the words striking Amelie like hammer blows.

Silently, Tammy-Jo placed her newborn babe in the hands of the Dark Man, who turned and laid the baby on the altar like an offering, unfolding the blanket in which it was wrapped, until its pale body was uncovered in the candlelight.

From the folds of his robes the dark man withdrew an object. Amelie couldn't quite make it out, until the light of the tapers reflected from it as from the blade of a knife.

"Whose child is this?" the Dark Man asked, the blade held high above the baby's naked body.

"Yours," Tammy-Jo replied, her voice flat, her eyes fixed on the Dark Man.

Though his face was invisible, the girl in the canoe shivered as she felt the Dark Man's cold smile.

She wanted to turn away, but knew she couldn't. Fascinated with the black-clad image of the Dark Man, she watched unblinking as he raised the instrument in his hands high, poising it over the tiny infant on the altar. The candlelight flickered, and tiny brilliant stars flashed from the tip of the instrument.

It began to arc downward.

It hovered for a moment, just over the child's breast.

There was a short scream from the infant as the tip of the blade entered its chest, a scream that was cut off almost as quickly as it began.

The glinting metal sank deep into the child's body.

Involuntarily, a shriek rose in Amelie's throat, a small howl of pure horror that she cut off almost as quickly as the Dark Man had cut off the infant's scream.

The Dark Man looked up, gazing out over the fire and the water, and Amelie imagined that his unseeable eyes were boring into her, fixing her image on his mind.

My baby, she thought. *He wants my baby, too.*

Silently she dipped her paddle into the water and backed the canoe away. But even as she moved noiselessly through the black shadows, she could still feel the eyes of the Dark Man following her, reaching out to her, grasping at her.

No.

Not at her.

At the baby within her.

As she turned the canoe, intent on fleeing into the darkness, she heard the Dark Man speak once again.

"George Coulton," the heavy voice uttered. "When will you bring me what is mine?"

There was a moment of silence before Amelie heard her husband reply. When at last he spoke, George's flat, expressionless voice was clear.

"The night he's born. The night he's born, I be bringin' him to you."

Kelly Anderson could feel his presence close by, feel him searching for her, reaching out to her.

He'd been there, usually hovering just out of sight, for as long as Kelly could remember. Even when she'd been a tiny baby, long before she could walk or talk, she'd caught glimpses of him.

In her dreams, his face would come to her out of the darkness of sleep, leering at her, horrible features twisted into a malicious smile, his fingers—the clawed talons of a carnivorous bird—stretching toward her. She would awaken screaming, and her mother would hurry to her, lifting her from her crib, cradling her, soothing her, whispering to her that she was safe.

Those words were the first she learned.

You're safe.

Safe.

Even now, at sixteen, she could remember speaking the word.

Safe.

But she hadn't been safe. Not then, when her mother had whispered to her that everything was all right, that she'd only had a terrible dream, and not now, when even wide awake she could feel him creeping closer to her, reaching out, reaching. . . .

For what?

What was it he wanted from her?

She knew nothing about the monstrous figure of her night-mares; had no idea who he was, nor where he'd come from.

All she knew was that he was there, never far from her. Waiting. And he wanted something.

Tonight, as Kelly moved restlessly around the small house she shared with her parents, she knew he was closer than ever.

It was an oppressive night, unseasonably hot for early June, the kind of thick, muggy night that hung heavily, threatening to suffo-cate her. She'd opened the windows an hour before in the vain hope that even the faintest of breezes might stir the air, might cool her skin, might even drive away the madness that threatened to destroy her tonight.

She knew that's what it was.

There was no man; there were no hands reaching out to her.

It was in her mind, all of it.

That's what she'd been told, first by her mother, and then by the doctors her mother had taken her to.

The man who pursued her, who skulked eternally on the fringes of her life, existed only in her own mind. She'd made him up sometime long ago, and should have forgotten him, too, some-time almost as long ago.

She'd talked to the doctor for an hour a week, and tried to do what he'd told her, tried to figure out why she might have invented the man. For a long time the doctor had insisted that it was because she was adopted, telling her that she was imagining a father to replace the real father she'd never known. Kelly hadn't believed him — after all, if she was going to create a father, he wouldn't be anything like the terrible image she saw in her dreams. And why wouldn't she have imagined a mother, too? Besides, she'd seen the man long before she'd ever known she was adopted, long before she'd begun to understand how different she was from everyone else.

Finally, when the nightmare man refused to go away, and she'd known he never would, she stopped talking about him, stopped trying to think of reasons why he might be there. Instead, she'd simply reported to the psychiatrist that he was gone, and at last she'd been allowed to stop going to the doctor.

For almost five years, she hadn't mentioned him at all. But the frightening image that haunted Kelly's nights had not gone away.

She'd stopped crying out in the night when he suddenly appeared out of the darkness of her slumber; stopped telling her mother when she caught glimpses of him at the veiled edges of her sight.

She stopped talking about much of anything, terrified that somehow she would slip, and her parents, or her teachers, or the other kids she knew, might find out that she was crazy.

For that's what she was.

Crazy.

Her terrible secret was that only she knew it.

But tonight it would end.

She stopped her aimless prowling of the house and went to the small bedroom that had been hers for as long as she could remember. The hot, humid night seemed even more cloying in the confines of the room, as Kelly glanced over the few objects that stood against its faded walls.

It was, she thought, a tired-looking place, filled with worn-out furniture that had never been any good, even when it was new.

Just like herself: tired, worn-out, never any good even to start with.

A few months ago Kelly had covered the walls with posters—strange, dark images advertising the bands whose records she collected but rarely bothered to play.

Another of her secrets: she didn't care about the bands, didn't really like the music, didn't even like the posters very much. But they covered the dullness of the walls, just as the clothes she wore—mostly black, decorated with metal studs and large ugly pins—were meant to cover up the aching emptiness she felt inside.

Except that Kelly wasn't empty anymore.

She could almost feel the baby she knew was growing inside her.

Where had it come from?

Could the man have put it there?

Could he have taken her one night, creeping up on her when she was asleep?

Wouldn't she have known it? Wouldn't she have wakened, feeling him inside her?

No, she wouldn't.

She would have shut it out of her mind, refusing to recognize what was happening, for had she allowed herself to experience it, she would have screamed.

Screamed, and wakened her parents, and then they would have seen how crazy she was.

No, she must have kept silent, must have retreated into sleep while the man took her. But she knew he'd been there, knew what he'd done.

She'd known it a month ago, when she'd begun being sick every morning, fighting not to let herself throw up, terrified of letting her parents know what had happened to her.

Last week, when she'd missed her period, Kelly had begun planning what she was going to do.

She wasn't sure where the idea had come from. But now that the time had come, and she was alone in the house, and had made up her mind, she had the strange idea that she'd *always* known it would end this way—that some night, when she could no longer stand the sight of herself, she would end it all.

She left her room, not bothering to turn off the light, and entered the tiny bathroom that separated her room from her parents'. She stood in the gloom for a few minutes, staring at the image in the mirror. Only half her face was lit, illuminated by the dim light that filtered from the hall. She could see one of her eyes—the eyes her mother insisted were green, but that she knew were only a pale brown.

The eye stared back at her from the mirror, and she began to have the peculiar sensation that it wasn't her own reflection she was seeing at all. It was someone else in the mirror, a girl she barely knew.

A stranger.

A stranger whose features looked older than her own sixteen

years, whose skin seemed to have taken on the pallor of age, despite her youth.

She saw a lifeless face, devoid of the joy and eagerness of youth. The face of the orphan she truly was, despite what the parents who had adopted her tried to tell her.

And then, over her own darkened shoulder, another image appeared.

It was the man. The man Kelly had seen so often in her dreams but only caught glimpses of when she was awake. Now she saw him clearly.

He was old, his loose skin hanging in folds, his eyes sunken deep within their sockets. He was smiling at her, his lips drawn back to reveal yellowing teeth.

Kelly gasped and spun around.

Except for herself, the room was empty.

She reached out, switched on the light, and instantly the gloom was washed away. She stood still for a moment, her heart pounding, but then her pulse began to ease. Finally, controlling her panic with the same grim will with which she had hidden her madness for the last few years, she turned back to the mirror once more.

He was still there, leering at her, his aged, ugly face contorted, the claws that were his fingers reaching for her throat.

"No!" Kelly screamed. "No more!"

Her hands clenched into fists and she smashed them into the mirror above the sink. The mirror shattered and most of the glass dropped away. But a single shard, razor-sharp and shaped like a sword, remained where it was.

In the bladelike fragment Kelly could still see her ancient tormentor, mocking her, laughing at her, reaching out for her.

Another scream rose in her throat, but this time there were no words. Only a final cry of anguish echoed in the house as Kelly reached out and snatched the fragment of glass from its frame.

Clutching it in both hands, she stared at it as if mesmerized, then raised it up. Now. Now the time had come. In one swift motion she plunged the blade into her belly, determined to end the life of the monster that was growing inside her.

End its life, and end her own.

"Well, that was a major waste of time," Mary Anderson sighed as she settled herself into the passenger seat of the five-year-old Chrysler. She regretted having said it instantly, knowing her words had been motivated by the heat of the Georgia night, combined with the five hours of effort she'd just put in doing her best to be charming to people she neither knew well nor liked. But it was too late. Before she could even apologize, Ted lashed out at her.

"It might not have been, if you had at least made the effort to be civil." He started the engine, slammed the transmission into gear, and listened with satisfaction as the tires screeched in protest before shooting the car out into the streets of Atlanta. He glanced over at Mary, ready to continue the tirade that had been building in his mind for the last hour—ever since Bob Creighton had told him that, despite his *personal* regard for Ted, there was no job available for him in Creighton Construction. "Personal regard," huh? It was bullshit, that's what it was. Creighton was going to give the supervisor's job to his own brother-in-law, and the hell with who was the better man! But that was what it always boiled down to—connections. It wasn't what you could do, but whose ass you kissed, or who you were buddy-buddy with, or—

His thoughts were interrupted as he felt Mary slip her hand into his and squeeze it gently. "I'm sorry," she said softly. As if she'd read his thoughts, her soothing voice went on, "If you ask me, he was never going to give you a fair shot at that job. He was always going to hire Elaine's brother."

"Then why the hell did he invite us over there tonight?" Ted asked. All the anger drained from his voice, replaced by a note of defeat that wounded Mary more than his rage had frightened her.

Her grip on his hand tightened. "Because he wanted to pick your brains. I figured it out an hour after we got there—all he wanted to do was find out how you'd deal with the marsh on that condo site. He knows where you're from, and he knows how much you know. And he didn't even have to hire you to get your advice—you gave it to him for nothing."

"Dumb!" Ted erupted, pulling his hand free of his wife's to

slam it angrily on the dash. "Why didn't you stop me? Why didn't you—"

Suddenly, in spite of herself, Mary started laughing. "Stop you! Since when have I ever been able to stop you from doing anything? Besides, you're not dumb—you're very smart. You're just too generous sometimes, that's all. You give away ideas that you could sell, and then wonder why no one wants to buy them. And don't argue with me, Ted—you know it's true."

When he remained grimly silent, she went on, "Please, Ted, relax. Stop worrying, and stop being mad at the world. You've always been able to find work before. You'll find something this time, too."

"Yeah," Ted groused. "And in the meantime, my daughter looks at me like I'm a total incompetent, and my wife—"

"Your wife loves you very much," Mary finished for him. "And if Kelly acts as though she thinks you're incompetent, at least she acknowledges that you're alive. In case you hadn't noticed, she's practically stopped speaking to me."

Ted smiled thinly in the darkness of the car. "Maybe you should consider yourself lucky. At least she doesn't tell you you're stupid when you object to pink hair."

"She did that three months ago, when she dyed it." Mary sighed. "Besides, haven't you seen the kids she hangs out with? Some of them have purple hair. And rings in their noses."

"What the hell are they thinking of? Don't they know—"

"They know they want to look different," Mary interrupted. "For most of them, it's just part of growing up. But with Kelly . . ."

She lapsed into silence as Ted turned the Chrysler into their driveway. She frowned, staring at the small house. Every light had been turned on. She should have been relieved; usually if she and Ted came home after midnight on a Friday night, the house was dark and empty. But tonight, even aside from the bright lights, she could sense Kelly's presence.

Sense that something was wrong.

She sat still in the car, making no move to open the door even after Ted had switched the engine off. Her feeling of unease was growing.

"Mary?" Ted finally asked. "What is it? You okay?"

His words seemed to bring Mary back to life, and she groped for the door handle. The door stuck for a second, then opened. She got out, moved along the cracked sidewalk, then stopped at the front door. She should have reached out and tried the knob—Kelly practically never remembered to lock it—but didn't. And when Ted came up beside her, she reached out to touch his arm, almost as if to prevent him from opening the door either.

"What is it?" Ted asked again.

Mary shook her head, as if to rid herself of the strange premonition she was having. "It—I don't know," she breathed. "There's something wrong. I can feel it."

A slow grin spread over Ted's face, and his voice took on a drawl that was even broader than usual. "What could be wrong? I got no job, and my daughter hates me, and my wife thinks I give the farm away." He reached out and tried the knob. The front door swung open.

About to go inside, he hesitated. Now he, too, felt a chill wash over him. His grin fading, he crossed the threshold. "Kelly?" he called out.

Silence.

And yet the house didn't feel empty.

"Maybe she's in her room," Ted said, hearing the lack of conviction in his own voice.

Mary, firmly putting aside the fear that was crawling inside her, moved past her husband, starting toward Kelly's room. But as she reached the hallway she paused, glancing into the bathroom.

She froze, her mouth open, an unvoiced scream constricting her throat. On the floor, lying still in a pool of blood, her face deathly pale, lay her daughter, a large, jagged fragment of the smashed mirror still clasped tightly in her right hand.

The scream died before it left her lips. Only a faint whisper emerged. "Kelly? Oh, no—Kelly—*nooo* . . ." She moved forward, dropping to the floor, staring helplessly at her daughter's limp form, and then she sensed Ted standing behind her. "Do something, Ted," she whispered. "Call an ambulance—"

A numbness seemed to fall over her then, and she thought she must be going into shock. No! she told herself. Kelly needs you! Don't start crying. Don't scream. Don't faint. Take care of your daughter!

She reached out and opened Kelly's right hand. The shard of glass fell away, breaking into smaller pieces as it hit the floor. Blood surged from the cuts on Kelly's palm. Oddly, the sight of blood streaming from the wound made Mary feel better, and then she knew why.

If Kelly were dead, she would have stopped bleeding.

Mary snatched a towel from the bar on the wall, wrapping it securely around the injured hand, then began tearing at Kelly's bloody clothes.

She found another wound in Kelly's torso, a deep gash. Kelly had clamped her left hand over the wound as she'd lain bleeding on the floor. Coolly, almost feeling detached from what she was doing, Mary pried her daughter's fingers away from the cut, then wiped the blood away from the laceration and inspected it for broken glass. Seeing none, she packed another towel against the abdominal cut, then looked up to find Ted standing in the doorway, his face ashen.

"She's alive," Mary whispered. "Did you—"

"I called the police," Ted replied. "They're sending an ambulance. I—" His gaze shifted away from Mary, fixing on the pale mask of his daughter's face, and his eyes flooded with tears. "She can't die," he whispered. "God, don't let her die. . . ." He sank down next to his wife and gently took Kelly's left hand in his own. Time seemed to stand still. An eerie silence settled over the house.

In the distance they heard the sound of sirens.

━━━━

Mary felt the ache of exhaustion as she stood up from the orange Naugahyde sofa in the waiting room of Atlanta General Hospital. She walked toward the front doors and looked outside to see the first light of dawn breaking. Had she really been sitting here all night?

No, of course not.

The Andersons had only arrived at the hospital after one A.M. For at least two hours Mary had paced nervously around the emergency room until the doctor—she couldn't even remember his name—had come out to tell them that Kelly was out of danger. The wound in her abdomen, despite how it had looked, wasn't deep, nor had the piece of glass with which Kelly had stabbed herself penetrated any vital organs. She'd lost a lot of blood, but the wounds had been stitched up.

She was alive, and she was conscious, and they had been allowed to see her.

With Ted steadying her, Mary had walked down the hall, abstractly wondering how it was that now, when she knew Kelly was going to be all right, she herself was falling apart. Yet when she'd thought Kelly was dying, she'd controlled herself, tending to Kelly's wounds, shedding not a tear, simply dealing with the situation.

They'd paused outside the room, and instinctively she and Ted had looked at each other. Until that moment, neither of them had spoken aloud about what had happened. Once again, Mary had found herself putting her emotions aside. When she spoke, her voice had been steady.

"She tried to kill herself, Ted."

Ted had shaken his head. "Not Kelly—" he'd begun, but she'd pressed a finger against his lips, silencing him.

"She did. That's why she's been so quiet. She's been thinking about it. And tonight, that's all we're going to do. We're going to think about it, but we're not going to talk about it, not unless she wants to. All we're going to do is let her know that we love her, that we're here for her."

Inside, their daughter lay listlessly in bed, her face pale. Next to the bed stood an IV pole, from which hung a bag of blood. A tube led from the bag down to a needle inserted into the vein of Kelly's right arm. She looked up at them, her eyes large and wary, like those of a terrified rabbit. Mary felt tears threaten to overwhelm her.

Her daughter was frightened, afraid that they were mad at her.

Mary controlled her tears and forced a smile. "How do you feel?"

Kelly licked nervously at her lips, and her eyes went to the bandage on her hand. "Okay."

"Do you want to talk about it?" Ted asked.

Once again Kelly's tongue flicked over her lips. She shook her head without looking up.

"Well, then I guess there isn't much to be said, is there?" Ted went on. Kelly shrank back into the pillows slightly, but then looked up.

"Are you very mad at me?" she asked, her voice quavering.

Ted was silent, and Mary could see his conflicting emotions passing through his eyes. Finally, he forced a smile. "I don't see how being mad at you's going to help anything. I just guess you must be pretty mad at your mom and me, and maybe yourself, too. But don't worry about it. Don't worry about anything." He leaned over to kiss his daughter's forehead. "Just go to sleep. We'll be here."

Mary stayed a few minutes longer, then kissed Kelly's cheek. "I love you."

Kelly made no reply, simply staring up at her mother with the strange, vacant gaze that Mary had never been able to fathom, a look that, at times, made her wonder if her daughter felt anything at all.

Tonight was one of those times.

Now, still standing in front of the glass doors, Mary heard a door open and close behind her. Turning, she saw the doctor from the emergency room coming toward her. She moved back toward the sofa, where Ted had risen to his feet, and slipped her arm through her husband's. The doctor glanced around the waiting room and, satisfied that it was empty except for the Andersons, motioned them to sit down. He dropped into a chair opposite them.

"Is Kelly all right?" Mary asked. "Has something else—"

The doctor raised his hands reassuringly. "She's fine," he said; then, as if realizing the inappropriateness of his own words, he amended them. "Given the circumstances, that is."

Ted leaned forward. "Has she talked about it, Doctor . . . ?" His voice trailed off.

"Hartman. Yes, she has talked about it." He paused, as if uncertain whether to go on, then seemed to come to a decision. "She seems to have been trying to abort herself."

Mary felt a sinking sensation in her stomach, and gripped Ted's arm, feeling his muscles stiffen under her fingers.

"Abort—" she breathed. "You mean, she wasn't trying to—" She hesitated, then made herself complete the sentence. ". . . to kill herself?"

Hartman shook his head. "I think it was both, Mrs. Anderson." His eyes darted from Mary to Ted, then back to Mary again. "I'm afraid your daughter has some pretty serious problems."

"Not nearly as serious as the kid who got her pregnant," Ted said, his voice dark with anger. "She's barely sixteen years old. When I get my hands on—"

Hartman's hands rose again, this time in protest. "Take it easy, Mr. Anderson. The thing is, Kelly isn't pregnant. I've given her a careful examination, and there's no question about it—as far as I can tell, your daughter has never had sex."

Confusion clouded Ted's face. "I—I don't get it. You said—"

"I know what I said. All I can tell you is that your daughter thought she was pregnant. She was afraid to tell either of you, and she couldn't remember when or how it had happened. So she decided to kill herself."

Mary closed her eyes, as if the act could protect her from Hartman's words. "Dear God," she whispered. "Why didn't she talk to us?" But of course she knew the answer—it was the adoption. No matter what she and Ted had ever told Kelly, they had never been able to convince their daughter of their love for her. Reluctantly, Mary had come to believe that from the moment Kelly had learned she was adopted, she had been waiting for her "real" parents to appear and claim her. And in the meantime, it was as if she refused to love them, refused to trust them. Her eyes filled with tears. "Why couldn't she ask us to help her?"

Hartman shook his head helplessly. "She's frightened. Frightened, and confused." He leaned forward, and his voice dropped slightly. "She thinks she's going to be locked up because she's crazy. She says nobody loves her, and she doesn't blame them." He glanced away, then forced himself to meet the Andersons' gaze directly. "What she said was that she's already dead, that she's always been dead, and that she just didn't want to pretend to be alive any longer."

For several moments neither Mary nor Ted said anything. Then, finally, Ted spoke. "What can we do?" he asked.

"Show her she's wrong," Dr. Hartman replied.

The jangling of the telephone made Carl Anderson groan softly and roll over in bed. The second ring brought him fully awake. He sat up, feeling a twinge of protest from his right hip, and reached out to pick up the receiver, at the same time glancing at the clock on his nightstand.

Six-thirty.

He should have been awake half an hour ago, and by now he should be dressed and in the kitchen, scanning the newspaper while he ate his customary plate of grits, accompanied by half a dozen sausages. "Anderson." He spoke the single word into the receiver in a carefully developed monotone that would give the caller no hint as to his mood: Carl had learned long ago that the less someone knew about how you were feeling, the less he could manipulate you. But when he heard his son's voice telling him what had happened the night before, the monotone disappeared. "Oh, Jesus," he moaned. "Is she going to be all right?"

"The doctor says she'll heal up in a couple of weeks," Ted replied. "Anyway, the cuts will."

Carl frowned, his eyes drifting to the framed photograph on his dresser. His son and daughter-in-law, with his granddaughter between them. He'd looked at the picture a hundred times since Ted had sent it to him last Christmas, his eyes always lingering longest on the image of Kelly, her pale face framed by the strange pink hair, her black clothes making her complexion even pastier by contrast.

But it was Kelly's eyes that always arrested his attention. They had an empty look to them, as if nothing in the world interested her. There was no sparkle to them, nor even any hostility.

Only a strange lassitude.

Ted's voice cut through Carl's momentary reverie. "Dad? You still there?"

"I'm here," Carl replied, his gaze still fixed on the picture. "What can I do?"

Now it was Ted who was silent for several long seconds. When he spoke, his voice had a reluctant note to it. "The job we talked about last month," he said finally. "Is it still open?"

Carl frowned. "What about Mary? You know what she says about Villejeune."

"That was last month," Ted replied. "After last night . . ." He left the words hanging, and Carl remembered again the problems he had always had in talking with his son. Indeed, after Bessie had lost her fight with cancer when Ted was still in his teens, he and his son had lived together in a peculiar silence, working together—when there was work—but rarely sharing much in the way of their private thoughts. But at least Ted had been there, his presence a comfort of sorts. It wasn't until his son had married Mary and moved to Atlanta that Carl began to feel the loneliness of his solitary existence. Then, five years ago, Villejeune had begun to change. Suddenly Carl's struggling contracting business had taken off.

With that early success, he had started his campaign to bring his son home. A campaign that, until now, had failed completely. The day Ted and Mary had left Villejeune, Mary said she'd never come back. She'd hated the town, hated the swamp, hated everything about the place. She had only agreed to marry Ted on the condition that they move away. And she'd stuck to her word. Obviously, though, everything had changed.

"The job's here," Carl said now. "I've got a lot going on, and not enough men who know what they're doing." He fell silent for a moment, then pressed his original question once more. "Ted, has Mary agreed to all this?"

When Ted replied, Carl could hear the strain in his voice. "She's not thrilled about it, no. But—look, Dad," he went on in a rush, as if afraid that if he didn't spill the words out quickly, he wouldn't be able to say them at all. "I haven't worked for a while now, and there just aren't any jobs. And with the kids Kelly's been running around with—well, we know we have to get her out of here, and there just doesn't seem to be anyplace else to go."

Carl felt a pang of resentment—it wasn't that they wanted to come home at all. There was just no place else to go. Still, he told himself, at least he'd have them here. And maybe, once Mary saw how Villejeune had changed, she'd want to stay.

After all, like Carl himself, and his dad before him, it was the place she'd been born. It was home.

"Okay," Carl said aloud. "Just let me know what I can do and when you'll be here."

"Thanks, Dad," Ted said. "It—well, it's nice to know I can count on you."

"Nothin' to it, son," Carl replied. "If you can't count on your dad, who can you count on?"

He hung up the phone and got out of bed. Hurriedly, he showered, dressed, and fixed his breakfast, but by the time he stepped out of the house into the damp, hot Florida morning, he was already more than forty minutes behind schedule.

Still, it didn't matter. He was going to have to see Dr. Phillips about the pain spreading from his hip, so his schedule was in the dumper anyway.

The important thing was that Ted and Mary were finally coming home, and bringing Kelly with them.

The heat was beginning to build as Carl drove through the village. Carved out of the Florida swamps on the northern edge of the Everglades so long ago that no one really knew when it had been founded, Villejeune had survived for more than three hundred years. Though it had had a few ups, most of its times had been downs, with the people of the town scratching out a living any way they could. There had been a few brief booms—the first during the nineteenth century, when there had been a flurry of plantation development, though the plantations had soon failed, cultivation overtaken by the ever encroaching swamps and marshlands. Prohibition had helped, for the lowlands had offered endless hiding places for small stills that pumped out moonshine night and day, and for a while Villejeune made a good living on the rum-running trade. The Florida land boom had followed, even reaching Villejeune for a few months before people had stopped buying land that was three feet under water. But when Prohibition died, so did the good times for Villejeune. For the next half century it went into a slow but extended decline, the cypress of its buildings slowly succumbing to the inexorable onslaught of the climate, while the people who lived in the buildings did their best to survive an economy as soft and treacherous as the mud beneath the swamp.

Then, a few years back, some people from California had begun quietly buying up large tracts of land to the north, outside of Orlando, and when their work was done, Disney World had emerged out of the marshlands. Suddenly the whole area began to thrive, and it wasn't long before Phil Stubbs, who had been eking out his living for thirty years by guiding adventurous—and very occasional—tourists through the swamp in his single leaky scow, had been able to buy a new boat, and then another and another.

Carl Anderson had taken one look at what was going on around Orlando, and seen that the boom would move southward. Acting quickly, he'd taken on partners and bought options on as much swampland as he could get. During the last five years he had begun exercising those options, draining the land and developing it into retirement communities. He'd started with a few small houses, but quickly expanded into condominiums. Already, a whole system of canals had been built, and even the smallest of his developments had tiny marinas attached to them. The larger developments allowed for private docks in front of rambling Florida-style houses, and the newest, his pride and joy, would include a golf course as well. As he'd expected, he had no trouble selling the developments—the weather was perfect for the retirement crowd, and a home in Villejeune all but guaranteed the buyers regular visits from their children and grandchildren. The fact that the kids had come to see Disney World rather than their aging relatives was beside the point. The point was that they came, and Villejeune was both close enough to Orlando to make the drive there easy and far enough away so it was still uncrowded and had a sense of its own identity. Carl wasn't certain how long that would last, but in the meantime everyone was making money for the first time in decades. Most of all, Carl Anderson.

Even the village, after its centuries of somnolence, was beginning to change. The buildings were being repaired and fresh paint applied to ancient cypress siding. Some new buildings had appeared, but Carl, as chairman of the Villejeune Preservation Committee, had seen to it that the new architecture matched what was already there, so by the time a new shop opened its doors, it appeared to have been there just as long as everything else. Indeed, Carl himself had come up with the idea of building these commercial structures with slightly sagging floors, so that despite their newness, they were all a little out of plumb, just as were their older counterparts.

Ted and Mary, Carl decided as he drove slowly along Ponce Avenue, were going to be surprised by what they found. Then, as Carl spotted Judd Duval lounging in front of Arlette Delong's café, his mood soured. Judd might be a deputy sheriff now, but as far as Carl was concerned, he was still nothing more than a swamp rat. And Carl Anderson didn't like swamp rats.

But that, Carl supposed, would never change. As long as there was a swamp next to the town, the swamp rats would be there too, appearing in the village every now and then, buying a few supplies, then disappearing back into the marshlands, to the crumbling stilted shacks in which they lived. Judd nodded to Carl as he passed, and Carl automatically nodded back, despite his dislike of the man.

A few minutes later the village was half a mile behind him, and as he pulled the truck into the parking lot of the small clinic that had been built only last year, Carl was relieved to see that Warren Phillips's Buick was there, even though it was Saturday. He parked the truck, wincing as he swung himself out of the cab. When he stepped into the receiving room a moment later, Jolene Mayhew raised one heavily plucked eyebrow. "Looks to me like you're here to see Dr. P," she observed. "Did you do something to yourself, or are you just getting old?"

Carl grinned at the nurse. "Come on, Jolene—don't you read my ads? No one gets old in Villejeune. That's why everyone's moving here. It's the weather."

"Right," the nurse replied archly. "Almost a hundred, with humidity to match. And we're barely into June. Gonna be some summer." She glanced down at the calendar on her desk. "Did you make an appointment?"

"Do I need one?" Carl peered exaggeratedly around the empty waiting room. "Doesn't look like you're doing what I'd call turn-away business. Maybe you should just close up shop and run away to Acapulco with me."

"And maybe you should act your age." Jolene tipped her head toward the closed door to Warren Phillips's office. "Go on in. He was supposed to take the day off, but you know him. Anybody needs a doctor around here, they always know where to find Dr. P."

Fifteen minutes later Phillips finished his examination of Carl. "Anything else, besides the hip?" he asked.

Carl, sitting up on the examining table, shook his head. "Feeling fine, just like always. Then this morning the thing started acting up on me." He watched as Phillips prepared a hypodermic, then stretched out and rolled over on his side. "Last thing I need right now is a bum hip. Ted's coming home and—" He winced as the needle slid into his hip, then rubbed at the sore spot when Phillips pulled the needle out a moment later. "Jesus. That felt like it went right into the bone."

Phillips grinned. "It almost did. Cortisone. The hip should be fine in a day or so. Now, what's this about Ted coming home? I thought Mary hated this place."

Briefly, Carl explained what had happened. Phillips shook his head sadly. "I don't know what goes on with kids these days."

"Well, if you ask me, it's not too hard to figure out," Carl replied as he pulled his pants up and fastened his belt. "The whole world's just gotten too complicated, and the kids get scared. But there's nowhere to run away to anymore, so they kill themselves."

Phillips looked doubtful. "You think that's what happened to your granddaughter? She got scared?"

Carl chuckled darkly. "Oh, I s'pose the doctors in Atlanta have a lot of fancy names for it, but when you get right down to it, I think she'll be just fine once she gets down here."

Phillips's frown deepened. "I wish I agreed with you."

Now it was Carl Anderson who looked uncertain. "You think I shouldn't have told Ted to bring her down here?"

The doctor shrugged. "It's hardly for me to say what Ted should or shouldn't do. But it seems to me that there's not much for Kelly to do around here."

"Maybe she's had too damned much to do in Atlanta," Carl growled. "You don't notice any of our kids killing themselves."

Phillips sighed. "There aren't that many around at all anymore, are there?" he countered. "This whole town's turning into a retirement center."

"Well, you can't blame the young folks for moving away. What were they supposed to do? The whole place was dying." He glanced at his watch, then grinned. "Well, not anymore. Can you believe me living my life by my wristwatch? Ten years ago, I was lucky to have anything to do at all. Now there's barely enough time to keep up. Speaking of which," he added, "I'm due for my regular shot tomorrow. Any reason not to have it right now?"

Phillips shrugged. "None at all." He turned back to his cabinet, picked up a small vial, and filled a second needle. A moment later he slipped it under the skin of Carl's forearm and pressed the plunger. "That's it," he said as he pulled the needle out and dropped it into the wastebasket. "That should keep you on schedule for a while."

As he left the clinic a few minutes later, the pain in his hip was already beginning to recede, and the vitamin shot—the one he'd been taking regularly for years now—was making him feel ten years younger.

Still, the fact that he felt as though he were going to live forever didn't make him change his mind about what he'd decided to do today. He pulled the truck back out onto Ponce Avenue and turned left, heading out toward the house he'd built for Craig Sheffield three years ago. As of this afternoon, his son would be a full partner in Anderson Construction Co.

In fact, he just might have the lawyer change the name of the company. Carl Anderson & Son. Sounded good to him. No, there was something even better.

Anderson & Anderson.

That was it—equal billing.

All in all, he decided, this was turning out to be a pretty good day. He was feeling great again, and his son was coming home.

Then he remembered Kelly, and his mood faltered. But that was going to be all right, too, he decided. Once she got away from Atlanta and onto the right track, whatever problems she had would simply disappear. Besides, he thought, his mind racing, there was even something he could do for her. What she really needed was a boyfriend. A nice kid, about her own age. Someone like Craig Sheffield's son.

Yes, everything was going to work out perfectly. By the middle of summer, even Mary would be glad she'd come back to Ville-jeune.

＝＝＝＝

Thirty minutes after Carl Anderson left his house, Craig Sheffield sat at the desk in his den, drafting the papers that would change the name of Anderson Construction Co., giving Ted Anderson the partnership Carl had ordered. It was, Craig realized, a sizable gift that Carl was giving his son. Over the last few years, Carl had become a very wealthy man. His net worth, Craig figured, was already well over two million dollars, and would rise substantially as soon as the newest development was well under way. And there was no end in sight, given the direction Villejeune was headed.

But even as he worked, Craig found himself thinking about the questions Carl had been asking him about his own son, Michael. Far more than the usual polite inquiries. Crafty old Carl was up to something, that was for sure. But what? Maybe he was thinking of offering the boy a summer job. Couldn't be. Carl's strict policy was to give jobs first to local men with families, and though things were improving, there were still plenty of men looking for year-round work. In fact, Craig was well aware that Michael had already asked Anderson about a summer job, and the situation had been explained to him. Nor had Michael been able to find work anywhere else. Everywhere he'd gone it had been the same story: "I'm just finally making enough to support myself. Maybe next summer, when the town's grown a little more . . ."

All very well for Villejeune, but for Michael the problem was *this* summer. If Carl Anderson could do something for Ted, Craig thought, then he himself should certainly be able to do something for Michael. Then, as he leaned back in his chair and gazed out the window across the lawn and the canal to the swamp, it suddenly came to him.

The swamp tour.

Phil Stubbs.

Why hadn't he thought of it before? Only last week Stubbs had been talking to him about a new liability policy. He was adding yet another boat to the tour fleet, and that meant more help as well as more insurance. Craig picked up the phone and called Stubbs. Ten minutes later it was all set up.

Craig left the den to find his son. Michael was upstairs in his room, stretched out on the bed, a pair of headphones clamped to his ears. He was leafing through a magazine, which he tossed aside as his father came into the room.

"I think I might have found you a job," Craig said as Michael pulled the headphones down to hang around his neck.

Michael frowned. "Where? In Orlando? I've already talked to everyone in town."

"Did you talk to Phil Stubbs?"

Michael rolled his eyes. "Twice."

"Well, try again. I just talked to him, and he wants to see you."

"How come?" he challenged, his voice suspicious. "He told me he has enough people already."

Craig shrugged casually. "He's putting on another boat."

"You pressured him, didn't you?" Michael shrewdly guessed.

Craig felt a twinge of annoyance. "What if I did? You need a job, don't you?"

"I should be able to find one myself," Michael replied, flushing. "How am I supposed to feel, knowing the only reason he hired me is because you conned him into it?"

Craig felt his temper rising. "How are you going to feel when you can't use that motorcycle your mom and I let you talk us into buying for you? You know the deal—you pay the upkeep and insurance, or you lose the bike. If I were you, I'd be on my feet getting ready to go talk to Stubbs, instead of lying on that bed, arguing with your father."

Michael's flush deepened, but he scrambled off the bed, pulling the earphones off his neck and dropping them onto the nightstand. "I didn't mean I wouldn't go—" he began, but his father cut him off.

"You're right," he snapped. "You *will* go, and you'll take whatever job Stubbs offers you, and you'll do it well. Christ, with your attitude, no wonder no one wanted to hire you." Turning away before his son could respond, Craig left the room.

Alone, Michael stripped off the torn jeans he'd donned that morning and pulled a clean pair of chinos off a hanger in his closet. He ran his eye over the row of shirts, then grinned, pulling out one he'd talked his mother into ordering through a catalog. It had been advertised as an expedition shirt, and had four pockets on the front, one on each sleeve, and epaulets. Until today, he'd only worn the shirt once, putting it away after someone at school had cracked that he was too skinny to try to look like a movie star. But the shirt seemed right if he was really going to work on the swamp tour.

Dressed, he went into the bathroom, washed his face, then began combing the unruly shock of blond hair that never seemed to want to stay where he put it. He brushed at it, then began working on it with his comb. A single lock kept falling down over his forehead, and after trying three times to make it stay up, he gave up, deciding to let it lie. He was about to turn away from the mirror when he saw a flicker of movement.

He froze, willing it to go away, but knowing it wouldn't.

Instead, as his eyes remained fixed on the glass, an image slowly began to take shape over his shoulder.

A face.

The face of an old man, with red, rheumy eyes peering at him out of deeply sunken sockets.

Instinctively, Michael closed his eyes against the image, but when he opened them again, the face was still there.

Now he could see the old man's hands reaching out toward him, as if to grasp him.

His breath caught in his throat, and he felt his heart begin to pound, but suddenly the door flew open and his six-year-old sister Jenny glared at him, her fists firmly planted on her hips.

"Mom says you're not supposed to stay in here more than ten minutes," she said.

Michael's eyes shifted from the mirror to his sister, but for a moment he didn't trust himself to speak, afraid his voice would betray the fear inside him. "If you have to go, there's a bathroom downstairs," he finally countered.

"But I want to use this one," Jenny complained. "It's not just yours. It's both of ours, and I have just as much right to—"

"Fine," Michael said. "There's the toilet. Go ahead and use it while I finish combing my hair. I don't care."

Jenny's eyes widened with outrage. "I'm going to tell Mom what you said!"

Michael moved to the door, lifted his sister up and put her down in the hall, then closed the door in her face, locking it. As he went back to the sink, Jenny began pounding on the door, wailing indignantly.

Michael, ignoring the pounding and the shouts, gazed into the mirror once again.

The strange image was gone. All that he saw now was his own reflection.

But where had the image come from? Had it really been there at all?

He wasn't sure.

But it wasn't the first time he'd seen it.

Indeed, he couldn't really remember when he'd first seen it. For a long time, it had happened so rarely that often he'd forgotten all about it. But now it seemed to be happening more frequently.

Sometimes he'd barely catch a glimpse of the face; it would be no more than a flicker in the mirror.

Other times he'd see it in his dreams, and wake up frightened.

Recently, he'd begun seeing the face more clearly, and more often.

For a while he'd tried to convince himself the house was haunted. Once, he'd even talked to his mother about it. She'd listened to him, but in the end she'd laughed it off.

"As far as I know, new houses don't get haunted. First you have to have someone die—preferably get murdered. And unless you've killed someone and not told me about it, that hasn't happened here."

He'd argued with her a little, but not much, because the more he'd talked about it, the more stupid the whole thing had sounded. And yet, the face seemed to be coming to him more and more lately.

He studied the mirror for a few seconds, now consciously willing the image to reappear, as if to convince himself that the specter existed only in his own imagination. But except for his own face, the mirror reflected only white, shiny tile.

Leaving the bathroom to Jenny, he hurried down the stairs and out into the heat of the morning. But as he started toward the garage and his motorcycle, he glanced back at the house.

What was the truth of face he'd seen in the mirror?

Was it in the house, or was it in his own mind?

As he mounted his bike and rode away, he decided that he didn't really want to know the answer to his own question, for one answer was as frightening as the other.

elly Anderson sat silently in the backseat of the Chrysler, staring unseeingly out the window. Though the scenery had slowly changed from the red earth and pine trees of Georgia to the marshy flatland of Florida, Kelly had been unaware of it. Her thoughts had been turned inward, remembering the two weeks she'd spent in the hospital.

She hadn't needed to be there—her wounds had healed quickly, and even the stitches in her stomach had been removed after only a week. What they'd really been trying to do was to figure out if she was crazy. She'd convinced them she wasn't, although she herself wasn't at all sure it was true. But the idea of being locked up in a hospital somewhere had terrified her even more than the image of the old man that she'd seen in the bathroom mirror the night she'd tried to kill herself, so instead of telling the psychiatrist about it, she'd made up a story. And the story wasn't really a lie, because she *had* been worried about her father not working, and she *had* felt she could never do anything right. So when she told them she'd just decided that maybe it would be easier for everyone if she weren't around anymore, they'd believed her.

She hadn't told them about the nightmare man—she knew better than that.

She'd talked her way out of telling Dr. Hartman about thinking she was pregnant, too. That hadn't been too hard—she just said she'd been feeling really bad lately, and when she missed her period, she automatically thought she must be pregnant. She even claimed she'd been drinking with some friends one night, didn't remember what had happened, and just assumed she must have gone to bed with someone. That part hadn't been true at all—she hated the taste of liquor—but they'd believed her.

And they hadn't locked her up.

They sent her home instead, and a week later her mother told her they were moving to Villejeune.

There'd been a long story about the job her grandfather had found for her father, but Kelly knew it wasn't true. Or even if it was, it still wasn't the real reason they were moving.

What they really wanted to do was get her out of Atlanta, and away from her friends.

Her friends, she thought hollowly. It was kind of funny, really, since she never thought of the kids in her crowd as friends. They were just other kids, people to hang out with so she wouldn't have to be by herself all the time. She never really talked to any of them very much.

If she had, they might have found out how crazy she really was.

Maybe she should have let them lock her up after all. At least that way her mother wouldn't have had to move back to Villejeune. She recalled her mother's words, last week: "I always hated it. It always felt like everyone there was just waiting to die. Nothing ever changed, nothing ever happened. And it wasn't just me. A lot of the other kids felt the same way. Most of us could hardly wait to get out, and a lot of us did. There wasn't any reason to stay—Villejeune was just like all those other little towns on the edge of the swamp. Nobody had any ambition, nobody had any dreams." Then, as Kelly watched, her mother's eyes had wandered over the fading wallpaper in their living room, taking in the worn furniture they'd never been able to replace. She'd sighed, and smiled wanly at Kelly. "Well, I guess my dreams never came true, did they? And your father says the town's changed, so maybe it's time I gave it another chance." She'd fallen silent, as if trying to convince herself that she believed what she was saying, and then she brightened, though Kelly had seen her force the smile onto her lips. "Anyway, it's time for you to have a change, isn't it? Meet some new people, make new friends! It'll be fun." The words had struck Kelly like tiny knives. An overwhelming sense of guilt had descended on her.

It was her fault that her mother had to go back.

"Well, for heaven's sake, will you look at that?"

The words from the front seat startled Kelly out of her reverie. She sat up, focusing for the first time on the landscape beyond the confines of the car, as her father slowed the Chrysler. Ahead of them on the highway was a large billboard, featuring a panoramic vista of a golf course and marina, dotted with houses and condominium units. In bold letters above and below the scene, the legend proclaimed:

VILLEJEUNE LINKS ESTATES

ANOTHER PROJECT FOR GRACIOUS LIVING

FROM ANDERSON & ANDERSON

Kelly stared at the sign, uncertain what it meant. Then she heard her father's voice.

"Do you believe it? He never said a word. He just said to keep an eye out for a new project he was starting."

"But—" Mary began, her words instantly drowned out by Ted's delighted laugh.

"He went all the way! He didn't just give me a job. He made me his partner!" He stepped hard on the gas pedal, and the car lunged forward. And when her mother turned to look back at the sign through the rear window, her eyes fell on Kelly.

She winked.

"Maybe this is going to work out after all," she said. "It's starting to look like Villejeune might not be quite the town I remember."

This time, there was nothing forced in her mother's words, and for the first time since the night she'd tried to kill herself, Kelly truly felt better.

Ten minutes later the Chrysler came to a stop in front of Carl Anderson's house. For several long moments Ted, Mary, and Kelly simply stared at it. Ted finally broke the silence: "Not much like the house I grew up in, is it?"

Mary shook her head, but her eyes remained fixed on a large split-level structure that sat well back from the road on an acre of landscaped grounds. There was a wide front porch, with bougainvillea climbing a trellis, and the front of the house was banked with a profusion of azaleas and jasmine. The expanse of lawn was broken by several clumps of palm trees, and near the house were two large magnolias that—judging from their size alone—must have been transplanted from somewhere else. As for the house itself, it had to be at least four thousand square feet, and though its lines were modern, the architect had softened the structure with a shake roof, so that despite its broad expanses of glass, it had a cozy look to it. Beyond the house she could see the canal that drained the property. There was even a small dock with a motorboat tied up to it.

An image flicked through Mary's mind of the house Ted and his father had lived in when she had first started dating him. A tiny, two-bedroom affair, smaller even than the house they had just left in Atlanta, the Anderson place had always seemed on the verge of collapse, no matter how hard Carl had worked to keep it in repair. The repairs back then had been makeshift, for Carl's work had been so sporadic that he'd never dared spend the money it would have taken to put the old house to rights.

And now—this.

The front door opened, and Carl Anderson strode out. Crossing the lawn as the occupants of the Chrysler scrambled out, he ignored Ted and Mary as he wrapped Kelly in a bear hug. "So you finally decided to come see your old grandpa, huh?" he asked. Before she could answer, he held her away. "Let me look at you."

Kelly felt a wave of self-consciousness, and tried to resist the urge to hide her right hand behind her back, with its still-visible scars as an ever-present reminder of what she'd done. Then she braced herself for whatever her grandfather might say about her pink hair and her black clothes. But instead of criticizing her, he only grinned. "I always wondered what pink hair would look like. It's not so bad. Pink and black was real big back in the fifties, you know."

Kelly felt the unfamiliar sensation of a smile playing at the corners of her mouth. "Mom and Dad hate it," she blurted out without thinking.

"Of course they do," Carl replied. "That's what parents are for. Half their job is to disapprove of their kids. Hell, when your dad was your age, I barely even spoke to him. Now, why don't you go up and take a look at your room. It's the big one above the garage." Kelly's eyes shifted back to the house and the windows above the three-car garage. Even from here she could see that the room went all the way through to the back of the house; and through the sheer curtains, she was certain she saw the blades of a ceiling fan. Suddenly she remembered all the hot nights she'd spent in her tiny room in Atlanta, sweltering in the still air despite the fact that she always kept the window wide open. As her grandfather turned his attention to her parents, she started across the lawn.

Maybe, just maybe, things were going to be all right after all.

———

Dusk was gathering, and Michael Sheffield was getting ready to close up the swamp tour. Everyone else—even Phil Stubbs—had already left, for after the first week it had been apparent to Stubbs that despite the pressure he'd been put under to hire Michael, the boy was the best worker he had. For the first two weeks, before school had let out, Michael had shown up every day promptly at three-thirty, and had not only done what he'd been told, but looked for additional work to do as well. The second day, when Stubbs had told him it was quitting time, Michael had shaken his head. When he'd been feeding the nutrias, he noticed that one of the furry little rodents was about to give birth to a litter, and he was in the process of fixing her a special nest away from the rest of the exhibit. "She'll get nervous with all the people watching her," he'd explained. "I'll just fix her up a box in the storeroom, and after a couple of weeks maybe we can set up a special cage for the babies. Sort of like a children's zoo.''

Stubbs had shrugged disinterestedly and let Michael do what he wanted, pretty much forgetting about the whole thing within a few days. But two weeks later Michael had stayed late again, and the next morning Stubbs had found a whole new exhibit next to the nutria cage. Inside a glass-fronted box were the new mother and her babies, who were now tumbling around like puppies. All around the box Michael had placed a series of neatly-lettered signs describing the life cycle of the little animals, from the period of their gestation to their expected life span, explaining what they ate and what their economic value was, as well as a clear description of their place in the ecosystem of the swamp. Stubbs had frowned at the exhibit, wondering why Michael had bothered with it, but that day he'd noticed that the baby nutrias had attracted more attention than any of the other cages at the headquarters, and on the tours that afternoon, people seemed more interested in the nutrias than the alligators.

By the third week Stubbs had stopped bothering to tell Michael what to do, since the boy was always busy and invariably stayed late, usually saying only, ''There's a couple things I still need to do.'' The next morning Stubbs would find another of the animal exhibits revamped, or new docking lines on the boats, or a fresh coat of paint on whatever had started looking shabby. By now it was simply assumed that Michael would be the last to leave, and that whatever anyone else forgot to do, he would take care of.

For Michael, the job was the closest thing he could imagine to paradise.

He'd always known there was something different about him, something that separated him from the other kids.

At first, when he was Jenny's age, he'd tried to be like them, tried to join in the spontaneous play of the rest of the children his age.

But his classmates seemed to sense that Michael was somehow different, and as he'd grown up, he had yet to make a genuine friend, yet to find one single person whom he felt he could tell about the peculiar emptiness that yawned inside him like a vast chasm threatening to swallow him up.

Over the years, he'd learned to pretend that he was like everyone else, laughing at the other kids' jokes, pretending to have emotions he didn't quite feel.

And as long as he could remember, he'd been fascinated with the swamp and everything in it. By the time he was ten, and he'd begun to accept the fact that he was never going to make any real friends, he started going out into the wilderness by himself, poking around among the bayous, watching the animals and identifying the plants. To him, there'd never been anything frightening about the marshes and bogs, nor had he ever gotten lost. Although he knew that for most people the waterways—and the endless tiny islands they surrounded—were a confusing, even frightening, maze, he saw each island as an individual. He knew every bend in the bayous.

Now, thanks to his father, he was being paid to spend even more time in the swamp, with its profusion of fascinating wildlife.

This evening he'd decided to go frog hunting. The big bullfrogs were peaking this time of year, and he'd already set up a terrarium to hold half a dozen large ones. If he was lucky, he might even still find an egg mass. Then he would be able to set up an entire life-cycle exhibit. Taking a large bucket with a mesh cover, and a flashlight, he got into a rowboat and set out, handling the oars expertly and silently, so that the little boat slid through the swamp without disturbing anything around it. Within a few minutes the dense vegetation closed around him, and his ears throbbed with the soft symphony orchestrated by the insects and frogs that teemed in the wetlands.

Then, slowly, he began to hear another sound, a sound that seemed to beckon to him. Obeying the call that drifted out of the swamp's depths, he pulled a little harder on the oars.

The boat slid faster through the water . . .

———

Kelly sprawled across the bed in her new room and stared for a moment at the large fan that turned slowly above her. Enjoying the feel of its breeze on her skin, she looked around the room once more, still scarcely able to believe it was hers. It had windows on three sides, and her very own bathroom in one corner. And the best part was that there were two doors—one leading to the rest of the house, the other opening onto a small deck with a flight of stairs down to the backyard. Her grandfather had told her that it was supposed to be a guest room, but since it had turned out that he rarely had guests, he'd decided it should be hers. "Girls your age need their own bathroom," he'd told her. "That way you can spread all your junk around without getting in anyone's way. But no sneaking out at night," he'd added, glancing meaningfully toward the door to the deck. "I wouldn't want your mom to make me nail that shut."

Kelly had blushed, wondering if her grandfather had actually been able to read her mind, and promised him she wouldn't.

Not that it was a promise she intended to keep, since she'd been going out in Atlanta whenever she felt like it for two years now. Of course, so far it didn't look like there was anything to do in Ville-jeune anyway. As they'd come through the town that afternoon—if you could really call it a town—she hadn't seen any interesting-looking kids at all. In fact, they'd all looked like the kind of boring jerks she'd laughed at in Atlanta.

The kind of boring jerks who'd never bothered to speak to her.

Putting the thought out of her mind, she finished unpacking her clothes, which didn't come close to filling the walk-in closet, and filled the medicine cabinet with all the cosmetics that had been stuffed in the top drawer of her dresser back in Atlanta. Finally, she unrolled a couple of the posters she'd peeled from her walls at home; but when she held them up against the brightly flowered wallpaper, she changed her mind and stuffed the whole bunch of them into the wastebasket. The room, she decided, was just perfect the way her grandfather had done it.

She went to the window, gazing out across the lawn and the canal toward the swamp. The daylight was beginning to fade, but there was still an hour before it would be completely dark. Maybe she should go out and take a look around. She started toward the door, then remembered her grandfather's words.

I'm just going outside, she told herself. It's not like I'm meeting someone. Why would they forbid her to go out for a little while?

Leaving the room through the interior door, she went down the stairs to the main level, and found her parents and grandfather in the den. "Is it okay if I go for a walk?" she asked. There was a brief silence as her parents looked uncertainly at each other. Kelly was sure she knew what they were thinking.

Where is she going?

What is she going to do?

Is she going to get into trouble?

Is she going to try to kill herself again?

The good mood she'd been feeling all afternoon evaporated, and she turned away. "N-Never mind," she murmured, starting back out of the den. Her grandfather's voice stopped her.

"What the hell's going on?" she heard him ask. "She's sixteen years old. Can't she go for a walk at seven o'clock in the evening?"

She froze, then slowly turned around. Her mother was staring at her grandfather, her face pale, her eyes frightened.

Her father was licking his lips nervously.

For what seemed to her an eternity, no one said anything.

Then her grandfather looked straight at her.

"You planning to do anything stupid?" he asked. "Like jump in the canal?"

Kelly's eyes widened at the shock of his words.

"Dad!" Ted said sharply, but Carl Anderson held up a hand to silence his son.

"Now come on," he rumbled. "We all know what happened, and I don't see how it's going to hurt to ask a simple question. If you're planning to try to watch her every minute of every day, then maybe you should have locked her up."

"Carl," Mary began, "you don't understand—"

"No, I don't," Carl broke in, his voice much gentler. "I don't understand at all. But I know you brought Kelly down here to give her a chance at a new life, and it seems to me you might as well start right now."

Mary hesitated for a moment, her eyes never leaving her father-in-law's face. It was a strong face, unlined, looking at least twenty

years younger than its sixty-four years. His hair, the same bur-
nished chestnut as Ted's, showed not a hint of gray, and his blue
eyes were as bright as those of any young man just starting out in
the world. That, she supposed, was the result of his ultimate tri-
umph—he'd hung on, and finally made a success of his life, and it
had given him a strength she'd never really noticed before.

The words he'd just spoken, she realized, had the ring of truth.
They were here to start over again—all of them—and they might
just as well start now. She turned to her daughter.

"How long will you be gone?"

Kelly felt a surge of hope. "N-Not very long. I just thought I'd
walk along the canal and look at all the houses Granddaddy built."

Mary took a deep breath. "All right. But come home before it
gets too dark, okay? And stay away from the swamp."

Kelly nodded, hurrying out of the house before her parents had
time to change their minds. She crossed the lawn, paused when
she came to a narrow footpath that edged the canal, then turned
right. She walked slowly, studying the houses strung along the
waterway. They were much smaller than her grandfather's, occupied by retired people who didn't need nearly as much space as her
grandfather had.

"I don't need it either," he'd said that afternoon. "I guess I built
this big place just because I could afford it, and I've been rattling
around in it ever since. No fool like an old fool. Still, it seems like
it's finally come in kind of handy."

She walked about a quarter of a mile, slowly realizing that the
houses were all alike—there were only four models, and two of
those were simply mirror images of the other two. Bored with the
houses, she turned her attention to the swamp on the other side of
the canal.

She'd heard about it from her parents all her life, but now that
she was actually seeing it, it didn't look at all as she had imagined.
She'd always thought of it as a scary place, filled with a tangle of
vines and infested with snakes and insects. But now that she was
close to it, it didn't appear frightening at all. There were vines, all
right, twisting up into the cypress trees, and the mangroves looked

strange with their branching roots, but there was something about the swamp that struck her as vaguely familiar.

As if she knew it, although she'd never seen it before.

Her pace slowed as the hypnotic drone of tiny creatures drifted out of the wilderness. Finally she stopped walking altogether and stood listening, beginning to sort out one sound from another. There were bird songs rising above the drone of insects, and the high whistles of tree frogs contrasted sharply with the lower tones of the bullfrogs.

A flicker of movement caught her eye. She peered across the canal, straining to see through the failing light. Then, almost hidden in the foliage, she saw a face.

As quickly as it appeared, the face was gone. For a moment Kelly thought she had imagined it.

Had the man—the man she'd seen in her dreams, and in the mirror that night a month ago—followed her here?

No. This face had been younger.

A boy's face.

And it had been real. Real, and somehow—in a way she didn't understand—connected to her.

Her eyes swept the area again, and she caught sight of a footbridge a few yards up the canal. Without thinking, she hurried up the path and crossed the bridge.

She paused on the other side. There was still enough light so she could clearly make out a narrow track leading through the foliage. She hesitated, then made up her mind. It wouldn't be fully dark for at least another half hour. Certainly it couldn't take her more than a few minutes to find the boy.

She started along the path.

As she walked, a new sound came to her.

A sound that seemed to lead her on.

═══

Amelie Coulton sat in the rocking chair on the porch of her shanty, a worn baby's dress in her lap. Her fingers, nowhere near as clever as her mother's, worked uneven stitches into the tear in the material—a tear her mother had told her she herself had put there seventeen years ago. As she gazed at the work, a feeling of hopelessness came over her. She was going to have to start all over again, and there were still so many holes in the garment that by the time she finally finished mending it, her baby would already be a year old.

If it survived being born, which would be any day now.

And if George kept his promise.

Usually, evening was Amelie's favorite time in the marshland. At the end of the day, when she'd finished all her chores, and George had gone off to get drunk on moonshine with one of his friends, she could sit in her chair and listen to the wilderness around her. She never got lonely, even when George didn't come home all night. She had the swamp to keep her company, and she never tired of watching the animals. Sometimes alligators would drift up close, haul themselves out on the mud next to the house and bask for a while. She would talk to them, and though she knew it was silly, sometimes she imagined that they were actually listening to her, understanding her.

Sometimes, if she had a little extra food, she'd toss one of the 'gators a bit of chicken, then watch as it contentedly crushed the bones and swallowed the whole thing.

But it was the sounds of the evening she liked best, and each day she looked forward to the setting sun, and the short minutes of quietude after the day creatures had gone to sleep but before the swamp's nocturnal inhabitants had begun their own songs. Then the night music would begin, and Amelie would sit still, enjoying it, before picking up her endless mending.

Tonight, though, there was something different in the air, an expectant stillness that suggested that something was going to happen.

George must have felt it too, for he suddenly stepped out of the shanty's door to stand beside her on the porch, his lifeless eyes peering out into the darkness. Amelie could feel the anger inside him, the anger that had almost made him slap her earlier, when she'd once more made him repeat his promise.

"He ain't gettin' my baby," she'd said, her voice quavering as she spoke the words. "You ain't givin' him away like Tammy-Jo an' Quint gave theirs!"

"You're crazy," George had told her a month ago, when the argument had begun. "You didn't see nothin' out there. That baby just died, Amelie. Ain't nothin' else happened to it at all!"

Then he'd told her she hadn't seen anything out at the island at the far side of the swamp, that she must have dreamed the whole thing. And sometimes she'd half believed him, for when she went looking for the island, she wasn't able to find it. But still she'd made him promise not to give her baby to the Dark Man.

"I cain't promise nothin'," he'd said at first. "Even if'n he's real—an' he ain't—ain't nothin' I can do about him."

"You promise," Amelie had told him, her voice implacable. "You promise, or I'm gonna kill you myself. See if I don't!"

And finally he promised. But ever since he'd made the promise—and she'd made him do it in front of Tammy-Jo, whose face had gone so pale Amelie had known right away she hadn't dreamed anything at all—he'd been acting so scared, she'd almost been afraid he was going to run off and leave her alone.

And tonight, when she made him repeat the promise one more time, she thought he was going to hit her, just the way her daddy always did when he accused her of being sassy. But he hadn't. Instead he just nodded his head, as if afraid to say the words, and had not said anything else. Now, as he stood on the porch, she could feel his anger turning into fear.

"Someone be comin'," he murmured.

Amelie frowned, her eyes scanning the darkness, her ears searching for the sound of a boat in the strange silence of the evening. Though she saw nothing, a sense of dread began to fill her soul, and she felt her skin crawling.

At last, from the depths of the darkness, a shadow even blacker than those surrounding it emerged from the night.

The shadow became a boat, rowed silently by Jonas Cox, a boy Amelie had known all his life. But in the prow, standing erect, was the tall figure of the Dark Man, clad in black, his face obscured by his black shroud, the cloth pierced only by the holes through which he gazed. Amelie's breath caught in her throat, and she thought her heart might stop beating.

The boat drifted to a stop in front of the shanty. For several long minutes time seemed to stand still as the black figure gazed steadily at George Coulton. Finally the Dark Man's right arm came up, his black-gloved finger pointing at George.

Saying nothing, moving with the steady rhythms of an automaton, George Coulton climbed down from the porch of the shack and stepped into the boat. A moment later the boat disappeared back into the blackness of the night, the Dark Man still standing silently in its prow, and except for the fact that George was no longer there, Amelie wouldn't have been certain that anything had happened at all.

Refusing to think about what it might mean, terror beating louder in her heart with every passing second, she forced herself to begin working once more on the tiny garment in her hands.

But even as she worked on it, the certainty grew within her that her baby would never wear it.

Unless . . .

A thought flickered in her mind, but she turned away from it as quickly as it came. Despite what she'd said, she didn't want George to die.

———

The boat drifted to a stop, and Jonas Cox shipped the oars. He looked up at George Coulton, seated in the stern, seeing George's bloodless face glowing ghostlike in the first light of the rising moon. Jonas could feel the fear that had seized George, and knew that the Dark Man, standing behind him, still had his eyes fixed on the boy Jonas had known all his life.

"You have disobeyed me," the Dark Man said, and though he spoke softly, the words chilled Jonas.

"I didn't—" George Coulton began, but before he could go on, the Dark Man spoke again.

"You belong to me. You do what I tell you. I did not tell you to marry Amelie Parish."

"She were havin' my baby," George whimpered.

"*My* baby," the Dark Man corrected him. "Your children are mine, as you are mine."

"An' I'm givin' him to you," George whined, desperate now.

"You promised your woman you wouldn't," the Dark Man stated. "You belong to me, and your children belong to me. It is why you live."

George said nothing, his eyes widening as he began to realize what was going to happen to him.

"I will not be disobeyed. My children will not promise that which is not theirs to give." The Dark Man opened his cloak and drew a long knife from a sheath at his belt. Leaning over, he placed it in Jonas Cox's hand. "Release George Coulton from the Circle," he said.

George gasped as he saw the knife, but it was already too late. Before he could utter even a single word, the knife in Jonas Cox's hand flashed in the moonlight, and its blade, razor-sharp, plunged deep into George's chest.

A scream rose from George's throat, rending the silence of the night, building as pain shot through his body, then fading into a low, horrible gurgling sound as blood bubbled from his lips.

As the life drained from his body, he began to change.

His eyes sank into his skull, and his skin withered into leathery folds. His muscles, lean and firm only a moment ago, turned flaccid, and his strong young bones turned suddenly brittle, his hip breaking under the weight of his own body.

Jonas Cox twisted the knife in response to a quiet order from the Dark Man, plunging it deeper, then ripping it upward to slice through George's heart.

George's body toppled from the stern of the boat, dropping into the shallow water.

Jonas, ignoring the corpse in the water, washed the blood from the blade of the knife, then returned it to the Dark Man. He put the oars back into the water, and the boat slipped away, disappearing once more into the darkness.

At first it was nothing more than a faint gasping sound, as if somewhere nearby in the darkness some unseen creature had been taken by surprise. Then, in an instant, Amelie heard the gasp turn into a scream of utter terror. It built, rising to a crescendo, then was suddenly cut off.

For a moment Amelie thought it was over, until she became aware of an agonized gurgling sound, a sound that died slowly.

Silence once again hung over the swamp. Amelie sat still, not daring to move until slowly, tentatively, the night sounds began to rise again.

For the creatures of the bog, whatever had happened was over.

For Amelie it had just begun, for as the scream had risen in the night, she had been seized by a gripping certainty about what had happened.

She put her sewing aside and moved into the small house, emerging a moment later with a lantern held high, its wick glowing softly. She climbed clumsily down off her porch into the canoe that was tied to one of the pilings supporting the house, and set the lantern in the prow. Untying the line, she cast the boat adrift, then began moving it forward, a single oar slipping silently in and out of the water.

She followed her instincts, moving through the narrow channels of the bayous. After a few minutes she found what she was looking for. Holding the lantern high, she peered down into the water.

Lying faceup on the bottom of the shallow channel, its face only an inch or so beneath the surface of the water, was a body.

The open eyes stared up at Amelie, but she could see there was no life in them.

The eyes were wide. The mouth was still open in a silent, flooded scream, the lips drawn back in an expression of frozen terror.

And from the wound in the chest, ripped wide nearly to the throat, blood still flowed, staining the water around Amelie's boat a ghastly shade of pink.

Amelie stared wordlessly at the body. An odd sense of relief came over her, for though she had been right in her presentiment, she had also been wrong.

She'd found the body she'd come looking for, but it wasn't the body she'd expected.

The body in the shallow water didn't look anything at all like George Coulton.

Slowly, she began making her way back through the swamp.

She came to her house and passed it by.

Soon, in the distance, she came to another shack, very like her own, crouched at the edge of the swamp.

But this house was different. This one had electric lights brightening its windows. And in this house there was a telephone.

Amelie sighed. It was going to be a long night.

Kelly Anderson gazed at the footbridge uncertainly. Was it really the same bridge she'd crossed earlier? And what had she been doing for the last hour?

She couldn't remember.

The only thing she was certain of was that it had still been light when she'd crossed the canal and set out along the path that wound through the tangled foliage of the island. It didn't seem as if she'd walked very long; indeed, she could barely believe it had taken more than fifteen minutes before she found herself back where she'd started. And yet the sky was black, and the full moon hung well above the horizon.

Why hadn't she noticed that night was falling?

She was in for it now. She could already hear her parents, telling her how irresponsible she was, demanding to know where she'd been and what she'd been doing.

The thing that frightened her most was that she couldn't tell them.

It wasn't just that she'd promised to stay away from the marshes.

It was that she couldn't really remember what had happened.

She searched the corners of her mind for some clue.

There had been a sound, almost like music, but not quite. The tones had struck a chord in her, and she'd felt herself drawn . . . drawn where?

She didn't know.

There were only fragmentary images, nothing she could put her finger on.

But now, as she thought about it, she had a sense that she hadn't been alone.

There had been others near hear . . . but who?

No faces came to mind. Only images of indistinct figures, figures that drifted past her, going somewhere.

Somewhere she could not find.

Something had been happening, something she should have been part of but was shut away from. She could bring none of it into focus, yet all of it had an eerie sense of familiarity.

The people around her—whoever they had been—were people like her.

Like her.

The phrase echoed in her mind. How could they have been people like her? She'd never met anyone like herself before, never known anyone who shared the lonely inner emptiness that had always pervaded her.

But now, as she looked back at the wilderness, she had a compelling feeling that somewhere, lost in the tangle of growth, she'd found other beings like herself.

Yet there were no clear memories of anything. The fragments in her mind seemed nothing more than remnants of a dream.

She started across the footbridge, but came to a sudden stop as she heard the wail of a siren. She listened, frozen, as the sound grew. Had her parents called the police? They couldn't have—she wasn't *that* late.

Unconsciously, she held her breath until the sound began to recede. Letting her lungs collapse in a sigh of relief, she ran across the bridge and started back to her grandfather's house, already searching for a story that would cover her lateness.

A few minutes later she opened the back door and stepped inside. From the den she could hear her parents' voices, still talking with her grandfather. Maybe, if she was lucky, she could slip up to her room and, if anyone came looking for her, claim that she'd been there for nearly an hour. But as she passed the open door to the den, her mother called out to her.

"Kelly?"

Kelly went to the door, bracing herself for the tirade. But her mother was only looking at her anxiously. "Honey? Are you all right? We were starting to get worried."

Kelly hesitated, then suddenly found herself blurting out the truth. "I'm sorry. I just lost track of time. All of a sudden it was dark, and I wasn't anywhere near home."

To her surprise, neither of her parents said anything, neither of them pointed out that she'd broken her promise to be back before nightfall. They simply accepted her words. In the silence that followed, Kelly found herself once again speaking with no forethought. "I like it here," she said. "I'm glad we came."

After Kelly went up to her room above the garage, Ted gazed questioningly at his wife. "Well, what do you think? Did we do the right thing?"

It was his father rather than his wife who answered him. "Of course you did," the older man said. "Kelly's exactly where she belongs. If you ask me, this is just what the doctor ordered."

———

Michael Sheffield's boat slipped silently around a bend in the bayou, gently bumping into the dock at the tour headquarters. He dropped the mooring line over the cleat, but instead of getting out of the boat, remained where he was, staring at the bucket of frogs.

There were half a dozen of them in the bucket.

Half a dozen—all of them dead.

And he'd been gone almost an hour and a half.

It was fully dark now, and Michael gazed around, feeling puzzled. Puzzled, and frightened.

This had happened before.

There had been many times when he'd gone out into the wetlands, intent only on exploring, and lost track of time. Over and over, when he'd come home, his mother had been waiting for him, demanding to know what he'd been doing. "Just looking around," he'd invariably told her. "I wasn't lost or anything."

"You said you'd only be gone an hour!" his mother would protest. "For heaven's sake, Michael, you know how dangerous it is out there."

"But I wasn't in any trouble," Michael would insist. "I always knew where I was."

Which was almost the truth, for often, when the mysteries of the swamp would close around him and time would begin to telescope in upon itself, he would find himself sinking into a world of his own, only to come out of his reverie in a completely different place from where he had begun.

Never a strange place, never an unfamiliar place.

Simply a different place from where he'd started.

He'd never told his parents about that, certain that if they were aware of his unconscious wanderings in the swamp, they would forbid him to go into it again.

Besides, nothing had ever happened to him. He'd always come out of his daydreams, packed up whatever specimens he'd collected, and gone home.

And he'd certainly never killed anything he'd collected.

He got out of the boat, tied off the stern line, then, still uncertain about what had happened to the frogs, emptied the bucket into the water. The dead frogs floated on the surface and slowly began drifting away.

The night was hot and humid, and a full moon flooded the clearing in which the tour headquarters lay. Still wondering about the frogs, and knowing he was already late getting home, he moved quickly through the darkness, checking the animal cages one last time.

The large terrarium containing the water moccasins was locked, and the other snake tanks were securely fastened shut.

In the alligator enclosure the three large reptiles that comprised the exhibit lay half out of the water, their eyes, glittering in the moonlight, fixed on him. As he approached the fence, two of them raised their heads, making tentative motions forward.

Michael shook his head. "Not tonight, guys. You've had plenty to eat. You don't want to get fat, do you?"

The 'gators bobbed menacingly up and down, but as Michael turned away, they settled back down into the mud. A moment later one of them slithered into the pond, cruising silently just below the surface, only its nostrils and eyes disturbing the stillness of the water.

Michael came to the nutria cages, flicking on his flashlight to check the water and food containers. One of the females, the mother of the pups, whom Michael had named Martha, came over to sniff at him through the wire mesh. Switching the light off and sliding it into his hip pocket, Michael unlocked the cage door and picked the little creature up. She nestled into his hands, and he raised her up to rub her soft fur against his cheek.

"Not so bad, is it, Martha?" he whispered. "Plenty of food and water, and nobody to hurt you. A lot better than being turned into a coat, huh?"

Then, as he held the little rodent close, a new sound drifted out of the night.

A siren, rising in the distance, abruptly silenced the droning of the insects.

Michael froze, listening.

The scream of the siren rose, dropped, then rose again. His pulse quickening, Michael moved away from the nutria cages, closer to the road.

As the wailing grew, he could see the flashing red and blue lights of a police car coming toward him.

His body went rigid, an icy chill passing through him as the car approached.

He realized he was holding his breath, every muscle in his body growing more tense by the second.

The car passed.

The sirens began to fade away.

Slowly, the tension drained from Michael's body. For the first time he became aware of the pounding in his chest.

Inexplicably, the approach of the police car had terrified him.

Why? He'd done nothing wrong—he'd never been in any trouble with the police in his life.

Yet just now, as the car drew closer, he'd had an unnerving feeling that it was coming for him.

He closed his eyes for a moment, willing the panic away. Slowly, his heartbeat returned to normal and the icy fingers that were clutching his chest retreated.

"Dumb," he murmured, partly to himself and partly to the little animal he still held in his hands. "Who'd care about a bunch of dead frogs? It's not like you need a license to hunt them."

When his voice brought no responding movement from Martha, he looked down at her.

His hands were tight around her throat, and her body hung limp and still.

He stared at the dead animal, a lump rising in his throat. As the panic he'd just quelled rose back up, threatening to overwhelm him, he hurried back to the cage, deposited the nutria inside, and relocked the hasp of the enclosure.

A minute later he was on his motorcycle, racing homeward through the night.

Marty Templar brought the police car to a halt in front of the tiny house Judd Duval occupied on the fringes of the swamp. It was a couple of miles out of Villejeune, set back from the road, approachable from the land side only by a rotting wooden causeway whose planks threatened to collapse under Templar's ample weight. Templar hated Duval's house; hated it almost as much as the bogs that surrounded it. Every time he came out here, which was as rarely as possible, he felt as if he was strangling, as if the vines and trees that surrounded the shack were creeping up on him, reaching out to him. But tonight he'd had no choice.

"Dunno what's goin' on," Judd had told him over the radio. "All's I know is Amelie Coulton is here, and says there's a body in the swamp."

"Well how the hell are we supposed to find it tonight?" Marty had complained. He'd been sitting at the counter in Arlette's, mopping up the last of some biscuits and gravy, when the radio on his hip had come to life. "Jeez, Judd—you can barely find anything out there in the daylight. At night . . ." He'd let the words trail off, knowing there was no use arguing with Judd Duval. He'd go into the swamp anytime, day or night. To him, as to the other swamp rats, it didn't seem to make a difference. So when Judd had told him to "shut up and move his fat butt," he'd stuffed the last of the biscuits in his mouth, dropped some money on the counter, and headed for the car. He supposed he hadn't really needed to turn the siren on, but what the hell—at least it let him drive as fast as he wanted.

He picked his way across the glimmering muck to the back door of Judd's place, banged on it, then let himself in. The cabin was only two rooms, and the door opened onto the larger of them, the one that served as both Judd's living room and kitchen. A television glowed in one corner of the room, but its volume was turned down. Judd was sitting in his big reclining chair, and Amelie Coulton was seated heavily on a sagging sofa, her face pale, but her narrow features bloated only a little by her advanced pregnancy. As Marty came inside, Judd rose from his chair and glared sourly at the other officer.

"Took you long enough," he groused. "Time we get out there, there won't be enough left of whoever it is to identify."

Templar's gaze shifted to Amelie. "You didn't recognize him?"

"I didn't hardly look long enough," Amelie said nervously. Though her eyes met his, there was a veiled look to them that made Templar wonder if she was telling the truth. "All's I know is whoever he is, he be dead. Lookin' up at me outta the water. Like to give me a turn, I can tell you."

"Let's not sit here workin' our jaws," Duval broke in. "The longer we wait, the harder this'll be."

The three of them went out to the porch, and Templar stared with distaste at the tangle of foliage. Despite the heat, a shiver went through him. He could already imagine the snakes that lay coiled in the branches of the trees, waiting to drop out of the darkness.

"Nothin's gonna get you," Judd Duval mocked, easily reading

the fear in Marty. "Maybe a 'gator or a moccasin, but nothin' to worry about." Chortling at his own joke, he stepped off the porch into the aluminum boat that was tied to the railing and started the outboard while Amelie Coulton and Marty Templar settled themselves onto the center bench.

"Move forward, Marty," Judd ordered, knowing full well how much Templar hated both boats and the swamp. "You don't give us some weight up there, we're gonna foul the prop and have to wade home."

Templar shifted his weight onto the small seat in the boat's bow, but twisted himself around so he could see where they were going. Judd cast off the line, gunned the engine. The boat shot away from the house and a moment later was lost in the twisting courses of the waterways.

With Amelie pointing the way, they moved steadily through the maze of islets. Then, signaling Duval to stop with her right hand, Amelie pointed ahead with her left. Judd cut the throttle, killed the engine, and let the boat drift silently ahead.

Amelie pointed into the water, and Marty Templar shined his light down into the darkness below the boat.

The face stared back at him.

An ancient face, so old and gnarled that had it not been for the expression of terror that contorted its features—and the gaping, ragged hole in the man's chest—Marty's first thought would have been that whoever it was had simply come out here and died of old age.

The mask of fear, and the wound, belied the notion.

"Let's pull him out," Duval said. Using an oar, he pushed the boat onto a small islet a few feet away, and Marty scrambled out to pull the dinghy higher out of the water. Despite hating the feel of the muck beneath his shoes, Marty waded in to help Judd pull the body out of the water.

When they had hauled the corpse onto the mud at the island's edge, all three of them stared down into the twisted face. "Either of you know him?" Marty asked.

Amelie gazed at the body for nearly a minute, but finally shook her head. "Don't look like anyone I ever seen."

Marty glanced up at Judd Duval. "What do you think happened to him?"

Duval shook his head. "Some kind of animal. Don't look like a 'gator, though. Mebbe a panther. There's still a few of 'em around here."

Amelie Coulton's eyes narrowed and her lips tightened. "Or mebbe it were somethin' else."

Though her words had barely been audible, they commanded Marty Templar's full attention. "Something else?" he repeated. "Like what?"

Amelie's gaze moved back to the corpse. When at last she replied to the deputy's question, her voice was uncertain. "I thought it was George," she said. "When I heard 'im scream, I was sure it was him."

"George?"

"My husband," Amelie went on, her eyes never leaving the body in the mud. "He came for George tonight, an' took him away. I figured he kilt him."

Templar's brows knit into a deep frown. "Who?" he asked. "Who came?"

Amelie's gaze finally shifted, her frightened eyes fixing on the deputy. "The Dark Man," she said.

Templar turned to Judd Duval. "The Dark Man?" he repeated. "What's she talking about?"

Duval shook his head. "Nothin'," he grunted. "Just an old story—been around the swamp forever. But there ain't nothin' to it. Just a crazy story. Seems like it just about dies out, and then somethin' like this turns up. Someone wanders out in the swamp an' gets themselves killed, an' no one wants to believe it was just one of the critters."

"Then what do they believe?" Templar pressed when Duval seemed reluctant to go on. When the answer came, it wasn't from Judd Duval. It was Amelie Coulton who spoke.

"The Dark Man," she repeated. "Don't matter what Judd says. I seen him, and he be real. Him, and his kids, too."

Marty Templar stared at her, but she said no more.

Barbara Sheffield glanced pointedly at the clock as Michael came through the back door, but his lateness was immediately overridden by both his appearance and the scent that wafted into the kitchen from his clothes. "Stop!" she commanded before he'd crossed the threshold between the kitchen and the laundry room. "If you track through this kitchen in those clothes, I swear, you'll mop the floor yourself. And you smell like something that died last month! What on earth have you been doing?"

Michael gazed down at his filthy pants, covered to the knees with mud and slime. His sneakers, which he always wore over bare feet when he went into the swamp, were stained dark brown. He grinned crookedly at his mother, "Well, at least I get paid for messing up my clothes now," he offered. "I was out collecting frogs."

Barbara uttered an exasperated sigh. "Did it occur to you at all to call and say you'd be late? Supper's ready, and your father and sister are already at the table." She glanced toward the open door to the dining room and her voice dropped. "And your father says the next time something like this happens, you can fix your own supper."

Michael stripped off his pants and shoes, dumping them into

the washing machine. Without measuring, he poured some detergent over the heap of dirty clothes and started the machine. "Is he really mad?" he asked.

Barbara hesitated. It wasn't just Craig who was annoyed—she was, too. In fact, she'd had an angry speech all prepared, and had been ready to deliver it when her irritation had dissolved in the face of Michael's grin. But wasn't that the way it had always been? Ever since he'd been a baby, he'd always been able to melt her with his dimpled smile and his bright blue eyes. Nor had he ever been in any real trouble.

Except for the strange empty look she'd noticed in his eyes sometimes, when he thought he was unobserved. That had troubled her, as had his refusal to cry, even when he was an infant.

From the first moment he had been put into her arms, Michael had always been an easy child to deal with. Even now, as he watched her warily, she couldn't see that there was any real reason to be angry with him—after all, he'd done nothing more than to work late, and he'd done that every single night since he'd gotten the job at the swamp tour. Nor had he left his filthy pants and sneakers for her to clean up. "No, I guess he's not really mad," she finally replied to his question. "But couldn't you call us if you're going to be late?"

"But I'm always late," Michael reminded her. "You know how it is. I get involved in something, and I just lose track of time."

Barbara shook her head helplessly. "Just go get a fast shower, and be at the table in ten minutes. Okay?"

Michael nodded, darting out through the dining room, calling a quick hello to his father and sister as he passed. He saw his father's mouth open, but decided that whatever his father was going to say to him could wait—besides, by the time he got back downstairs, his mother would have straightened the whole thing out.

He paused at the bathroom to start the hot water running in the shower, then went on to his own room, stripped off the rest of his clothes, wrapped himself in a towel, and went back to the bathroom. Steam was pouring from the shower stall, and the mirror was already fogged with condensation. Still, as Michael glanced at the misted glass, the memory of what he'd seen there before leaped once more into his mind.

But why tonight?

He got into the shower, shampooed his hair, then soaped the washcloth and began scrubbing the perspiration off his body. Suddenly he froze, his skin crawling with the feeling that he was being watched. He shut off the water and listened for a few seconds, finally pulling the curtain open.

The bathroom was empty.

Feeling ridiculous, he turned the shower back on, letting the stream flow full force over his soapy body.

Less than a minute later he was done, but as he stepped out of the stall and grabbed his towel, he once more had the sensation of unseen eyes fixed on him. He dried himself quickly, trying to rid himself of the eerie feeling, telling himself it was all taking place in his imagination.

He started out of the bathroom, then paused, his eyes fastened on the clouded mirror.

There was something there.

He could feel it.

Reaching across the sink with the towel, he wiped away the moisture on the glass.

It disappeared almost as quickly as he saw it, but the image stuck in his mind.

A face.

An old man's face, staring at him.

The face of a dead man, with empty eyes.

Michael stood rooted in front of the mirror, his mind numb. Where had the image come from? Had it even been real?

It couldn't have been, for when he'd seen it, his own reflection hadn't been there at all. It had been replaced by the grotesque image of the old man.

No, it had to have been some kind of strange refraction caused by the wetness on the mirror. He'd seen only himself, distorted by the steam in the room.

Yet as he hurriedly dressed and joined his family at the supper table, he found himself unable to rid himself of the dark image he'd glimpsed in the mirror, and when he finally went to bed that night, he stayed awake a long time, the reading light on, a book propped in his lap.

But the book remained unread, for no matter how hard he tried, the memory of what he'd seen in the mirror refused to ease its grip on him. Twice he went back to the bathroom, closed the door, and stood in front of the mirror, not only searching the glass for any remnant of the vision, but studying his own reflection as well, trying to see the old man's face in his own features, trying to envision himself as a wizened relic of what he was now.

But all he could see were his own familiar features, his clear blue eyes and strong jaw, the hints of dimples in his cheeks, which deepened when he smiled, and his unruly blond hair, rumpled from the pillow.

What he'd seen that night—and the other times, too—had to be nothing more than tricks of his own mind.

At last, back in his bed once again, he put the book aside, switched off the light, and pulled the sheet over his body.

Outside, the moon still shone brightly, and the insects and frogs filled the night with their music.

It was a music that Michael had always before found soothing, but tonight he tossed restlessly, resisting sleep.

When sleep finally came, the face dominated his dreams, looming up at him out of the darkness, leering at him, reaching for him with gnarled clawlike hands.

Three times during the night he awakened, his body sweating, his muscles tense, still caught in the nightmare.

The fourth time he awakened, it was dawn, and the morning light finally seemed to drive the night specter away.

═══════

Clarey Lambert hadn't slept at all that night. Clarey was past ninety, she was sure of that, but how much past she no longer bothered to reckon. After all, it didn't matter. All that really mattered was that she was still alive.

Still alive, and still looking after things.

Clarey lived alone, five miles from Villejeune. Five miles as the crow flew, anyway. A lot farther when you went by boat. You had to wind through the bayous, watching all the landmarks, or you'd never find the place. And, in fact, very few people ever did find Clarey's house. Often weeks would go by without Clarey seeing anyone, but always, just when she was running low on food, someone would show up and her stores of flour and rice, or whatever else she needed, would be replenished. For vegetables, she'd long ago cleared out a little patch on the island behind her house, where she raised okra and beans, and some sweet potatoes. Not enough to sell for money, but enough for herself, with a little left over to trade with the other swamp rats for whatever else she needed.

As the gray light of dawn began to brighten, Clarey stirred in the chair on her porch and stretched her bones. There were a few aches, but not too bad, all things considered. She heaved herself out of her chair, went into the shack she'd lived in most of her life— the shack in which she'd borne her children, and raised the only one who'd survived—and poked at the dying coals in the stove she used for cooking. She added a chunk of cypress to the fire, then put on a kettle of water.

Coffee—thick and black, well-laced with chicory—would drive the arthritis out of her bones.

She was still standing at the stove when she sensed someone approaching and she moved stiffly back out onto her porch, her still-sharp eyes scanning the bayous.

Sure enough, less than a minute later a rowboat emerged from the reeds and slid across the water. There were two boys in the boat, both of them in their late teens, both wearing dirty overalls held up by a single strap. Quint Millard feathered the oars, and the boat turned, drifting to a stop a few feet from Clarey's sagging porch. From the bench in the stern, Jonas Cox gazed up at Clarey through eyes that barely seemed to focus. But though his expression revealed nothing, Clarey knew exactly what was in his mind.

George Coulton.

"It warn't your fault, Jonas," she told him. "You didn't have no choice. You understand that?"

Jonas's brow furrowed slightly. "Me and George was friends. I didn't—"

"You done what the Dark Man made you do," the old woman declared. "Ain't nothin' anyone can do about that. So you just remember that you didn't do nothin'! You hear me?"

Jonas nodded mutely, and Clarey turned to Quint Millard. "You got somethin' to tell me, too?"

"Saw someone new last night," Quint replied.

Clarey's body tensed. "New?" she repeated. "Where?"

"By the canals, where they's buildin' all them houses."

The old woman's countenance darkened at the mention of the development. She knew who the developer was—she knew who everyone in Villejeune was—and she didn't like Carl Anderson. And it wasn't just for what he was doing to the swamp, chipping away at it, draining a few acres here, a few acres there, ruining it for all the people and animals who'd lived in it peacefully for hundreds and hundreds of years. No, she had other reasons for hating Carl Anderson. His name had gone on her list years ago, long before he'd started encroaching on her beloved marshes.

"Who was the person?" Clarey asked, though after last night, she was almost certain she knew.

The children had been out last night, prowling through the swamp, guarding their master as the Dark Man went about his punishment of George Coulton. And Clarey, though she'd never left her house, had been there, too, her mind reaching out, sensing their wanderings, tracking their movements. Last night, though, she had felt a new presence in the swamp, felt the vibrations of someone seeking her out.

Her, and the children.

And the Dark Man.

Clarey had been aware of such a presence before, and always known who it was.

Michael Sheffield.

She'd followed Michael for years. She'd sensed him often, feeling his way through the swamp, unconsciously searching for something of which he had no understanding. And for years she'd kept him away, refusing to reach out to him, unwilling to guide him to the tiny island at the far edge of the swamp, where the Circle gathered.

Perhaps if he knew nothing of who he was, if he took no part in the rituals of the Circle, he would be able to escape.

Escape unscathed, from the evil into which he had been born.

But last night Clarey had felt another presence, a new presence. It wasn't nearby, nowhere near close enough to be sensed by anyone but herself, but much closer than she'd ever felt it before.

"It's a girl," Quint said now, and Clarey closed her eyes for a moment, hearing the words she'd been expecting.

"She's come back," she breathed, barely aware she was speaking aloud. "He promised me she wouldn't. He promised me he'd leave her alone."

She stopped speaking, feeling Quint Millard's eyes upon her.

"But she's one of us," Quint said. "Soon's I seed her, I knowed."

"Did she see you?" Clarey asked.

Quint hesitated, then nodded, knowing he couldn't lie to Clarey. "She tried to follow me. But she couldn't, 'cause she don't know how. I kept close to her and didn't let nothin' happen to her."

A heavy sigh escaped Clarey's throat. "You done right, Quint. But I reckon the police'll be snoopin' around, and I don't see no good in them talkin' to either one of you two. So you just lay low, hear?"

Quint nodded, but Jonas's empty eyes narrowed. "If'n they find me, what'll I tell 'em?"

Clarey's lips tightened bitterly. "You don't tell nobody nothin'. Ain't nobody's business what goes on out here. An' if'n you say anything, I cain't help you anymore'n I could help George Coulton. So you just lay low an' keep quiet, just like always."

Jonas was silent, staring sullenly at his lap. "It ain't right," he finally said.

A great wave of pity washed over Clarey. No, it wasn't right. None of it was right. But that it wasn't right made no difference. It was the way things were. "Go on, Jonas," she told him softly. "Go on and find somewheres to hide. And don't you fret yourself none. Ain't none of it your fault."

Jonas Cox frowned slightly, as if uncertain whether to believe her words or not. But at last he nodded as Quint Millard dipped the oars back in the water and leaned into them. Once again the little boat turned, and a moment later was swallowed up by the dense foliage.

Clarey waited until Jonas and Quint were gone, then went back into her house. The kettle of water was boiling on the stove, and she threw a handful of coffee grounds into the pot, then poured water over them. The grounds floated to the surface, and Clarey added a pinch of salt. In five minutes or so the grounds would sink to the bottom and the coffee would be ready, just the way she liked it.

In the meantime, she had some thinking to do.

She knew who the girl Jonas had seen was, and had prayed that this day would never come. But the girl had come back, and now the last of the children was in the village.

The boy and the girl would find each other, recognize each other the minute they met.

And when they did, they would begin to understand what they were.

They would come looking for her.

Her, and their brothers and sisters.

And the Dark Man.

They would be taken into the Circle, no matter the promises the Dark Man had made.

The evil she had been able to contain for so long would finally begin to spread.

The boundaries of the swamp would no longer restrain it, and once it was loose . . .

She put the dark thought out of her mind. It had begun here in the swamp, and it would end here, too.

For there were things Clarey understood that even the Dark Man did not.

Tim Kitteridge pulled into the parking lot outside the clinic at a few minutes after eight that morning. He lingered in the car, putting off the moment he would have to go inside and look at the body in the back room that served as a morgue.

This was the part of the job he hated most, and it didn't seem fair that it had cropped up only a couple of months after he'd come to Villejeune. In fact, it was one of the reasons he'd taken the job as police chief of the little town in the first place. He'd considered it carefully, checking out the town thoroughly before making his decision. And he'd liked what he'd seen—a sleepy Florida back-water. Growing, but growing with retired people, a notoriously peaceful group. Not like San Bernardino at all, where the city was booming and the problems were growing even faster. The southern California city had changed in the years he'd been there, from a quiet farming town into yet another Los Angeles suburb. But with San Bernardino's growth had come drug problems, and with drugs had come gangs. A year ago Tim Kitteridge had finally decided he'd had it, and begun looking for another job. He'd had two basic requirements: warm weather and little crime. The second condition had eliminated all the major cities of the South. Villejeune, though, had been perfect. Though he supposed there might be a little drug traffic in the swamp, it was just that. Little. With no good landing strips in the area, and the nearest metropolitan center fifty miles away, Villejeune held little attraction for drug lords.

Indeed, after looking over the records, he had concluded that there was little crime of any sort in Villejeune. That was fine with Tim Kitteridge.

Now, only two months later, a body had been pulled out of the swamp.

Kitteridge worked himself out from behind the wheel and wondered, not for the first time, if he should have just retired. Still, at fifty-five he had another ten years in him, and though he could have lived on his retirement pay, it would have been tight. On the other hand, retirement would have definitely precluded having to look at corpses, which was something he truly hated.

He slammed the car door shut, crossed the parking lot, and nodded a greeting to Jolene Mayhew, but said nothing else, knowing that if he spoke to the nurse at all, he would proceed to stall even further. Better just to get it over with. He passed through the emergency room, then went down the long corridor. At the end lay the small room that was the morgue. Orrin Hatfield, the coroner, was already there, waiting for him. To his relief, the body was covered, and he made no move to remove the shroud. Instead, he picked up the clipboard on which Hatfield had made his notes and scanned it quickly.

The first space, where the victim's name should have been filled in, was blank. He glanced questioningly at Hatfield.

The coroner, whom Kitteridge judged to be in his mid-forties, shrugged helplessly. "No identification at all."

"And neither of the boys recognized him?"

Kitteridge shook his head. "Seems like nobody here's ever seen him before."

Just then the door opened and Warren Phillips walked in, "Chief," he said, nodding to Kitteridge. "Orrin. Jolene tells me we have an unidentified body."

"Duval and Templar brought it in around midnight. No ID, and nobody recognizes him."

Phillips frowned, moving to the table, where he pulled the covering back from the corpse's face. Taking a deep breath, fighting the nausea that rose in his gut, Tim Kitteridge made himself look, too.

The old man's eyes were still open, and the rictus of fear that had twisted his features as he died remained frozen in place. But what startled Kitteridge was the man's age. His hair—only a few straggling wisps—was snow white, and the heavily creased skin of his face was draped loosely around his skull. Most of his teeth were gone, and his body, what Kitteridge could see of it, was little more than skin and bones.

Phillips, a deep frown creasing his brow, pulled the cover farther back, exposing the wound in the man's chest. A gaping slash, several inches long, laid the man's rib cage open. Once again Kitteridge fought to control his churning stomach.

Phillips uttered a low whistle. "Whatever got him, it tore his whole sternum out."

"You mean *who*ever got him, don't you?" Kitteridge asked,

looking at the doctor. To him, the cut had looked exactly like a knife wound. "Any idea who he is?"

Phillips, still examining the wound, shook his head. "No one I've ever seen before." He glanced up at Orrin Hatfield. "What do you think? Is it a homicide?"

The coroner shrugged. "Probably. But offhand, I'd say the odds are pretty good we'll never even find out who this is, let alone why somebody might have killed him. If he was poaching on someone else's trap line, no one will ever talk about it."

"Any identification on him?" Kitteridge asked.

"Nothing at all." Hatfield's eyes met Kitteridge's. "Did Judd or Marty find anything out there?"

"If they did, they haven't told me yet. But, Christ, how old was this guy? Ninety?"

Warren Phillips's lips curved into a thin smile. "Hard to tell with these old swamp rats. And this is sure one of them."

Kitteridge sighed silently. He was already well aware that the marshlands harbored a closed community of people who shared nothing of their secrets with the townspeople of Villejeune, and in fact were rarely seen in the village at all.

But the swamp sometimes seemed full of them—sallow-faced men in rotting boats, running trap lines and setting nets, scratching a living out of the wilderness. Many of them, he knew, barely existed at all. No birth certificates, no school records, nothing. Most of the women, Phillips had told him, still gave birth at home.

When Kitteridge had objected that they were running insane risks, Phillips had agreed. "But they still do it," he'd insisted. "It's primitive, but it's the way they do things. If the babies die, no one ever knows about it. No one ever even knows they were born. Same with the old people. They die, and their families bury them. Sometimes they even kill each other, and nobody ever hears a word about it. Rumors, but nothing else."

Now, in the tiny morgue, Kitteridge remembered those words, and gazed at Phillips. "You're telling me what we have here is the body of a man who probably never existed at all?"

Phillips shrugged but said nothing.

"It's not the first time something like this has happened, Tim,"

Hatfield replied. "I know it sounds crazy, but every now and then a body turns up in the swamp, and no one can identify it. Hell, there're probably a lot more bodies out there than we even know about. If Amelie Coulton hadn't heard a scream, this one would still be out there, too. Except by now the animals would have finished him off, and none of us would ever have known what happened."

Or cared, Kitteridge thought a few minutes later as he left the clinic. But as he drove back to the police headquarters next to the post office, he wondered if it was so strange after all.

Southern California wasn't really so different. Even there, Mexicans and other illegal aliens were lost among the masses of other citizens, living outside the system, disappearing into society just as completely as the swamp rats of Villejeune faded into the marshes.

And if people had been living in the swamp for generations, neither knowing nor caring what went on in the outside world, why would they change?

Why wouldn't they just go on living, keeping to themselves, living their lives the way they always had?

Suddenly he remembered a conversation he'd had with Judd Duval, no more than a week after he'd arrived in Villejeune. He'd asked the deputy if he'd grown up in the town, and Duval had laughed. "Not me," he'd said. "I'm a swamp rat. Not a real one, 'cause I like a few things the swamp don't have. Like electricity, and liquor I didn't make myself. But I'm part of the swamp. Always was, and always will be." He'd grinned. "And don't ever ask me what goes on out there, 'cause I won't tell you. Not me, or any of my kinfolk, either."

"Sounds mysterious," Kitteridge had remarked.

Judd Duval's eyes had narrowed slightly. "It ain't no mystery," he'd said. "Folks like us just like to be let alone, that's all. We got our own ways, and they ain't none of nobody else's business."

An attitude, Kitteridge reflected, that was apparently shared by Warren Phillips and Orrin Hatfield. As far as they were concerned, the case was closed. An unidentified man had been killed by an unidentified assailant, and that was that.

Except that Kitteridge wasn't satisfied.

No matter who the man in the morgue was, he had died within Tim Kitteridge's jurisdiction, and his death would be investigated.

It was time for him to go into the swamp, find some of the people who lived there, and ask them some questions.

P hil Stubbs gazed up at the new sign that hung over the entrance to his tour headquarters. It had only been there a week, but despite his complaints at how much it had cost, the expenditure had already proved itself worthwhile. The lettering, done in the ornate style of circus posters, was in red edged with gold, and stood out brightly against a white background.

SEE SWAMP MONSTERS UP SO CLOSE YOU CAN ALMOST TOUCH THEM IF THEY DON'T KILL YOU FIRST!

When Michael had first suggested the sign, Stubbs laughed at the idea. "Seems to me like you're tryin' to turn this place into a tourist trap."

"But isn't that what it is?" Michael had asked, blurting the words out before he realized quite how they sounded. He'd reddened, but floundered on. "I mean, what about all the people who are afraid to go out in the swamp but still want to see the animals? How are they going to know what we have?"

Stubbs had thought about it, finally deciding the boy might be right. Since Michael's signs had turned the animal cages into real displays, business had already picked up. But he'd balked again when Michael had shown him a sketch of the sign he had in mind. "Now come on," he'd protested. "We don't let anyone touch anything but the nutrias, and old Martha wouldn't bite a thing."

"But the sign only says you can 'almost' touch them," Michael pointed out.

So Stubbs had given in. The day after the sign went up, business had immediately improved. People were coming in with their kids, and spending a couple of hours wandering around the cages, watching the animals. A lot of them, after getting a preview of what was in the swamp, signed up for the tour as well. Business was booming, and for the last couple of days Stubbs had even been considering adding an admission fee for the people who just wanted to see the animals.

All in all, he decided as he unlocked the office and started getting ready for the first batch of tourists who were already on their way down from Orlando, hiring Michael hadn't been a bad move at all. The boy worked harder than anyone he'd ever seen, and always seemed to be coming up with new ideas.

And yet, despite how hard the boy worked, there was something about Michael Sheffield that made Stubbs a little bit nervous. Not that he didn't like the kid—he did. It was just that over the last month, as he'd gotten to know Michael, he'd gotten the feeling that there was something about Michael that he didn't understand, something that Michael kept carefully hidden.

He'd finally talked to Craig about it last week, but Michael's father had assured him there was nothing to worry about. "Michael's always been like that. Sort of a loner, if you know what I mean. I think he'd rather go off into the swamp by himself than do practically anything else."

Stubbs hadn't pushed the matter, but he'd found himself watching Michael a little more carefully. And finally he'd figured out what it was. Sometimes, around dusk, as the light began to fade and the long shadows of evening darkened the wilderness, Michael seemed to have periods when he lost track of what he was doing.

A few days ago, for instance, Phil had been toting up the accounts in the office, and looked up to see Michael washing one of the tour boats. For a few minutes there had been nothing extraordinary about the scene at all. Using a bucket and a mop, Michael had been swabbing down the long benches that ran, back to back, down the center of the boat. But suddenly something invisible to Stubbs seemed to catch the boy's attention, and he simply stopped what he was doing, the mop clenched tight in his hands, his eyes staring into the tangle of growth across the bayou. Stubbs had followed Michael's gaze but still seen nothing. As the seconds turned into minutes, he'd begun to wonder if Michael was all right. Leaving the office, he'd walked down to the dock. Just as he arrived, Michael had suddenly come to life again, his grip on the mop relaxing. "Michael? You okay?" Stubbs had asked.

Turning, Michael looked puzzled. "What?"

Stubbs had repeated the question. "I saw you staring off into the mangroves over there," he went on, nodding in the direction of the island across from the dock. "Thought you must have seen something."

That was when Michael's eyes had changed, a veil dropping over them as if he was afraid Stubbs might see something he wanted to conceal. "I—I don't know," he'd said. "I guess I was just daydreaming."

Stubbs had let the matter go, but nonetheless had kept his eyes open. He'd seen the same thing happen three or four times more. Michael would be in the midst of doing something—always as night was gathering—and suddenly he would simply freeze, his hands clenching, as if he was looking at something, or hearing something. A few minutes later it would be over, and Michael would go on with his work as if nothing had happened.

Phil Stubbs was beginning to worry about Michael. What was he doing, those nights when he worked late, hanging around the little complex where the tours were headquartered long after everyone else had left? Of course Stubbs knew how most of Michael's time had been occupied—the evidence of his work was usually obvious the next morning. But was there something else? Something Michael might not even be aware of, that held him there each evening?

Stubbs finished counting the morning till, observed with satisfaction that all the tour boats for the day were fully reserved, and made a note to himself to keep track of the turn-aways. Perhaps it was time to buy yet another boat. His thoughts were disturbed by the sound of a little boy's voice, shouting excitedly.

"It's not either asleep, Mommy! It's dead!"

Stubbs looked out the window to see a clump of tourists clustered around the nutria cages. They were buzzing amongst themselves, and several of them seemed to be pointing at one particular cage. Stubbs hurried out to see what was going on, elbowing his way through the crowd until he was in front of the cage where Martha lived with her litter of pups. The pups, as usual, were tumbling around, scrambling over each other as they struggled to get to the food dish.

Martha lay unmoving on the floor of the cage, just inside the door.

"Well, if you ask me," he heard a heavyset woman whisper loudly to her companion, "it's cruel to keep the animals caged up this way. Of course they die—they probably die every day."

Ignoring the woman, Stubbs unlocked the cage, opened the door, and lifted the lifeless nutria out of the pen.

"Did something kill it?" the little boy who had yelled a few moments earlier demanded, his eyes staring accusingly up at Phil Stubbs.

"Nope," Stubbs replied, returning the little boy's gaze. "Martha here just got old, that's all."

"*I'll* bet she starved to death," the heavyset woman observed.

Well, that's not something you'll ever have to worry about, Stubbs said silently to himself as he took the nutria away. Returning to the office, he examined the animal.

What *had* happened to it?

He picked it up again, fingering it carefully, searching for a wound. When he set it down once more, the head flopped over at an unnatural angle. Frowning, he explored the creature's neck with his fingers. Even to his unpracticed touch, he could tell the nutria's neck had been broken.

An unbidden memory came to his mind of Michael, standing perfectly still, the mop clenched tightly in his fists.

If it hadn't been a mop in his hands a few days ago, but instead one of the nutrias . . .

There was a rumbling noise outside, and a moment later Michael himself appeared, pulling his motorcycle to a stop outside the gates. Stepping outside, Stubbs beckoned him over to the office.

"Got something I want you to look at," he said as Michael approached. He led Michael back into the office, then stepped aside so that the boy could see the dead nutria on the desk. "You know what might have happened to her?" he asked.

Michael stared at Martha's limp body. He couldn't explain what had happened, since he still wasn't sure. And if he told the truth, he knew he would be fired. But he couldn't lie, either. "I—I don't know," he stammered. "Last night, she didn't look too good—"

Stubbs's eyes fixed on him. "Her neck's broken, Michael."

Michael swallowed. "Oh, God. I thought she was going—I thought—" He fell silent, staring helplessly at Stubbs.

Stubbs's anger eased in the face of the Michael's obvious torment. "Now just take it easy, boy. Tell me what happened."

"But—But I don't know what happened," Michael stammered. "I was petting her, like I always do, and I heard a siren. And it scared me." His eyes flicked around the room, as if he were searching for a way out. At last his gaze came back to Phil Stubbs. "I didn't do anything to her," he said. "At least I didn't mean to. But after the police car went by, and I looked down at her again, she'd stopped moving." He fell silent for a few seconds, his eyes fixing on the nutria. He took a deep breath. "I—I guess I must have killed her."

Stubbs said nothing, frowning deeply as he tried to figure out what to do. His first impulse was to fire the boy. Yet Michael was so obviously miserable about what had happened that Stubbs was certain he hadn't intended to hurt the little animal. Indeed, Michael always became angry with anyone who even teased the creatures in their cages. "Well, I don't know," Stubbs said at last. "But if you can't even remember what happened, I guess I can't say you did it on purpose."

Michael stared abjectly at the floor. "I'm sorry," he said. "Are—Are you going to fire me?"

Stubbs considered it. Once again he remembered those strange lapses when Michael seemed to lose himself. But he also remembered how much his business had improved since he'd hired the boy. "No," he said, making up his mind. "But I think maybe you'd better take the rest of the day off—without pay—and think about keeping your mind on your work from here on out." When Michael looked puzzled, Stubbs went on, "I've seen you daydreaming before, Michael. It's like you've just gone somewhere else, like you're in some kind of trance or something. So starting tomorrow, I don't want you working after hours anymore. Can you understand that?"

Michael nodded, finally looking up. "Are you going to tell my dad?" he asked.

Stubbs hesitated. What if Craig Sheffield demanded proof of what Michael had done? Guys could be funny about their sons—never wanting to admit their own flesh and blood could be less than perfect. And Sheffield was a lawyer, and despite the fact that he was Stubbs's own lawyer, that could lead to trouble. Besides, when you got right down to it, Michael was old enough to be responsible for himself. "Seems to me this is just between us," he said. "So let's just keep it that way, okay? Now get out of here, and make sure you're on time tomorrow."

Michael left the office, his head still down. Stubbs heard the motorcycle roar to life, and watched from the doorway until the bike disappeared around a bend in the road. Returning to his desk, he picked up the dead nutria. He stared at it for a moment, then shook his head and tossed it out the window into an open Dumpster a few yards away.

"Get Craig Sheffield upset over a lousy nutria?" he muttered to himself. "I may be dumb, but I'm not that dumb."

═══

Michael gunned the engine of the motorcycle, feeling an exhilarating burst of speed as the machine responded to his command.

Leaning forward into the wind, he tried to put the scene with Phil Stubbs out his mind. But an image of the dead nutria lying on his boss's desk stayed with him. This morning, on his way to work, he'd let himself hope that Martha would still be in her cage, munching on her food and looking after her pups. Maybe nothing had happened last night at all—maybe his memory of the limp animal he'd returned to the cage had been no more real than the strange image he'd seen in the mirror.

But as soon as Stubbs had called him to the office, he'd known the truth.

Somehow, last night, he'd killed the little creature.

But why couldn't he remember doing it?

He slowed the motorcycle, banking it into a curve.

Well, at least he hadn't been fired, and Stubbs wasn't even going to tell his folks what had happened. He could imagine what his father would say if he'd lost the job—the motorcycle would be gone, and he'd probably be grounded for the rest of the summer as well.

But it wouldn't happen again. From now on he'd keep his mind on what he was doing, and not let himself be distracted by anything.

But what about today? He couldn't go home—if he did, he'd have to explain why he had the day off.

And he couldn't spend the day in town, either. Even if his father didn't see him, everyone else would, and his dad would be bound to hear about it sooner or later.

Maybe he'd just head out on the bike and spend the day riding. He had plenty of money—he might even head up to Orlando and go to Disney World. Except he'd been there last year and hadn't liked it very much. Nothing had seemed real, and while Jennifer had run from one ride to another—screaming about everything— he'd wished he'd stayed home and spent the day by himself, poking around in the marshes.

Maybe that's what he would do today. There was a place he knew about, a few miles out of town, where he could hide the bike. There weren't any boats out there, but there were paths and trails.

Yes, that's what he'd do. Spend the day exploring. And he'd keep his mind on the time, so he wouldn't be late getting home.

As he gunned the bike once more, a horn blared behind him. Startled, he automatically glanced into the rearview mirror, expecting to see a car overtaking him.

Instead, he saw the hideous visage of the ancient man, leering at him.

Stunned by the image in the mirror, he swerved the bike, realizing almost too late that the car behind him was now passing. As the car's horn blasted a second time, Michael jerked the bike the other way. The motorcycle skittered toward the edge of the pavement; then, as the car disappeared around a bend, the cycle slid off the asphalt into the soft earthen bank of the drainage ditch that paralleled the road. The narrow tires began to sink into the mud as Michael struggled to pull the bike back onto the road. Throwing his weight onto the handlebars, he twisted the front wheel around. The bike remained mired in the mud. The rear end rose up, pulled free of the muck, then swung around, throwing Michael onto the ground, the toppled bike beside him.

═══

The day before, Kelly Anderson had had only a glimpse of Villejeune from the car. Now she realized just how little there was to it. Only few stores, a café, and the post office with a police station tucked in behind it. A block away she found the school she'd be going to in the fall, which didn't look like much, either. There were only two buildings, one of which seemed to be a gym, and she didn't see any sign of a swimming pool. Still, as she wandered around the village she decided she kind of liked it. It didn't feel at all like Atlanta, but that was all right.

As she came around the corner, onto Ponce Avenue, she saw the kids.

There were four of them, two boys and two girls, and the moment she saw them, she felt her guard going up.

They looked like the kids she'd always avoided back home.

Hicks, that's what they looked like.

Not one of them was wearing any interesting clothes, and the girls both wore their hair in styles Kelly wouldn't have been caught dead in, like they'd just fallen out of some old beach blanket movie starring Annette Funicello.

She felt them watching her.

Maybe she should walk right up to them and demand to know what they were staring at.

Except that she already knew.

She'd put on three pairs of earrings that morning, and two sets of cuffs. And even though the weather was hot, she was wearing a black turtleneck shirt and a pair of black jeans that she'd sewn some sequins onto. Back in Atlanta the outfit had looked cool, and not really very weird, compared to what a lot of the kids wore.

But here in Villejeune she stuck out like a sore thumb.

Her first impulse was to go home, but to do that she'd have to walk right past the kids. Even if she crossed the street, it would still be obvious that she was avoiding them.

Making up her mind on the spur of the moment, she turned and went the other way, walking quickly, as if she knew exactly where she was going. Once she was out of the village, and away from the kids who were staring at her, she began to feel better again.

The road, built up like a causeway, wound through the swamp here, with deep ditches on each side. Everywhere she looked there seemed to be water, with only a few patches of soggy-looking land rising above the surface here and there. Dense thickets of mangrove stood above the water, and odd stumplike objects protruded from its surface, as if this had once been some kind of forest.

Birds were everywhere, bobbing on the surface of the water, wading in the shallows, and soaring overhead. Twice she saw alligators basking in the mud, but they seemed unaware of her presence, ignoring her as she passed.

As she moved farther from the town, a feeling of peace began coming over her. After a while she realized what it was. Back in Atlanta there had been the continuous noise of the city all around her: the hum of cars, trucks grinding as they shifted gears, rock music pouring out of boom boxes—a steady stream of sound that, though she'd never really been aware of it, had simply always been there.

Here there was nothing but the songs of birds, the rustle of the wind in the cypress trees, and the splashing of fish and frogs in the water.

Then, from ahead, she heard the roar of a motorcycle approaching. A moment later there was the blast of an automobile horn, quickly followed by another, and then a car came roaring around the bend in the road, shooting past her so fast she barely had time to get off the pavement.

"Creep!" she shouted, glaring at the car as it raced away.

Silence. Where was the motorcycle?

Kelly stood still, listening.

What had happened?

Had the car hit the bike? But the driver would have stopped, wouldn't he? And wouldn't there have been a crash?

Then she knew what had happened. The car had almost run her down—it must have run the motorcycle right off the road.

She broke into a run, and found what she was looking for a few seconds later.

The motorcycle lay in the ditch; the body of a boy lay beside it. Kelly froze for a second, afraid that the person might be dead. If he was—

But before she had time even to finish the thought, the person by the bike moved, slowly sitting up. Kelly darted over to him. He looked up at her, and when their eyes met, Kelly's stomach tightened.

She knew him.

But that was crazy—she'd never seen him before in her life.

And yet something inside her insisted she knew him.

"You're from Atlanta, aren't you?" she blurted.

Michael shook his head, his eyes still on the odd-looking girl who was standing a few feet away. He had the strangest feeling, as though she were someone he knew. But that was crazy, because from the way she looked, she couldn't be from around here. None of the girls in Villejeune dressed the way she did, and there sure weren't any with pink hair. "I've never been to Atlanta. I mean, I've been there, but just to the airport. We were going to Chicago once, and we changed planes there."

Kelly frowned. It was really weird. He didn't look like anyone she knew, and yet somehow she was certain they knew each other. And then she remembered the boy in the swamp last night.

She hadn't gotten a good look at him, really. It had already been getting dark, and she'd only seen him for a second. "Were you out in the swamp last night?" she asked.

Michael frowned. How had she known? Had she seen him there? And if she had, why hadn't he seen her?

Maybe he had.

Maybe it was one more thing he didn't remember.

A chill crawled up his spine, and he shifted uneasily. "Were *you?*" he countered.

Kelly hesitated, then nodded. "I was walking along the canal near my grandfather's house, and I saw someone. I thought it might have been you."

Now it was Michael who hesitated, searching his mind for any hint that he might have seen the girl before.

There was nothing.

Except that there was something familiar about her.

It was her eyes. There was something in her eyes that he recognized. But what?

"I was out there," he said at last. "But not by the canals. They're on the other side of town." But he might have been there. He was in a boat, and he might have gone anywhere.

Kelly gazed at the boy, feeling his eyes fixed on her, too. If he didn't know her, then why was he looking at her that way? And then she remembered. He was dressed the same way as the kids she'd seen in town—a pair of khaki pants and plaid shirt, and even though his clothes were stained, and there was mud in his hair, she could tell he wasn't any different from them at all.

He thought she was some kind of freak.

"How come you're staring at me?" she demanded, summoning all the hostility she could muster.

Michael took a step back. "I—I keep feeling like I know you, too."

Kelly hesitated—was he just trying to get to her? "Well, if it was you I saw, then you saw me, too," she finally challenged.

"I guess maybe so," Michael said uncertainly. Then, without thinking about it at all, he told her the truth of what had happened to him in the swamp.

Kelly stared at him. It was exactly what had happened to her last night! Maybe they *had* met, even though neither of them remembered it! Maybe they'd even talked to each other.

"M-My name's Kelly Anderson," she said, suddenly feeling shy.

Michael grinned crookedly. "Now I know who you are. My dad's your grandfather's lawyer. I'm Michael Sheffield."

Together, the two of them pulled the bike back onto the road, and after checking it for damage, Michael tried to start it. On the third attempt the motor caught. Michael stole another look at Kelly. He'd never seen anyone who looked quite like her before, except on television.

Yet there was something about her that appealed to him, despite her pink hair and strange jewelry.

Something about her that was different from any of the other kids he knew, something in her eyes that set her apart.

That was familiar.

Then he knew what it was.

Despite her looks, he was certain that inside, behind the strange clothes and makeup, she was just like him.

Filled with those awful feelings of being somehow different from everyone else.

"Y-You want a ride?" he asked, expecting her to refuse.

But instead of refusing, she nodded. "I think I'd like that," she said. "Where should we go?"

Something flickered in Michael's eyes, then was gone. But when he spoke, Kelly had the feeling he wasn't quite telling her the truth. "I have the day off," he said. "Maybe we should get some food and have a picnic." He turned the bike around and climbed on, then steadied it while Kelly mounted the buddy seat behind him.

"If we're going to buy food, don't we have to go back to town?" Kelly asked.

Michael said nothing, simply putting the bike in gear and pulling away.

But as they rode away from Villejeune, each of them was thinking the same thing.

I know this person. I've known this person all my life. This is the friend I've never met before.

Though neither of them understood it, both of them felt the instant bond that drew them together the moment they had met.

Somehow, they were connected.

Tim Kitteridge was beginning to wonder if he'd made a mistake. He'd been in the swamp for two hours now, and though he'd followed the map Phil Stubbs had given him, he knew he was lost.

The trouble was, it all looked the same. There were tiny islands everywhere, poking up from the shallow water of the bayous, each one of them identical to all the others. He glanced up at the sun, but even that was no longer of much use. It was noon, and the sun was so high it seemed to be almost overhead. He could be going in any direction at all and would never know the difference.

He was moving slowly, the small outboard motor at the stern of the boat puttering quietly. Suddenly he felt the underside of the boat touch bottom, and quickly cut the engine entirely. But when he tried to tilt the motor up, lifting the propeller above the surface, he realized it was too late. The prop was already stuck in the mire that lay, completely invisible, only a few inches beneath the dark brown water. Using the oars, he tried to push the boat back, but the stern only dug deeper into the mud. At last he laid the oars aside, knowing what he had to do. Taking off his shoes and pants, but leaving his socks on, he slipped his legs into the water. Even through his socks he could feel the slime of the bottom. As he shifted his weight out of the boat, his feet sank into the ooze. For a moment he panicked, afraid he'd stepped into quicksand. But when the muck was halfway up his calves, his feet touched more solid ground. He stood still for a few seconds, hating the feel of the mud sucking at his feet, hating the thoughts of what might be lying unseen in the water.

Still, he had no choice.

He grasped the transom of the boat, heaving it upward, and felt the prop come loose from the quagmire. Twisting sideways, he dropped the boat back into the water and tested it. The tip of the outboard still touched the bottom, and it would rebury itself if he climbed back into the little skiff. He moved the boat a few more feet until he was certain it would float free even with his weight added to it.

He climbed back into the boat, but left his bare legs, covered with mud, hanging over the side. As he began rinsing them off, his hand touched something firm and slimy and he reflexively jerked it away. Swinging his legs into the boat, he stared at the leech that clung to his left calf.

Three inches long, it looked like a slug, except that its head, instead of being raised up, was pressed tightly against his leg. He stared at the hideous creature for a second, then, with a shudder of revulsion, snatched it from his leg, hurling it overboard in the same movement.

There was an angry red welt on his leg, where the leech had been in the process of attaching itself to him.

Still queasy, Kitteridge examined his other leg, then quickly pulled his pants back on. He stripped off his socks, dropped them into the bottom of the boat, and rowed away from the shallows into deeper water. He shipped the oars once more, deciding to let the small boat drift, for even out here where the water seemed to be totally stagnant, there were still gentle currents wafting through the shallow channels.

Once again he remembered Judd Duval's words just before he'd taken off into the swamp: "If you get lost, just let the boat drift. It don't look like it, but that water's movin', and if you let the current take you, you'll get out." The swamp rat had grinned sardonically. " 'Course it'll take a few hours, and you'll wind up maybe fifteen, twenty miles from Villejeune, but it's better'n spendin' the night out there, right?"

Well, at least he'd listened, and remembered. He watched the maze of islets drift by. Here there was less cypress, and the landscape was far more open than it was closer to Villejeune. Marsh grasses grew in profusion; flamingos and herons stood in the shallow water, their beaks searching the bottom for food. As he drifted around a bend, he heard a low snorting sound, and looked around just in time to see a wild boar disappear into the reeds.

Then the landscape began to change again, and he was back under the canopy of moss-laden cypress trees. The current picked up slightly, for here the islands were larger, the channels narrower and deeper.

A house hove into view—if you could call it a house. Actually, it was nothing more than a shack, propped up at the water's edge on rotting stilts. Its floor sagged badly at one corner, and its walls were pierced with glassless window frames.

At first Kitteridge thought it was nothing more than a fishing shelter, and a long-abandoned one at that. But as he drew abreast of the structure, a slight movement caught his eye, and he dipped the oars into the water, stroking lightly against the gentle current. His eyes fixed on the sagging structure, and he studied it carefully. For a few moments he thought he must have been wrong, that he had only imagined that someone was inside the building. Then, in a sudden flurry, a form darted through the shadows of the building's interior and out through a back door. Kitteridge pulled hard on the oars, and the skiff shot forward, but by the time he had gained a view of the thicket behind the house, the figure was already disappearing.

He hesitated, considering the possibility of following whoever had faded away into the undergrowth, but quickly abandoned the idea. In the boat, at least the current would eventually carry him out. On foot, he was certain he would be hopelessly lost within a matter of minutes.

He moved on, rowing now, following the current as it drifted through the islands. The islands were still larger here, and he began to see more and more of the dilapidated shacks, spaced well apart, as if whoever lived in them valued their privacy.

Occasionally he saw people—thin, narrow-faced women, their faces sullen and weathered, clad in faded cotton dresses, some of them with children clinging to their legs. They watched him suspiciously as he drifted by, and he could feel their hostility. A few times he tried calling out a greeting, but no one answered him. At the sound of his voice, they simply disappeared into the gloom of their shanties, herding their children before them.

As he rounded yet another of the endless bends in the slow-moving stream, he saw still another of the wooden shanties. On the porch of this one, though, a lone woman stood, her torso distended in the last stages of pregnancy, and even as he spotted her, Kitteridge knew who she was.

Amelie Coulton, who had led Judd and Marty to the body last night.

And today, from the way she looked, Kitteridge was almost certain she was expecting him. His feeling was confirmed as he drew closer to the house and Amelie gazed down at him, her eyes filled with suspicion.

"It warn't me that killed that man last night," she said. "Onliest reason I went out there at all was I thought it might be George. But it warn't."

"You said George went off last night. With someone called the Dark Man."

Amelie's sallow complexion turned ashen, and a veil dropped behind her eyes. When she spoke, her voice was flat. "I don't know nothin' about that."

"But that's what you told Judd Duval and Marty Templar," Kitteridge pressed.

Amelie shrugged. "I warn't feelin' too good last night. I don't remember what I said."

Kitteridge sensed that he was on the verge of losing the woman entirely, and decided to change tactics. "But George was out last night?"

He could see Amelie relax a tiny bit. "He's always out. Out

fishin', out drinkin'—don't make no difference, long's he ain't here."

There was a silence as the man in the boat and the woman on the porch eyed each other suspiciously. "Where is he now?" Kitteridge finally asked. "Did he come home last night?"

Amelie shook her head, and Kitteridge had the distinct impression that she would be just as happy if George Coulton never came home at all.

"You don't believe me, do you?" Amelie asked as if she'd read his mind. "You think I be lyin', and it were George I found out there last night."

Kitteridge said nothing, but met her gaze steadily.

"Okay," she said. "Come on inside. I got a picture of George. You tell me if'n it's the same man."

Kitteridge climbed up onto the porch and followed Amelie into the shanty. Inside, though it barely seemed possible, the house was even more decrepit than outside. There was a tattered sofa covered with a worn blanket, and broken recliner. In one corner stood a splintering pine table and two more chairs. A wood stove filled another corner, and a makeshift counter had been built along the wall next to it. Through a door, he could see a second room, containing a bed frame on which lay a sagging mattress. There was no sign of a bathroom, and the police chief knew better than to ask about it. Here in the swamp there simply was no plumbing. Through an empty window frame he could see a lopsided outhouse, against which leaned a pile of traps. Well, at least he knew how George Coulton earned whatever money he made. Shaking his head at the poverty of the place, he turned around to find Amelie holding a picture. He studied it carefully, taking it out onto the porch to hold it in the sunlight.

It was a photograph of a couple, and the woman was clearly Amelie Coulton. The man next to her, a lean, gangling figure almost a foot taller than she, had the narrow face typical of the swamp, and empty eyes. His chin was covered with a stubble of beard, and a shotgun was cradled in the crook of his arm. His other arm was draped possessively over Amelie's shoulder. Kitteridge flipped the picture over and read the scrawl on the other side:

"Wedding day—me and George." It was dated seven months earlier.

Kitteridge studied the picture again. Even allowing for the pre-
mature aging of the swamp rats, George Coulton couldn't have
been more than twenty-five when the photograph had been taken.

The man in the morgue had to have been at least eighty.

Silently, Kitteridge handed the picture back to Amelie, who had
followed him out onto the porch. But as she reached out to take the
snapshot from him, her face paled, her eyes widened, and her hand
went to the great bulge in her belly. Unsteadily, she sank down onto
the rocking chair.

"Oh, my," she gasped as the sudden spasm of pain drained out
of her. "I think mebbe it's time."

Kitteridge knew immediately what was happening. "Was that
the first contraction?"

Amelie nodded. "I told George it was gettin' close," she said,
her voice bitter.

Nice son of bitch, Kitteridge observed silently, thinking that if it
had indeed been George Coulton whose body had been carried out
of the swamp last night, at least he had found someone with a
motive. But after talking to Amelie for a few minutes, he suspected
killing Coulton would have been justified. When he spoke, though,
he revealed none of his thoughts. "If you're starting labor, we'd
better get you into town. Do you have a suitcase packed?"

Amelie uttered a high-pitched, brittle laugh. "A suitcase? Ain't
nobody out here got one of them, an' even if'n I did, ain't nothin'
to put in it. All's I got is—" Her words were choked off as another
contraction seized her. When it had passed, she struggled to her
feet.

Kitteridge helped her down the ladder to his boat and got her
settled in the bow, then started the engine and cast off. But before
he moved out into the channel, he glanced once more up at the
house. "You sure you don't need anything to take with you?" he
asked.

Amelie laughed tightly again. "Like what? I ain't even got a
purse. Out here, nobody's got nothin'. You're born, you live awhile,

and you die." Her voice turned bitter. "Sometimes it seems like it's the lucky ones that die young."

As Kitteridge pulled away from the shanty, Amelie cocked her head and, for the first time, her eyes seemed to come alive. Kitteridge reflected that when George had married her—if, indeed, he really had—she must have been pretty.

Amelie laughed out loud, genuinely this time. "You're lost, ain't you?" she asked.

Kitteridge felt himself redden, but nodded. "How'd you know?"

"Easy," she said. "You be goin' the wrong way. Villejeune's back there," she went on, pointing past Kitteridge's shoulder. "Not far, neither. Mebbe half a mile." As he turned the boat around, she went on. "You take the main channel straight ahead, an' cut through a little gap after the second island. Then bear left till you come to a big stump. After that, you can see the town."

Ten minutes later they were there, and as they pulled up to the dock where Kitteridge had left his car, Amelie glanced nervously around, as if she expected someone to be waiting for her. Seeing him watching her, a veil dropped behind the young woman's eyes and her lips twisted into a smile. "Thought he mighta been waitin'. He wanted me to birth the baby to home, but I won't. Ain't no way I'm lettin' nothin' happen to my baby."

Kitteridge helped her out of the boat and led her up to the police car. Another contraction seized her just as she crept awkwardly into the passenger seat. "Take it easy," he told her. "We'll have you at the hospital in a couple of minutes." Closing the door, he hurried around to the driver's side, got in, and started the engine. As he pulled away from the dock, Amelie turned to him, her face almost pretty as she managed a small smile. "Leastwise, it warn't a complete waste of time, you comin' out to my house today."

Kitteridge smiled wryly. "But I still don't know who the body is."

Amelie shrugged. "You know who it ain't," she said. Her lips compressed once more into the bitter smile that seemed almost second nature to her. "Frankly, I was kinda hopin' mebbe it were George. Leastways, if he was dead, I guess it'd be my house, wouldn't it?"

Kitteridge shrugged noncommittally, not wanting to get in-volved in whatever domestic arrangement George and Amelie had evolved. But after less than an hour with Amelie, he was all but certain that there were no documents anywhere registering a mar-riage between them. Which, he suspected, was just the way George Coulton wanted it. As long as Amelie pleased him, fine. But if she didn't, he could simply throw her out.

He pulled into the clinic parking lot, helped Amelie inside, and got her admitted. Promising to look in on her later, he left her in Jolene Mayhew's care and started back to his office.

Dead end, he thought, as he began filling out the forms neces-sary to dispose of the body in the morgue. Fingerprints had already been made, and before the body was interred, pictures would be taken and a dental chart prepared. But by this evening, before it could begin to rot in the heat and humidity, the nameless body would be in the Villejeune cemetery, laid to rest in one of the anon-ymous crypts owned by the village for just such purposes as this.

And yet, even as he set the bureaucratic wheels in motion, Tim Kitteridge couldn't shake the feeling that the corpse was, indeed, George Coulton's.

Once more he remembered the words Marty Templar had spo-ken that morning, as he'd been giving his own report of what had happened in the swamp last night: "You want to hear something really weird, Chief? The woman who found the body—Amelie Coulton—was talking about someone called the Dark Man. Sounded like some kind of spook who came and took her husband away with him. Do you believe those people out there? They must be nuts!"

And he remembered the look on Amelie's face when he himself had mentioned the Dark Man. Despite her claim not to remember what she'd said, he knew she was lying.

Lying, and frightened.

Amelie Coulton, he was sure, knew a lot more than she'd told him. But he was also sure, despite whatever motive she might have had, that she hadn't killed the man from the swamp. Given the advanced state of her pregnancy, it seemed impossible for her to have attacked anyone.

No, someone else had killed him.

Someone he already suspected he would never find, given the refusal of all the swamp rats—except for Amelie—even to speak to him.

Yet Amelie knew something.

She had gone into the swamp alone, fully expecting to find the corpse of her husband. It wasn't as if she'd simply stumbled upon the body and gone into a panic.

Making up his mind, he left his office and started back toward the hospital.

———

Amelie lay in bed, waiting for the next contraction to seize her. She was trying to keep track of how long it was between them, but she couldn't concentrate.

She was still thinking about the police chief coming out to talk to her about George.

She knew he hadn't quite believed her this afternoon—knew he suspected that the body she'd found last night was her husband, no matter what she'd said.

And what she'd told him hadn't really been a lie, for until Clarey Lambert had appeared that morning to tell her that George wouldn't be coming home again, even she hadn't been certain the body was his. Indeed, Clarey herself had never quite said that it was.

Of course, when she'd looked into the lifeless eyes of the corpse in the water, she'd recognized George right away. It was the eyes— flat and dead. But when she'd finally been able to look at his face, instead of just his eyes, she hadn't been so sure.

The man's face had looked so old.

And George, when he'd left last night, hadn't looked any different than he ever had. But he had looked scared.

So she'd gone off and found Judd Duval, which she probably shouldn't have done at all.

What she should have done was just gone home, and never told a soul what she'd found. But she hadn't, and then, when she'd come back with Judd and the other fellow, she'd seen the gaping wound in his chest.

Whether the body was George's or not, she'd known what happened to him.

She shouldn't have given herself away like that, talking about the Dark Man.

Still, the police chief hadn't pushed her when she'd lied to him.

And, thank God, neither had Clarey Lambert.

This morning Clarey had rowed up and climbed onto the porch. Amelie knew right away why she'd come, so the old woman's words hadn't come as a surprise.

"George won't be coming home no more," Clarey had told her, easing her bulk into the rocking chair on the porch. She'd reached out and squeezed Amelie's hand. "I don't s'pose that's the worst news you could've heard, is it?"

Amelie had said nothing, waiting for the real reason for Clarey's visit. It hadn't taken long for it to come. "I heard the people from town found a body last night," she said, and Amelie was certain the old woman had deliberately not told her it was George. "So I figure they'll come around askin' everyone questions." Her eyes had fixed on Amelie, two dark embers that felt like they were burning into Amelie's very soul.

Amelie had thought quickly. If the old woman didn't know it had been she herself who had led the police to the body, then she wasn't going to be the one to tell her. "What you want me to do?" she'd carefully asked.

Clarey had been silent for a while, her tongue poking around in her mouth where her molars had once been. At last the old woman's gaze had fixed on her again. "Don't say nothin'. If they ask, you tell 'em George ain't here and you don't know where he be." Amelie's head had bobbed up and down, and Clarey heaved herself out of the chair. "They come around, don't you say nothin', you understand me?"

And she hadn't said anything, not really.

She'd said only as much as she had to, and denied that the body she'd found was George's.

Another contraction wrenched Amelie's body, and she clamped her eyes closed in an attempt to shut away the pain. A few seconds later, as the pain began to ease, she opened her eyes again.

And froze.

Standing a few feet from the bed, framed by the doorway, was Tim Kitteridge. Instinctively, she turned her head away, but the police chief came and sat down by the bed, taking her hand.

"It *was* George you found last night, wasn't it?" he asked.

Amelie tried to pull her hand away. "You got no business comin' in here."

Kitteridge's grip tightened. "I need to know, Amelie. Was it George? Do you know what happened to him?"

Amelie's eyes darted around, searching for help; but of course she found none. Another contraction seized her. When it finally subsided, she felt exhausted, too tired to defend herself against his question. "Maybe it were," she breathed. "But I didn't do nothin' to him. An' I cain't even swear it were him. He didn't look nothin' at all like George. George warn't old."

"All right, Amelie. I won't argue with you about that anymore. But do you know what happened to him?"

Amelie's jaw set stubbornly, and Kitteridge felt her shudder under his touch. Now, in the face of her obvious fear, he repeated back to her once more the words she herself had spoken to Marty Templar the night before. "What did you mean, Amelie? Who is this Dark Man?"

Her face draining of color, Amelie shrank back into her pillow. "Don't ask me," she pleaded. "If you're gonna ask anyone, ask Clarey Lambert. Or Jonas!"

"Jonas?" Kitteridge repeated. "Who's Jonas?"

"He's one of 'em," Amelie breathed. "Just like George was."

Kitteridge reached out to take Amelie's hand, but she snatched it away. "I'm not sure what you're talking about, Amelie," the police chief told her. "*What* are they?"

Amelie gazed bleakly at him. "*Dead*," she breathed. "They be the Dark Man's children, and they all be *dead!*"

"This is pretty," Kelly said, stretching languidly on the thick mat of grass that spread across the deserted picnic ground. They were twenty miles away from Villejeune, and they'd just finished the lunch they'd bought at a little store-and-bait shop that was all but hidden in the wilderness five miles away. When Michael had turned into the narrow lane leading to the picnic ground, Kelly had wondered if maybe she shouldn't have come at all—the place was deserted, and she had the creepy feeling that if something happened to her, nobody would find her for years. But when she'd seen the pond that had been dredged out of the lagoon, and the sandy beach that edged it, she'd changed her mind.

"How come nobody ever comes here?" she asked now.

Michael shrugged. "I don't know—I guess most people don't like the swamp, and hardly anyone even knows about this place. Since I got the bike, I've been coming here a lot, and I've never seen anyone else."

Kelly fell silent for a moment, then grinned mischievously. "Want to go for a swim?"

Michael cocked his head, wondering if she was kidding. "We didn't bring any bathing suits."

"So? Haven't you ever heard of skinny dipping? You said no one ever comes out here, didn't you?"

As Michael's face turned scarlet, Kelly wished she hadn't suggested the idea, even though she herself had intended to back out if Michael took her up on it. "I was just kidding," she said quickly. "I just wanted to see if you'd do it."

Michael gazed curiously at her. He still wasn't used to the way she looked, and when she'd suggested taking off their clothes and going into the pond, he'd been certain she meant it. "Did your friends in Atlanta go skinny dipping?"

Kelly started to tell him that of course they did, but then found herself telling him the truth instead. "I—I didn't really have any friends in Atlanta. There were some kids I hung out with, but I hardly even knew them. You know what I mean? I always felt like . . ." Her voice trailed off, and there was a silence for a moment before Michael, his eyes fixed on the ground a few feet away, finished the thought for her.

". . . like you were different from them? Like they were sort of all together, but you weren't part of the group?"

Kelly stared at him. "How did you know?"

" 'Cause that's the way I always feel, too." For some reason he didn't quite understand, he felt that Kelly would know exactly what he meant, even though he'd never talked about the strange emptiness inside him before. "I always feel like everyone else knows something I don't know, like there's part of me missing."

"But that's the way I feel, too," Kelly breathed. "It's been that way ever since I can remember. I've always felt like there's something wrong with me, you know? Like I can't—" She hesitated, searching for the right word. ". . . like I can't *connect* with other people."

Michael said nothing for a few minutes, as he sorted out her words, examining them carefully. That was exactly how he'd always felt, too—as if he was missing some connection with everyone else.

Except in the swamp. When he was out there, all by himself, he sometimes felt that he wasn't alone after all, that somewhere very close to him there were people who understood him. But he'd never seen or met anyone during his wanderings, and he'd finally decided the idea was crazy, that he was only trying to deny his own loneliness.

Now, sitting here with Kelly Anderson, he didn't feel alone at all. Despite her pink hair, black clothes, and the weird jewelry covering her ears and wrists, he felt as though he was with someone who truly understood him.

He sensed Kelly's eyes on him, and looked at her.

"Are you mad at me?" she asked, her voice shy, carrying none of the bravado he'd heard when they first met.

Michael shook his head. "I was just thinking, that's all."

Kelly smiled. "You want to meet me tonight?"

Michael hesitated, uncertain exactly what she meant. "I—I don't know," he stammered. "I'll see."

A few hours later, when he finally dropped her off at the same place he'd met her that morning, he still hadn't made up his mind.

———

"Dad?"

Craig Sheffield looked up at his son, his brows arching in an exaggerated expression of surprise. "The Sphinx speaks," he said. Michael flushed, and Craig immediately regretted his teasing tone. "Well, you haven't exactly been talkative tonight."

"Usually he talks too much," Jenny piped up from her chair opposite Michael's. "I hardly ever get to talk at all. And all he ever talks about are those dumb animals he finds in the swamp." She regarded her brother with all the scorn she could muster. "Sometime you're going to go out there and a big snake's going to eat you all up!"

"Jenny!" Barbara did her best to glare at her daughter, but wound up laughing instead at the little girl's obvious delight at her imagined fate for her brother. Jenny, taking the laughter as a victory for herself, stuck out her tongue at Michael, who pointedly ignored her.

"Do you know Mr. Anderson's granddaughter?"

Before Craig could reply, Jenny piped up again, chanting: "Michael's got a girlfriend, Michael's got a girlfriend."

This time her brother glared at her. "Can't anyone ask a simple question around here without you making a jackass of yourself?"

Instantly, Jenny's eyes turned stormy. "You take that back!" she demanded. "Mommy, tell Michael he's not supposed to call me names!"

Barbara groaned, leaning back in her chair and putting her napkin on the table. "Enough," she said. "If you tease him, you have to expect him to tease you back." Jenny opened her mouth, ready to push the argument further, but Barbara held up a warning hand. "I said that's enough, Jenny. If you want to stay at the table, you can be polite and finish your dinner." Before Jenny could reply, she turned to Michael. "Now what's this about Kelly Anderson?"

"She came around today," he hedged, deciding it wasn't quite a lie. After all, she'd been walking toward the tour headquarters when she found him by the ditch. If she'd kept walking, and he'd still been at work, he probably would have met her anyway.

"Well, stay away from her," Michael heard his father say, his voice sharp.

Startled, Michael turned. His father was frowning deeply.

"Stay away from her?" Michael echoed. "How come?"

"Now, Craig, you're not being fair—" Barbara began, but her husband didn't let her finish.

"The girl tried to kill herself, Barb. She—"

"Craig, please!" Barbara broke in, glancing pointedly toward Jenny, who was watching her father eagerly.

Craig hesitated, then grinned crookedly at his daughter. "Looks like you're about done with your dinner. Why don't you go on in and watch television?"

"I want to *hear*," Jenny objected.

"And I *don't* want you to," Barbara said firmly. Jenny glanced from one parent to another, and realized there would be no appeal.

"Well, it's not *fair*," she complained, moving sulkily toward the door. "When I'm a grown-up, I'm going to let kids hear everything!" She slammed the door on the way out, but neither of her parents responded. Craig, in fact, was already facing Michael, his expression serious.

"Kelly Anderson decided she was pregnant a month ago, and

tried to kill herself," he said. "The fact of the matter was that she wasn't pregnant at all. She simply imagined the whole thing."

Barbara took a deep breath, hating her husband's habit of making judgments before he had all the facts. And she hated even more that he only did it with his family, never with his clients. "Craig, that's not fair. We don't know exactly what happened—"

Craig held up a warning hand. "I know enough that I'm sure she's not the kind of girl I want Michael mixed up with. She's got a lot of problems, and from what Carl Anderson tells me, she always has. There are plenty of perfectly nice girls around here who—"

"Great!" Barbara exploded. "Of course she has problems! Why do you think Ted and Mary brought her down here? Did it ever occur to you that maybe Carl told us about her problems in the hope that we might be able to *help*? But the way you're talking, they might as well go back to Atlanta. You haven't even met the poor girl, and you're already condemning her. It seems to me the least we can do is give her a chance!"

Craig Sheffield glared at his wife. "Spoken like a true social worker! All the chances in the world for everyone else. But what about your own son? You really want him exposed to some fruitcake punker from Atlanta? You don't have any idea what she might be up to! From what I've heard, it sounds like she's some kind of druggie, and if she thought she was pregnant, she must be a tramp!"

The argument between his parents raged on. Certain they'd forgotten all about him, Michael stood up from the table, picked up the dishes from his place and took them into the kitchen. He started to go back into the dining room to finish clearing the table but changed his mind.

Neither of his parents had ever met Kelly, yet here they were arguing about her. Well, the hell with them. He'd make up his own mind.

He went out the back door, crossed the lawn, then walked out onto the Sheffields' dock where two boats were tied up. One, a small runabout with an inboard engine, he was forbidden to use unless his father was with him. The other, a rowboat powered by a small outboard, was his to use anytime he wanted. He untied it, jumped in, and pushed it away from the dock. He pulled the starter rope twice as the boat drifted out into the canal, then the engine caught. He gunned the engine, speeding away from the house. As he turned into another canal, he wondered if his parents had even noticed he was gone.

In the delivery room of the small clinic, Warren Phillips glanced up at the face of his patient. Her hair, long and blond, lay in damp tangles, half covering her right eye. Despite the air conditioner, it was hot in the operating room, and Phillips wiped the perspiration from his brow with the sleeve of his greens. Amelie's labor had been going on all afternoon. An hour ago he'd had her brought to the delivery room. But only now did he finally get a glimpse of the baby's head.

"Push, Amelie," he urged. "We're getting there. Just a few more minutes."

Amelie strained, battling the fatigue that seemed to have drained the last of her energy.

"C-Cain't," she sighed.

"Shh," the nurse standing next to her head said, wiping at Amelie's brow with a damp cloth. "Don't try to talk, honey. Just concentrate on the baby."

Another violent contraction seized Amelie's body, and it felt like someone had shoved a hot poker into her belly.

It hurt too much. It wasn't supposed to hurt this much, was it? Another contraction seized her, and a wave of nausea passed over her.

She couldn't throw up. Not now.

She concentrated on the baby, and tried to push like the nurse had showed her.

"Get the needle ready," she heard Dr. Phillips saying. He was saying it soft, hoping she wouldn't hear, but one thing she had was good ears. "We're in trouble."

She wanted to scream out, to beg him not to let anything happen to her baby, but then another awful spasm of pain struck her, and though a sound rose from her throat, there were no words. Instead, it was a piercing scream of agony.

"It's all right," the nurse told her. "You just let it out, honey. Just let it out."

She screamed again, and once more her body felt as if it was being torn apart. And then, oddly, she felt something moving, moving quickly, slipping away from her.

The pain eased.

"The needle," she heard Dr. Phillips say again, and could tell by the sound of his voice that something was wrong. Then he spoke once more. "Tie off the cord. Quick." His voice rose. "Come on, nurse! Now!"

A moment later she heard the nurse speak.

"Is he all right, Dr. Phillips?"

Silence.

An unending silence, a silence that seemed to go on forever.

Then the sound of the doctor's voice.

"He's not making it . . ."

His voice went on, but Amelie wasn't listening. She knew what the words meant.

Her baby had died.

After all these months, her baby had died.

But it couldn't have happened.

It wasn't right.

It wasn't dead! It wasn't! She wouldn't let it be!

A new kind of pain washed over her. Not a physical pain this time, but a pain that seemed to engulf her whole being.

"Nooo!" she screamed. "No! I want my baby. Give me my baby!"

The nurse—whose name she couldn't even remember—tried to comfort her.

"It's too late, honey," she whispered. "He's gone. Your baby's gone, but you're going to be all right."

"No!" Amelie screamed again. "I want my baby! Give me my baby!" By sheer force of will she sat up on the birthing table, her eyes darting around, searching for her baby.

But except for herself, Dr. Phillips, and the nurse, the delivery room was empty.

"I'm sorry," Dr. Phillips said gently, coming around to take her hand and ease her back down onto the table. "There was nothing we could do. Even last week, if we'd taken it, we couldn't have saved it. It's not your fault, Amelie. Just remember that. There's nothing you could have done, and nothing I could have done. It's just one of those things that happen sometimes."

Amelie listened to him numbly, heard him offer her a shot, something to make her sleep.

She shook her head.

Then she started to cry.

The argument between Craig and Barbara was still raging when the telephone rang, and only when Jenny appeared in the dining room doorway, gazing uncertainly at her parents, did they finally interrupt themselves.

"Someone wants to talk to you, Mommy," Jenny said shyly. When her mother was gone, she went and scrambled into her father's lap. "Are you and Mommy going to get a divorce?" she asked, her voice quavering.

Craig, immediately sorry for the fight the little girl had been forced to overhear, hugged her close. "No, of course not. Mommies and daddies just do that sometimes. Don't you ever argue with your friends?"

Jenny nodded, but said nothing.

"Well, it doesn't mean you're not friends anymore, does it?" Jenny's arms tightened around his neck, but he felt her head shake. "And that's the way it is with mommies and daddies. Just because they don't agree on something doesn't mean they don't love each other."

Barbara reappeared in the doorway, her expression tense. "I have to go to the hospital," she said. "It's Amelie Coulton. She's just had a stillbirth, and they need me."

Instantly, the last of Craig's annoyance with his wife evaporated, and when he looked at her, his eyes reflected his concern. "Can you handle it all right? Do you want me to go with you?"

Barbara shook her head. She'd been prepared for this—Warren Phillips had told her a week ago that it looked like there might be complications with Amelie's pregnancy. Indeed, he'd recommended a cesarean section, but Amelie had refused. "It'll be fine," she'd whispered in her odd, little-girl voice. "The Lord'll look after me an' my baby. An' I wanta have him the regular way."

Barbara, who had been counseling Amelie from the moment the young woman had first appeared in her office six months before, shyly asking if there was any way she could see a doctor even though she didn't have any money, silently reflected that the Lord hadn't been looking out for Amelie when he let her get pregnant. But by last week she had known her well enough to keep the thought to herself. Despite the fact that Amelie was barely eighteen and lived with a husband who frightened her in one of the shacks in the bayous, she was much stronger-willed than the other swamp-rat women, most of whom never ventured into Villejeune at all.

"I know what'll happen if I have my baby at home," she'd said. "He'll die, just like everyone else's. An' I want my baby, Miz Sheffield."

"It's going to be hard for Amelie," Barbara said now, picking up her purse from the sideboard and kissing both her husband and her daughter. "Her husband didn't even bother to come into town with her."

Craig's eyes clouded over. "Her husband? George Coulton?"

Barbara's lips tightened. "That's the one. From what I gather, he's not much of a husband."

"He may well not be a husband at all," Craig observed, his brows arching. "Tim Kitteridge's boys brought a body out of the swamp last night, and Tim thinks it might be George Coulton."

Barbara stared at her husband, her mind racing. Did Amelie know? Was that what had brought on her labor? But then for some reason she found herself focusing in on a single word that Craig had uttered. "Thinks?" she repeated. "You mean he doesn't know who the body is?"

Craig shrugged helplessly. "Apparently it didn't look like Coulton, and there wasn't any ID. But Coulton's gone, and Tim says that even Amelie admitted the corpse might have been him."

"Dear God," Barbara breathed. "If it's true, then that baby was all she had." She forced a smile. "And no matter what I can tell her, she's going to be devastated."

She left the house and drove to the clinic, where the evening nurse told her to go directly to Amelie's room. "How's she doing?" Barbara asked.

The nurse spread her hands helplessly. "No better or worse than you could expect."

Barbara took a deep breath, gripped her purse and proceeded to the patient's wing. From a room at the end of the hall, she heard the sound of a woman sobbing. She hurried toward the room, knowing how Amelie must be feeling.

Exactly as she had once felt herself.

"Amelie?" She spoke the name softly, but there was no response from the distraught woman who lay on her side, her face to the wall, her body shaking with her grief. Barbara crossed the room, dropped into the chair next to the bed, and laid a gentle hand on Amelie Coulton's shoulder. "Amelie, it's me. Barbara Sheffield."

"G-Go away," Amelie moaned.

"Amelie, I'm here to help you."

Amelie shrank away from Barbara's touch. "Cain't nobody help me," she sobbed. "My baby . . . I want my baby."

"I know," Barbara crooned. "I know. But sometimes these things happen."

Suddenly Amelie rolled over, her eyes feverish and angry, fixing on Barbara. "Why won't they let me have him?" she asked, her voice pleading.

Barbara's heart wrenched as she drew the young woman into her arms. "Oh, Amelie, I'm so sorry."

"They won't bring him," Amelie sobbed. "How kin I take care of him when they won't even bring him? He wants his ma!"

Barbara stroked Amelie's damp and tangled hair. "It's all right, sweetheart. The Lord's taking care of your little baby."

Amelie stiffened in her arms. "No," she wailed. "It ain't so! It's 'cause of me! They won't let me have him 'cause they don't think I'm a fittin' mama!"

Barbara felt tears well up in her eyes. It was the same thing that had happened to her, when they'd first told her about her own baby so long ago. She hadn't believed them—hadn't wanted to believe them.

Not her little girl—not the little girl she'd planned for since the day she'd found out she was pregnant. It couldn't have been born dead.

She'd refused to believe it, even when Craig had explained to her what had happened, that the umbilical cord had gotten twisted around the baby's neck and strangled it even before it could take its first breath.

"No, Amelie," she said, wondering how she could comfort the girl. "It's nothing to do with you, darling. It's just something that happened. And I know how you feel. Really I do."

Now Amelie drew away slightly, and her eyes gazed into Barbara's. "No you don't," she gasped. "You cain't. Cain't nobody understand, less'n it's happened to 'em."

Barbara took a deep breath, her own memories, even after sixteen years, bringing tears to her eyes. "It has happened to me," she said softly. "And I won't tell you you'll ever get over it. When my baby died before I even got to hold her in my arms, I wanted to die, myself. And I still think about her every day. I think about what she would have been like if she'd lived, and all the things we would have done together."

Amelie's eyes narrowed suspiciously. "You're lyin' to me, Miz Sheffield," she said. "Your baby didn't die. You got a boy sixteen years old, an' a little girl be seven. You told me last week."

Barbara nodded. "That's true, Amelie," she said. "But Michael isn't the baby that was born that night. After my little girl died—when I thought I might die, too—Dr. Phillips brought Michael to me. He was two weeks old. Just a week older than my little girl. His mother had decided to give him up, and Dr. Phillips brought him to me. At first, when I saw Michael, I was sure I couldn't take him. But then, when I held him, I knew. I needed him as much as he needed me. And I started getting over my hurt. But that first week, before Dr. Phillips brought Michael to me, I just wanted to die. I felt just like you feel now."

Amelie's whole body trembled, and Barbara felt her struggling to control her churning emotions. But then she went limp, dropping back against the pillows, covering her face with her hands. "It ain't gonna happen that way for me," she said hollowly.

Barbara took her hand. "You don't know that, Amelie."

Amelie dropped her other hand to her lap and turned, her eyes—deep pools of grief and hopelessness—fixed on Barbara. "It ain't going to," she repeated. "You're a nice woman, Miz Sheffield. But don't lie to me. I ain't educated, but I ain't stupid, neither. Ain't no one gonna give a baby to someone like me. I ain't got no job, an' my man's gone, an' I live in a shack in the swamp. There ain't no babies for the like of me. And the Lord knew it. That's why he took away my little boy. Even God don't got no use for someone like me."

Barbara sat with Amelie for an hour, doing her best to comfort her, but she knew that the other woman was right. There was going to be no miracle for her, no tiny golden-haired baby placed in her arms to take the place of the child she had lost. Still, she was certain, in time Amelie's wounds would heal.

At last, exhausted not only by her labor, but by her grief as well, Amelie seemed to drift into sleep, and Barbara turned down the light and made her way out of the room. But as soon as Barbara was gone, Amelie's eyes opened.

"He ain't dead," she whispered into the silence of the empty room. "If he was dead, I'd know it."

Instead, deep within the innermost reaches of her soul, she knew her baby was still alive.

Alive, and yet somehow already dying, his own soul slowly being stolen away from him.

Kelly sat in the den with her parents and grandfather. The television was on, but she wasn't watching it. She stared out the window, her attention drawn to the gathering dusk outside. The sun had set half an hour ago, and the twilight was just beginning to fade. The noises from the swamp across the canal began to change, growing louder, and the heavy fragrance of jasmine drifted through the open door to the patio. There was a stillness to the warm evening air, and Kelly began to feel as though she would suffocate if she stayed in the den any longer.

And there was Michael.

She was absolutely certain he was coming tonight.

She didn't know why—he hadn't even looked at her when she'd suggested it that afternoon. All he'd done was mumble something noncommittal and then ride away.

Yet she *knew* he was coming.

But she didn't want her father cross-examining him, acting like he was some kind of jerk who was going to try to rape her or something.

Nor did she want her father demanding to know where they were going, or what they were going to do.

She got up from the sofa, stretching. "I think I'll go up to my room," she said to no one in particular.

Her father spoke, his eyes never leaving the television screen. "So early? The movie's barely started."

"It doesn't look very good," Kelly replied. "I'm gonna listen to some tapes and read." She kissed her parents good night and hurried upstairs. If either of them came to check on her, it wouldn't be for at least a couple of hours. By then they'd think she'd gone to sleep.

In her room, she pulled the coverlet off the bed, shoved some pillows under the sheets, then checked how it looked from the door. If no one turned on the light, it would look as if she were in bed, sleeping. Satisfied, she switched all the lights off, leaving through the outside door to the deck at the top of the stairs. She descended the steps carefully, but they were new and solidly built—there wasn't so much as a squeak to betray her. Coming to the lawn, she darted across to the canal, then turned right, moving a few yards away from her grandfather's house.

She came to a bench and sat down to wait.

A cloud of gnats hovered just above the surface of the canal, and a school of small fish gathered, leaping up from the water to feed on the tiny insects, their movements leaving the surface covered with an intricate pattern of tiny ripples. A bird dropped down out of the sky, plunging into the water, emerging a moment later with one of the fish in its mouth. Another bird swooped, and then another, until soon there was a small flock of them, feeding on the fish that fed on the gnats. Kelly watched in fascination, until the birds rose as one into the air, as if heeding an unseen signal, wheeled, and soared away, their wingtips barely clearing the tops of the cypress trees. Kelly searched the wilderness across the canal, but could see nothing that might have disturbed them. Then she heard a noise, a soft puttering that floated above the drone of the frogs and insects.

A boat came around a curve, and Kelly instinctively knew who it was. She stood up from the bench, moving to the water's edge. A moment later the boat glided to a stop beside her and she recognized Michael in the stern, gazing at her curiously.

"How did you know I was coming?" he asked as she climbed into the dory and settled herself on the center bench.

Kelly shrugged. "I don't know. I guess I just had a feeling. Doesn't that ever happen to you? You know what's going to happen before it does?"

Michael's brow furrowed slightly. "But I didn't even know myself, till I left my house." He hesitated, then went on. "My folks were having a fight."

Kelly knew without being told that the fight had been about her; she could sense it in the way Michael's gaze suddenly shifted away. She waited for him to go on, but he didn't elaborate, merely turning the boat around to go back the way he'd come.

They cruised slowly along the canal, the darkness gathering steadily about them. And yet, despite the coming of the night, Kelly felt no fear. Ahead, a narrow channel veered off to the left, and even before they came to it, Kelly knew Michael would steer the boat into it. A few seconds later, as they passed through the narrows and the overhanging trees closed around them, Kelly felt a subtle change come over her.

She felt safe, as if the swamp itself were somehow nestling her in its arms. The feeling she'd always had in Atlanta—the strange sensation of never quite belonging—was gone. Here, in the swamp, she felt as if she'd come home.

The channel, only a few feet wider than the boat itself, snaked between two islands, then branched.

Again Kelly knew before they arrived at the fork which way Michael would go.

It was, she realized, as if some unseen force, some sentinel neither of them could see, was guiding them.

The boat moved slowly and steadily. As they coursed deeper into the tangled bayous of the marshland, Kelly became aware once more of the nearly inaudible siren song she'd heard last night. She turned, looking at Michael, and found that despite the gloom within the swamp, she could see him clearly.

His eyes, expressionless, were fixed on her, but then she realized that he wasn't looking at her at all. Rather, he seemed to be gazing beyond her, as if seeing right through her. Saying nothing, he cut the engine and lifted oars from the bottom of the boat. Except for the music of the swamp, they moved forward in silence now.

The eerie strains of the subliminal aria reached deep into her mind, and she responded to its call, letting herself drift with the unearthly music, letting it imbue her with the sense of peace its notes brought.

=====

They were no longer alone.

Other boats were around them now, shadowy forms drifting around the edges of Kelly's vision. She had no idea how many there were, nor did it matter, for each of the boats contained someone else like herself, someone else whose mind was obeying the gentle summons of the music.

Slowly, barely visible at first, Kelly saw a glow of light flickering in the darkness ahead. Like a beacon, it pierced the darkness, and even though it was still far away, Kelly imagined she could feel its heat on her face. She felt drawn to it, as a moth to a flame, and as the boat moved steadily toward it, a sense of anticipation grew within her.

Tonight, something special was going to happen.

Tonight, she was certain, she was finally going to find out who she was, and why she had always known she was different from anyone else.

At last the boat touched the shore. Without needing any instruction at all, Kelly stepped out of the bow and fastened the line to a low-hanging cypress branch.

Other boats were already there. In the darkness beyond the island on which she stood, Kelly could sense the presence of still others, each of them homing in on the glowing signal.

The music was more compelling than ever: a low drumbeat pulsed in the air, and above it a high voice keened a melody.

With Michael beside her, and other shapes drawing closer in the night, Kelly moved toward the beckoning light.

=====

Clarey Lambert felt the children drawing near. Shortly after dusk she had journeyed to the island hidden deep in the wilds of the swamp, and begun the preparations for the ceremony that was to come.

Last night George Coulton had died.

Tonight, a new child would join the Circle.

Now, on the island from which the Circle had begun its spread so many years ago, the preparations were all but complete. The altar was ready, the candles waited to be lit.

The Dark Man was nearby.

Clarey's mind concentrated now on the call she had sent out an hour ago, the call only the children could hear, the call that would draw them to the Circle.

Someday, she supposed, she, too, would die. What would the Dark Man do then? Without her, would it all end, as he had always said?

She doubted it.

No, he would simply find someone else to take her place, some-one else to don the robes and summon the children.

But it wouldn't be someone like her, who loved the children, who felt a small piece of herself die each time a new child was taken into the Circle.

Still, despite all the tiny fragments that had died within her over the years, she still lived, still clung to the hope of destroying the Circle. Still searched for a way to destroy the Dark Man and release the children from the living death to which he had condemned them.

She stiffened, sensing something different in the clearing where the children were gathering.

Long ago she had tuned her mind to sense each of them, so that always she knew where they were, what they were doing.

Except for the two.

The two the Dark Man had released from the swamp sixteen years ago.

Those two had been experiments. The Dark Man had wanted to watch them, wanted to see what would happen to them if they grew up beyond the Circle.

One of them he had sent far away, but the other one he had kept close by.

And Clarey Lambert knew why.

He wanted to watch Michael Sheffield, wanted to see how far the summons could reach.

On each of the nights when there had been a ceremony, she had watched the Dark Man scanning the faces of the children, searching for Michael.

Until tonight, Michael had never been there.

She'd felt him sometimes, felt him in the swamp, searching for the island where they were gathered. But he'd never found them, for she had never reached out and guided him.

But now the girl had come back. Today, the two of them had met, and tonight, together, they had heard the summons clearly, and responded.

From the shelter of the trees that concealed her, Clarey saw them in the clearing, waiting with the others. Saw them and felt a terrible dread.

The fire in the center of the clearing was not big, but it blazed brightly, its flames licking at the darkness, illuminating the altar in front of which it had been built, its damp wood spitting embers outward toward the semicircle of children who stood in motionless silence around it. There were twenty-five of them, ranging in age from four to nearly twenty. They wore tattered clothes, clothes that had been worn by other children before them, and there was a sameness to their faces.

The narrow faces of the swamp rats, framed by scraggly, ill-kempt hair.

They were thin children, their bony frames a product of the poverty in which they lived, and though their eyes reflected the light of the fire, still there was a dullness to them, as if the inner light of their youth had long since gone out.

They looked old, not so much in the tiredness of their stance, for many of them stood straight and tall, but old in spirit, as if their lives were already over.

Kelly and Michael, standing close together toward one end of the semicircle, were unaware of the stark contrast they made to the others in the group, for already they had been mesmerized by the hypnotic call emanating from Clarey Lambert's mind. All they were aware of was that somehow they belonged here, that somehow they shared a kinship with these children they'd never seen before.

With the others, they waited.

Something was about to happen, and though neither of them was aware of what it might be, they both knew they would be a part of it.

There was a movement in the trees beyond the altar, and a figure stepped out of the shadowed darkness. A figure clad in flowing robes of scarlet velvet, embroidered in gold and silver. The figure paused, staring out at the children, and then its arms rose, spreading wide.

Clarey Lambert's voice rang out. But it was no longer the weak and rasping voice that outsiders heard. Now her voice rang with the pure clarity of a young woman in her prime. "Are all my children gathered?"

"We are here," the children answered in a single voice.

Clarey turned, facing the altar, and dropped her arms to her sides. Slowly, she began lighting the candles, each of which illuminated a doll. The dolls had been made by hand, and each of the faces was different. And yet they had a certain sameness about them, just as did the children who now stood gazing raptly. The eyes of the dolls glittered brightly in the shimmering light.

Clarey Lambert stood silently before the altar for a few moments, then turned to face the gathering of children.

"He is with us," she spoke, her words rolling from her lips in the measured cadence of a chant.

"He comes to bless us," the children replied in a single voice.

The black-garbed figure of the Dark Man emerged from the trees, stood silent before the altar for a moment, then turned to face the assemblage outside.

The Dark Man's face, like his body, was shrouded in black, but in the glimmering light of the fire, his eyes glowed brightly from two holes in the hood that concealed his features.

The Dark Man gazed out at the children, his eyes finally fixing on Michael and Kelly.

"My children return," he said, his voice carrying in the hushed darkness. Striding away from the altar, he crossed the clearing, his eyes never leaving the faces of Michael and Kelly.

Neither of them moved, neither of them shrank away. Rather, they stood as if carved from stone, gazing steadily at the black-shrouded face. The Dark Man stopped a few feet from them. He held out his arms.

"Come," he said. "I have missed you."

Taking their hands in his, the Dark Man led them to the altar. "You have a gift to give," he said, his words resonating in the silence that had fallen over the clearing. "Why have you withheld it?"

Unbidden, words rose in the throats of Michael and Kelly.

"We were lost," they said. "Now we have come home again."

Laying a hand on each of their shoulders, he turned them around to face him. He began speaking again, his voice dropping so that only they could hear, taking on a new rhythm, soft and soothing, a rhythm that reached inside their minds and put them gently into a hypnotic sleep. At last, when he saw that their last vestiges of will had been surrendered, he directed them to lie on the ground before the altar.

He approached Michael first.

From the folds of his robe he took a large syringe. As Michael unbuttoned his shirt and laid his chest bare, the Dark Man gazed down at the tiny, almost invisible scar that had been on his chest since the night he was born. He smiled with satisfaction, then shifted his attention to Michael's glazed eyes. "Are you afraid?" he asked.

"No."

"Will you feel pain?"

"No."

"Do you give your gift freely?"

"I do."

Slowly, the Dark Man lowered the needle, sinking it deep into Michael's chest. He paused, then slowly began drawing the plunger upward.

From somewhere within Michael's body a single drop of murky fluid seeped into the syringe's chamber.

When he was finished, he moved to Kelly, unbuttoned her shirt, laid her chest bare and repeated the ritual. At last he stood before the altar and held the needles high.

"Youth," he intoned. "Youth, freely given."

Laying the syringes on the altar and covering them with a cloth, the Dark Man turned back to face the children who watched in silence from beyond the glowing fire. "Rise," he commanded. "Rise, and join your brothers and sisters."

Kelly and Michael rose up from the ground, re-covering their bare chests, and silently returned to the semicircle.

———

Jonas Cox stood next to Loretta Jagger, his arm draped around her shoulders as she cradled the baby against her breast. In silence he'd watched the ceremony in which Kelly Anderson and Michael Sheffield presented their gift to the Dark Man, knowing that when it was over, it would be his turn.

His and Loretta's.

But their gift, he knew, was far more valuable to the Dark Man than that of Kelly and Michael.

The Dark Man valued babies more highly than anything else.

And though Jonas and Loretta had not yet produced a child of their own to give to the Dark Man, they had been honored in being allowed to present the baby in Loretta's arms to him.

In fact, they might even be allowed to keep this baby and raise it in their own house, the house he and Loretta had moved into last year after his grandfather had died.

He and Loretta weren't married yet, but that would come. As soon as Loretta was pregnant, there would be a special ceremony here on the island, in front of the altar of the Circle, and the Dark Man would marry them.

But not until Loretta was pregnant, for the Dark Man never allowed his children to marry until they had proved their faith in him by making him a baby.

Making him a baby, and presenting it to him the night after its birth.

That, Jonas knew, was why George Coulton had been released

from the Circle. Even now, Jonas didn't think of George as having died, for Jonas, like all the Dark Man's children, believed that George had been born in the darkness of death, and that only by serving the Dark Man, and obeying him, could life finally be given to him.

For the baby in Loretta's arms, the long journey toward life was about to begin. Tonight the baby would be inducted into the Circle, and the Dark Man himself would take him, nurturing him for the first months of his life. Then the baby would be given to one of the women of the Circle, who would raise him in the knowledge that he was different from children beyond the Circle.

Someday, if his obedience was perfect—as perfect as Jonas's had always been—and if he fathered new children for the Dark Man—as Jonas intended to do—Jonas would be released from the Circle.

He would join the others.

Jonas knew who some of them were. Important men, men who didn't live like swamp rats. And when it was time, and if he was worthy, he, too, would benefit from the Circle's gift.

But if he wasn't worthy, if he disobeyed the Dark Man . . .

An image of George Coulton flashed into his mind, but evaporated almost instantly.

His thoughts were interrupted as he heard the Dark Man speak his name.

With Loretta at his side, he stepped out of the semicircle around the fire and moved toward the altar where the Dark Man waited.

Jonas Cox took the baby from Loretta Jagger and placed it into the Dark Man's waiting arms.

The Dark Man turned to face the altar, holding the baby high. "Jonas Cox and Loretta Jagger offer this child. Do you accept him?"

The voices of the children again spoke as one. "We do."

The Dark Man placed the baby on the altar, unwrapping the blanket in which it was wrapped. It lay in the light of the candles, naked, reaching out with its tiny hands, its eyes blinking in the flickering glow.

Again the Dark Man reached beneath his cloak, and when his hand was once more revealed to the watching children, it held an ornately carved instrument, its handle worked from ivory, from which protruded a glistening needle.

The Dark Man held the device high, poised it over the infant's breast, then began to bring it downward. There was a long silence as he held the needle still, but then he plunged it suddenly downward.

The child uttered a scream as the point passed through its skin, then pierced its sternum to sink deep within its chest.

But as the needle found its mark, the baby's scream died away, a sigh drifting up from its throat when the Dark Man's dagger entered into the core of its being.

Though its body remained unharmed, the baby's spirit began to die, impaled on the tip of the Dark Man's weapon.

As the child's sigh died away, the Dark Man unscrewed the ivory handle, leaving the needle in place.

When he was finished, he held the baby high. "Behold your brother," he said to the gathered children. "Care for him, as I have cared for you."

The ceremony was over.

In her room in the clinic, Amelie Coulton woke up screaming. In her dreams, she had just seen her baby.

And her baby was not dead.

It was in pain, and it needed her.

"I just wish I knew what to do,"
Mary Anderson told Ted the next morning. She was standing in
front of her sink in the master bathroom, gazing dispiritedly at her
own image. "I must have been awake until after three." The lack
of sleep showed: there were dark circles under her eyes, and the
skin beneath her chin seemed to be sagging. Her eyes shifted to
her husband, who was watching her studying herself, a small grin
playing around the corners of his mouth. "Well, I'm sorry," Mary
groused. "But it's not easy lying awake worrying about your daughter all night, then getting up at dawn to fix breakfast for your husband. It ages a girl."

"Not that much," Ted observed, playfully reaching out to pinch
her rump. But his smile quickly faded. "Maybe we should have
talked to her when she came in last night."

Mary's brows arched. "On that one, I have to agree with your
father. You know how she can get, and the last thing I wanted last
night was to set her off. I wouldn't have gotten any sleep at all."

"Do you want me to talk to her this morning?"

Mary hesitated. A month ago she would have said yes, but now
she wasn't sure. What if Kelly thought they'd been spying on her?
But wasn't keeping track of your daughter part of being a mother?

She'd thought things couldn't get any worse after Kelly's suicide attempt, but she was no longer so sure.

For a month she'd felt as though she was walking on eggs, doing her best to make Kelly feel good about herself, but always worrying that something was going to happen, something that would set Kelly off again. And if Kelly thought they were watching her . . .

Anger roiled up in her. Why *shouldn't* they be watching her? They were worried about her! And Kelly had said nothing about going out last night. All she'd said was that she was going up to bed.

But she'd sneaked out.

Mary probably wouldn't have found out about it all if it hadn't been for the fan. When she'd stopped at Kelly's door on her way to bed, she'd only peeked in, planning to say good night if her daughter was still awake. In the dim glow of the moonlight she'd seen Kelly in bed, apparently sound asleep, and had been about to close the door when she noticed how hot and stuffy the room was.

Though the window was wide open, Kelly hadn't turned the fan on, and there wasn't a breath of movement in the warm night air.

So Mary had reached for the switch in the darkness, but her fingers had found the wrong one. The light had gone on instead, and she'd instantly realized that the form in the bed wasn't Kelly at all.

It was only some pillows stuffed under the sheet.

She'd told Ted and his father about it, and Ted had wanted to call the police immediately. Carl, though, had suggested that they wait. "How's she going to feel if you send the cops after her? And Villejeune's not like Atlanta. There's just not that much trouble she can get into." Finally he had suggested a compromise. "It's a little after eleven now. Let's wait until midnight. If she's not home by then, we'll decide what to do."

Mary had reluctantly agreed, certain they were simply putting off the inevitable by an hour. But just before midnight they heard footsteps on the stairs outside, and Carl had smiled at her. "See? She's back. Nothing to worry about."

The comment rankled more in retrospect than when Carl had uttered it. What did he mean, nothing to worry about? Kelly had been gone for almost four hours, and they hadn't a clue as to where she'd been or what she'd been doing. And it had kept Mary awake most of the night, wondering.

At last she made up her mind. "We'll both talk to her," she decided. "We'll let her know that we certainly don't mind her going out, but that we want to know where she's going, and who she's with." Which, she thought but didn't say, will get us one of Kelly's patented glares, and a complaint about invading her privacy. And maybe it was true, she reflected as she splashed cold water on her face in an attempt to wash away her sleepiness. Things had changed since she was a girl. She'd never even thought about going out without telling her mother where she'd be. But nowadays a lot of parents simply didn't seem to care.

But Mary did.

When she got downstairs a few minutes later, Carl was already at the table, finishing the breakfast he'd made for himself. "I'm sorry," Mary apologized. "I'm afraid I didn't sleep very well last night."

Carl shrugged, his attention still focused on the morning paper. "No problem. After this many years, I guess I'm used to fending for myself." Only when Kelly came in a few minutes later did he push the paper aside. "There's my angel!" he boomed, but as he saw the pallor in Kelly's face his words trailed off. "Kelly?" he said. "You okay?"

Hearing the change in her father-in-law's tone, Mary turned to look at her daughter. Kelly, as usual, was dressed in a black turtle-neck and torn jeans, her ears decorated with an array of the jewelry that Mary suspected Kelly wore more as a way of irritating her elders than because she really liked it. But this morning she seemed to have put on some makeup that made her complexion look absolutely pasty, and her eyes were glazed over, almost as if she wasn't aware of where she was.

Drugs.

The word flashed into Mary's mind instantly. But she rejected the idea as quickly as it came to her. To the best of her knowledge—and over the last few weeks, it had become intimate—one problem

Kelly had never suffered from was drugs. "Kelly, what is it?" she asked. "What's wrong?"

Kelly's eyes instantly focused, but as she sat down at the table, she shook her head. "I—I just don't feel very good, I guess. I didn't sleep very well."

"Perhaps you would have, if you'd been in bed before midnight." As soon as she uttered the words, Mary regretted them, knowing that not only her comment, but the archness in her voice would undoubtedly set Kelly off. But Kelly's reaction surprised her.

"Midnight?" she echoed. "But we didn't—"

"We?" Despite her good intentions, Mary's voice cracked like a whip. "Who were you with?"

Kelly's face reddened. "A—A boy I met yesterday."

Kelly had said nothing of meeting anyone. "You didn't mention having a date last night," she said more sharply than she intended. "You said—"

"I said I was going to bed!" Kelly shot back. "So I didn't go to bed. So I changed my mind and went out for a walk. What's the big deal? And I didn't have a date!"

Now it was Carl Anderson who spoke, his voice heavy. "Just hold your horses, young lady," he began. "There's no need to talk to your mother in that tone of voice. And it sure sounded to me like you had a date. Now who was it with?"

Kelly glared angrily at her grandfather. "It was Michael Sheffield, all right? His father is your lawyer." She turned furious eyes on her mother. "And I didn't have a date with him. I just thought he might come over, and he did. So I went out with him for a while. I'm sixteen, Mom. I can go out if I want!"

Mary felt all her good intentions of keeping the conversation rational slip away. "But couldn't you have asked us?" she demanded.

Kelly was on her feet now. "Would you have let me go?" she countered. "And what's the big deal? I went out with Michael and I lost track of time! Why can't you just leave me alone?" Turning, she stormed out onto the patio, then disappeared around the corner of the house.

As Ted came into the kitchen, Carl was on his feet, ready to go after Kelly, but Mary stopped him. "Don't," she said, biting her lower lip. "When she gets like this, there's no reasoning with her." She turned to Ted, forcing a wan smile. "Well, so much for my good intentions. I asked her about last night, and she blew up."

Ted's expression set grimly. "How the hell are we supposed to show her we love her when she won't even let us talk to her?"

Mary sank into one of the chairs at the breakfast table. "I don't know," she sighed. "I just don't know."

"Well, I know," Ted replied darkly. "Tonight, after Dad and I get home from work, Kelly and I are going to have a little chat. I'm going to tell her what the rules are around here, and she's going to by-God abide by them! And if she doesn't—"

"And if she doesn't, what?" Mary broke in, her eyes moistening with tears. "She's never obeyed any of our rules, Ted! What makes you think she's going to start now?" She buried her face in her hands and sobbed quietly. "It was supposed to be different here," she said. "That's why we came. But it's not different. We're the same, and Kelly's the same, and I can't stand it. I just can't stand it!"

Ted and Carl gazed helplessly at Mary as she sobbed.

Finally Carl spoke into the silence. "Michael Sheffield's not a bad kid," he said. "He's kind of a loner, but he's never been any trouble to anyone. If Kelly's hanging out with him, there's nothing to worry about."

Mary, hearing the words, wiped her eyes and managed to look up. "Is that what you think, Carl?" she asked.

Her father-in-law nodded.

"Well, I wish I thought you were right. But right now I'm not so sure. Just now I think that maybe Craig Sheffield should be worrying. After all, it's his son who's hanging around with my daughter."

Carl's expression darkened. "You don't mean that, Mary," he said. "That's a terrible thing to say about your little girl."

Mary nodded miserably. "But she's not my little girl, is she?" she asked brokenly. "She's a stranger who lives with me, and I hardly know her. And it's always been that way. Always."

Two hours later, as he and Ted were inspecting one of the houses in Villejeune Links Estates, Carl paused halfway up the temporary stairs to the second floor and found himself panting. Ted, already on the landing above, looked down at him. "Dad? You okay?"

Carl took a deep breath, nodded, and continued on upward. But his legs felt heavy, and by the time he reached the top, he needed to sit down. "Getting old," he said. "Just give me a minute, and I'll be okay."

Ted eyed his father carefully. Carl's face had gone pale, and wrinkles Ted had never noticed before were etched around his eyes. "You don't look so good," he said. "I think maybe we'd better get you over to the clinic. Does your chest hurt?"

Carl glanced up at his son and chuckled hollowly. "Thinkin' maybe your old man's going to have a heart attack?" he asked. "Well, don't get your hopes up. I don't have any plans for dying."

"I didn't mean it that way," Ted said quickly. "But at your age—"

"At my age, I'm in better shape than most men twenty years younger'n me!" He struggled to his feet, but his legs still felt rubbery. "Huh," he muttered. "Maybe you're right. Maybe it wouldn't hurt to go see Warren Phillips."

Allowing Ted to steady him, Carl made his way carefully down the stairs. As he came to the bottom and started toward the front door, his vision began to blur slightly, and suddenly he knew what was wrong. "Shit," he muttered under his breath.

Ted, still holding the older man's arm, tightened his grip. "What is it?" he asked.

"Nothin'," Carl replied. "I just need to go see Phillips today, that's all. I'm feeling puny 'cause I'm due for a shot."

Ted said nothing until they were in the truck and heading toward Villejeune. He glanced over at his father. Though Carl was sitting straight up in the seat next to him, he looked even worse than he had a few minutes before. "What's wrong, Dad?" he asked.

Carl's head swung around, and his eyes, suddenly looking dull, fixed vacantly on Ted. "Huh?" he grunted.

"You said you need a shot, Dad," Ted went on, trying not to betray the concern he was feeling. "What shot? What's wrong with you?"

Carl made a dismissive gesture. "It's nothing. Just a vitamin shot Warren Phillips gives me."

Ted frowned. Whatever was wrong with his father, it didn't look like a vitamin shot would take care of it. Indeed, Carl seemed to be getting worse by the minute. His breath was rasping now, and he was beginning to cough every few seconds. Ted pressed his foot on the accelerator, and the truck shot forward. When they came to the clinic, Ted ignored the parking lot, pulling up to the emergency entrance and hurrying around to help his father out of the truck.

"I can make it," Carl complained, brushing Ted's hand away as he struggled to get out of the truck. He felt his limbs stiffening, as if his arthritis were flaring up again. Clenching his jaw against the pain, he walked into the clinic, Ted beside him.

Jolene Mayhew looked up from her computer terminal, a welcoming smile on her face, which faded into a look of concern when she saw Carl Anderson. "Carl! What's— My goodness, let me call Dr. Phillips." She picked up the phone, punched two digits into it, then spoke rapidly. A moment later she hurried out of her cubicle and took Carl's left arm. "Let's get you right in."

Carl irritably shook the girl off. "Leave me alone, will you?" he rasped, his voice querulous. "I'm not dying, young lady."

Jolene fixed him with an exaggerated glare. "Well, you couldn't tell by me," she said. "You look gray as a ghost. If I didn't know you better, I'd swear you were having a heart attack."

"Well, I'm not!" Carl snapped, moving toward the corridor that led to Warren Phillips's office. "Ted, you stay here. I don't need you fussing while I'm talking to Warren."

Ted, ignoring his father's words, started after the older man, but Jolene stopped him. "I wouldn't, if I were you," she said. "I've seen your pa like this before, and he'll bite your head right off if you cross him. Just sit down. He won't be but a few minutes."

Ted looked at the nurse curiously. "This has happened before?" he asked.

Jolene shrugged. "Not often. Your pa's real good about making his appointments."

Ted felt a twinge of foreboding. "How often does he come?"

Jolene shrugged. "Every other week, regular as clockwork. And don't you worry. Dr. P will fix him right up."

Ted sank into a chair, his mind spinning. What was going on? His father had never been sick—in fact, as far as Ted knew, he was in perfect health. But if he was taking shots every other week . . .

He sat numbly, waiting for his father—or the doctor—to reappear.

Fifteen minutes later Carl walked back into the waiting room, smiling now, his color back to normal. "See?" he teased Jolene Mayhew. "Fit as a fiddle. Even had Warren give me an EKG, just to prove to you that I was right. Probably cost me fifty bucks, but what the hell?" He turned to Ted. "Come on, boy. Let's not waste the day sittin' around here waiting for people to die. There's work to be done."

Ted stared at his father, stunned. It was as if the incident had never happened. Carl's breathing was back to normal, there was a spring to his step again, and he was once more the man he'd been early this morning.

As they left the hospital and returned to the truck, Ted had the uncomfortable certainty that he knew why. "Dad," he said as he started back to the construction site, "about those shots . . ."

Carl chuckled. "I know what you're going to say," he interrupted. "You think Warren Phillips is a Dr. Feelgood, and your old man's hooked on drugs, right? Well, forget it—he's not!"

Ted pursed his lips. "Whose word do you have on that?" he asked. "Seems to me that if Phillips was shooting you up with something, he'd be the last person to tell you."

Carl laughed out loud. "Well, I guess we know whose son you are, anyway! First time he gave me one of those shots, way back when my arthritis first hit, I got suspicious. Never thought I'd say this, but I felt too damned good. So the next time, soon as I was done with him, I hied myself up to Orlando and got a blood test.

Didn't name any names—just told them I'd been given a shot and wanted to know what was in it." He chuckled softly. "Figured it was amphetamines, at least, and probably a whole lot else. Well, score one for Warren Phillips. All they found was cortisone, along with some traces of hormones."

Ted stared at him incredulously. "Hormones?" he repeated. "What kind?"

"How the hell would I know?" Carl boomed. "I don't know shit from hormones, and don't want to. Probably some kind of sheep's balls or something, like that guy in Switzerland used to use on the movie stars. All I know is, it keeps me feeling good and looking good, and the doctor in Orlando said there was nothing wrong with it. And there damned well shouldn't be, considering the price Phillips gets for it." He grinned at Ted. "Who knows? If I can afford it, maybe I can live forever."

Ted said nothing more, but his father's words didn't sound right. If the shots were nothing more than hormones, how could they have made his father rebound so quickly? And why did they cost so much? From what his father had said, the shots didn't sound like they should be that expensive.

But drugs were.

And only drugs, as far as he knew, could affect anyone the way Dr. Phillips's shot had affected his father.

———

"How the hell do you know where you are?" Tim Kitteridge asked Judd Duval.

He was sitting in the prow of Judd's boat. For the last hour he had been certain they were going in circles. Everywhere, the tangle of moss-laden cypress and bushy mangroves looked the same. Half the time, the foliage had closed in so tightly around the boat that the mangrove roots scraped against its sides as they passed. Every now and then Tim had spotted snakes—thick, green constrictors—draped over the tree limbs under which they'd passed. He'd shuddered as he imagined one of them dropping down on him, coiling itself around his body, slowly crushing him. In addition, alligators lay in the water, their yellow eyes staring greedily as they passed.

"Lived here all my life," Judd replied. "When you grow up in a place, you get to know it real well. Just have t'know what t'look for." He chuckled, an ugly, cackling sound. " 'Course, they say us swamp rats have some extra senses, too," he added. "There's them's as think we can see in the dark."

"Well, I'd just as soon not find out," Kitteridge observed. "Not today, anyway. You sure you know where this Lambert woman lives?"

Judd's chuckle rumbled up from his throat again. "Less'n she's moved, I know the place, and she ain't likely to move till the day she dies. If she ever dies."

Kitteridge glanced back at the deputy. "How old is she?"

"Who knows? Been here as long as I have, and she was an old lady back then." He grinned wickedly at the chief. "Lots of folks say she's a witch. Or maybe a voodoo princess."

Kitteridge wondered, not for the first time, if he wasn't just wasting the morning. Still, if he could get a line on Jonas Cox, it would be worthwhile. He'd asked Judd about Jonas first thing that morning, as soon as Judd had reported for the day's duty.

"Kid's half cracked," Judd had told him. "Lives out in the swamp somewhere, and nobody hardly ever sees him. Just as well, if you ask me. Mean as shit, and twice as dumb."

"According to Amelie Coulton, he and George both have something to do with this person she called the Dark Man."

Judd had rolled his eyes. "Amelie's almost as dumb as Jonas. Anyway, that sure warn't George we found out there."

"Amelie thinks it was," Kitteridge replied.

A dark look flashed across Judd's face, then disappeared. "Well, there ain't no such person as the Dark Man. You cain't hardly believe nothin' a swamp rat says. They'll tell you anythin' you want, then shoot you in the back."

Kitteridge had stared pointedly at Duval. "Not much of a recommendation for you, is it?"

The comment had not been lost on the deputy, but he'd merely shrugged. "You're the boss. You want to see Clarey Lambert, it's my job to get you there. But the onliest way we'll find Jonas is if we stumble onto him."

Now, as they rounded yet another of the myriad tiny islands, a house came into view. Kitteridge had become accustomed to the shacks the swamp rats lived in, and this one seemed no different from any of the others. Propped up out of the mire on stilts, it was built of cypress, patched here and there with bits of corrugated tin. On the porch, a woman sat in a rocker, her hands busy with some mending. "That's her," Judd said from behind him. "Settin' in her chair, just like always."

As the boat drew near, Clarey Lambert's fingers stopped working and her eyes fixed on the two men. She knew Judd Duval— had known him for years. The other one she'd never seen before, but recognized anyway.

"Mrs. Lambert?" Kitteridge asked as the boat came to a stop a few feet out from the porch and Judd cut the engine.

Clarey nodded, but said nothing.

"I'm Tim Kitteridge. I'm the police chief in—"

"I knows who you be," Clarey said, her eyes dropping back to the work in her lap.

"I want to talk to you."

Clarey shrugged.

"I heard a story about some people who live out here."

Clarey's head tilted disinterestedly.

"Amelie Coulton said I should talk to you about them."

Clarey remained silent.

"Do you know Jonas Cox?"

Clarey nodded.

"Do you know where he is?"

Clarey shook her head.

As Kitteridge's eyes fixed on the old woman, she returned his stare, unblinking, and he knew he was going to get no information out of her at all. He had no idea how old she might be, but her eyes were almost hidden in the deep wrinkles of her skin, and her hair, thin and wispy, barely covered her scalp. "Amelie said her husband and Jonas Cox were the Dark Man's children." He watched the old woman carefully as he spoke, but if she'd reacted to his words, she gave no sign at all. He hesitated, then went on, "She said they were dead, Mrs. Lambert. And she said I should ask you about them."

Clarey's lips creased into a thin semblance of a smile. "If Jonas be dead, why ask me where he is?"

Again Kitteridge hesitated. Then: "That's not what she meant. I think she meant it more like they were zombies or something."

Clarey's eyes fixed on the police chief. "If'n I was you, I'd be careful who heard me talkin' like that. Folks might think you be crazy."

Kitteridge held her gaze. "I didn't say I believed her, Mrs. Lambert. I'm just doing my job."

Clarey Lambert smiled once more. "Then I reckon you better git on with it. And I'll git on with mine." Dropping her eyes, she went back to her mending, her fingers working the needle deftly through the fabric in her lap. Kitteridge watched her for a moment, but he knew that no matter what he said, she would say no more. He signaled Judd to start the engine, and the deputy pulled the boat away from Clarey's shack. Though the police chief watched her as long as he could, she never looked up from her sewing.

Kitteridge had the eerie feeling that as far as she was concerned, he'd never been there at all.

———

Tim Kitteridge signaled Judd to slow the boat. "There's a boat up ahead," he said, as the deputy cut the engine and he himself slipped the oars into their locks.

A moment later, as they drifted through a clump of mangrove and emerged into a quiet lagoon, he could see the boat clearly. It was empty, floating in the shallows fifty yards away. Across its stern he could make out a single word, scrawled unevenly in black paint: COX

He glanced inquiringly at Judd Duval: "Jonas Cox?"

The deputy shrugged. "Could be. Mebbe not—must be a dozen Coxes out here. 'Sides, boat's empty."

Kitteridge frowned. "Where would he have gone? And why just leave the boat?" But even as he spoke the words, an idea formed in his mind. "Tell you what we're going to do. I'll row us over there, and get in that boat. Then the two of us will talk about hanging around, and decide not to. Then you row away."

Judd, mystified, did as he was told. They pulled alongside the rowboat, and he held it steady while Kitteridge, talking loudly, carefully transferred himself from his own boat into the other one.

"I don't know," he said, seating himself on the center bench of the dory. "Looks like whoever was here just took off. Probably in the next county by now."

"Maybe we oughta take his boat," Judd suggested.

"Forget it. Looks like it's ready to sink, and I don't see any point wasting time trying to tow it out of here. Let's just leave it."

He waved Duval off, and the deputy started the engine, steering their boat across the lagoon into a narrow channel on the other side. Tall reeds closed around him, and a minute later he could barely make out Tim Kitteridge sitting silently in Jonas Cox's small dory.

For nearly twenty minutes Kitteridge didn't move. The water around him was as flat and still as a mirror, and the reflection line had all but disappeared. It was as if he was suspended in a green sphere, totally alone in the world.

But he could feel someone close by, sense him with all the instincts that had protected him through his long career in California, where he'd always known which of the seedy apartments he was breaking into were empty and which held armed men, ready to shoot him on sight.

Suddenly, from the side of the boat, a ripple ran out over the surface of the water.

A moment later two hands appeared, clasping the boat's gunwale.

And then a narrow-faced, stringy-haired boy of around nineteen, with two short pieces of hollow reed clenched in his teeth, rose out of the shallow water. His ferretlike eyes widened as he saw

Tim Kitteridge in the boat, and he tried to hurl himself away, but it was too late.

The police chief grabbed him by his lanky hair, twisting him sharply so he lost his balance. He dropped back into the water from which he'd just emerged, struggling wildly.

"Got him!" Tim yelled, but the shout was unnecessary. Judd Duval had already started the engine of his boat and was speeding across the lagoon. A minute or two later Jonas, his hands cuffed behind his back, was sitting in the deputy's boat, glowering sullenly at Tim Kitteridge.

"How'd you know he was there?" Duval asked as he fastened the line from Jonas's boat onto the stern cleat of his own.

"Saw it in a movie a long time ago," Kitteridge said, chuckling. "The water's so murky you can't see two inches into it. So if you want to hide, all you do is stick a couple of reeds in your mouth and lie down. People can pass you a foot away and they'll never see you." His eyes fixed on Duval. "Seems to me you should have thought of it yourself."

Duval's jaw tightened, but he said nothing. As the deputy started the engine and began maneuvering the boat back into the narrow channels toward Villejeune, Kitteridge shifted his gaze to Jonas. "Why'd you hide from us, son?" he asked.

Jonas's eyes, flat and lifeless, seemed to look right through him, and he made no reply to the chief's question.

"Okay," Kitteridge sighed. "You sit and think about it. But by the time we get back to town, believe me, you're gonna talk to me. There's a lot I want to know about you, Jonas, and I'm gonna find out."

He turned away, completely missing the look that passed between Jonas Cox and Judd Duval.

11

Kelly stepped out of Arlette De-
long's café, where she'd been sitting by herself for most of the
morning, nursing three Cokes and leafing through magazines
she'd picked up from the rack by the front door. Finally sensing
that the woman behind the counter—a middle-aged woman with a
bleached blond beehive hairdo she assumed was Arlette—was
about to tell her either to purchase the magazines or put them back
on the rack, she'd put some money on the counter for the Cokes
and left. Outside, away from the air-conditioning, the humid heat
of the morning closed around her, and she began wondering where
to go next.

As she moved quickly down the street, the one thing she was
certain of was that she didn't want to go home, where she would
once again have to listen to her mother's accusations.

Except she knew they weren't empty accusations. She *had*
sneaked out last night, and she'd been caught.

But that wasn't so bad—she'd been sneaking out at night since
she was fourteen, and been caught lots of times. And nothing much
had ever happened. Her folks had told her they wouldn't put up
with it, but in the end they always did.

The problem this morning was that she wasn't really certain

what had happened last night. What she could remember was so strange that when she had awakened this morning, she thought the whole thing must have been a dream.

She and Michael had gone into the swamp—that part she remembered clearly.

But after that things were fuzzy. There had been some kind of ceremony, almost like a religious service. And she and Michael had been part of it. They'd been led up to an altar, and a priest, all dressed in black, had spoken to them.

Then he'd laid her down on a bed and put a needle in her chest. But there had been no pain—no pain at all.

That was why, when she'd remembered it this morning, she assumed it must have been a dream. But then she looked at herself in the mirror, and there on her chest she'd seen the mark.

A red spot, in the center of which was the tiny round circle of a puncture wound. The spot had been tender to her touch.

All she'd thought about since then was finding Michael and asking him if he remembered what had happened last night.

Asking him if he, too, had a strange red mark on his chest.

Except that the whole thing was crazy. Over and over she'd told herself that the mark could have been made by a mosquito and that she must have dreamed the whole thing.

Or hallucinated it.

Was that it? Was she going crazy again, and hallucinating?

Now, as her mind whirled in confusion, she suddenly wished she hadn't gotten into the fight with her mother. All she'd have had to do was apologize for sneaking out. And then maybe she could have talked about the dream, and how frightened she was this morning.

Except that she'd never been able to talk to her mother.

She'd never been able to talk to anyone, really. Always she'd felt like an outsider, set apart, unable to touch anyone around her.

Until yesterday, when she'd met Michael.

And last night . . .

An image rose up in her memory of the swamp, and the circle of children around the fire.

The circle that had opened to include her.

Her, and Michael, too.

When she'd awakened this morning, that was the first thing she remembered: the feeling that they had somehow belonged in that circle.

Michael.

She had to find him, had to talk to him.

She glanced around and saw a phone booth in front of the post office. Crossing the street, she found a thin directory sitting on a shelf below the instrument. She rifled through its pages quickly and found what she was looking for. From the address, it seemed that the Sheffields' house couldn't be more than a few blocks from her grandfather's.

And it must face on one of the canals.

Leaving the booth, she started down Ponce Avenue, back the way she'd come this morning.

After turning down two wrong cul-de-sacs, she found the house. She was on the pathway that fronted the canal, less than half a mile from where she herself lived, and although she couldn't see the street number, she recognized the boat Michael had been in last night, now tied up to a small dock at the canal's edge. She gazed across the lawn at the house, a long, low, vaguely Mediterranean structure, with a tile roof. On a patio shaded by trellises twined with wisteria, a little girl was playing. Feeling eyes on her, the child looked up, then trotted across the lawn, coming to a stop a few yards from Kelly. Cocking her head, she stared quizzically at the older girl.

"I bet you're looking for my brother, aren't you?" she asked.

Kelly felt herself blushing. "Is your brother Michael Sheffield?"

Jenny nodded. "But he's not here. He's at work. My name's Jenny."

"My name's Kelly."

Jenny's eyes widened. "Kelly Anderson? My daddy says—" But before she could finish, another voice called out from the house, and a woman stepped out onto the patio.

"Jenny? Where are you? Jenny . . ." Her words faded away as she saw her daughter, and then she, too, crossed the lawn. "Hello,"

Barbara said, smiling at Kelly. "I hope Jenny isn't bothering you. Sometimes she thinks the pathway belongs to us, too."

"This is Kelly," Jenny interrupted. "Michael's girlfriend!"

"Jenny!" Barbara exclaimed. "She's not Michael's girlfriend. She's just a friend of his, who happens to be a girl." She smiled with embarrasssment at Kelly. "I'm afraid she just blurts things out."

"I do not!" Jenny protested. Turning back to Kelly, she started talking again. "Last night, Daddy said—"

"That's enough, Jenny," Barbara said sharply, and suddenly Kelly realized she had been correct; Michael's parents had been fighting about her last night. She felt her blush deepen.

"I—I better be going," she murmured, but Barbara shook her head, pulling Jenny close and clamping her hands firmly over the girl's mouth.

"No, don't. I just made some lemonade for Jenny, and there's plenty for you, too. Come and visit with us for a while, and I promise I won't let Jenny say anything terrible. Please?" she added, when Kelly still seemed on the verge of hurrying away.

Kelly hesitated. "I—I was just looking for Michael. If he's not here—"

"Then we can get acquainted without him saying 'Oh, *Mom!*' every two seconds. Now come on. It's hot and sticky, and I can't think of anything better to do right now than sit in the shade and sip lemonade." She looked down at Jenny. "And if I let go of you, you'll keep your mouth closed, won't you?" Jenny nodded vigorously, and as Barbara released her, Jenny clamped her own hands over her mouth, giggling happily. "See?" Barbara laughed. "She's not really awful—she just seems like it when you first meet her."

Chattering on, sensing that if she stopped talking Kelly might still dart away like a frightened rabbit, Barbara led her to the house, taking her inside while she poured the lemonade, then leading her back to the patio. "There," she said as she sank into one of the cushioned chairs that sat around a glass-topped table, "isn't this nice?"

Kelly gazed up at the wisteria that hung in bright blue clumps from the trellis. Around the patio's edge a border of pink petunias were in full bloom, and the scent of honeysuckle wafted through the air from a vine growing up a wall a few feet away. "The flowers are nice," she said shyly. "Especially the petunias. I like pink."

"Is that why you dyed your hair that funny color?" Jenny asked.

Barbara glared exasperatedly at her daughter. "Jenny! You promised not to say things like that."

"But it's true!" Jenny wailed. "Her hair *is* a funny color."

"*You* may think it's a funny color, but that doesn't mean everyone thinks it is," Barbara told her daughter. She smiled apologetically at Kelly. "I'm sorry. I guess we're a little backward around here. Jenny's never seen hair like yours, except on television."

Kelly's eyes clouded. "There's nothing wrong with my hair. Just because it's different doesn't make it bad. Why does everyone have to have the same color hair?"

Barbara held up her arms in an exaggerated gesture of defense. "Hey, wait a minute! I'm on your side! I think you should have your hair any color you want it. Who cares? It's your hair, and you shouldn't have to please anyone but yourself!"

Kelly felt her brief flash of angry defensiveness collapse in upon itself and studied Barbara carefully. Did Michael's mother really not care what her hair looked like? But everyone's parents cared. "Y-You don't think it looks weird?" she asked, suddenly uncertain.

Barbara shrugged. "I wouldn't pick it for myself, but the only question that matters is, do *you* like it?"

Kelly felt confused. She'd never really thought about whether she *liked* her hair or not—when all the kids she'd known in Atlanta had started dyeing their hair, she had, too. And none of them had ever talked about whether they liked it. All they'd ever talked about was how mad it seemed to make everyone. The whole idea was to watch the expressions on people's faces when they walked down the street. "I—I don't know," she heard herself saying. "I guess I never really thought about it before."

Barbara chuckled. "Well, it doesn't matter, does it? It's your hair, and you have a right to have it any color you want. And if people say you don't, ignore them. They're just plain wrong. Anyway," Barbara said, fingering a strand of her own honey-blond hair and inspecting it with distaste, "I was thinking of changing mine. Maybe auburn? Don't you think this color is kind of boring?"

Kelly hesitated. Did this woman really care what she thought? The way she was talking, it seemed as though she did. "Actually," she finally said, "I like your hair the color it is. I always wished I had hair that color. And auburn wouldn't be right with your eyes. They're like mine—sort of blue, but not really, and with auburn hair they'd just sort of die away."

Barbara sighed. "I guess maybe you're right." She tilted her head, eyeing Kelly thoughtfully. "If you like honey blond so much, why don't we dye your hair?"

Now Kelly gaped openly at Barbara. "Are you kidding?"

Barbara shrugged. "I've got plenty of dye, and nothing better to do. Maybe we'll dye Jenny's, too. What do you think? Hair party? Just us girls?" She glanced from Kelly to Jenny, and Kelly found herself turning uncertainly to the six-year-old.

"She's kidding, isn't she?" she asked.

Jenny shook her head. "Mom'll do anything."

Kelly thought it over. Why not? The worst that could happen would be that her mother would be mad at her again, but it seemed like her mother was always mad at her anyway.

And Kelly knew why her mother was mad at her, too. It was because she wasn't her mother's real daughter. She was just someone whose real parents hadn't wanted her or loved her, and had given her away. And the people who had taken her, and called themselves her parents, didn't love her, either.

Maybe they'd wanted to, at first, but it hadn't lasted very long. Now she was pretty sure they didn't really want her at all anymore.

But if she could only find her real mother, everything would be all right.

Indeed, she'd often fantasized about what her real mother would be like.

It would be someone who understood her, and didn't always find things to criticize about her.

Someone, she suddenly realized, like Barbara Sheffield. "Okay," she said, grinning. "Let's do it. Let's make my hair look just like yours."

Tim Kitteridge leaned back in his chair, studying Jonas Cox carefully. If he had to guess, he'd figure the boy's IQ somewhere around eighty-five. Not real bright, but not quite retarded, either. Jonas, his worn overalls still damp from the time he'd spent lying in the water, was sitting on a straight-backed chair on the other side of the table, his eyes fixed dully on the police chief. They'd been talking for almost an hour now, and Tim was about ready to give up. Jonas had continually insisted he didn't know anything about what had happened to the man whose body had been brought out of the swamp two nights before.

"Did you like George Coulton, Jonas?" Tim asked now, taking a new tack.

Jonas's expression remained impassive. "Didn't hardly know 'im," he said. " 'Sides, way I heard it, that were an old man you found in the swamp. George ain't much older'n me."

"You just said you hardly knew him," Kitteridge reminded him.

"I know who he be," Jonas growled. "Ain't no reason I shouldn't. There ain't that many folk in the swamp."

Kitteridge decided to take a shot in the dark. "But you and George were some kind of brothers, weren't you? Amelie Coulton says you're both the Dark Man's kids."

Jonas's eyes narrowed, his lips curling into a sneer. "Amelie don't know nothin'! Hell, I don't hardly even know who my folks is!"

Kitteridge took a deep breath. "Now, come on, Jonas. You must know who your parents are."

Jonas shook his head. "Lotsa kids in the swamp don't know who their folks is."

"Come on, Jonas," Tim repeated, but Judd Duval interrupted him.

"It's true, Chief. There's all kinds of kids out there bein' raised by folks who ain't their parents. Since they won't come into town to have their babies, some of 'em just die a-birthing, and other people take the kids. After a while, you don't hardly know who belongs to who."

Tim shook his head. It was almost unbelievable that people could live like that at the end of the twentieth century. And yet he'd seen their houses, scattered through the swamp, seen the way they lived. Hell, it was a miracle any of them survived at all. Then he had an idea.

"Are those the kids Amelie was talking about? The ones she called the Dark Man's kids? Is he the one who decides who gets the kids?"

Though he was speaking to Judd Duval, his eyes were on Jonas. He thought the boy stiffened at the mention of the Dark Man's name.

"That's it, isn't it?" he asked. "Those are the kids Amelie was talking about. The Dark Man's kids, she said. And she said you're one of them."

Jonas's face remained impassive. "I don't know what you be talkin' 'bout."

Tim leaned forward. "Sure you do," he said, boring into the boy with his eyes. "You know exactly what I'm talking about."

"No," Jonas whispered, his own eyes flicking toward Judd Duval as if searching for help.

But Tim wouldn't let him go. "That's it, isn't it, Jonas?" he pressed, his voice dropping. "Amelie told me about you and George. She told me you were dead. Not just George. You, too."

Jonas's eyes widened. "No," he breathed again, but now his voice was shaking.

"And you are, aren't you, Jonas? You've got no mama, and you've got no papa, and you never did have. Isn't that what the Dark Man tells you? That you're dead, because you've got no folks?"

Jonas's eyes took on the look of a cornered rat. "Who told you that?" he demanded.

Tim ignored the question. "It's true, isn't it? It's not just George Coulton. It's you, too! You're dead!"

Jonas shrank back, and Tim knew he'd struck a nerve. But it was crazy, all of it! Jonas wasn't dead—he was sitting right there. Was it possible that there really was something going on out there in the swamp? That somehow, for some reason, someone calling himself the Dark Man had convinced a bunch of kids that they were dead?

But why?   •

And what about the others? The adults? Could they really be so superstitious that they believed in something so crazy?

And then he remembered the voodoo cults of the bayous in Louisiana, and the zombie cults of the Caribbean. There were still people who believed in all of it, and there was no reason for him to think that some of those people might not live right here in the swamp outside Villejeune.

But it still didn't solve the problem of what had happened to George Coulton.

He didn't believe that Jonas had killed Coulton—hell, he didn't really have any proof that the corpse in the cemetery *was* Coulton. And even if he could prove the identity of the corpse, how could he connect it to the slack-jawed, ferret-faced, empty-eyed boy who sat across from him now? Nowhere, he was sure, would he be able to find out anything about Jonas Cox. From what he'd learned the past couple of days, anyone in the swamp could be related to anyone else, in ways that would form family trees more tangled than the vines that hung from the cypresses these people lived among.

And no one in the swamp, he was quite certain, would talk to him about any of it.

He was beginning to regret having gotten involved at all. After the little investigating he'd already done, he now understood much more clearly what went on around Villejeune. Orrin Hatfield and Warren Phillips, both men who had spent most of their lives in the area, had known perfectly well what he would run up against in the swamp.

Hostility.

Secretiveness.

Supersition.

A tangle of myths that he would never be able to sort out.

And for what?

Even Amelie Coulton didn't care if her husband was dead— assuming the corpse was her husband at all.

No one else had even asked about what had happened. Indeed, what had happened to the old man in the swamp apparently wasn't even that unusual.

So why not let it go? If no one else cared, why should he?

And no matter what he thought, no matter what confusion and myth he might eventually be able to sort out, he was absolutely certain he would never be able to prove a thing.

"All right, Jonas," he said, eyeing the boy once more. "I guess that's it." He glanced up at Judd Duval. "Take him back to his boat."

As if he feared the police chief might change his mind, Jonas darted out of the little room where the interrogation had taken place.

When he was gone, Judd Duval eyed his boss questioningly. "Well?" he drawled. "What do you think?"

Kitteridge shook his head tiredly. "I think we just wasted most of a day on a wild-goose chase. That boy may not be crazy, but he's about the closest thing to it I've seen in a long time. You think he really believes he's dead?"

Duval shrugged. "That's swamp rats for you. Believe anything anyone tells 'em, no matter how dumb it is." He turned and left the room. In the hall, he signaled Jonas to follow him, but said nothing more until both of them were back in the squad car and he was on his way down to the dock where the boats were tied up. Finally he glanced over at Jonas. "It's okay," he said. "He thinks you're nuts."

Jonas glared at him. "You in big trouble, Judd," he growled. "When the Dark Man finds out you helped him find me—"

"He ain't gonna find out, less'n you tell him," Judd snarled. "You understand me, boy?"

Jonas sank into a sullen silence, not speaking until they were back at the dock. But as he got into his boat, Jonas's eyes fixed on Judd once more and his pale, empty gaze made Judd shudder.

His words chilled Judd's very soul.

"Mebbe he'll turn me on you, Judd," he said. "Mebbe he'll turn me on you, just like he turned me on George."

Getting into his boat, he untied it, then looked up at Judd once more as he grasped the oars in his strong, callused hands.

"I'm gonna rip it out of you, Judd," he said softly. "I'm gonna reach inside'a you, and rip your life out. See if I don't."

Judd, frozen by the ice-cold words, stood where he was long after Jonas had disappeared back into the swamp.

12

Amelie Coulton looked up as the door to her room opened, but when she saw who it was, her eyes shifted immediately back to the open window that looked out onto the garden outside.

"How are you doing this morning, Amelie?" Warren Phillips asked. When the girl in the bed made no reply, he picked up her wrist, quickly checking her pulse. "You know," he went on, "there's no reason for you to stay here, Amelie. If you want, you can go home this afternoon."

Amelie turned to glare darkly at the doctor. "I ain't leavin' 'thout I got my baby," she said.

Phillips sighed heavily and lowered himself into the chair next to the bed. "Amelie, you know what happened."

"I don't know what happened," Amelie replied. "All's I know is I woke up last night and my baby was cryin'."

"It was a dream, Amelie," Phillips told her. "Believe me, I understand how you feel—"

Amelie's voice rose. "No you don't. Ain't no way you kin tell what I'm feelin'! An' my baby ain't dead! I'm his mama, an' if'n he was dead, don't you think I'd know?"

This was the part of his practice that Phillips hated most. But when a mother lost a child, he was always there to talk to her, and listen to her. "Amelie, let me try to explain what happened—" he began, pressing the girl's hand comfortingly.

Amelie snatched her hand away as if his touch had burned her. "I *know* what happened," she told him. "You decided I wasn't a fittin' ma, and gave my baby to someone else!" Her eyes met his now, and he could see her anger glowing brightly in them. "That's it, ain't it? You think I be just a dumb swamp rat, but I hears things, too. You took my baby. You think just 'cause I ain't got no schoolin' and don't live in some fancy house in town I ain't a fittin' ma!"

"Now, Amelie, you know that isn't true," Phillips replied. "Why would I want to give your baby away?"

"Money!" Amelie spat. "You think I don't know there's women who'll pay for babies? An' I bet nice blue-eyed, blond-haired ones fetch a real good price, don't they? Ain't that what everyone wants? Pretty blue-eyed blond babies? Well, I got blue eyes and blond hair, and so'd my baby's daddy!"

Phillips took a deep breath, wondering how to argue with the bereaved mother, who was little more than a child herself. "Amelie, think about it. Didn't I spent a lot of time talking to you about taking care of your baby? Didn't we talk about what to feed it, and what to do if it got sick? Now, why would I have done that if I were planning to steal your baby?"

Amelie's jaw set stubbornly. "You was just foolin' with me, so I wouldn't figure out what happened." She faced Phillips once more. "I let you take care'a me, an' I came in here to have my baby 'cause I trusted you." Her voice began to rise, crackling with emotion. "An' you stolt him! You just took him away, thinkin' I'd believe whatever you told me. Well, I don't believe it! I don't believe you, and I want my baby!"

Her hand came up as if to slap him, but Phillips's fingers closed on her wrist, bringing her arm back down to the bed. At the same time, he pressed a buzzer on the bedside table. Jolene Mayhew appeared at the door.

"Amelie?" she began, but then recognized Warren Phillips as he turned to glance at her. "Dr. P! What is it? Is something wrong?"

"Get Amelie some Thorazine," he said. "Fifty milligrams." As Jolene hurried out of the room, he spoke to Amelie again. "I'm going to give you something to make you sleep, Amelie," he told her. "I know it's a terrible thing to lose your baby, and I know how much you're hurting right now. But after a while it will get better. You're young, Amelie, and you'll have more babies. It's going to be all right." Jolene came back into the room and handed a cup containing a pill to Phillips, then poured a glass of water for Amelie. "I want you to swallow this pill, Amelie," he went on. "Just wash it down with a little water, and in a few minutes you'll fall asleep. And when you wake up, you'll feel much better."

Amelie regarded Phillips with suspicious eyes, but finally took the cup and put the pill in her mouth. Accepting the glass from Jolene, she took several swallows of water, then laid her head back down on the pillow.

"That's my girl," Phillips said, pulling the sheet up and tucking it around Amelie's shoulders. "Now you just go to sleep, and when you wake up, we'll talk about sending you home again. Once you're home, you'll feel a lot better."

Amelie made no reply, but a sigh escaped her lips and she closed her eyes. Phillips signaled to Jolene, and the two of them left the room. "Keep an eye on her," Phillips told the nurse as they walked back toward the reception area. "She's come up with the idea that we stole her baby and sold it, and she was pretty hysterical for a few minutes there."

Jolene clucked her tongue sympathetically. "Oh, Lord. Maybe I better call Barbara Sheffield and ask her to come down again. Last night she was able to get Amelie right off to sleep."

Phillips nodded. "Good idea. At least it will give Amelie someone to talk to when she wakes up." He smiled wryly as a thought came to him. "Unless she's decided Barbara's part of our nefarious scheme, too." He glanced at his watch. It was eleven-thirty. "Anything on the books for the next couple of hours?"

Jolene shook her head. "Nothing till after lunch. Then you've got Judge Villiers, and Fred Childress, and that's it for the day."

"Then I'll see you after lunch." He left the hospital, got into his car and started home, glancing once more at his watch. It would be close, but there was time.

━━━

As soon as Phillips and Jolene Mayhew left her room, Amelie Coulton sat up and spit the pill they'd given her into her hand. She stared at it for a second, then got out of bed, went to the bathroom, and dropped it in the toilet.

How dumb did they think she was? Thinking they could talk her out of what she knew and put her to sleep by giving her a pill. Well, they were wrong. She'd had a dream last night, and she knew what dreams were. Everyone in the swamp did.

You could see all kinds of things in dreams.

Sometimes you could talk to dead people, people you thought you'd never get to see again.

Sometimes you could go places. Places you'd never get to go in real life. Amelie had had lots of dreams like that. She'd been to New Orleans, and Paris, and all kinds of places.

And sometimes you could see the future.

Amelie had had lots of those, too. She'd had dreams where she was a lot older than she was now, and had lots of children around her.

And last night, when she'd dreamed about her baby and woken up knowing he needed her, she'd known what that dream meant, too.

It meant her baby wasn't dead at all. It was still alive, and it was crying out for her.

Well, she wasn't going to hang around the hospital, that was for sure. Whatever they'd done with her baby, no one around here was going to give it back to her.

She found her clothes in the closet and pulled them on, then started for the door.

But what was she going to do? Just walk out there and tell Jolene Mayhew she was leaving? What if Jolene tried to stop her?

But Dr. Phillips had said she could go home today. That's what he'd been talking about when he first came in.

Except then he'd given her the pill, and she was supposed to be asleep right now.

She made up her mind, and turned away from the door, heading for the window instead. She unlatched the screen, pushed it out, and climbed out into the garden.

And suddenly felt weak.

She leaned against the wall for a moment, catching her breath and waiting for the dizziness to pass. Then, glancing both ways to make sure no one was watching her, she darted away from the building, across the parking lot, into the thicket beyond the asphalt. As the palmettos and saw grass closed around her, she began to relax a little. She wasn't back in the swamp yet, but at least she was out of the hospital.

She could get back to the swamp even without a boat.

And once there, she would start hunting for her baby—the baby Amelie believed with all her heart still lived.

━━━━

"Well, what do you think?"

Kelly gazed into the mirror. She could barely recognize the image that stared back at her.

Her features hadn't changed, but she looked like a different person. Barbara Sheffield had trimmed her hair as well as changed its color, and it was much shorter now, no longer hanging around her face the way it used to. Instead it was brushed back and seemed to have taken on a glow all its own. The new color, a light honey shade with a few darker streaks in it, didn't look dyed at all, and made her skin look healthier and her eyes bluer. She reached out for the earrings that she'd piled on the ledge above the sink before they'd started the project, then hesitated.

"What's wrong?" Barbara asked, frowning. Then she thought she understood. "Oh, dear, you don't like it, do you?"

"No!" Kelly protested. "I like it fine. It's just . . ." Her voice trailed off. The truth was that she *did* like her hair, but now all of a sudden her clothes looked wrong, and so did her jewelry.

"It's what?" Barbara urged. "I think you look very pretty. Doesn't she, Jenny?"

Jenny, who had been kibitzing through the whole session, bobbed her head enthusiastically. "She looks just like cousin Tisha."

Kelly frowned. "Who's cousin Tisha?"

"My sister's daughter," Barbara replied. "They live in Tallahassee." She cocked her head. "Jenny's right—you do look a lot like Tisha. I think I must have subconsciously cut your hair like hers, because she's my favorite niece." When Kelly made no reply, Barbara sighed. "Well, I guess this wasn't such a good idea after all. I'll tell you what—as soon as it grows out a bit, we'll put it back the way it was."

Kelly shook her head. "But I do like it," she said at last. "What I don't like is my clothes and stuff. W-Would you help me go shopping sometime? I mean, just to help me pick out the right things?"

Barbara felt her eyes dampen slightly. "Well, I don't know," she said, feeling uncertain. "What about your mother? Wouldn't she like to take you shopping?"

Kelly took a deep breath. "I don't like to go shopping with her," she said. "She never likes what I like, and always wants to choose everything herself. And now—" She hesitated, not sure how much Michael's mother might know about her. "Well, she acts real nervous all the time. Now, if I said I liked something, she'd say it was wonderful, even if she hated it."

Barbara, standing behind Kelly, laid a hand on her shoulder. "That's probably because of what happened last month," she said softly. "She'll get over it."

Kelly stiffened. "You know about that?" she asked.

Barbara shrugged. "Yes, Kelly, I know. But I also know you're going to be fine."

For a moment, neither of them spoke. Even irrepressible Jenny, sensing something happening between her mother and this girl, was silent. Finally, hesitating, Kelly asked, "You mean you don't think I'm crazy?"

Barbara took a deep breath. "No, I don't," she said. Her hand remained reassuringly on Kelly's shoulder. "Do you think you're crazy?"

Kelly considered her answer for a long time before she turned and faced Barbara. "I don't know," she admitted for the first time, to anyone. "Sometimes I'm afraid I might be."

Barbara slipped her arms around Kelly and gave her a gentle hug. "Sometimes, Kelly, we're all afraid we're crazy," she told her. "But you don't seem crazy to me. You just seem like a sixteen-year-old girl who isn't quite sure who she is yet, and is spending entirely too much time worrying about it. And," she added with a wide smile, "I'd love to go shopping with you sometime, and I promise you I'll tell you exactly what I think of everything."

But as she gazed at Kelly's reflection in the mirror, a thought came into Barbara's mind: This is what Sharon would have looked like. If she'd lived, this is how old she'd be, and this is how she'd look.

As quickly as the thought rose, she tried to put it aside. Kelly was someone else's daughter, not her own. Her own daughter was long dead, her body locked in a crypt in the family's mausoleum in the cemetery.

Yet even an hour later, after Kelly had left, the thought still clung to Barbara's consciousness, flitting around the edges of her mind like a persistent bee, impossible to get rid of.

═══

As she waited for the water on the stove to heat to exactly the right temperature—hot enough to feel warm when she dipped her finger into it, but not hot enough to scald her—Lavinia Carter looked admiringly around the kitchen. She never tired of it, even after two years. Like the rest of the house, it was so different from where she'd grown up that she still marveled at all the wonderful things it contained. At home in the swamp there'd been nothing but the squat little stove in the corner, which her parents had always insisted she keep lit, even when finding wood dry enough to burn was almost impossible. Worse, no matter how low she kept the fire behind the sooty iron door, the stove kept the house so hot it was unbearable most of the time.

House.

It hadn't been a house at all, except that until she'd come here, she hadn't really known it was any different from anything else, because until she was fifteen, she'd never been out of the swamp at all.

Her parents had kept her at home, and she'd always known what her life would be like. She would help her mother raise her sisters and brothers—some of whom her mother had birthed herself, and some of whom had come from the Dark Man, brought to her mother by Clarey Lambert.

Lavinia herself had been brought by Clarey Lambert, when she was so small she couldn't remember it. But as she'd grown up, her mother had told her she was special—that she was one of the Dark Man's children, and that someday she would marry another one of his children.

"You and the rest of his kids be different," her mother had explained to her. "The day you was born, the Dark Man chose you. You be special, and there's things the Dark Man can do for you."

But she hadn't felt special.

She hadn't felt anything at all, really.

She'd just grown up, doing as she was told.

And on some nights, when she felt the silent call summoning her, she'd gone out into the swamp and stood in the Circle with the rest of the children watching the ceremonies.

Watching the weddings.

Witnessing the inductions of the babies into the Circle.

And giving the gift.

Unconsciously she fingered the mark on her chest, the scar that bore witness to the gift she'd given, and the needles that had painlessly penetrated her body so many times when she was a little girl.

Then, two years ago, the Dark Man had singled her out for a special ceremony.

She had been dressed all in white that night, and when she'd been called to the altar, she had at first thought she was going to be married.

But that wasn't possible, for she wasn't pregnant yet. Indeed, the Dark Man had not even selected a boy for her to live with.

But she had obeyed the summons—as all the children obeyed the Dark Man—and gone to the altar, where the Dark Man had spoken only to her, his voice reaching into her mind, putting her slowly to sleep.

When she had awakened, her life had changed.

She was no longer in the swamp.

She was here, in this house where she'd been ever since.

And she could no longer speak.

During the ceremony, her voice had been taken from her.

The Dark Man had explained it to her, telling her that of all the children, she was the most special. Out of all of the children, he had chosen her to look after the babies.

Lavinia had accepted the loss of her voice as she accepted all things.

She hadn't cried, but like the rest of the Dark Man's children, she had never cried in her life.

Soon she had realized that it didn't really matter that she could no longer speak, for there was no one to speak to anyway. Most of the time she stayed in the house, looking after the babies, and the Dark Man, too.

And the house was wonderful.

In all her life she'd never seen anything like it.

Upstairs, there were six rooms on the main floor—beautiful rooms, with walls covered with polished wood and fuzzy paper. One of the rooms was lined with shelf after shelf of books, and though Lavinia couldn't read, she still loved to go into that room and touch the books, smell the aroma of their leather bindings and wonder what the words on the pages might say.

But most of her time was spent in the rooms under the house, taking care of the babies.

As the water came to the right temperature, Lavinia put a bottle filled with formula into the pan, then went into the nursery. It was a windowless room, painted white, containing a dozen cribs.

Four of them were occupied; the rest were empty.

She leaned over Tammy-Jo and Quint Millard's little son, and tickled him under the chin. His eyes opened sleepily and his arms began to wave around, his fingers finally grasping the tube that led from the needle in his chest to the bottle hanging from an IV rack next to the crib. Gently, Lavinia pried his fingers loose from the tube, slipping a rattle into his hands instead. Distracted, he fingered the rattle clumsily, finally inserting its handle into his mouth. Lavinia smiled—as long as he wasn't playing with the tube, trying to pull it loose, she wouldn't have to strap him down.

Two of the other babies—children who had been here almost a year now, and who would soon be going back to the swamp—were sound asleep, and as Lavinia hovered over them, she wished she could still speak, for she would have liked to be able to sing one of the lullabies she knew to them. Instead, she contented herself with tucking a blanket gently around one of them, and replacing the teddy bear that had slipped from the arms of the other. The sleeping baby stirred only slightly, then wrapped its arms around the stuffed animal before dropping back into a deep sleep.

Finally Lavinia went to the crib containing the newest baby, the one the Dark Man had brought to her only last night. She carefully detached the tube from the needle in its chest, then picked the baby up, carrying him with her back to the kitchen.

Testing the bottle against the skin of her wrist, she sat at the kitchen table, the baby in her lap, and held the nipple to its mouth. The baby tried to push the nipple away at first, but Lavinia gently insisted, and finally the child accepted it. As the infant began sucking the formula from the bottle, Lavinia cradled him against her breast, wondering if the time would ever come when she would have a baby of her own.

She suspected not.

Though there was no one to talk to about it, she was almost certain that she would spend the rest of her life here, tending to other people's babies, while having none of her own. But if that was the Dark Man's will, she had no choice but to obey.

Indeed, it had never really occurred to Lavinia even to think about disobeying him.

Suddenly, as she heard footsteps on the stairs, she stiffened, and her eyes automatically went to the clock on the wall.

Early.

It wasn't nearly time for him to come.

Yet she knew whose footsteps she heard, for not only did no one but she and the Dark Man ever come down here, but his tread was so familiar she would have recognized it even in her sleep.

A moment later the door opened and the Dark Man stepped inside. He stopped short, his eyes boring into her. In the bright light of the kitchen, they gleamed like polished stones.

"Put the baby back in the nursery," Dr. Warren Phillips ordered.

Lavinia, her face ashen, hurried to obey her master, and Phillips smiled as he left, pleased—as always—at her instant compliance with his wishes. Of all his children, only Lavinia had ever seen his face, had ever seen the man who lived behind the Dark Man's black mask. And she would never tell what she had seen, for he had removed her vocal cords during the ceremony in which he had called her to care for the babies in the nursery.

Except that there weren't enough babies.

As he started toward the nursery, the Dark Man's eyes automatically scanned the floor for leaks. The rooms beneath his house were carved out of the limestone bedrock itself, and though they had been sealed years earlier against the constant seepage from the nearby swamp, the pumps still seemed always to be running. Nevertheless, the chambers beneath his house served their purpose.

A few miles beyond Villejeune, the house was hidden in a dense wilderness that protected it well from casual visitors. And those few visitors he had saw nothing of the soundproofed complex that lay below the house, the chambers where he prepared for the ceremonies that took place in the swamp, the laboratories where Phillips worked alone, or the nursery where the babies were kept.

He stepped into the nursery just as Lavinia Carter was reattaching the plastic tube to the needle in the chest of Amelie Coulton's baby. Lavinia glanced fearfully at him as he came in, but he ignored her, moving quickly among the cribs, detaching the filled bottles that hung from the IV racks, replacing them with empty ones.

At last he came back to the crib where Amelie Coulton's baby lay on his back once more, his tiny arms held immobile by nylon straps, the needle still fixed to his chest.

The tube attached to the needle steadily dripped liquid—faintly brown, and viscous—into the collecting bottle on the rack.

Phillips gazed at the level in the bottle.

Not enough. Not nearly enough.

He glanced around the rest of the nursery, at the eight empty cribs.

They should have been full.

Always, until recently, he'd been able to keep the cribs full.

But for the last few years it hadn't been possible.

Too many babies had been born dead in the swamp, and too many fathers had insisted on being in the delivery room in town.

It had been easy before, working with only a nurse who paid most of her attention to the mother.

But the fathers paid attention only to their babies, never letting them out of their sight even for a moment, taking them from him almost at the moment he delivered them.

Still, last night Amelie had delivered her child, and already the baby had produced nearly ten cc's of the precious fluid. For the next several months, there would be nearly as much each day.

After that, as the baby grew, there would be less of the fluid, and he would be able to milk it only occasionally.

Eventually, as it approached adulthood, there would be only a few drops each year.

And finally nothing.

By that time, though, the child would be old enough to breed, and he would find it a mate from among the Circle, and the child would begin to procreate.

And there would be new babies to fill the cribs in the nursery, babies bred by him for a single purpose.

But for now, when only a few of the children were old enough to begin producing babies for him, the problem was becoming acute, for even as he was having trouble obtaining babies, he was finding that he needed more and more of the precious fluid with which they provided him.

Phillips disconnected the collecting bottle from the tube, re-placing it with another. Nodding to Lavinia, he left the room.

In the lab, he began the refining process, filtering and concentrating the fluid he'd extracted from the babies, sealing it into the glass vials he would eventually move to the safe in his office. But there was so little of it now that he was going to have to make some decisions soon.

Decisions about who would live and who would not.

He knew the criteria upon which his decisions would be based, and to him they seemed eminently fair.

To extend old life, he needed new life. And as time moved inexorably on, he was finding he needed more and more new life to battle the ravages of age.

Therefore, those who died would be those who could not bring him children.

Babies, to fill the cribs in the nursery once again.

George Coulton had tried to renege on his promise of the child in the nursery, and the Dark Man had punished him. George's death had served another purpose as well: it would serve as a warning to the others.

When his work was completed, Phillips left the lab. Half an hour later, at the helm of his own boat, he pulled up in front of Clarey Lambert's shanty. There, he listened silently as Clarey told him what had happened to Jonas Cox.

Though he said nothing to Clarey, by the time he left her, he'd already made up his mind.

Judd Duval had allowed one of the children to be interviewed by an outsider.

Judd would have to be punished.

And Warren Phillips knew how to punish Judd in the worst possible way.

Kelly was waiting for Michael when he finished work. At first he barely recognized her, but as he approached the motorcycle—on which she was seated—he gazed at her quizzically. "What'd you do to your hair?"

She grinned uncertainly. "I dyed it. Well, actually your mom dyed it."

Michael's mouth dropped open. "My mom?" he repeated.

Kelly explained what had happened, and listening, Michael rolled his eyes. "Weird," he pronounced when she had finished. "I mean, that doesn't sound like my mom at all."

Kelly giggled. "I like her. She's nice, and—" Abruptly, she fell silent.

"And what?" Michael pressed.

Kelly's eyes shifted to the ground. "She . . . well, she doesn't make me feel like a freak," she finished.

"Who said you're a freak?" Michael asked.

Kelly looked at him impatiently. "I didn't say anyone *said* I was a freak. It—It's just the way I feel sometimes. I mean, don't you ever feel like that? Like maybe you're going nuts or something?"

Michael slowly nodded. In fact, it had happened just this morning, when he'd awakened with a vivid memory of a dream.

So vivid that he was afraid it hadn't been a dream.

Then, when he'd looked at himself in the mirror this morning and seen the angry red mark on his chest, he'd become frightened.

Had everything he'd remembered really happened? Or was he going crazy?

All day, as he'd gone about his job at the swamp tour, he'd kept thinking about Kelly and wanting to talk to her. He'd put his thoughts aside, sure that she'd think he was crazy. But after what she'd just said . . .

Now it was he who found himself unable to meet her eyes. "I— I had a dream last night," he said. "It was really weird. It was about what we did in the swamp last night."

Kelly's pulse quickened. If he remembered the same thing she did— She stopped herself, not even wanting to think about what it might mean.

Michael's eyes met hers. Even before he spoke, she knew what he was going to say.

"There's a spot on your chest, isn't there?" she asked. "Like a mosquito bite, only bigger."

Michael nodded slowly. "It's . . . well, it's like someone stuck a needle into me. And it's sore."

Kelly glanced nervously around. There were still a few tourists coming out the gate, and she suddenly felt self-conscious. "Can we go somewhere?" she asked. Sliding back onto the buddy seat of the bike, she made room for Michael.

"Where do you want to go?" Michael called back over his shoulder as they took off.

"I don't know. Just someplace where we can talk, I guess." Her arms tightened around his chest. "Michael, I'm scared."

Michael made no reply, unwilling to admit that he, too, was frightened. If she also had a mark on her chest, then the dream hadn't been a dream at all.

═══════

An hour later, as they sat side by side on the edge of one of the ubiquitous drainage canals, staring across at the swamp, Kelly slid her hand into Michael's.

Today, unlike last night or the night before, the swamp had taken on an eerie look, with its moss-laden cypresses and clumps of palmetto lining the shallow bayous that seemed to lead off into nowhere. Kelly gazed into it, wondering how they could have felt so comfortable in its depths the night before, drifting through the darkness in Michael's boat. Even now she could glimpse snakes coiled in the trees, and see alligators basking in the mud, lying still, as if waiting for something—anything—to cross their path. Right now, with the sun still high in the sky, she couldn't imagine wanting to go into the suddenly terrifying wilderness.

They'd talked about what had happened last night, slowly and tentatively at first, but soon established that both of them remembered the same thing.

The ceremony, and the Dark Man, clad all in black, and the needles that had been inserted into their chests.

And the other kids.

The children who were nothing like either of them, who neither of them even remembered having seen before. Children with whom both Kelly and Michael somehow felt a strange kinship.

"But they're swamp rats," Michael had finally said. "They're not like us at all."

But what if they were? Kelly wondered, a thought suddenly coming to her. What if that was where she'd actually come from? She found herself cringing at the thought. In her fantasies, her natural mother was beautiful, not like the women in the swamp, with their pinched faces and stringy, lank hair.

"Did you ever think about being adopted?" she asked Michael now.

Michael frowned, looking at her in surprise. " 'Course I did," he said. "I *am* adopted."

Kelly stared at him. "S-So am I," she said. "And I was just thinking. D-Do you suppose that's where we came from?"

Michael's frown deepened as he watched Kelly staring across at the wilderness a few yards away. "The swamp?" he asked. "What do you mean?"

Kelly bit nervously at her lower lip, and when she spoke, she selected her words carefully. "I—I'm not sure. But those kids last night. I mean, what if we felt like we belonged with them because we really do? What if that's where we came from? What if that's where our parents got us?"

"But that's crazy," Michael protested. "Those people out there are all weird. Half of them don't even know who their fathers are—"

"But maybe that's it," Kelly said. "Maybe our real moms live out there somewhere. Maybe they didn't want us to grow up like those kids, so they gave us away."

"But all those people are half crazy—"

Kelly's eyes fixed on him. She did not speak. She didn't have to.

Michael said nothing for a few moments, Kelly's words echoing in his mind. Was that where the strange image in the mirror had come from? Some dark place in his own mind that he knew nothing about? When he finally spoke, he couldn't look at Kelly. "Do you ever see a face in the mirror?" he murmured, more to himself than to her. "An old man, who looks almost dead, and who's reaching for you?"

Despite the cloying heat of the afternoon, Kelly felt a chill race through her. "He's over your shoulder," she breathed. "Staring at you. But when you turn around, there's no one there."

Michael turned to her, his face ashen. "You *have* seen it."

She nodded.

"It's what I saw yesterday," Michael went on. "When I fell off the motorcycle. It wasn't the car that scared me. It was that face. It was in the mirror of my bike."

"I saw it the night I tried to kill myself," Kelly said quietly. Slowly, haltingly, she told Michael exactly what had happened that night, about how she'd seen the man in her dreams since she was a little girl, and how terrified she was of him. "I thought he'd made me pregnant," she finally admitted, telling Michael what she'd been too frightened even to tell the doctors. "That's why I did it. I thought I was going to have his baby."

Michael gazed at Kelly. "But that's not it, is it?" he asked.

Kelly shook her head. "It's something else. He wants something from us."

Michael's voice went hollow. "What if he doesn't?" he asked.

"What if he already has it? What if he already has it, and is afraid we'll try to get it back?"

Kelly's hand tightened in his. "But what?" she breathed. "What could he have taken?"

For that question, Michael had no answer, but his fingers unconsciously moved to the mark on his chest.

Craig Sheffield glared at his son as Michael came into the dining room and slid into his chair, then he looked pointedly at his watch. "You were supposed to be home an hour ago," he said. "The rest of us are almost done with supper. Would you like to tell me where you've been?"

Michael thought quickly. After last night, when his parents had been fighting about Kelly Anderson, he certainly didn't want to tell his father he'd been with her again.

"I was doing some overtime," he said. "There were some things I wanted to finish up."

Craig's eyes narrowed. "I'm going to have a talk with Phil Stubbs. Either you're not doing your job right, or he's overworking you."

Michael felt a knot of fear form in his stomach. If his father called Stubbs, his boss would be certain to tell him what had happened yesterday. "I—I wasn't really at work," he said. Better to tell the truth and get it over with. "Kelly Anderson was waiting for me when I got off, and we were just talking. I'm sorry I'm late, but—"

Craig didn't let his son finish. "Didn't I tell you I don't want you getting mixed up with that girl?" he demanded.

"Yes, but—"

"But nothing. I want you to stay away from her, do you understand?"

Michael's temper began to rise. "Jeez, Dad! You don't even know her!"

"No, but I know about her!" Craig shot back. "And don't raise your voice to me, Michael. You may be sixteen, but I'm still your father."

"Oh, for heaven's sake, Craig," Barbara said. "Michael's right! You don't know a thing about her except what you've heard, and if you met her, you'd like her!"

Craig's attention shifted from his son to his wife. "And I assume you know something about her that I don't?" he inquired coolly.

Barbara inclined her head, winking at Jenny, who tried not to giggle, but failed miserably. Instantly her father's eyes fixed on her.

"What's going on?" Craig demanded.

"Kelly was here today," Jenny blurted out. "And Mommy dyed her hair."

"You dyed Kelly Anderson's hair?" Craig echoed blankly, turning back to Barbara.

Barbara nodded. "She showed up looking for Michael, and we got to talking. And before you know it, we'd decided to change her hair color."

Craig pursed his lips. "Was there a reason?" he asked. "I mean, isn't it a little unusual for a girl you've never met to come wandering in, introduce herself, and ask that you dye her hair?"

Jenny giggled. "It was pink, Daddy," she said. "You should have seen it!"

Craig's eyes remained fastened on Barbara. "You're going to tell me she's a very nice girl, aren't you?" he asked, his voice indicating that he was prepared to argue the point with her. "Just a little mixed up, right?"

Barbara sighed. She hated it when Craig took on a patronizing tone, even though she knew it was one of his best assets in his practice. If Craig wanted to, he could always make anyone feel as if he had just made a fool of himself. But as she saw the anger blazing in Michael's eyes, she knew she couldn't let it pass. "Yes," she said coolly, "that's exactly what I was going to say. I was going to sound exactly like a social worker, which I'm sure is the next thing you were going to point out."

Craig opened his mouth, but Barbara gave him no chance to speak. "And it seems to me," she went on, "that you might want to examine the evidence before you make up your mind, counselor."

Craig's expression took on a defensive quality. "I didn't mean—"

"But you did," Barbara interrupted. "You've made up your mind about Kelly Anderson even though you've never met her. Well, you're wrong. Michael likes her, and I like her, and Jenny likes her. And we've all met her." Her eyes darted as though for reassurance toward Michael, but immediately returned to her husband. "I'm not saying she doesn't have problems. She does. She has next to no self-confidence, and it's a little hard to talk to her, but underneath, she seems like a very nice girl."

Craig surveyed his family, who suddenly all seemed to have lined up against him. "All right," he said finally. "I'll tell you what we'll do. I'll call Carl Anderson and set up a barbecue. We'll have the whole family over, and I'll meet this girl you all seem to think is so wonderful. But in the meantime," he went on, his voice hardening and his eyes fixing once more on Michael, "I want you to start taking some responsibility for yourself. No more overtime, and no more hanging around with Kelly or anyone else without calling to let your mother know where you are and when you'll be home. Is that understood?"

Michael nodded silently.

For a long time that night, he stared at his reflection in the mirror on his closet door, willing the hideous face to appear, certain that his knowledge that Kelly, too, had seen the strange image would make it less frightening.

Tonight, though, there was nothing.

———

The darkness surrounded her, but she could feel that she was no longer alone. There was a presence close by, a presence of something evil.

It was him, coming after her again.

She couldn't see him yet, but she could sense him there, hovering in the night, reaching out toward her.

She saw him.

Just a glimpse at first, a shadowy form in the blackness.

The face began to emerge.

A skeletal face, the skin stretched tight now, drawn back so the eyes—glowing, red, hungry eyes—shone brightly.

The lips were stretched back, too, and in his mouth she could see his rotting teeth.

Now she could hear the raling of his lungs and smell his fetid breath.

At last his hands, those terrifying fingers, reaching out to her, groping for her in the darkness.

Away.

She had to get away!

She wanted to run, but her legs wouldn't obey the commands of her mind, and her feet felt mired to the ground.

Mud.

There was mud all around her, sucking at her, pulling her down, trapping her so that he could get at her.

She opened her mouth to scream, but no sound emerged. Her voice had deserted her.

She redoubled her efforts, and felt a constriction in her throat as she tried to force a sound—any sound—from her lips.

Closer, he was closer, his fingers about to touch her.

Then they were on her—cold, reptilian skin that made her flesh crawl—and she recoiled, the scream finally coming.

"No!"

Kelly woke up, her whole body jerking spasmodically, and instantly she realized she'd had the dream again.

But that was all it had been. Just a dream. She was safe in her room over her grandfather's garage. From the open window she could hear the frogs and insects filling the night with sound.

She was all right.

No.

There was someone in the room with her.

Panic rose inside her as the terror of the dream seized her once more.

He was here, in the room.

Except it was impossible. She was awake now, and she should have been safe.

But she wasn't. She could still feel him, feel him standing next to the bed, looking down at her in the darkness.

She kept her eyes closed, willing him away.

She could hear the breathing again, the raling of dying lungs.

She waited, paralyzed, for his touch.

A hand grasped her.

"No!" she shouted, jerking away and sitting up, fumbling with the lamp, certain the bright light would wash away the lingering nightmare.

She blinked as the room filled with light, and another scream rose in her throat.

A figure loomed over her.

"Kelly? Kelly, are you all right?"

It was her grandfather's voice. Kelly took a deep breath, her lungs flooding with air. She shuddered and fell back against the headboard.

"I didn't mean to frighten you, sweetheart," Carl Anderson said. "I just came in because I heard you screaming."

Kelly squinted up, her eyes not yet adjusted to the light. In the bright glare she could almost imagine—

No! She put the thought out of her mind. It was just her grandfather. "What time is it?" she asked.

"Just a little after eleven," Carl told her. "I thought you'd still be reading."

Kelly shook her head. "I—I was having a nightmare."

Carl clucked sympathetically. "It's my fault. I shouldn't have come creeping in here, should I? Scared you half to death."

He bent over and kissed Kelly gently on the cheek.

His breath, the same fetid scent Kelly remembered from the dream, filled her nostrils once more. Instinctively, she shrank away.

Her grandfather straightened, stood still for a moment, then turned and left the room.

Kelly stayed awake most of that night—and the nights that followed—too frightened to sleep.

14

"**W**ell?" Barbara Sheffield asked.

It was Saturday evening, and the sun was poised on the western horizon, casting long shadows across the broad yard that separated the Sheffield house from the canal. Barbara and Craig were in the kitchen, Barbara garnishing a large bowl of potato salad with sliced hard-boiled eggs, and Craig fishing in the refrigerator for a couple of cans of beer. Outside on the terrace, Ted Anderson was tending the just-lit barbecue kettle, while his father and wife were stretched out on chaises. The afternoon had gone quickly, with the men watching a baseball game on television while Barbara Sheffield and Mary Anderson got acquainted.

"Well, what?" Craig countered, though he knew what Barbara was asking him. She tilted her head toward the window, and Craig looked out, then smiled wryly. Outside, a croquet court had been laid out on the lawn, and Kelly Anderson was bent over Jenny, helping her line up a difficult shot. As he watched, Jenny, with only a little help from Kelly, swung the mallet. The orange ball shot through the wicket, ricocheted off Kelly's ball, and struck Michael's.

"It worked!" he heard Jenny yell, bouncing up and down with excitement. "Now what should I do?"

While Michael and Kelly argued about Jenny's next shot—with Michael insisting that Jenny should knock Kelly's ball into the yard next door, while Kelly suggested that maybe they should find out if Michael's ball would float—Craig shrugged.

"Okay, so I was wrong. She seems like a perfectly nice girl." He dropped his voice, even though they were alone in the kitchen. "But I still don't get it—if she's as normal as she seems, why did she try to kill herself?"

"Kids can be under all kinds of stress."

"Well, she certainly looks normal enough now," Craig observed. "Maybe Mary and Ted were right—maybe all she needed was a new environment."

"You should have seen her a few days ago." Barbara chuckled. "With that pink hair—" She fell silent, her face reddening as Mary Anderson appeared in the doorway.

But Mary only smiled. "That *awful* pink hair?" she asked. "Is that what you were talking about?" Barbara's blush deepened. "It's all right, Barb," Mary went on. "It *was* awful, and I still haven't thanked you for talking her into changing it. Let me give you a hand with that." She picked up an egg and began peeling it, then glanced at Craig. "My husband and father-in-law are both grumbling about what they claim must be a beer shortage."

Taking the hint, Craig pulled three cans out of the refrigerator, leaving the two women alone in the kitchen.

"I do appreciate what you did," Mary said as she began slicing the egg she'd just shelled. "And I still want to know how you did it." She sighed and her smile turned wan. "I . . . well, sometimes I just don't seem to know how to talk to her."

"Well, don't ask me," Barbara replied. "As far as motherhood's concerned, I've always just winged it. I figure there's no training for the job, and all we can do is follow our instincts."

The last of Mary's smile faded away. "Maybe my problem is that I don't have any instincts," she said, her eyes carefully avoiding Barbara's. "Every since Kelly was a baby I've felt that I didn't have the slightest idea what she was all about. And it seems that it gets worse as she grows up, not better."

"Don't be silly," Barbara objected. "Every mother has instincts. Didn't you feel it when you first got pregnant?" She hesitated as Mary's face reddened, and suddenly, as comprehension dawned on her, she felt a wave of embarrassment. "That was stupid of me," she said. "I don't know why I didn't figure it out. Kelly doesn't really look like either one of you. She's adopted, isn't she?"

Mary nodded. "I couldn't have children at all. Ted and I tried, but I just can't conceive." Her voice took on an edge. "Sometimes I wonder if it might not have been better if we'd simply accepted the fact that we weren't going to be parents."

Barbara stopped working, and faced the other woman. "Mary, you can't mean that."

"Can't I?" Mary asked, her eyes glistening with tears. "Do you know what it's like, raising a child you don't even know? Every time something goes wrong—and with Kelly, it's seemed as though that's been most of the time—you wonder whether it's your fault. And then you start wondering where your child came from, if maybe it isn't your fault at all. You start thinking maybe it's something in your child's genes." A brittle, harsh laugh escaped her lips. "You wouldn't know about that, would you, with two perfect children of your own?" At the stricken expression on Barbara's face, Mary's words suddenly died on her lips. "Barbara? Now *I've* said something, haven't I?"

Barbara nodded mutely, trying to control the tears that had flooded her own eyes. "I guess we've been lucky," she breathed. "With Michael, there haven't been that many problems. He's always been a bit of a loner, but—"

Mary Anderson's jaw dropped open with surprise. "You mean he's not yours?"

Barbara swallowed the lump that had suddenly risen in her throat. "I—There was a problem. My first baby was stillborn," she breathed. "We adopted Michael before I even left the hospital."

Mary slipped her arms around the other woman, hugging her for a moment. "I'm sorry," she said softly. "I had no idea." Releasing Barbara, she stepped back, breathed deeply, then forced a smile. "Well, aren't we a pair. Known each other half a day, and here we are, crying on each other's shoulders."

The two women went back to work, and suddenly Barbara found herself telling Mary about losing her child. "I hadn't really thought about it for years," she said. "But the same thing happened to one of the swamp-rat women last week. Her baby was stillborn, and she almost lost her mind." She told Mary about the call she'd had from the clinic just a few minutes after Kelly had left that day, when Jolene Mayhew had told her what had happened to Amelie Coulton's baby, and how the young woman had reacted. "Didn't Kelly tell you?"

Mary shook her head. "I'm afraid Kelly doesn't tell either of us very much. She comes and goes, and eats and sleeps, but every time I try to talk to her about anything, she just gets defensive."

"I know," Barbara sighed. "Michael can be that way, too. He's always been a loner, sticking pretty much to himself." She glanced out the window to see Michael lining up a shot on Kelly's ball, while his sister did her best to ruin his concentration. "At least he was until Kelly arrived. I have a feeling she's about to become his first girlfriend."

"Well, it's fine by me," Mary declared. "I don't know what's happened since we came here, but Kelly seems happier. She still hardly talks to us at all, but at least she's not out running around all night long."

They watched the children for a few minutes, and suddenly Kelly, as if feeling their gaze, looked up and waved. Mary waved back, but then frowned. "If that isn't the strangest thing," she said.

Barbara looked at her inquiringly.

"Just now, when she looked up, Kelly looked just like you!"

Barbara felt a chill run through her, and Jenny's words of a few days ago echoed in her mind. *She looks just like cousin Tisha!* The memory of her brief fantasy about her long-dead daughter reared up once more, bringing with it thoughts of Jolene Mayhew's strange story that Amelie had insisted her baby hadn't died but had been taken from her.

It was the same thing that Barbara herself had thought when

she'd lost her little girl sixteen years ago. She, like Amelie, had been unable to accept her loss.

She'd denied it completely, until Dr. Phillips had put Michael in her arms, and the tiny boy had instantly filled the great yawning chasm that had opened inside her.

Now all those memories surged up in her once again. Before she thought about it, she heard herself speaking.

"Mary, where did Kelly come from?"

Mary, startled not only by the question, but by the odd tone of Barbara's voice, turned to face her, and instantly understood the thought that had come into the other woman's mind.

"Oh, no, Barb," she said quietly. "I certainly didn't mean to put a thought like that into your head. It's—well, it's just a startling coincidence, that's all."

Though she said no more about the strange idea that had popped into her head in the kitchen, Barbara could not keep from studying Kelly all through the rest of the evening.

And each time she looked at the girl, she thought the resemblance between Kelly Anderson and her sister's daughter was more and more remarkable.

———

Judd Duval got up from his chair and moved to the doorway of his shack at the edge of the swamp for at least the tenth time since darkness had fallen two hours ago.

He was imagining things.

He knew it, had told himself over and over again that none of the sounds he kept hearing was real. Still, each time he thought he sensed something approaching the cabin, he pulled himself up from his battered recliner and went out to look.

Each time it was the same.

He stepped out onto the porch, and the darkness closed around him. It was a frightening darkness, a blackness that reached out to him, as if it wanted to swallow him.

Deciding it was the lights of the cabin that made the surrounding blackness so impenetrable, he at last switched off the lights, leaving nothing to illuminate the interior of the cabin except the flickering gray light of his black-and-white television set.

After his eyes had adjusted to the darkness, he searched the shadows once more. Somewhere out there, hidden in the tall saw grass, or concealed behind a clump of palmetto, they were watching him.

The children, fixing him with their empty eyes, saying nothing.

Bullshit! he told himself each time.

It was nothing.

So each time he returned to the television, staring at the screen, but paying no attention to the images on the set, his mind filled with images of his own.

This time he was sure he heard the soft splash of an oar dipping into the water.

He flicked off the lights once more, then waited in the darkness.

He heard a rustling sound off to the right and froze.

Then he saw the eyes.

Bright, glowing eyes, staring at him.

Another pair, just to the right of the first.

Then another, and another.

His heart began to pound as he watched the semicircle of staring eyes.

Were they coming closer?

He couldn't tell.

Moving slowly, barely lifting his feet from the splintering planks of his front porch, he stepped backward, feeling for the door with his right hand.

He touched the wood of its frame and steadied himself.

Then he was inside, closing the door behind him and throwing the bolt.

He paused again, listening.

He could hear nothing, but could sense them moving closer to the house, surrounding him.

His breath catching in his throat, he crossed to the television and switched it off, plunging the cabin into total darkness, broken only by the slightly lighter areas where windows were cut into the walls.

He moved toward one of them, almost more afraid to look out than not to. His heart pounding, he peered out into the marshlands.

The eyes were still there, watching him, fixed on him.

A sound.

A soft, scratching sound, as if someone had crept onto his front porch.

He froze, the icy chill of panic creeping up his back.

It was Jonas.

Judd had been waiting for him for days now, ever since the boy had fixed him with those evil eyes and sworn to tear his life out of his body.

And tonight it was going to happen.

He could sense the boy's presence on the porch, and then heard a scratching at the door.

His gun.

He had to get his gun.

He thought furiously.

The table, next to the bed. That's where it was—he remembered putting it there when he'd come home from work this afternoon.

He crept soundlessly through the darkness, feeling his way. Finally, his hands closed on the revolver. Feeling for the safety, he flipped it off, then ran his fingers over the chambers in the drum.

Each of them held a cartridge.

He turned back to the front door.

Once again he heard the faint scratching sounds, as if whoever was out there was searching for a way to get in.

Judd moved to the door, pressing his ear against it. For a moment he heard nothing, then felt a slight bump as if whoever was outside had tested the latch and bolt.

The gun held tightly in his right hand, its hammer cocked, Judd felt for the bolt and carefully, silently, drew it back.

He stepped back, tensing.

Finally he reached out, turned the latch, and jerked the door open.

A form rose up in front of him, and Judd raised the gun and fired. There was a screech of agony as the slug ripped through skin and muscle, and then the dark form dropped to the porch, where it lay still.

Judd reached out and flipped on the light switch.

A raccoon, its fur soaked with blood from the gaping wound in its chest, lay on the pine boards of the porch.

Judd stared at it in disbelief for a moment, then swore under his breath. Still holding the gun, he kicked the dead animal off the porch into the water. It floated lazily for a moment, but then the water swirled, and an alligator appeared to snatch the dead animal up, disappearing back into the darkness with a flick of its huge tail.

"A 'coon," Judd muttered to himself as he went back into his cabin. "Nothin' but a damn 'coon!"

He put the gun back on the table by the bed, then glanced up in the mirror.

And froze once more.

His face looked gray and pasty, even in the bright light, and his eyes seemed to have sunk deep within their sockets.

Around his neck wattles of loose flesh were forming, and when he looked down at his hands, his knuckles had swollen and his skin was blotched with liver spots.

It couldn't be happening—he'd been to see Phillips just three days ago. He was in perfect shape.

Unless . . .

A thought formed in his mind.

What if Phillips knew about Jonas, about how he'd laid a trap for the boy so Kitteridge could talk to him.

But Phillips had said nothing.

He'd only given him his biweekly shot and sent him away.

He went to the phone, his fingers trembling as he pressed the buttons of Phillips's number.

On the fourth ring, as fear peaked inside the deputy, Phillips's voice came onto the line.

"It's Judd," Duval said, his voice rasping.

There was a momentary silence.

"Judd? How are you feeling?" Phillips's voice carried a faintly mocking tone that chilled Judd's blood.

"I—I ain't so good," Judd replied, doing his best to conceal the terror that suddenly gripped him.

"What seems to be the problem?"

"It's my skin, Doc. It's showing spots, and my knuckles are all swole up. I got wrinkles on my face, an'—"

"It sounds like you're getting old, Judd," Phillips said softly, and instantly Judd knew the truth.

"The shot," he breathed. "You didn't give it to me. You gave me something else."

"What did you expect, Judd?" Phillips replied. He was silent for a moment, then went on. "I don't like it when you let outsiders talk to the children, Judd."

He *did* know.

"I didn't do no harm, Doc," Judd whined, his terror now clear in his voice. "Kitteridge don't know nothin'! He thinks Jonas is nuts!"

Warren Phillips's voice turned icy. "What he thinks is immaterial, Judd. You know the rules. The children are protected from outsiders."

"But I need my shot, Doc." Judd was begging now, but he didn't care. "You can't just let me die. You—"

"Without me, you would have died years ago, Judd. And there's another problem, too."

Judd's chest tightened with fear. "What problem?" he demanded. "I've paid," Judd breathed. "I've always paid—"

"It's not that, Judd," Phillips replied. "It's the children. There just aren't enough of them anymore."

"I don't get it," Judd growled. "You said everything was gonna be fine. There's all kinds'a kids out there. Quint and Tammy-Jo had one last month, and Amelie—"

Phillips's cold voice cut him off. "It's not enough, Judd. There's just not enough to go around. Do you understand what I'm telling you?"

Judd's mind reeled. "What?" he breathed. "What do you want? I'll do anything."

There was a silence, and then Phillips spoke once more. "I just told you what I want, Judd. The nursery is almost empty. Supplies, Judd. I need supplies. Bring me supplies, and I'll give you your shot. A full-strength one."

The phone in Judd's hand went dead.

Shaking, he put the receiver back on the hook, but stood where he was for a moment, his mind reeling.

He knew what Phillips wanted, what the price of his error the other day was going to be.

But how?

How could he produce what the doctor was demanding?

He looked down at the watch on his wrist, and found his eyes could barely focus on it.

He squinted, then made out the numbers.

Eight-thirty.

Tomorrow.

Tomorrow he'd figure out a way.

He moved back toward the mirror, and felt a strange burning pain in his hips and knees.

Breathing hard, feeling exhaustion simply from the effort of crossing the room, he peered once more into the mirror.

Old.

He looked old, and he felt old.

But he'd live through the night.

He'd rest, and in the morning he'd find a new source for Warren Phillips.

And Phillips would restore Judd Duval's youth.

Life in Villejeune would go on—eternally.

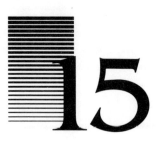

66It's time for you to go to bed, young lady," Barbara Sheffield told Jenny, who was curled up on the end of the sofa in the family room, all but asleep already.

Instantly the girl's eyes opened wide. She sat up. "I don't want to go to bed. I want to stay up until Michael and Kelly come back."

"Well, you're not going to," Barbara replied, glancing meaningfully at the clock. It was almost ten, and already Jenny had been up an hour and a half past her regular bedtime.

"But they said they'd be back by now," Jenny argued.

"I know what they said," Barbara agreed, her own annoyance etching her voice. When the two teenagers had left on Michael's motorcycle, it had been only a little after eight, and they'd promised to be back by nine-thirty.

"We're just going down to Arlette's for Cokes," Michael had told them.

Craig had eyed his son sternly. "See that that's the only place you go. Stay away from the park."

Michael had rolled his eyes scornfully. "Why would we go out there? I don't even like those kids." He was well aware of what went on out at the county park at the other end of town, where a lot of the teenagers of Villejeune gathered in the evening, drinking beer and playing their boom boxes at top volume. Most of the time they didn't do much but hang out, but every now and then the phone rang late at night and his father had to go down to the police department to help bail out someone else's son. And always, the next morning, Michael had to listen to a lecture about staying out of trouble. On this evening, he had seen his father's eyes shift meaningfully toward Kelly Anderson, and suddenly he'd understood. "Aw, come on, Dad," he groaned, his voice dropping so no one else would hear him. "Lighten up, okay? Kelly doesn't even *know* those kids."

Craig had finally agreed to let them go.

Now, as the clock in the corner struck ten, Mary Anderson stood up. "Well, Jenny may not be tired, but I am," she announced. "And look at Carl—he's sound asleep." She smiled fondly at her father-in-law, who was sprawled out in Craig's favorite recliner, snoring softly. "Come on, Ted, wake up your father and take us home."

Ted's jaw set stubbornly. "I think we should wait for Kelly."

"I'm sure you do," Mary observed. "And I'm sure that when she comes home, there's going to be a scene. So why don't we have it at our house, instead of here?" Though she tried to keep her tone light, the tension she was feeling showed clearly. "Please," she went on. "Michael or Craig can bring her home. And I *am* tired."

For a moment she thought Ted was going to argue with her, but then he stood, moving toward his father. "Come on, Dad," he said, shaking the older man gently. "The boss says we're going home."

Carl's snoring stopped and his eyes opened. "I wasn't sleeping," he said. "Just resting my eyes." He glanced at the clock, then frowned. "Where are the kids?"

"Not back yet," Mary interjected before Ted could say anything. "We're going home, so Barb can put Jenny to bed." She turned to Barbara. "Want me to help clean up the kitchen?"

Barbara, sensing Mary's tension, shook her head. "There isn't that much. You go on, and don't worry. I'm sure the kids are fine. Knowing Michael, he just lost track of time."

The Andersons left after Barbara promised to call Mary the minute Michael and Kelly showed up. When they were gone, she put Jenny to bed, then went to work on the mess in the kitchen. When that was finally done, she sat down with Craig to wait.

To wait, and to try to keep her husband's temper under control.

———

"Maybe it *was* a dream," Kelly said. She and Michael were sitting in the back booth of Arlette's café, where they'd been for almost two hours. Except for them, the café was empty, and Arlette, wiping down the long counter on the other side of the room, was eyeing them impatiently.

"But what about the marks on our chests?" Michael protested. "And the baby we saw—what if that was Amelie Coulton's?"

Kelly's mind felt muddled. They'd been sitting here for almost two hours, and hadn't talked about anything else except what had happened to them the previous night. And they still hadn't come up with any answers at all. "Maybe we'd better get out of here," she said, avoiding Michael's question entirely. "I think Arlette wants to close up."

Michael glanced up at the clock on the wall. "Oh, Jesus—we promised we'd be back half an hour ago." He pulled his wallet out of his pocket, put some money on the table, and slid out of the booth.

"What's the big deal?" Kelly teased. "It's hardly even ten o'clock yet. We're not in junior high anymore!"

"Except my dad's already mad at me for losing track of time at work."

They left the café, and as soon as they were gone, Arlette turned off the sign and pulled the torn shade down over the window in the door. They had started toward Michael's motorcycle when a car pulled up and a voice called out to them.

"Hey, Sheffield! Who's your girlfriend?"

Michael turned to the car and saw Buddy Hawkins behind the wheel of his five-year-old Trans Am, grinning mockingly at him. Next to Buddy was Melanie Whalen, who had been going steady with Buddy's cousin Jeff only a couple of weeks ago.

"This is Kelly Anderson," Michael replied uncertainly as a

pickup truck packed with four other kids pulled up behind Buddy's Trans Am. He recognized all the kids as being part of the crowd that hung out at the county park, and suddenly felt uneasy. What were they doing here? He warily introduced Kelly to Buddy and Melanie. "Where's Jeff?" he asked Melanie, but she shrugged disinterestedly.

"We broke up last week. I'm going with Buddy now." She grinned through the window and held up a can. "Want a beer?"

Michael shook his head.

"How 'bout you?" Melanie asked Kelly. "We got plenty."

Kelly, sensing Michael's sudden nervousness, shook her head, and Melanie's lips curled into a scornful sneer. "What are you?" she asked. "A goody-two-shoes like Michael?"

Kelly, slipping her hand into Michael's, felt him stiffen as the rest of the kids, now out of the pickup and gathered around the Trans Am, started laughing. Kelly's mind raced—maybe if she played along with the other girl, the kids would leave them alone. "I like beer," she said. "So does Michael." Leaving Michael's side, she walked over to the car and took the two beers that Melanie was now offering, then returned to Michael, handing him one of them.

"I—I don't think I better," Michael mumbled.

"Come on!" Kelly urged under her breath. "If we don't have one, they'll think we're dweebs. Besides," she added, even though it wasn't really true, "I like beer." She raised the can to her lips, filled her mouth with the bitter liquid and swallowed. A split second later she choked, and the beer that was still in her mouth spewed out, spilling down the front of her clothes.

"Been drinking long?" Melanie Whalen asked acidly, and turned to her friends. "Hey, you guys know who this is? It's the crazy girl who tried to kill herself!"

Kelly froze.

So they knew. They'd probably been talking about her all week.

Another car pulled up. Soon a group of teenagers had gathered around Michael and Kelly. Kelly could feel them looking at her, sizing her up. "Come on, Michael," she said softly, so only he could hear. "Let's go."

But Michael was glaring angrily at Melanie. "What do you

want to say something stupid like that for, Melanie?'' he demanded.

Melanie's eyes glittered mockingly in the glare of a streetlight. "It's true, isn't it? She tried to kill herself, didn't she?"

"So what?" Michael demanded. "You put out for every guy in town, but you don't want everyone talking about it, do you?"

Melanie's face darkened with rage. "You asshole!" she shouted. "Buddy, are you going to let him talk to me like that?"

The door of the Trans Am flew open and Buddy Hawkins positioned himself a few inches from Michael, his fist clenched threateningly. "You better get the hell out of here, Sheffield," he growled. "And take your crazy girlfriend with you!"

Michael stood his ground, though Buddy was three inches taller, and outweighed him by at least thirty pounds. "It's a public sidewalk, Buddy. We've got just as much right here as you do."

"Well, you don't have a right to insult my girl!"

"Who started it?" Michael shot back, his own anger building rapidly. "If you can't do any better than Melanie Whalen—"

Before he could finish the sentence, Buddy's arm came up and his fist smashed into Michael's stomach. Michael felt the wind shoot out of his lungs, and doubled over as pain spread out from his stomach. But then, abruptly, he straightened, his own fist coming up to connect with Buddy's chin. Buddy staggered backward, lurching into his car, where he hesitated a moment, eyeing Michael. Around them, the group of teenagers backed away, forming a circle.

"I'm gonna pound your ass, Sheffield," Buddy growled, rubbing the spot on his chin that was already beginning to swell.

"Big deal," Michael retorted, his voice hoarse as he still fought to regain his breath. "What do you think I'm going to do, run away from you?"

Buddy's eyes narrowed. "Last chance, Sheffield. Take your crazy girlfriend and get out of here, or your butt's gonna get kicked."

"Then you better start kicking," Michael replied, dropping down slightly, his eyes riveted on the bigger boy. " 'Cause until Melanie apologizes, we're not going anywhere!"

Buddy straightened up and moved away from the Trans Am, his knees flexing as he feinted first one way, then another. He ducked left, then moved quickly toward Michael, his right fist poised. Michael, seeing the blow coming, dodged away, then spun around to jab his left into Buddy's gut.

Buddy doubled over as a chant began to rise from the kids surrounding the combatants. "Fight! Fight! Fight!"

Buddy suddenly rushed Michael, his weight knocking the smaller boy to the sidewalk.

Kelly screamed as she saw Michael fall with Buddy dropping on top of him. "Stop him! Can't someone stop him?"

The crowd of kids ignored her, urging their friend on. "Come on, Buddy! Let him know who's boss around here!"

As Buddy raised himself up in preparation to smash his right fist into Michael's face, Michael drew his knees up and shoved hard, twisting at the same time. Throwing Buddy off, he scrambled to his feet, then spun around to face the other boy just as Buddy was rising from the ground. But before Buddy could get up, Michael's left foot lashed out, catching Buddy's cheek. A scream of pain mixed with outrage boiled up out of Buddy's throat, and he lunged toward Michael. Then a new sound rose out of the night, drowning out the shouting.

It was the scream of a police siren, and it was only a few hundred feet away.

"Cops!" someone yelled. Instantly the fight was forgotten as kids hurled beer cans into the narrow alley between Arlette's and the building next door.

Seconds later a police car screeched to a halt on the other side of Buddy Hawkins's Trans Am. "Hold it right there!" Marty Templar demanded, his voice amplified by the bullhorn on the roof of his car. Templar got out of the police car and approached the knot of kids who were now huddled silently on the sidewalk, his right hand resting casually on the butt of his pistol. "Well, well," he drawled. "What have we got here? Little gathering that got out of hand?" His eyes raked over Buddy Hawkins, then shifted to Michael, whose face was scraped, his clothes torn. "What're you doing hanging out with this bunch?" he asked. "Never had any trouble with you before."

Michael said nothing, his eyes fixing on the sidewalk at his feet.

Templar's attention shifted to Buddy Hawkins. "You wanta tell me what's going on, or shall we all go down to the police station?" Before Buddy could reply, Templar spotted the four six-packs of beer stowed behind the front seat of the Trans Am. "Okay," he said. "A fight's one thing. The beer's something else again. Hawkins, you and Sheffield get in my car." He scanned the small group of kids who, now nervous, were avoiding his gaze. "Any of you not drinking?" he asked.

Two of the boys and a girl stepped forward. After sniffing their breaths, he nodded curtly at them. "One of you bring Hawkins's car, and the other Sheffield's bike. Meet me at the station." He let his gaze run over the kids, one by one. "And don't any of you get any ideas about taking off," he added. "I know every one of you, and I don't want any bullshit. Got it?"

As he turned back to the car, he spotted Kelly. Frowning, he paused. "Who are you?"

Kelly hesitated. "K-Kelly Anderson," she finally stammered. Templar's eyes narrowed.

"Carl Anderson's granddaughter?"

Kelly nodded.

"Who're you with?"

"Michael. But we didn't do—"

Templar silenced her with a gesture. "Get in my car."

=====

Ted Anderson, his temper simmering, arrived at the police station behind the post office. Craig Sheffield was already there, and Ted, ignoring the other worried-looking parents clustered around the duty officer's desk, crossed the room to glower at him. "What the hell's going on?" he demanded. "If your kid took my daughter out and got her drunk—"

"Now hold on, Ted," Craig broke in. "I just got here myself, and we don't even know what happened yet."

"It was a fight," a third man said. "They was all out in front of Arlette's, and your kid got into it with Buddy Hawkins."

"Michael?" Craig asked. "I don't believe it. Michael's—" His words died on his lips as the door to one of the back rooms opened and Michael, his face smeared with drying blood, emerged. His jaw tight, Craig's hand clamped on his son's shoulder. "What the hell's going on, Michael?" he asked. "I told you—"

"Can we just go home, Dad?" Michael pleaded. "I didn't do anything, and neither did Kelly. She'll be out in a minute."

"No, we can't just go home," Craig replied. "Not until I've talked to Marty Templar myself. Sit." Turning, he strode back to the office from which Michael had just emerged, rapped on the door once, then let himself in. When he came out again, Kelly Anderson was beside him. He moved through the knot of parents, then spoke to Ted Anderson.

"They're done with our kids," he said. "But he's booking some of the others for possession of alcohol. I'm going to have to stay around—half these people are my clients. Will you drop Michael off?"

Ted nodded, and Craig turned back to face his son. "Don't think this is the end of it, Michael. The police may be done with you, but I haven't even started yet." Before Michael could say anything else, Craig turned away and began explaining to Billy-Joe Hawkins that beer had been found in his son's car.

Michael followed Ted Anderson and Kelly out to the parking lot and slid silently into the cab of the company truck, with Kelly between her father and himself.

"I—I'm sorry about what happened, Mr. Anderson," Michael said as Ted pulled out of the parking lot and swung down Ponce Avenue.

"I'd say you're not half as sorry as you're going to be after your father gets through with you," Ted growled. "If you know what's good for you, you'll keep your mouth shut before I decide to show you just how mad I can get."

Michael shrank down in the seat, saying nothing else until the truck pulled up in front of his house a few minutes later. As he opened the door, he turned to Kelly. "I'm really sorry," he said, but Kelly shook her head.

"It wasn't your fault. I was the one who took the beer. If you want, I'll tell your dad tomorrow—"

"You won't be talking to anybody for a while, young lady," Ted Anderson interrupted, reaching across Kelly to yank the door closed.

Only when the truck turned the corner at the end of the block and disappeared did Michael finally go into the house to try to explain to his mother what had happened.

And to wait for his father to come home.

That was when the real trouble would start.

═══════

"What the hell kind of kids are you hanging around with?" Ted demanded, the anger that had been building up in him since the police had called almost an hour ago boiling over. He pulled the truck over to the side of the road and turned to glare at his daughter.

"I don't even know those kids," Kelly replied. "We weren't even with them!"

"Right!" Ted snapped, etching his words with sarcasm. "You and that little son of a bitch just happened to be wandering by, and someone jumped you. I'm not an idiot, Kelly!"

"It wasn't that way!"

"Then how was it?" Ted demanded. "And don't give me any of your lies, Kelly. I've had it up to here with them!"

Kelly shrank back against the door. "It was a girl," she said, her voice quavering. "She—She was talking about me."

"What do you mean, talking about you? What did she say?"

Melanie's words echoing in her mind, Kelly said nothing, but stared out the window into the darkness beyond the cab of the pickup.

"I'm waiting," Ted said. "We're not going anywhere until I know what the hell was going on tonight, understand?"

"She—She said I was crazy," Kelly breathed.

"Who?" Ted demanded.

"Her name's Melanie. She was with the guy who was fighting with Michael. She told everyone I was the crazy girl who tried to kill herself."

"Well, what the hell did you expect, talking to kids like that? They're exactly the kind we're trying to keep you away from!"

"I—I was just trying to be friendly," Kelly pleaded. "I didn't know what was going to happen."

Ted's anger welled up in him again. "What do you mean, you didn't know? It's always the same thing with you, isn't it? You hang around with a bunch of no-good trashy kids, and then say you didn't know what was going to happen. Sometimes I think maybe you *are*—" He caught himself, clipping off the word before it escaped his lips, but it was too late. Kelly was staring at him.

"Crazy?" she said. "Is that what you were going to say? Well, maybe I *am* crazy! Maybe I've always been crazy, and always will be!"

"Kelly," Ted began, "I didn't mean that—" But Kelly jerked the door of the truck open, and scrambled out.

"Why didn't you just let me die that night?" she demanded. "Don't you think I know what I'm like? Don't you think I know how people talk about me and look at me? And it isn't any different here than it was in Atlanta. It's always the same! Why didn't you just let me die!"

Slamming the door, she dashed away from the truck, stumbling across a vine-choked field toward one of the canals. Ted, still reeling from his daughter's words, opened the driver's door of the truck, dropped to the pavement and started after her.

"Kelly!" he called. "Kelly, come back!"

He came to the center of the field, searching the darkness for any sign of her. For a moment he saw nothing, but then there was a movement near the canal. He took off again, running and calling out for her.

He came to the path that edged the canal and paused, breathing hard.

Then he saw her.

She was fifty yards away, at the near end of one of the footbridges that crossed the canal, linking the path with the wilderness on the other side.

"Kelly! Kelly, wait! I didn't mean—" He started running, but by the time he got to the bridge, she was out of sight.

At the other end of the bridge he could see nothing but the black darkness of the wilderness.

The last of his anger drained out of him as he crossed the bridge and saw the dense vegetation on the other side. In place of his anger a cold knot of fear began to form in his belly. "Kelly?" he called out yet again. "Kelly, where are you?"

He listened, silently praying that she would answer his call, but all he heard was the steady droning of the insects and frogs, and the hoot of an owl.

Kelly had disappeared into the darkness.

16

Mary, pale and shaken, listened numbly as Ted tried to explain what had happened. Her hand instinctively clutched at the lapels of her robe as a chill passed through her. "Why?" she demanded when her husband had finished. Her voice had gone hollow. "Why couldn't you have waited until you got home?"

Carl rose from his chair and went to the phone. A moment later, as Mary listened with growing panic, he said, "Kitteridge? This is Carl Anderson. We've got a problem. My granddaughter's gone into the swamp." There was a moment of silence, then: "It doesn't matter a damn *why* she went in, Kitteridge. What we have to do is find her while we still can . . . No, I don't know exactly where she started, but my son does . . . They had a fight . . . All right, we'll wait for you here. And get Judd Duval—he knows the swamp better than practically anyone."

He hung up the phone and turned to Ted. "I'm going to start calling everyone I can think of. If we're lucky, she won't have gone far, and we'll find her right away." As Mary and Ted sat numbly, feeling totally helpless in the face of what had happened, Carl began organizing a search party. Fifteen minutes later, as the doorbell rang and he went to let the police chief into the house, the phone began jangling. Mary, startled by the sound, stared blankly at the instrument for a moment, then felt a surge of hope.

"It's Kelly," she said, hurrying across the room and snatching up the receiver. "Kelly? Kelly, is that you?"

There was a moment of silence, and then she heard Barbara Sheffield's voice. "It's Barbara, Mary. Craig just called from the police department. What can I do to help?"

Mary felt herself floundering. "I—I don't know. The police chief just got here . . ."

"Craig's on his way home," Barbara told her. "We'll be over as soon as he gets here."

"You don't have to do that—" Mary automatically began to protest, but Barbara cut her off.

"Don't be silly, Mary. I'm not going to leave you sitting alone there. You'd go crazy. And don't worry. Judd Duval knows the swamp like the back of his hand. I'm sure they'll find Kelly within an hour or two."

"Will they?" Mary heard herself asking. "But what if she doesn't want to be found, Barbara? What if—"

"Stop it, Mary," Barbara told her. "Don't even think about anything like that. I'll be there as soon as I can."

Mary silently put the receiver back on the cradle as Barbara Sheffield hung up. She turned to find Tim Kitteridge gazing curiously at her.

"Mrs. Anderson? What did you mean just now?"

Mary frowned uncertainly. "Mean? I—I'm sorry . . ."

"What you just said, Mrs. Anderson. About your daughter not wanting to be found."

Mary closed her eyes for a moment and steadied herself against the table on which the telephone sat. "I—She—"

"My granddaughter had a problem a few weeks back." Carl Anderson spoke into the silence that had suddenly descended on the room. "She was very unhappy, and she tried to kill herself. But that's all over with now."

Kitteridge, his brows knitting, turned to Ted. "I need to know what happened. Did your daughter just take off?"

Unable to meet Kitteridge's steady gaze, Ted haltingly repeated what had happened, glossing over the worst of it. "She was really upset about being picked up by the police," he finished, but Mary broke in, her eyes fixed angrily on her husband.

"It wasn't like that at all, Ted! It was your fault! You blew up!" She shifted her attention to the police chief. "He told her she was crazy," she said, her voice trembling. "He told her— Oh, God, I don't know! What does it matter? Just find her." She began sobbing, sinking brokenly into a chair and burying her face in her hands. "Please—just find her. . . ."

═══

"I'm going, Dad," Michael said, his voice carrying a quiet determination that Craig Sheffield had never heard before. Craig had been home only a few minutes, and was about to leave with Barbara to go to the Andersons' when Michael appeared in the kitchen.

"You're not going anywhere," Craig replied. "You're going to stay right here and take care of your sister. She's too young to stay by herself, and your mother's going to sit with Mary Anderson."

Michael's features set stubbornly. "Let Jen go with Mom. I know the swamp better than practically anyone in town. Besides, I feel like it's my fault that Kelly's out there. If I hadn't gotten into that fight, none of this would have happened."

"So I'm supposed to reward you for your irresponsibility by letting you go out and prowl around the swamp all night?" Craig replied, intentionally infusing his words with as much sarcasm as he could muster.

Michael ignored his father's mocking tone. "I can help, Dad. I know my way around."

Craig looked to Barbara for support, but instead of backing him up, she nodded. "He's right, Craig. He knows the swamp as well as anyone, and he's never gotten lost. I'll go get Jenny."

While they waited for Barbara, Craig, still unconvinced, turned the matter over in his mind. Finally he spoke: "All right, but here's the deal. You don't take off by yourself, and you keep either me or someone else in sight at all times. Fair enough?"

Michael nodded his agreement. By the time Barbara appeared with Jenny, who, though dressed, was still rubbing sleep out of her eyes, he'd gathered two flashlights, some extra batteries, and some rope. "She could be caught in mud, and there might not be a way to get to her," he told his father.

"Who?" Jenny asked, the last of her sleepiness disappearing.

"It's Kelly, darling," Barbara explained. "She went for a walk in the swamp, and now people are going to look for her."

Jenny's eyes widened. "Is she lost?"

Barbara hesitated, but saw no reason not to tell her daughter the truth. "Yes, she is. And that's why I've always told you never to go into the swamp by yourself." She looked up at Craig. "Ready?"

They went out the back door and crossed the lawn to the dock, where Michael got into the outboard-powered rowboat while his parents and sister climbed into the larger Bayliner. Checking the gas supply, Michael jumped out of the boat again and ran up to the garage, returning a moment later with an extra tank. By the time he had it stowed under the bench of the dory, the engine on the Bayliner was already rumbling softly. "I'll meet you at the Andersons'," Michael called as his father cast the cruiser off and moved out into the center of the channel.

"We'll wait," Craig replied, letting the engine idle until Michael had started the outboard and maneuvered the dory away from the dock.

Five minutes later, after two more boats had joined them from other branches of the canal, they pulled up to Carl Anderson's dock and rafted their boats onto the three that were already there.

Inside the house, Tim Kitteridge was organizing the search, while Mary Anderson, her face pallid and her eyes rimmed with red, sat silently on the couch. She seemed unaware of what was happening, but as Barbara approached her, she came out of her reverie and stood up. "Thanks for coming," she said softly. "You were right—I think I would have gone crazy if I'd had to wait here by myself." Her eyes brimmed with fresh tears. "I'm scared, Barbara. I'm so scared."

Barbara slipped her arms around the other woman. "It's going to be all right," she assured Mary. "They'll find her." But as she listened to the men talking among themselves, she wondered.

"If she doesn't go far, we have a chance," Billy-Joe Hawkins said. "But I don't know—it's dangerous enough hiking in there in broad daylight, when you can at least see where you're goin'. At night . . ." His voice trailed off among murmurs of agreement.

At last they were ready. Ted Anderson would accompany Tim Kitteridge in the squad car to the place where Kelly had taken off. The rest of the men would go in boats, rendezvousing at the footbridge Kelly had crossed, then spread out from there, forming a loose net that would move out into the dark wilderness.

But even as they left, Barbara had the distinct feeling that the few of them who knew the swamp well, who had spent much of their lives exploring it and working in it, were feeling far less than optimistic about the search.

They knew the dangers of the marshy wilderness all too well.

Judd Duval glanced at his image in the mirror, seeing the deep wrinkles in his face and the collapsing of the tissue around his mouth. Thank God his mind had still been working when Kitteridge had called him a few minutes ago. If Kitteridge saw him like this—

But he'd thought fast, and the answer had come to him. "I'm startin' now," he'd said. "She can't be far from where she went in, and I know every one of them bayous. If'n I'm lucky, I'll have her home before you're even ready to start."

He had no intention of going into the swamp tonight—no intention of letting anyone see him until he'd found a way to get another shot from Dr. Phillips. So he left the house, but instead of taking his boat out to search for Kelly Anderson, he moved it only a hundred yards from his cabin, carefully hiding it deep within a tangle of reeds and mangrove. In the daylight it might be seen by someone passing this way, but in the darkness it was completely invisible.

Satisfied, he began making his way back to the house, slogging through the shallow water and mud.

Once again he felt eyes watching him as he made his way through the marsh.

The first tendrils of panic reached out to him, but he fought them off. He stopped, searching in the darkness for the evil presence that he sensed close by.

There was nothing.

And yet his fear only increased.

He tried to run, but the muck on the bottom clung to his feet, and his already weakening muscles began to tire.

No! he told himself. Ain't nothin' out here! Nothin'!

But he didn't believe his own words, and by the time he finally got back to the cabin, he was exhausted from fear as well as exertion. He dropped into his chair, his chest heaving and his breath coming in ragged gasps, terrified that his heart was about to fail him.

Slowly, though, he began to regain strength. He forced himself back to his feet, moving around the room, putting out all the lights and turning off the television.

If Kitteridge and the others came this way, the house had to look empty.

In darkness, he stripped off his filthy clothes and put on clean ones.

The waiting began.

Sitting alone in the dark was almost worse than being out in the swamp, for he dared not even turn on the radio to keep him company.

He began to lose his sense of time. As the minutes stretched into eternities, he imagined that dawn must already be at hand.

He began to see faces at the windows—children's faces, all of them looking like Jonas Cox, staring at him with dead, empty eyes.

When at last he heard the low puttering of an outboard motor, his first instinct was to throw open the door and call out to whoever was approaching. But the frightening image of his own aging face rose out of the darkness, and he resisted the impulse, cowering silently in the darkness, waiting for the flotilla of small boats to pass.

At last the murmuring of the engines faded away and the lights of the boats were swallowed up into the night.

Judd stirred, wondering what to do next.

And then it came to him—they'd been there, all of them, and seen his dark cabin, seen that his boat was not there. They thought he was in the swamp, searching, and they wouldn't be back this way.

Not for hours; perhaps not until morning.

He changed clothes again, pulling the mud-encrusted pants back on, and, taking his gun with him this time, crept back onto the porch.

He could still feel the children out there, watching him, waiting for him.

He told himself it was crazy, that if they were there, the search party would have seen them.

Maybe.

Or maybe not.

He knew the children of the swamp, knew them well. They moved through the wetlands anywhere they wanted to go, invisible unless they wanted to be seen.

He paused on the porch, his eyes darting around, searching.

Nothing.

At last he lowered himself onto the porch floor, then slipped into the water. It came up to his hips, and his feet, bare now, sank into the mud. Slime oozed up between his toes, and thick grasses swirled around his ankles. Clutching his gun, its safety already released, he moved slowly away from the house, feeling his way back toward the mangrove thicket.

Now he imagined he saw eyes everywhere. They seemed to be in the trees, looking down at him from the branches that stretched out toward him like skeletal arms.

They were in the water, staring up at him from the depths. He saw George Coulton, lying on his back, gazing blankly upward, a gaping wound torn in his breast.

The memory made him shudder, and he tried to move faster,

but the waters themselves seemed to be grasping at him now, and he felt as though in the grip of a nightmare.

He came at last to the mangrove thicket and hauled himself into the boat, his chest pounding, his breathing ragged. He fell back, resting against the gunwale, and waited for the exhaustion to pass. At last he pulled himself up onto the bench, untied the line from the mangrove root to which it was secured, and slipped the oars into the locks. Dipping the oars into the water, he slipped the boat out of the thicket.

And froze.

No more than ten feet away a silent figure sat in another row-boat, staring at him.

Pale eyes seemed to glow in the darkness.

Jonas.

He released the oars and reached for his gun, which lay on the bench beside him. But as his fingers closed on its grip, a low, hollow laugh drifted across the water from the other boat.

"Cain't kill me, Judd," Jonas said softly, but with a terrible clarity that rang in Judd Duval's ears. "Remember? I already be dead." There was a silence, then Jonas spoke again: "But I be comin' for you, Judd. Soon. Real soon."

The boy's dismal laugh sounded again, and then the boat slid away into the darkness. A moment later it was as if it hadn't been there at all.

Terror clutching at him once more, Judd's shaking hand dropped the gun and clasped the oars of his own boat.

The hundred yards back to the cabin seemed to take an eternity. Once he was inside again, Judd turned on every light in the place.

For him there could be no more darkness tonight.

Kelly stopped in her tracks, listening.

She wasn't sure how long she'd been in the swamp. For the first few minutes, after she'd fled from her father's stinging words, she'd paid no attention at all to where she was going. She'd dashed across the field and come to the canal, then seen the bridge off to the right. She'd heard her father calling after her, but ignored him, and run toward the bridge. She'd hesitated there, uncertain whether to cross into the wilderness beyond, but when her father had started toward her, still shouting, she'd stopped thinking and run across.

Across the bridge lay the swamp, where she could disappear in an instant. So she'd crossed the bridge, and plunged into the wilderness, her feet finding a narrow pathway that twisted through the undergrowth.

She'd stopped no more than thirty feet from the end of the bridge and waited, controlling her gasping breath by sheer force of will. She'd been able to hear her father's feet echoing on the wooden bridge as he crossed, and clearly heard his voice as he called out to her.

He didn't sound as angry now as he had in the truck.

He sounded almost scared.

But what would happen if she went back?

As soon as he found out she was safe, he'd be even madder than he'd been before.

So she'd kept silent, afraid even to move, for fear the rustling of the palmettos would give her away.

Finally, after what seemed an eternity, he'd stopped calling to her, and then she heard him gunning the truck's engine, a sound that had quickly died away.

Had he gone home?

She moved deeper into the wilderness, following the narrow track until it finally petered out, then pushing through the underbrush, guiding herself only by following the line of least resistance.

For a while—she wasn't sure how long—it was kind of fun, being alone in the darkness.

But slowly the night closed in around her and she began to feel frightened.

She moved faster, searching for a path in the darkness, but things looked the same everywhere.

She felt the ground under her feet growing softer, and finally felt water leaking into her shoes.

She turned back, trying to retrace her steps, but everywhere she turned, everything looked the same, and the farther she walked, the deeper the water seemed to get.

It was up to her ankles when suddenly she stepped out of a clump of mangrove and found herself at the edge of the island.

She stared at the channel a long time, trying to determine how deep it might be.

On the other side, the ground seemed higher. Over there, at least, she wouldn't be wading.

At last, breaking a stick off of one of the mangroves, she started across, testing the water's depth with the stick. In the middle of the channel she was knee deep, but then the bottom began to slope upward, and a moment later she was back on solid ground.

She waited, listening, wondering if her father might not be calling for her again.

But she heard nothing, and finally started moving again, searching for any trace of a path.

Now, with no idea how long she'd been wandering in the wetlands, she stopped once more, listening.

This time she heard something.

It was almost inaudible at first, just a faint rustling in the midst of a thicket of palmettos and saw grass.

It came again, louder this time.

There was something there, coming closer to her.

Kelly's heart began to pound and she felt a tightness in her lungs as panic rose inside her.

"H-Hello?" she asked, her voice trembling.

The instant she spoke, the steady droning of the insects came to a stop and the silence around her took on an eerie quality.

She felt as if she was being watched.

Tendrils of fear clutched at her, and she spoke again, unable to stand the hollow silence any longer. "Who is it?" she called. "I know someone's there."

Silence. Then, once more, the strange rustling noise. It was closer now, and she thought she could hear the sound of breathing as well.

"I'm not scared of you," she called out, but her voice, even to herself, sounded tiny, like the whimpering of a frightened animal. Her hand tightened on the stick she still held.

There was another rustling, and then, out of the darkness, she saw a pair of eyes glinting in the darkness and heard a low snorting sound.

A boar.

It stepped out of the thicket, its head lowered, its tusks glinting in the darkness. Above the tusks its eyes fixed on her, and Kelly's heart began to pound yet harder, as the animal snorted menacingly, pawing at the ground with its great cloven hoofs.

Her eyes flicked around, searching for somewhere to hide, or a tree to climb. But there was nothing around her except the low palmettos and the saw grass.

The boar's head weaved back and forth, and she sensed that it was about to charge.

"No!" she suddenly screamed, running toward the huge animal, the stick raised above her head.

Startled, the boar froze where it was, and suddenly Kelly was upon it, bringing the stick down, smashing it into the boar's snout.

Roaring in pain at the blow, the pig whirled, charging off into the underbrush, its immense body crashing through the palmettos. Birds burst up from the foliage, roused by Kelly's scream and the boar's bellow of pain, wheeling overhead while they squawked in panic, only to settle back into their nesting places.

Too terrified to move, Kelly remained rooted to the spot, her heart still racing, her breath catching in her throat.

Slowly, the birds fell into an uneasy silence and the insects began a tentative chirping once more.

Kelly felt her heartbeat slowing, and her breath returned to normal. She listened, straining her ears for any sound of the foraging boar, but it seemed to have disappeared into the darkness.

She gazed around, searching for anything that might yield a clue as to where she was, but there was nothing. The trees, the bayous, the islands—all of them looked alike.

She felt the icy fingers of panic reaching out for her again, but steeled herself against them, refusing, this time, to give in.

She'd been in the swamp before, twice.

Neither time had she felt any fear at all.

But she realized that there had been something different then.

The night she'd come into the swamp alone, and the next night, too, when she'd come with Michael, there had been another sound, a faint song rising above the steady monotone of the insects, a song that had somehow spoken to her, beckoned to her.

Tonight, that song was silent.

Tonight, she was totally alone.

She felt the panic edging its way back, grasping at her once again.

No! she told herself.

I'll be all right. I'll keep moving, and I'll find my way out.

But even as she spoke the words silently to herself, she knew she didn't believe them.

Deep in her heart, she wasn't sure she would ever get out at all.

Michael cut the engine on the outboard, letting the boat drift silently through the bayou. He played his flashlight over the foliage, the brilliant halogen beam slicing through the darkness, illuminating the trees around him. Insects sparkled and glittered in the shaft of light, homing in on the artificial sun until Michael finally switched it off as they swarmed around him.

"Kelly!" he called out. "Kelly, it's Michael. Can you hear me?"

He listened, but heard nothing except the sound of other voices, also calling. It was as if the whole swamp had become an echo chamber, with Kelly's name drifting back and forth.

But he knew that unless she was in the immediate area, Kelly wouldn't hear the searchers, for the thick mosses that covered the trees muffled sound quickly. Only a few hundred yards away, there would be no hint of the twenty-odd men who were combing the wilderness for her.

The cloud of insects that had answered the flashlight's beacon moved on, except for the mosquitoes that whined around Michael's ears, risking a landing every few seconds, only to be swatted away. At last Michael turned the light on again, its beam trapping a possum that clung to a tree a few yards away. The animal froze, mesmerized by the light, staring unblinkingly at Michael.

"It's okay," Michael crooned softly to the frightened creature. As if responding to his voice, the possum moved slightly. Suddenly a large green form dropped down from the branch above and a tree boa threw three quick coils around the possum's body. The possum, squealing loudly with surprise and pain, struggled in the grip of the reptile, but the snake, responding to the movement, only tightened its grip on the little marsupial, crushing its lungs.

In a few minutes the possum's wriggling began to weaken, and then as a final breath was squeezed from its body, it went limp in the snake's grip.

The boa began to move, never releasing the creature from its grasp as it worked itself around so that its mouth was at the possum's head.

Its jaws opened, stretching wide as it began working the dead creature into its maw. Michael watched, fascinated, as the boa's mandible dropped away from its maxilla to accommodate the impossibly large body of its prey. Michael had seen it before, and knew it would take the better part of an hour before the possum's long tail finally disappeared into the snake's craw and the serpent, sated, crept off to coil in the crotch of a tree while it digested its meal.

At last, as the insects once more began swarming around him, he cut the light again and restarted the outboard. Shifting it into forward, he opened the throttle, and moved on.

He left the light off for a while, his eyes slowly adjusting to the dark. Around him other lights blinked intermittently through breaks in the foliage, and as he moved from one channel to the next, rounding small islands and crossing the wider lagoons, other boats drifted around him in a surreal, random pattern.

He knew where he was, so intimately acquainted with the geography of the swamp that each time he made a turn, another familiar landmark appeared.

But there was no sign of Kelly.

Once more he let the boat drift to a stop and cut the engine while he sat and thought.

He knew where she'd gone into the swamp, knew the island the footbridge she'd crossed led to. He'd explored every square foot of it years ago, when he'd first started going into the wilderness by himself. It was a long, narrow, strip of land that barely rose six inches above the water. Only at the near end was it truly solid; as it extended into the swamp, it became boggier and boggier, until at last you were wading.

In the darkness Kelly would have been unable to retrace her steps. Even in the full light of day, it would have been difficult, for Kelly had no familiarity with the area.

So she would have followed her feet, testing the bottom, feeling her way. And since she hadn't come back to the end of the island at the bridge, she must have stumbled onto the one other spot where the island could be left: a narrow, shallow channel, too shallow for anything but the lightest of boats to navigate, with a second, larger island, on its other side.

Perhaps Kelly was still on that island.

Michael gazed around. The rest of the boats had momentarily disappeared, and he was alone. But at least he knew where to go.

Restarting the engine, he began threading his way through the maze of waterways.

Though Kelly was wandering on foot, Michael was confident he could follow her with his mind. In the swamp there simply weren't that many paths she could follow.

Unless she made a misstep and stumbled into one of the great patches of quicksand that dotted the area.

Michael refused to think about that possibility.

"Help!" Kelly called out. "Someone, please help me!" Though she shouted at the top of her voice, even to herself the words sounded pitifully weak, seeming to die away into the heavy humid air almost as quickly as she uttered them.

She was tired now, but she kept moving, afraid even to sit down, for the last time she stopped to rest, lowering herself onto the damp earth, she felt something wriggling beneath her and leaped up, yelping with fright. So she kept walking, and finally, off to the right, she saw a faint glow in the sky.

Villejeune!

She quickened her pace, and the light grew steadily brighter.

Her spirits began to rise.

Just a few more minutes and she'd be out, emerging from the tangle of trees and reeds to find the canal, and the village beyond.

And then just as she was certain she was nearly there, the moon rosc in the east and all her fears crashed in on her once more.

"Please?" she called out. "Can't anyone hear me?"

No one answered her plea.

How long had she been walking, and in which direction?

Or had she simply been going in circles?

She didn't know.

There was a high whining sound in her left ear, cut off as the mosquito settled on her forehead. She raised her right hand, slapping at it, then brushed at another as she felt it pierce the skin of her left hand.

Suddenly they were all around her, seeming to come out of nowhere, and she batted at them in the darkness.

She could feel their pricks everywhere on her skin now, and feel them in her hair, as well.

"No," she whimpered. "Get away! Leave me alone!" Her arms windmilling as she tried to fend off the attacking insects, she broke into a run. Her foot caught in a root, and she sprawled out, feeling a sharp pain in her ankle. She lay still, waiting for the worst of the pain to pass, then sat up, gingerly pulling her foot free from the root, massaging it with her fingers.

Suddenly she sensed rather than saw a movement in the grass a few feet away. Instinctively freezing, she held her breath as she waited for the movement to repeat itself.

For a long moment nothing happened, and then a snake, weaving back and forth as it rippled over the ground, slid out of the grass and into a patch of moonlight that shone through the tall cypresses. Its head rose up from the ground, its mouth wide open, showing its fangs in the moonlight. From the whiteness inside the mouth, Kelly knew immediately what it was.

A water moccasin, hunting in the darkness.

It had sensed her, and now it was waiting, searching in the moonlight for the slightest movement at which to strike.

Kelly's heart began to pound wildly.

Time stretched into an eternity as she sat on the ground, her eyes fixed on the reptile, every muscle in her body threatening to betray her.

The snake bobbed and weaved in the gloom, its tongue darting in and out of that hideous white mouth.

It moved forward, slithering toward her silently, as if it were now certain where she was.

Kelly tensed, willing her throat to constrict the scream that rose from her lungs.

The snake paused again, coiling back on itself, darting first one way and then another.

It crept still closer, and Kelly felt a shudder go through her as it neared her outstretched leg.

But as it touched her skin, and all her instincts screamed at her to jerk away, something reached into her mind.

Don't move, an unseen presence spoke silently. *Don't move at all.*

The unheard voice calmed her, and Kelly stared mutely at the serpent as it rippled over her calf, its scales making her skin crawl.

And then, as quickly as it had appeared, the snake slithered off into the foliage, its thick black body and yellow tail moving through the reeds with barely a sign that it was there at all.

Her teeth chattering with the sudden release of tension in her body, Kelly stayed where she was until the reeds stopped moving and she was certain the snake had gone. Slowly she raised herself up and carefully tested her weight on the injured ankle.

A sharp pain shot up her leg, but the ankle held, and she took a tentative step forward.

The pain eased slightly, and on the second step, the shock of her weight on the joint was less severe.

She could still walk.

But now she felt creatures lurking everywhere in the darkness, lying in wait, ready to strike out at her. Every vine she saw became a snake, and with every soft rustle she heard in the undergrowth she froze, searching in the faint moonlight for signs of the animals she was certain were there.

She trudged on. Now, straight ahead of her, a pair of eyes glowed brightly, low to the ground.

Another pair appeared beside the first, and then a third.

She stopped short, once again holding her breath.

The eyes moved, and then a raccoon, accompanied by two babies, crossed a small patch of moonlight. As Kelly uttered a sharp laugh of relief, the raccoons, startled, leaped into a tree and scrambled upward, pausing finally on a branch midway up, where they gazed warily down at her.

Kelly lingered there for a few minutes, watching the raccoons until they moved on, scrambling through the trees, where they disappeared.

And then, in the distance, Kelly saw a light, moving slowly, as if it was floating above the water.

Ignoring the pain in her ankle, she ran forward, calling out, "Help! I'm here! Help me!"

Abruptly the light stopped moving, hanging stationary in the darkness.

Ignoring everything but the light, Kelly bolted through the night. She felt her shoe flood with water but gave it no heed, stumbling on toward the glowing beacon, which now seemed to be coming toward her.

Her right foot struck a log that was half submerged in the shallow water, and she was about to step over it when, abruptly, it moved. The water roiled and an alligator rose up out of the mud and spun around, its tail lashing as its jaws gaped wide.

Screaming, Kelly twisted away as the 'gator lunged at her, and she felt a sharp tug as its jaws snapped closed on the loose tail of her blouse. Her voice rose in another scream and she jerked hard, feeling the material of the blouse give way.

The 'gator dropped into the water, then started after her, rising up once more on its stubby legs, lumbering through the mud. Kelly hurled herself forward, but once more she slipped, lost her balance, and flopped into the water.

The alligator was closing again, its jaws wide, and Kelly raised her arm to shield herself from its attack.

And then, just as the 'gator was starting its final lunge, a shot rang out.

The 'gator stiffened, then dropped back into the water, its tail lashing spasmodically.

Kelly stared at it, a third scream rising in her throat. Kicking out with her legs, her fingers clawing at the soft bottom, she tried to pull herself away from the thrashing beast.

Hands closed on her shoulders and she felt herself being lifted up.

"He's dyin'," someone said. "He's dyin', an' I got you."

Kelly looked up. Above her, gazing down at her in the dim moonlight, was a narrow, pinched-looking face, its pale, deep-sunk eyes all but covered by a battered hat.

Kelly, already on the verge of exhaustion, felt a wave of dizziness overwhelm her. Then the blackness of the night closed around her as her mind began to shut down.

———

"This is nuts," Tim Kitteridge muttered as Marty Templar turned their boat into yet another of the endless bayous. "I hope you know where the hell we are, because if it were up to me, I'd never get us out of here."

Templar chuckled, but the laugh died away quickly. It had been almost two hours, and there hadn't been so much as a trace of Kelly Anderson. He glanced at the chief out of the corner of his eye, then returned his gaze to the swamp. "Seems like maybe we ought to wait till morning," he said. "We're almost back where we started from, and if we're going to keep on looking, we'll have to do it on foot. Only places we haven't been are where it's too shallow to take a boat like this."

Kitteridge nodded. "I've been thinking the same thing. Let's head back to the bridge." He raised his bullhorn and called out to the next boat in the loose network, telling its occupant what they were going to do and asking him to pass the word along.

The search party began gathering at the bridge, the boats arriving one by one until there was a small flotilla rafted together in the canal. The men scrambled ashore, gathering around the chief.

"Marty and I think it's time to call it off until morning," Kitteridge said. "The way I see it, if Kelly'd been able to hear any of us calling her, she'd have answered, so wherever she is, she's not where we've been looking, or she doesn't want to be found."

Ted Anderson pushed his way through the crowd to stand angrily in front of the police chief. "You mean you're giving up!"

"I didn't say that, Mr. Anderson," Kitteridge replied patiently. "All I said is that I think we'd have a hell of a lot better chance of finding your daughter if we do it in the daylight. You can't see a thing out there—"

"So you're just going to quit?" Ted demanded. "What the hell kind of crap is that? She could be hurt out there! By morning she could be dead!"

A silence shrouded the group. Each of the men was unwilling to voice what he was thinking, but the silence itself spoke clearly enough.

"You all think she's already dead, don't you?" Ted said, his voice low and trembling.

Kitteridge shifted uncomfortably, but finally spread his hands helplessly. "I think it's something we have to consider," he said, unwilling to lie to Kelly's father. "There's a lot that can happen to someone out here, even in the daytime. At night . . ." His voice trailed off, but before Ted Anderson could say anything more, Craig Sheffield moved forward.

"I think we have another problem, Tim," he said, his expression clearly reflecting the fear he was feeling. "Michael didn't come back with the rest of us."

Kitteridge started at Craig. "Michael?" he repeated. "Are you telling me your kid was out there, too?"

Craig's voice took on a defensive edge. "Why wouldn't he have been?" he demanded. "He knows the swamp better than any of the rest of us, and he knows Kelly, too. Do you really think I could have stopped him?"

Kitteridge took a deep breath, then slowly released it in a long sigh. "All right. So now we have two kids missing. Just what is it you want me to do? Keep this search up until every one of us is lost?"

Craig's eyes fixed icily on the police chief. "I expect you to do whatever is necessary to find our children."

Kitteridge felt his temper beginning to fray. He understood exactly how the two fathers felt, but he also was all too aware of the futility of night searches. Unless the person they were hunting for was able to respond—and wanted to respond—the task was next to impossible. He made up his mind.

"I intend to find these kids, Craig. We'll start again at dawn, with more men."

"What about dogs?" someone called out from among the men around him. "B. J. Herman's got some of the best hounds in the county."

Kitteridge sighed. "We'll sure try 'em," he agreed, but privately wondered how anyone could expect a hound to follow a scent through a marsh. Still, he was willing to try anything.

"I'm not quitting, Tim," Craig Sheffield said quietly. "And I don't think Ted and Carl Anderson are going to give up and go home, either." He glanced toward the two men, who nodded their agreement. Then he raised his voice so the rest of the search party could hear him. "Anybody else willing to keep looking?"

The men glanced uneasily at each other, then one by one nodded. "Seems like we can't just leave them out there," someone said.

Kitteridge hesitated, but knew he'd already lost control of the search party. They'd stay out all night, and by morning, when they'd actually have a chance of finding the two missing kids, they'd be exhausted.

Which meant that he'd have to find more searchers. Still, he understood how they felt. "All right," he agreed. "Anyone who wants to, keep looking. But remember, if you don't find them tonight, we start again at dawn." He turned to Marty Templar. "Come on. You and I have some work to do. We've got to get the state troopers lined up, and maybe we can borrow some boys from up at Fort Stewart." As the group of men started moving back toward the boats, he turned to Craig Sheffield and Ted Anderson. "I'll go by Carl's house and let your wives know what's happening. And as for you, Craig," he added, "I won't try to stop what you're doing, but I'm going on record right now as telling you it's both stupid and useless. I don't want anyone else getting lost out there. Do we understand each other?"

Craig was silent for a moment, but finally offered the chief his hand. "I know what you're saying, Tim, and if it weren't our kids out there, I'd probably agree with you. But Michael's my son, and I can't just sit up all night worrying about him. I have to *do* something."

Kitteridge and Marty Templar watched as the search party set out once more, then returned to the squad car. As they headed toward the Anderson house, Kitteridge frowned.

"I never saw Judd Duval out there," he said.

Templar chuckled. "I never expected to. He knows places in that swamp you and I could never hope to find. And if I had to bet, I'd bet that when those kids are found, it'll be Judd who finds them."

———

Michael knew he was close to Kelly now—he could feel it.

It had been nearly an hour since he'd turned away from the rest of the search party, slipping off into the narrow bayous, guiding his boat almost by instinct through the maze of islands, threading his way between sunken logs, raising the motor twice to row through water so shallow that the hull of the boat scraped against the mud bottom.

Ten minutes ago he'd heard a muffled shot, and knew it must have been fairly close by—even a gunshot carried only a few hundred yards in the swamp before dying away without so much as a trace of an echo.

He'd turned the boat in the direction of the shot, and finally had to get out and pull it over a bar between two of the islands, but now he was on his way again, every nerve in his body attuned to the slightest alien noises.

Suddenly, ahead of him, he heard a splashing in the water and switched on his light, playing its beam over the rippling surface.

Ahead, the water was frothing as an alligator thrashed spasmodically, rolling over on its back, its tail lashing weakly.

Michael frowned.

At night the 'gators were usually lying in the shallows, all but covered by the water, waiting for an unwary water bird to cruise too close. Or asleep.

He moved the boat closer, until he was only a few yards away from the big reptile.

It was lying on its back now, but suddenly the tail thrashed again and it flipped over.

He played the light over its body, then held it steady as the beam revealed a hole in the creature's head.

He frowned, then understood.

Someone had shot the 'gator, apparently from close range. From the look of the hole, the animal must have been charging, and whoever held the gun had fired it straight into the 'gator's mouth.

He moved the light forward, and his breath caught in his throat.

A piece of cloth, stained and muddy, was caught in the corner of the 'gator's mouth.

Kelly.

Kelly had been here, and the 'gator had attacked her.

But someone else had been here, too, and fired at the 'gator.

He cast the beam of light around, searching for any sign of Kelly, but there was none.

Who had been here?

It was none of the searchers, of that he was certain. The rest of them, he was sure, had stayed together, combing through the swamp as best they could, never losing sight of each other.

One of the swamp rats.

It had to be.

One of them had been out here and found Kelly.

But who?

Had it been a coincidence? Had one of the men who hunted the swamp at night simply stumbled onto Kelly?

And then he knew.

Turning away from the dying alligator, he opened the throttle on the outboard. The engine roared to life, the stern of the boat dropping low as the bow rose up. A minute later, climbing up onto the plane, the boat skimmed across the water, moving deeper and deeper into the wilderness.

Only in the heart of the swamp, Michael knew, would he find Kelly.

18

Jenny Sheffield woke up as a car door slammed outside the open front window of the room in which she'd been sleeping. For a minute she wasn't sure where she was, but as she rubbbed at her eyes and came fully awake, the doorbell chimed and she remembered. Kelly Anderson had gotten lost in the swamp, and, Jenny recalled, her father and brother had gone looking for her. Maybe they were back now.

She slid out of the bed and went to the back window, looking out at the dock, hoping to see their boat tied up there.

The dock was empty, and though she looked as far up and down the canal as she could see, it, too, was deserted.

Turning away, she scurried across the room to the other window, the one that overlooked the driveway, and peered down. There was a police car in the street in front of the house, its headlights on and a flashing light revolving on the roof. But if her father and Michael hadn't come back yet, why were the police here?

Clad in one of Kelly's pajama tops, she went to the door and opened it a crack, pressing her eye to the narrow gap. From where she was, she could barely see down the stairs to the front door. But she could hear voices in the living room, and then there was a muted scream.

"No!"

There was just the one word. For a split second Jenny thought someone had seen her and was telling her to shut the door. But before she could do anything, she heard another sound.

It sounded like someone crying. Pulling the door open, she tip-toed to the landing at the top of the stairs and looked down. Now she could see into the living room. Two policemen were standing near the coffee table, and her mother was sitting on the couch, with Kelly's mother next to her.

It was her mother who was crying.

Frightened, Jenny ran down the stairs, then scuttled over to the couch, climbing up into her mother's lap. "Mommy? What's wrong?"

Barbara, wiping away the tears that had overwhelmed her when Tim Kitteridge had told her the news, hugged Jenny close.

"It's nothing for you to worry about, sweetheart," she said, not knowing whether she was trying to reassure her daughter or her-self. "Michael just went off by himself while everyone was looking for Kelly, and now they can't find him, either."

Jenny gazed worriedly up into her mother's face. "Are you scared?"

"No, darling, of course not," Barbara lied. Forcing a tiny, shaky smile, she added, "Well, maybe a little."

"But Michael knows all about the swamp," Jenny told her. "He goes there all the time."

"I know, honey," Barbara sighed, sniffling and wiping her eyes with the Kleenex Mary Anderson had handed her. "I'm just being silly. Your daddy's out looking for him, and by now they're probably all together again." She eased Jenny off her lap and stood up. "And if you don't go back to bed, you're not going to want to get up in the morning. Come on." With an apology to the two officers, and a promise to be right back, she led Jenny back up to Kelly's room and tucked her back in the bed. "Now I want you to go back to sleep," she said, leaning over to kiss the little girl.

Jenny frowned up at her mother in the darkness. "Is something bad going to happen to Michael?"

"No," Barbara insisted, putting a conviction into her voice that she wished she felt. "He just went the wrong way, and now Daddy has to look for him, That's all." Barbara kissed Jenny again and gave her a final tucking in. "Try to sleep, honey. All right?"

"All right," Jenny replied, turning over and closing her eyes. But as soon as her mother was gone she sat up, slid out of the bed, and crept back out to the landing so she could hear whatever was going on downstairs.

"I don't understand why you're not out there with them," she heard her mother saying.

"Mrs. Sheffield, there are still five men out there, but searching that swamp at night is like looking for a needle in a haystack."

"But our children—" Mary Anderson began.

The police chief cut in. "Believe me, I know how you feel, Mrs. Anderson. And whether you believe it or not, we're doing everything we can. By sunup Marty and I are going to have enough men out here to search the swamp inch by inch. But that takes some organization, and I can't do that and be out there in a boat, too."

"I know," Barbara sighed, determined not to give in to the fear that was threatening to overwhelm her. "Just let us know what's going on."

"You can count on it. And try not to worry. Michael knows the swamp, and Kelly just might walk out anytime." His gaze shifted to Mary Anderson. "If she was as mad as it sounds like, it seems to me there's a pretty good chance that she doesn't want to be found. I have an idea she might just know exactly where she is, and come back home once she cools down."

"Or she might do something else," Mary replied, her voice trembling. "If she believes her father thinks she's crazy, she might try to kill herself again. But we can't even find her to tell her that no one's mad at her." She shook her head sadly. "And even if we could, I don't think she'd believe a word any adult said to her."

Barbara managed a sorrowful, wry smile. "Maybe we sent the wrong people out to look for her," she said. "Maybe Jenny and I should have gone."

As her mother and the policemen started toward the front door, Jenny silently darted back into Kelly's room, quietly closing the door behind her. But instead of getting back into bed, she pulled off the pajama top and began putting on her clothes. She put her underwear on backward in the darkness, but didn't notice it, then got into her jeans and pulled her T-shirt over her head. Shoving her bare feet into her shoes, she fumbled with the laces, but finally got them tied.

As she carefully opened the outside door and stepped onto the landing, she felt a pang of fear.

What if she got lost, too?

She gazed apprehensively at the swamp in the distance and almost changed her mind. But then she saw the path along the edge of the canal, and the bright pools of light that flooded from the lamps that lined it every hundred feet. If she stayed on the path, nothing bad could happen to her. And she could call out to Kelly from there. And if she actually *found* Kelly—

She felt a surge of excitement. The last of her fear evaporated as she set out on her adventure.

Kelly felt as though she was drowning in a sea of blackness. It was all around her, pressing down on her, constricting her. She had to struggle, had to free herself from its grip. She tried to move, but it felt as if she was mired in quicksand. But then, far off, there was a faint glimmer of light. If she could reach it—bring it into focus— she'd be all right. But it was so far away, and she was so tired.

She moaned softly, and then felt her arms move.

The light brightened, and she realized her eyes were open.

The moon.

It was the bright crescent of the moon she saw, and, as she came slowly back to consciousness, she began to remember.

Running through the swamp, her terror growing every minute.

The alligator attacking her. The shot exploding only a few yards away from her.

The hands lifting her out of the mud, pulling her into the boat.

The face.

The swamp rat's face.

Her breath caught in a gasp of sudden fear. Almost involuntarily her eyes shifted from the bright light of the moon to the face of the man who sat at the center of the boat.

Not a man.

A boy.

A boy she'd seen before. And then it came back to her.

"I know you," she said. "I saw you the first night I was here. You were at the edge of the swamp."

Jonas nodded. "I was watchin' out for you."

Kelly frowned. "But I was looking for you. I couldn't find you."

Jonas pulled at the oars, and the boat slid silently into a narrow passage between two islets. "Don't matter. I was there, and made sure nothin' happened to you. Like tonight."

Kelly's frown deepened. "You mean you were looking for me?"

"Didn't have to look. I knowed where you was at."

"But—"

"There's lots of other folk lookin' for you, too. But they didn't know where you was."

Kelly fell silent, studying the boy in the faint light of the moon. His clothes were little more than rags, and he looked half starved, with his hollow cheeks and sunken eyes.

If she'd seen him in Villejeune, she knew she would have been afraid of him.

And yet now, in the middle of the night, in the swamp, she felt no fear of him at all. Indeed, she felt as if she knew him.

"You're one of them, aren't you?" she asked.

Jonas gazed at her with his strange, empty eyes, but said nothing. Instead he silently kept rowing the boat, guiding it effortlessly through the tangle of waterways.

Lights began to glimmer here and there, the soft, warm glow of oil lanterns. They were passing the strange, stilted houses of the swamp rats now, but although the boy did not say a word, Kelly was certain that wherever they were going, it was not here.

It was somewhere else, somewhere even deeper in the swamp.

They moved on, Jonas handling the oars with such skill that not even the faintest splashing betrayed their presence. When they were gone, only the rippling of the water from the boat's bow gave evidence that they had been there at all.

And only Amelie Coulton, sitting silently on her porch, saw them pass.

Something stirred inside her as she watched the small boat move slowly through the bayou, and she rose up from her sagging chair, then climbed down from the porch into the worn skiff that was tied up to one of the pilings.

There was just enough moonlight to let her follow the rippling trail of Jonas's boat.

———

"Kelly?" Jenny called out, her voice barely more than a whisper. "Kelly, it's me!" She paused, listening, but heard nothing except the chirping of the insects.

She wasn't sure how far she'd come, but finally the paved path along the canal came to an end. Ahead of her lay a field, dotted with pines and choked with kudzu, with only a narrow trail edging the drainage channel. She had stopped, wondering if maybe she shouldn't go back home, when she suddenly realized where she was.

Her own house was on the other side of the field and two blocks farther down. Though she'd never been on this side of the field before, she and her friends often played along the other edge, hiding in the vines, pretending they were in the jungle.

And there was a house right on the canal, halfway across the field, that she used to think was a scary place, where a witch lived. But her father had taken her there one day and told her that it wasn't a witch's house at all.

"A policeman lives there," he'd told her. "And if you're ever playing out here and see a stranger, or get lost, you go there and he'll take care of you. There's nothing in that house to be afraid of."

She'd looked at the house, with all its paint worn off, and propped up on stilts that looked like they might fall down, and wondered how anyone but a witch could live in anything like it. But then her father had gone right up to the back door and knocked, and a man had opened it.

His name was Mr. Duval, and he wasn't scary at all. He'd even told her he'd take her out and teach her how to fish sometime, if she wanted.

She still hesitated, searching in the darkness for a light in the house. From where she was, all she could see was the roof, barely visible through the trees.

But if Kelly was lost, maybe she knew to go to that house, too.

Resolutely, she started along the dirt trail, trying not to think about how far away the lights of the subdivision behind her were getting, or what might be hiding in the kudzu, waiting to jump out at her.

Off to her right she heard something move in the bushes, and she broke into a run.

And then she was there. The house stood at the edge of the canal, its front porch jutting out over the water just like she remembered it. She ran around to the back door and knocked loudly. "Mr. Duval?" she called out. "It's me! It's Jenny Sheffield!"

Her heart was still beating fast, and she listened hard, certain that whatever she'd heard in the bushes might be coming after her. But then she heard a sound from inside the house, and a second later the door opened a crack.

"Mr. Duval? It's me. I'm looking for Kelly. She's lost and I thought maybe she came here."

Judd Duval gazed down at the little girl, his mind racing. When he'd first heard the pounding at the door, he'd been certain it was Kitteridge, come looking for him. But when he'd heard the little girl's voice, an idea had suddenly come to him. He'd struggled to his feet, every joint aching now, and steadied himself with trembling hands for a moment before he'd been able to get to the back door. Now, as he looked down at Jenny, a surge of adrenaline energized him.

"She's not here," he said. "But I know where we can find her. Would you like me to take you there?"

Jenny nodded eagerly, and Judd Duval stepped out onto the back porch, pulling the door closed behind him. "We have to go in the car," he explained.

Jenny frowned. The car? But Kelly was in the swamp. And there was something funny about his voice, too.

Then Judd turned and the light of the moon fell onto his face.

Jenny's eyes widened as she stared at the wrinkles in his skin, and his deeply sunken eyes. He didn't look anything like she remembered him at all.

He looked old and sick, and there was something about the way he was staring at her that frightened her. Instinctively, she backed away, but Judd reached out and grasped her wrist. "Don't run away, Jenny," he said, his voice rasping.

Jenny struggled, trying to pull away from him, but Judd's grip tightened. He picked her up, and carried her into the house. Fumbling in the dark, he found the nylon ties he carried instead of handcuffs, and, twisting Jenny's arms around behind her back, bound her wrists.

"Stop that!" Jenny screamed. "I want to go home!"

Judd's hand clamped over the little girl's mouth, and he reached for a dish towel, tying it around her head as a makeshift gag. Thirty seconds later two more of the nylon ties bound her ankles together, immobilizing her. Picking her up again, ignoring her struggles, he took her out the back door and carried her the ten yards to his squad car, which was parked under one of the pine trees. He opened the trunk, put her inside, then closed the lid again.

Trembling more violently than before, he hurried around to the driver's door, got in, and started the engine. Putting the car in gear, he made a U-turn and steered quickly up his rutted drive to the main road. He paused there for a moment, his own lights out, searching for any other cars. But the highway was deserted, and finally he turned on his headlights. He wasn't too worried—his destination was in the opposite direction from the village. With any luck at all, he'd have the road completely to himself.

Warren Phillips switched on the porch light and looked through the window to see Judd Duval standing outside, his sunken eyes glowing maniacally in the light from the globe above the door. Unlocking the bolt, he opened the door and pulled Judd inside. "What are you doing here?" he demanded.

"My shot," Judd croaked, his voice rattling in his throat. "I got to have my shot. Look at me! I'm dying."

Phillips's voice hardened. "I told you the price. I need children, Judd."

"I got one," Judd said, his lips twisting into an ugly grin.

Phillips's eyes narrowed. "Who? There aren't any—"

"Not a baby," Judd interrupted. "But she's young enough. She's in the trunk of my car."

Fury welled up in Phillips. "Are you out of your mind?" he demanded. "What have you done, Judd?"

"I got you what you wanted," Judd insisted.

"Where?" Phillips spat. "Who is it? How did you get her?"

"Craig Sheffield's kid," Judd replied. "And I didn't do anything. She came right up to my back door."

"In the middle of the night?" Phillips demanded. "I'm not a fool, Judd."

Duval's lips curled into a malevolent smile. "She was lookin' for the Anderson girl," he explained. "There been people lookin' for her all night, out in the swamp. And then this kid came up to my door, askin' me if she was there. She was alone, Doc. I figure she musta snuck out."

Phillips glared furiously at the other man. "And you don't think anybody will miss her? For Christ's sake, Judd!"

"So what if they miss her?" Judd whined. "All they can do is look in the swamp, and they can't find what ain't there. And you need her. You told me you need kids."

Phillips's mind raced. Jenny Sheffield was only six years old, and the magical gland inside her had barely begun to atrophy. But if they started searching the swamp for her and didn't find her, they wouldn't give up. Not until they either found Jenny or her body.

And then he realized there was a way.

If they found her body . . .

"All right," he said. "Take the car around to the back and bring her in."

Judd held his palsied hands up. His fingers were shriveled and curling in upon themselves, the nails cracking with age. "I don't know if I can, Doc. I'm getting weaker."

"Do it," Phillips ordered him. "I'll meet you in the back."

Three minutes later Judd carried Jenny through the back door. She was still struggling, and incoherent screams, muffled by the gag in her mouth, rose from her throat.

"Put her down," Phillips told Judd Duval, who immediately lowered the terrified child to the floor. Phillips knelt down and slid a hypodermic needle into the vein of Jenny's forearm. Jenny's eyes widened in fear as she watched him press the plunger on the needle, but a few seconds later she slumped to the floor, her eyes closing.

Phillips cut away the nylon straps that bound her wrists and ankles, then removed the gag from her mouth. Picking her up, he carried her into the library and laid her on the couch. Finally he went to one of the pictures that hung on the walls, swung it away, and opened a wall safe, from which he removed a small vial of clear fluid and another hypodermic needle. Filling the needle carefully, he slid it into Judd Duval's arm and pressed the plunger. "Lie down," he told Duval. "Get some sleep. By sunrise you'll feel a lot better."

Judd sank gratefully onto the sofa opposite the one on which Jenny lay, already feeling the rejuvenating effects of the shot. The aching in his joints was fading away, and the deathly raling in his lungs was easing. He could feel the years rolling away as the shot restored his youth, as it always did.

It was like emerging from quicksand, struggling back from the black paralysis of death to the full light and vigor of life.

Smiling, he drifted into a peaceful sleep.

19

Clarey Lambert waited, her eyes closed, her mind turned inward to focus on the children. They were close now—she could feel Kelly and Jonas drawing near, sense that Michael was not far behind. Clarey was tired—it had been hours since she'd first sensed Kelly's presence in the swamp, knowing instantly that the girl was alone and frightened. She'd tried to reach out to Kelly, tried to show her the way back, but Kelly's mind, confused, had stayed just beyond her reach, and the best she'd been able to do was steer the child out of danger, keeping her away from the worst of the quicksand and sink holes that lay like traps, concealed by rings of apparently sheltering trees, inviting the unwary.

Then the cottonmouth had appeared, and she'd had to struggle against Kelly's urge to run from the snake, finally seizing control of her mind, willing the girl not to move. But in the end she'd succeeded, at last searching for Jonas and guiding him through the swamp, sending him ever closer to Kelly.

Now they were only a few hundred yards from her house, and she finally let herself relax. She opened her eyes, blinking in the soft glow of the lantern light that filled the room, and pushed herself out of her chair.

She felt every year of her age tonight, and wondered how much longer she would be able to stay alive, how much longer she would be able to keep her vigil over the children.

Of course the Dark Man had promised that she could live forever, but she had refused the elixir he offered, disbelieving his promises.

The Dark Man had promised her the fountain of youth so many years ago.

Now she was old, and he was still young.

Young, because of what he stole from the children of the swamp.

She didn't pretend to understand all of it, but knew well enough what the needles inserted in the chests of the babies were for.

"It's only a little blood," he'd told her. "It doesn't hurt the children at all."

Clarey knew better. What he was stealing from the children was not just their blood, but their youth.

Their youth, and their very souls, as well.

She knew—she'd watched them grow up, seen their empty eyes, watched them follow the Dark Man's will, doing whatever he told them to do. No, it wasn't merely blood he took from them.

It was the essence of their being, delivered to the men of Villejeune.

The men who paid the Dark Man, and did his bidding.

The men who should have died years ago, and were living on the youth of their own children.

The men she'd come to hate almost as much as she hated the Dark Man himself.

———

Kelly gazed up at the old woman who stood on the porch. The woman's face was lost in shadows, yet despite the darkness, Kelly still felt a deep certainty that she knew this woman.

"Come up, child," Clarey said, her voice rough with age. Kelly rose shakily and climbed up the ladder that led from the bayou's surface up onto the porch six feet above. The woman turned toward her, and lamplight from the open door flooded onto her face.

Kelly gasped.

The skin of the woman's face, dry as parchment, hung in deep wrinkles, and her thin hair was drawn back in a knot at the nape of her neck. She wore a black dress that hung loosely over her bony frame, and when she reached out toward Kelly, her hands, with their swollen knuckles and crooked fingers, had the look of a crow's claws.

But though the hands and face of the woman were as grotesquely distorted with age as the image Kelly had seen so often in her dreams and her mirror, there was something in the crone's eyes that instantly quelled the wave of fear that had risen inside her.

These eyes had no cruelty to them at all, gazing out of their deep sockets with a warm compassion that made Kelly want to put herself into the woman's arms and be held by her.

"Come, my dear," Clarey said softly, both her arms extended now. "Come and let me hold you again."

Silently, Kelly moved to the old woman. As Clarey's arms closed around her, she felt a sense of well-being come over her.

"So pretty," Clarey crooned softly, her shriveled fingers gently stroking Kelly's hair. "Always the prettiest. Always the sweetest."

Kelly stood still, resting her head against Clarey's withered breast, hearing the old woman's heart beat softly within.

Again that strange sense of familiarity passed over her, as though this woman had held her before.

The low throbbing of an outboard sounded in the darkness, and then a second boat appeared. Its occupant cut the engine almost as soon as it came into view, and a moment later the craft drifted up to the house.

Jonas silently took the bow line from Michael, fastening it to one of the pilings. The two boys climbed up the ladder, and as they stepped onto the porch, Clarey released Kelly from her embrace, took her hand and led her into the house.

Michael and Jonas followed.

Clarey closed the door when they were all inside, then turned the lantern up so that its bright glow washed the shadows from the room. She turned and smiled at Kelly.

"Do you remember my little house?"

Kelly gazed curiously around the single room, which held a coal-burning stove in one corner, a sink and cupboard against the back wall, and a sagging bed in the corner opposite the stove. At the foot of the bed there was an old-fashioned iron bathtub, barely large enough for a single person to crouch in. There was a worn sofa against one of the walls, and a rocking chair sitting close to the stove. A braided rug, little more than a rag, covered the floor.

Never had she seen anything like the tiny house, and yet, like the woman herself, it seemed strangely familiar.

"I—I don't know," she faltered.

"Come here, child," Clarey said, leading Kelly to the sink. She worked the handle of a pump, and water spurted into the sink. Taking a washcloth from a hook at the counter's edge, she put it into Kelly's hands. "You'll be even prettier with the mud gone from your face."

Kelly gazed into the cracked mirror above the sink. Her face was smeared with mud and slime, and her hair was caked with it as well. She bent over, putting her head beneath the pump's spout, then began working the handle, letting the water gush over her, washing away the grime from the swamp. At last she used the washcloth to wipe away the last flecks from her face, then groped for the towel that hung from the same hook from which Clarey had taken the washcloth. Wrapping the towel around her hair, she straightened up.

In the mirror, she saw the image of the ancient being who had haunted her all her life. She gasped, but then heard the old woman's gentle laughter.

"It's all right," Clarey told her. "It's not him. It's only me. Only Clarey."

Kelly felt the blood drain from her face, and turned to face the old woman. "H-How do you know about him?"

Clarey smiled, revealing worn teeth. "Now, never you mind how I know. There's lots I know." Her eyes fixed on Kelly. "Do you want me to tell you who you be?"

Kelly said nothing, watching the old woman mutely.

"He stolt you," Clarey told her. "The Dark Man stolt you from your mama, and brung you to me before you was even a day old. Then he took you away ag'in, and said you wouldn't never be back, that he were lettin' you go." Her chin quivered and a tear ran down her cheek. "But it were too late, warn't it?" she asked. "He'd already took your soul, an' I couldn't give it back to you."

Kelly's eyes darted toward Michael, who was listening raptly. "That's what's wrong with us, isn't it?" he asked softly. "That's why we never feel like other people."

Clarey nodded. "It's what he takes from you. He says it ain't true, but I know it is. It's how you feel, ain't it? Like you're dead?"

"It's always been that way," Kelly breathed. "Ever since I was a little girl. I—I thought I was crazy—"

"Hush," Clarey told her. "Don't you go thinkin' that. It ain't you that's crazy—it's him! And now it's time to stop it, if'n we can."

She began talking, her voice droning softly in the night. "I know who they be, all of 'em." Her eyes came to rest on Kelly once again. "And that's why you come back. He said you wouldn't never come back, but he was wrong. You *did* come back, and now it's time."

Michael's brows knit. "Time?" he echoed. "Time for what?"

Clarey Lambert's voice hardened. "Time to end it. It's time to take your souls back from thems as stole 'em."

There was a long silence in the room, and then Michael spoke, his voice barely audible. "Did the Dark Man bring me to you, too?"

Clarey's eyes turned to twin fragments of glittering stone. "Oh, yes," she whispered. "He brung you to me. But I know'd he wouldn't keep you in the swamp." There was a heavy silence, and Michael sensed what she was about to say even before she spoke the words. "He's your papa," she finally said. "You be the Dark Man's son."

———

Outside, Amelie Coulton carefully dipped her oars into the water and silently pulled her boat away from Clarey Lambert's house. She'd heard it all, listened to everything Clarey had said.

And now she knew.

Her baby hadn't died at all.

Hers, and who else's?

But who could she tell?

Who would believe her?

———

Craig Sheffield glanced at his watch. It was almost four in the morning, and not only Kelly Anderson, but now Michael, too, seemed to have been swallowed up by the swamp. Until an hour ago he'd maintained the hope that if he went just a little farther, rounded one more bend, circled one more of the endless tiny islands, he would come upon Michael's boat and find that nothing more serious than an empty gas tank had befallen his son.

But hope had finally begun to drain away, and though he kept on searching, he felt as if his mind had been dulled by the long night. He still stopped every few yards, cut the engine, and listened for the sound of a motor puttering in the distance.

But there was nothing. Nothing except the endless droning of the insects, a droning he'd long since stopped hearing, except when he wanted to hear the sound of Kelly's voice, or Michael's boat.

Then the night sounds seemed to rise to a deafening level, drowning out anything else that might be there.

He rounded another curve and cut the engine yet again. A hundred feet away he could see the glowing green light of Carl Anderson's starboard lamp, and farther away he could make out the white stern light of one of the other boats that had lingered in the swamp, its occupant refusing to give up until the sun rose and brought with it the searchers that Tim Kitteridge had promised. But all of them were as tired as Craig himself was now, and he wondered if perhaps, unknowingly, they'd passed Kelly by, her own calls drowned out by the engines of the boats and the eternal insects.

The Bayliner drifted to a stop, and Craig sat behind the wheel, listening. The moon had risen high in the sky now, its reflection glimmering on the surface of the water. Every now and then Craig could see the glowing eyes of nocturnal animals, foraging for food, pausing in their hunt to stare at him.

Once, half an hour ago, a screech had rent the night and the insects had gone suddenly silent. A chill had passed through Craig, but whatever had been attacked in the darkness made no more sounds, and soon the insects had resumed their endless song.

Now, though, as he sat in the darkness, a new song came to him.

Barely audible at first, it grew steadily louder.

A boat, coming toward him, its engine throbbing in the night.

He waited, unconsciously holding his breath, certain he recognized the unique rhythm of the motor. At last, from out of one of the narrow channels, a shadow appeared, a white froth of wake spreading out behind it.

Craig stood up in the Bayliner, hope surging once more. "Michael? Michael!"

The boat turned, and sped up, and a moment later the little skiff, with Kelly sitting on the center seat and Michael astern next to the engine, pulled alongside. "Dad? Dad, I found her!"

Tears of relief flooded Craig's eyes and a lump rose in his throat. "You're okay?" he cried, his voice cracking. "Both of you?"

"We're fine," Michael replied.

Craig gaped helplessly at his son, not sure whether to laugh or cry or vent the rage he felt at Michael for going off alone and frightening him so. Bone-tired, he'd been wandering through the swamp for hours, searching for his son, fearing the worst. But now, that didn't matter. Michael was safe. And he'd found Kelly. Craig reached down to the dash of the Bayliner and began flashing his navigation lights. All around him the other boats turned toward him, moving quickly closer.

"They're back," Craig yelled as Carl Anderson's boat came near. "Michael found Kelly!"

Carl pulled his boat alongside Craig's and tossed a line to the other man. Michael pulled his boat up to Carl's.

"Kelly?" Ted Anderson said, his voice shaking. "Honey, are you all right?"

Kelly looked up at her father. "Are you still mad at me?"

Ted took a deep breath, then let it out in a long sigh. "How can

I be mad at you? I thought you—" He cut off his words, unwilling to complete the thought. "I'm just glad you're back. Where did you go? We've been hunting for hours." He held out his hand and helped Kelly move from Michael's boat into his father's.

"I got lost," Kelly told him. "I was just running at first, and then I was afraid to come out. And when I decided to come home, I didn't know where I was. If Michael hadn't found me . . ." Her voice trailed off as she remembered what her father had said about Michael only a few hours before.

But Ted looked down at her, then his arms went around her and he pulled her close.

"Maybe I was wrong," he said. "Maybe he's not such a bad kid, after all. The important thing is that you're both back, and you're both fine."

But we're not fine, Kelly thought silently. Michael's not fine and I'm not fine. Then she shivered in her father's arms as Clarey Lambert's words echoed in her mind.

It's time to take your souls back from thems as stole 'em.

Only then would they be truly fine again.

"Listen," Barbara Sheffield said. "Do you hear something?"

But Mary was already on her feet, moving toward the patio door. Barbara followed her, and as Mary slid the wide glass panel open, they heard the sound of a boat coming along the canal.

"That's the Bayliner," Barbara said, her voice vibrant as hope washed away the fear that had been building in her as the long night had worn on. "They must have found them!"

Mary gazed anxiously at Barbara. "Are you sure?"

"It has to be," Barbara replied. "Craig wouldn't come back for any other reason."

They ran across the lawn, coming to the dock just as the three boats pulled up.

"They're safe!" Barbara cried, tears streaming down her cheeks as she ran out onto the dock. "Michael, what were you thinking of? Do you have any idea of how frightened I've been? You promised you'd stay within sight of your father!"

But like Craig's, Barbara's brief spate of anger dissolved at the sight of Michael's grin, and she threw her arms around him, nearly toppling both of them into the water as his skiff shot away from the dock.

"Jeez, Mom! Let me get tied up before you drown both of us!"

A few minutes later they were all in the house, and Mary, seeing Kelly in the bright light of the kitchen, gasped.

Kelly's clothes were soaked with mud, and her legs, scratched and bleeding, were covered with slime. "Darling, what happened?" she asked.

Kelly looked ruefully down at her ruined clothes, then up at her mother. "I—I guess maybe running away in the swamp in the middle of the night isn't the best thing I've ever done, is it?"

Mary stared at her daughter for a moment, then the tension that had been building in her all night suddenly snapped and she began laughing. "Well, I guess it isn't," she said when she finally regained control of herself. "Go dump those clothes in the washer and take a shower, and I'll get you a robe." She hurried out of the kitchen, returning a few seconds later with her own favorite bathrobe, which she took to Kelly, who was already in the small bathroom Carl had built behind the kitchen so he wouldn't have to track mud through the house when he returned from work each afternoon. When she came back, she sank into a chair across from Michael.

"How did you find her?" she asked.

Michael said nothing, knowing there was no way to explain the strange things that had happened to him in the swamp. Indeed, even after listening to Clarey, he barely understood it himself.

"It don't matter how it works," the old woman had told him. "Alls I can tell you is I always know where the children is, and what they's doin'. And I can call 'em, too, like I called Jonas tonight, and sent him out to get Kelly. And I was talkin' to you, too, tellin' you where to go, tellin' you where to look." She'd gazed deep into him then. "You think you know the swamp, but you don't know half of

what I know. So don't you be thinkin' you can always do anythin'
you want, you hear? I might not always be lookin' out for you!"

"I—I guess I was just lucky," he said at last, feeling the eyes of
his own parents, and Kelly's, too, on him. "I sort of pictured where
she went into the swamp, and where she'd have had to go. I
mean—well, there's only so many places you can go on foot."

Finally Kelly came out of the bathroom, her mother's robe
wrapped around her, and joined the group around the table. She
tried to tell them everything that had happened, but when she
came to the snake, she stopped, shuddering at the memory.

"Kelly?" Mary asked. "What is it?"

"A—A snake," Kelly stammered. "It was a water moccasin, and
it crawled right over my leg."

Mary stifled a scream.

"What did you do?" Carl Anderson asked.

Kelly looked up at her grandfather. "I didn't do anything," she
said softly. "I just held still. I didn't move, and the snake went
away."

Carl's eyes held on Kelly. She felt her flesh crawl as, just for an
instant, a peculiar look came into her grandfather's eyes. A look
that somehow frightened her.

"How did you know to do that?" he asked.

Kelly hesitated for only a split second. "Michael told me," she
said. "Remember? A few days ago, when we went out into the
swamp together? He told me that if I ran into a snake, I should
hold still. He said it couldn't see me if I didn't move."

Carl's gaze held hers for a second longer, then he nodded.
"He's right. They can sense you, but they don't strike at what's not
moving. If something's not moving, they think it's dead and they
leave it alone."

Once again Kelly felt her skin crawl, and when she glanced
quickly at Michael, she was certain he was having the same feeling.

But neither of them said anything.

Finally Barbara stood up. "I have to go home," she announced.
"I'm not sure I'm going to be able to sleep, but at least I can go to
bed and try to get some rest. I'll go up and get Jenny."

The group in the kitchen moved toward the family room and

were just starting out onto the terrace when Barbara, her face ashen, appeared at the top of the stairs.

"She's not here," she said, her voice cracking. "Craig, Jenny's gone!"

The chatter of conversation died as everyone in the room stared at Barbara in stunned silence.

20

"**W**ake up, Judd." Warren Phillips spoke the words harshly, shaking the sleeping man's shoulder. "Come on, Judd, it's almost dawn."

Judd groaned, pulling away, but when Phillips prodded him once more, his eyes opened and he groggily sat up.

The first thing he noticed was that the pain in his joints was gone. His limbs were once more as supple as they had ever been.

He looked at his hands; the liver spots had disappeared, and his cracked nails had smoothed out again. His knuckles, grotesquely swollen last night, were their normal size, and the skin on his fingers was that of a man in his late forties.

Rising from the sofa, he crossed to the mirror over the fireplace and stared in relief at his own reflection. His face had smoothed out; only the small crow's-feet around the corners of his eyes remained. His eyes, dull and sunken only hours ago, looked perfectly normal, and when he spoke, there was no trace left of the crackling rasp that was all he'd been able to manage when he'd arrived at Phillips's house a few hours earlier. He breathed deeply, feeling the rush of air into his lungs, then released his breath in a long clear sigh. He turned, grinning. "It worked. I feel great again."

"Of course it worked," Phillips replied. "It's worked for twenty years—why wouldn't it work now?" Without waiting for a reply, he began issuing orders to the deputy. "Jenny Sheffield is in the bathroom upstairs. You're going to use the radio in your car to call the hospital and tell them you found her in the canal and you're bringing her in."

Duval shook his head. "Wouldn't do that. I'd call for the medics. It's procedure."

Phillips lips curled in a thin smile. "If she's already dead?"

The deputy stared at the doctor numbly. "You killed her?"

The doctor tilted his head toward the stairs in the foyer. "Why don't you go take a look, and tell me what you think."

Duval hesitated, but left the library, and with Phillips following behind, mounted the stairs. When he came to the landing, he glanced uncertainly around.

"Second door on the left," Phillips said.

Duval moved down the hall, hesitated, then opened the door to the bathroom. For a moment he saw nothing, but then his eyes gravitated to the tub.

It was filled, a layer of ice cubes floating on the surface. But beneath the translucent ice he could make out the form of a body.

Jenny's body, clad in jeans and a T-shirt, her hair floating around her head in the form of a grotesque halo.

"Holy Jesus," Duval whispered, gazing in shock at the face that peered up from beneath the water's surface. He dropped down to his knees and pushed the ice cubes aside.

She lay on her back, her empty eyes wide in a pale, bluish face. Duval blinked, and instinctively reached for the body, intending to lift it out of the tub.

"Not yet," Warren Phillips snapped. "Not until you know exactly what you're going to do."

Duval, his eyes still fixed on the body in the tub, spoke numbly. "The canal," he repeated, the words coming slowly as he tried to grasp what Phillips had done. It was wrong—he'd brought Jenny Sheffield as the price of his shot. She wasn't supposed to be killed—Phillips needed her! "I was on my way to work, and I found her in the canal. I don't need an ambulance—she's dead already."

"That's right," Phillips told him. "And you take her to the morgue, just like you would any other body."

Duval nodded.

"All right," Phillips went on. "We're ready."

Duval reached into the icy water and lifted Jenny's limp body, cradling it in his arms as he stood up. Phillips held the door open, and Duval carried her out to the hallway, then down the stairs and through the back door. Outside, Phillips held the door open while Duval laid Jenny onto the backseat.

"Go," Phillips said, his voice low, but leaving no room for disobedience. "Keep your lights off, and get to the canal as fast as you can. Then make the call, turn on your lights and siren, and head for the hospital. And one more thing, Judd."

Judd turned in the predawn darkness to face Phillips. "Tell them to call me. Tell them who it is, and tell them to call me."

Duval's brows creased into an uncertain frown. "But she's dead," he began. "They'd call Hatfield."

"They will, Judd. But I want them to call me, too. After all," he added, a cold smile twisting his lips once more, "I'm her doctor, right?"

Judd Duval, his mind still not fully comprehending what Phillips had done, nodded. A few seconds later, the lights of the squad car switched off, he disappeared into the darkness.

═══

When the phone rang in Warren Phillips's house, he waited until the sixth ring before he picked up the extension by his bed. And when he spoke, his voice was groggy, as though he'd just been roused from a sound sleep.

"Phillips," he mumbled.

"Dr. P?" Jolene Mayhew's voice was brittle with tension. "Dr. P, it's Jolene. We need you down here right away! At the clinic!"

"Jolene?" Phillips repeated, as if not quite grasping who it was. "What time is it? It must be the middle of—"

"It's almost dawn, Dr. P. It's Jenny Sheffield. Judd Duval just called. Dr. P, he found her in the canal. He says she's dead."

"I'll be right there!" Phillips snapped, dropping the sleepiness from his voice, knowing that Jolene's words would have brought him wide awake instantly.

He hung up the phone, then quickly changed his clothes, pulling on khakis and a polo shirt, stuffing his bare feet into a pair of tennis shoes. Less than two minutes after Jolene's call, he was on his way, arriving at the hospital just as Judd Duval was helping Jolene and the night orderly load Jenny's body onto a gurney.

The ring of the Andersons' phone shattered the tense silence that hung over the living room of Carl Anderson's house. Mary Anderson and Barbara Sheffield glanced at each other. It wasn't until Michael, forbidden by his mother to join the men as they began hunting for Jenny, moved to the phone, that Barbara spoke. "No!" she said, her voice sharp. "Let Mary get it."

Michael sank back onto the sofa where he'd been sitting with Kelly, and watched as Mary quickly crossed to the phone, picking up the receiver on the third ring. Her face paled as she listened, then she spoke. "I'll bring Barbara right away. The men are still out looking . . . No, I'm not sure where. They were going to start by the canal . . . All right." She slowly hung up the receiver, then turned to face Barbara, tears streaking her cheeks.

Barbara closed her eyes for a moment, steeling herself in preparation for the words she knew Mary was about to utter.

Her fault.

Whatever had happened—and she was certain it was bad—was her fault.

She'd known it almost from the instant she'd found Kelly's empty bed. In that first eternal moment of terror, she had heard her own words echoing in her mind.

Maybe Jenny and I should have gone looking for her.

Her own words.

As the words rang in her head, she'd known what had happened. Jenny hadn't been asleep at all. Instead, she'd crept out of bed and sneaked back onto the landing to listen.

She had heard what Barbara herself had said.

And gone looking for Kelly.

How long had she been gone?

Hours, certainly.

Craig had called Tim Kitteridge, finding the police chief at his desk, and explained what had happened. Then, while Kitteridge began reorganizing the plans he'd been making through the long night, Craig, Ted, and Carl had gone out once more. Craig had insisted that it would be all right, that this time, at least, they didn't have to worry about the swamp.

Even in broad daylight, and with her father in the boat with her, Jenny hated the swamp. Her child's imagination saw alligators and snakes everywhere; to her the swamp was a place where every living thing was a threat, and when her friends told her stories of other things that might live there—ogres and ghosts, zombies and witches—she sometimes lay awake all night, afraid even to sleep for fear of dreaming about the swamp.

"She'll stay by the canal," Craig had insisted. "You know how she is—I had to take her to Judd Duval's house myself last year and prove to her that Judd isn't a witch. She's probably hiding somewhere, three blocks away, too terrified of the dark even to come back here."

Barbara had tried to believe her husband's words, but after he'd left with Ted and Carl, she'd sat silently, certain in her heart that something dreadful had happened to her daughter, and that it was her own words that had sent the little girl out into the night.

At last she forced herself to face Mary Anderson. "What is it?" she asked. "What's happened?"

Mary crossed to her, crouching down by the chair in which she sat, and took her hand. "It was Tim Kitteridge," she said. "He just heard a call from Judd Duval. H-He's found Jenny."

A flash of hope surged through Barbara, then ebbed away as quickly as it had come. The sadness in Mary's voice betrayed the truth.

"She's dead, isn't she?" she said, her voice breaking.

Mary bit her lip, praying that perhaps Kitteridge had misunderstood the radio call he'd overheard. If Judd was taking Jenny to the hospital, there must still be hope. "I—I don't know. Apparently Judd found her in one of the canals—"

Barbara gasped, her right hand covering her mouth.

"He's taking her to the hospital," Mary said quickly, recognizing her own cowardice in being unable to tell Barbara exactly what Kitteridge had told her.

Barbara clutched at Mary's hands. "I have to get there," she said, lurching to her feet. "My baby—"

"I'll drive you," Mary said.

Michael was on his feet again, this time moving toward the patio door. "I'll find Dad—"

"No!"

The single word resounded through the room like a shot. Michael froze. "No, Michael," Barbara went on, her voice breaking. "I can't stand the idea of you going out there again. I want you with me . . ." Her words trailed off into a sob, and Michael went to his mother, clumsily slipping his arms around her.

"I'll go," Kelly said. Then, before her own mother could say anything, she spoke again. "Don't worry, Mom. I won't go anywhere near the swamp. Dad and Grandpa said they were going to look by the canals, and if I can't find them, I'll get help. Just take Mrs. Sheffield to the hospital. Please?"

Mary hesitated, but then made up her mind. There was something different about Kelly, as if the hours in the swamp had not only terrified her, but made her grow up in some strange way. "All right," she agreed. As Kelly left through the patio door, Mary led Barbara and Michael through the kitchen into the garage.

Five minutes later Mary pulled into the parking lot next to the clinic. Barbara was out of the car even before it came to a full stop, running across to the emergency entrance. Judd Duval's squad car still sat in front of the door.

Inside, Barbara's eyes searched frantically for a nurse, but she saw only Judd, sitting alone on a chair, writing on a sheet of paper attached to a clipboard. When he looked up, his eyes widened in surprise, but then he rose to his feet.

"Miz Sheffield—"

"Where is she?" Barbara cried. "Where's Jenny? Where have they taken her?"

Judd moved toward her. "Miz Sheffield, maybe you better sit down." His hand closed on her arm and he tried to guide her to a seat, but Barbara pulled herself free as Jolene Mayhew, looking harried, pushed through the doors from the treatment rooms in the rear, and Michael, followed by Mary Anderson, rushed through the front doors.

"Jolene?" Barbara asked. "Where's—" She froze when she saw the look on the nurse's face, her last shred of hope dying within her. "No," she sobbed. "Oh, please, no . . . not my little Jenny. Not my baby . . ."

Jolene hurried across the room to her while Michael stood frozen just inside the door. "Oh, Barbara. I'm so sorry. Dr. P's in with her, but . . ." Her voice trailed off.

"No," Barbara sobbed. "She can't be dead. Not Jenny! I want to see her." She started toward the treatment rooms, and Jolene tried to stop her. Michael, too, stepped forward, but Mary Anderson intercepted him, putting her hand on his arm.

"Let her go, Michael." For a moment it seemed as if Michael hadn't heard the words, but as his mother disappeared through the swinging doors that led to the back of the building, he nodded mutely and let Mary lead him to a chair. He sank into it and looked up to see Judd Duval sitting across from him.

"My sister," he breathed. "Jenny . . . is she—"

Judd's head bobbed slowly. "She was in the canal," he said. "Right near my place. I was just leavin', on my way to work. She—"

But Michael had stopped listening. There was something about Judd, something in his eyes, that was wrong.

With a deep certainty, Michael knew the deputy was lying.

———

When Barbara came into the room, Warren Phillips was bent over Jenny's body, his stethoscope pressed to her bare chest. Barbara gasped as she stared at her daughter, and the truth finally closed in on her. Jenny was so still, her skin so horribly pallid.

"No," Barbara sobbed, lurching toward the examining table on which her daughter lay. "Oh, no . . ." She reached out and touched her daughter's face, her hand reflexively pulling back as she felt the coldness of Jenny's flesh.

"Barbara," Warren Phillips said, coming around to support the distraught woman, easing her into a chair next to the door. "Barbara, I'm sorry. There's nothing we could have done. When Judd found her, she must already have been in the water for nearly an hour."

Barbara heard the words, but her mind refused to accept them. She sat still, her eyes fixed on her daughter. When she finally spoke, her voice was nearly inaudible. "But there must be something—she can't be dead. Not Jenny. She was in bed—I put her to bed. I tucked her in." Her eyes finally strayed from Jenny, coming up to peer desolately at Warren Phillips. "She's sleeping. She's not dead. She's just sleeping."

Phillips laid his hand gently on Barbara's shoulder. "Where's Craig, Barbara? Is he with you?"

Barbara's head swung slowly from side to side. "He—He's out looking for her," she said hollowly. "He's out looking for Jenny." It wasn't possible—she couldn't be sitting here, staring at her daughter's corpse, while Craig was out somewhere in the barely dawning light, searching for their little girl, hoping to find her any minute. But it was true.

It was Jenny lying on the table.

Her beautiful daughter, whom she'd kissed good night only a few short hours ago.

She stood up, willing her legs to support her, and moved slowly to the table, looking down into Jenny's face.

She reached out again and gently stroked the little girl's forehead, then bent, brushing the cold lips with her own. She backed away, her eyes never leaving Jenny's expressionless face, and sank once more onto the hardness of the chair. "Can I stay here?" she asked. "Can I sit with her until Craig comes?"

"Of course," Dr. Phillips replied. "And I'll get you something—"

Barbara shook her head. "No. Please, no. Just let me sit with her. I'll be all right. I will . . . I know I will . . ." As tears began to run down her cheeks, Phillips silently left the room, closing the door behind him.

Thirty minutes later Craig Sheffield arrived, accompanied by Ted, Carl, and Kelly Anderson. As the Andersons joined Mary in the waiting room, Craig spoke to Jolene Mayhew, then went to the room where his wife still sat with Jenny. He paused at the door, his eyes fixing on his daughter, trying to comprehend the reality of what had happened. He heard Barbara's broken voice, murmuring quietly: "My fault. It's my fault."

"No," Craig said, turning to his wife, dropping down next to her, gathering her into his arms. "Don't say that, darling. Don't even think it. It was an accident, honey. It was just a terrible accident."

Barbara shook her head, refusing to be consoled. "It wasn't, Craig. If I hadn't been so *stupid*—if I'd only realized she might be listening!" Her arms went around him, and she clung to him. "Take me home, darling. Please take me home."

Craig helped Barbara to her feet and led her down the hall to the waiting room, where Warren Phillips was talking quietly to Michael and the Andersons. As Craig and Barbara came in, Phillips rose to his feet.

"I'm taking Barbara home," Craig said, sounding dazed, as if he wasn't quite sure what he was saying. "Then I'll come back. I'll come back and . . ." His voice trailed off. Come back and what? She was dead. His baby, his princess, was dead. He gazed at Phillips, who immediately knew what was going through Craig's mind.

"You don't have to come back, Craig," he said. "We'll take care of everything here. There will be some papers, but right now they don't concern you. Just take Barbara home. If you need anything, call me." He scribbled on a prescription form and tucked it into Barbara's purse. "Just in case she can't sleep."

Craig nodded and turned away, the shock of what had happened numbing his mind. Immediately Carl Anderson stood up. "I'll drive them," he told Ted. "You take Mary and the kids. We'd better all go to the Sheffields'. I don't think they should be alone right now." He glanced at Phillips. "If there's anything that needs to be done, you let me know. Craig's been a good friend for a long time, and I don't aim to let him down now."

Phillips nodded agreement, and a moment later the waiting room emptied out. When they were alone, with only Judd Duval still there, Phillips spoke to Jolene. "Call Orrin Hatfield, and tell him we need him," he said. "I can sign the death certificate, but given the circumstances, we'll need a coroner's report."

"I already called him," Jolene replied. "He's on his way."

Phillips nodded, turning immediately to Judd Duval. "There's no need for you to stay," he told the deputy. "Orrin can pick up your report after he's finished his own examination."

Judd, looking relieved, hurried out of the hospital. Phillips turned back to Jolene. "Call Fred Childress," he said. "Have him send a hearse."

He was just starting back toward the room in which Jenny Sheffield lay when Orrin Hatfield arrived, his eyes still puffy from sleep. "What's going on, Warren?" the coroner demanded. "Jolene says you got a six-year-old girl who drowned in the canal?"

Phillips beckoned the other doctor to follow him, and led Hatfield into the examining room. "I want this done quickly, Orrin," he said. "Jolene's calling Fred Childress, and by the time his hearse gets here, I want your report to be ready."

The coroner frowned uncertainly. "I don't know, Warren. Given what Jolene said, there'll have to be an autopsy, and that takes some time."

Phillips's eyes hardened. "There will be no autopsy, Orrin. Look her over if you want to, but don't touch her with a scalpel. We need her, Orrin. All of us."

Orrin Hatfield, who had already bent over Jenny, beginning his examination, straightened up. As he saw the expression in Warren Phillips's eyes, he slowly began to understand.

"I see," he said softly. "How much time do we have?"

Phillips glanced at his watch. "None. If we don't start now, she might really be dead."

Going to the cabinet against the wall, he found the syringe he'd brought with him to the hospital less than an hour ago, carefully putting it away even before he started forcing water from Jenny's lungs.

Now, slipping the needle into Jenny's arm, he administered the shot of naloxone, which would counteract the morphine he'd used to put Jenny into a coma even before he'd immersed her in the tub of ice water.

The morphine had slowed her metabolism nearly to the point of death, and that, combined with the hypothermia induced by the ice water, had kept her barely alive through the last hours.

With luck, there wouldn't even be any brain damage.

Not that it mattered, really, for Warren Phillips wasn't the slightest bit interested in Jenny Sheffield's mind.

It was her thymus he was after.

Her thymus, the large mysterious gland above the lungs, whose use he'd finally discovered so many years ago.

There would be enough of the precious secretion from Jenny Sheffield's thymus to stave off the aging processes of at least three of his patients. And she was young enough that he could milk her for at least another year.

As long as she didn't die before he got her to Fred Childress's funeral home.

There were no lights on in the house, but she knew there was someone inside, waiting for her. Though the house was barely visible in the darkness of the night, still she could see it clearly; the worn, splintered boards of its siding glowing unnaturally, as if they had somehow come alive. Vines crept up the walls, but though the air was still, the vines moved like serpents, rippling around the windows, creeping toward the roof.

She wanted to run from the house, but something drew her toward it, and though she struggled to turn away, her legs refused to obey her, carrying her steadily closer.

At last she was on the porch, and now she could feel the vines reaching out for her, their tendrils twisting, searching. One of them brushed against her skin, and she wanted to shrink away, but again her body seemed paralyzed. As the vines began to enfold her, binding her arms to her body, the terror inside her threatened to overwhelm her.

She opened her mouth to scream, but no sound came out.

The door opened, and in the darkness a figure appeared.

A man, so old he seemed barely alive at all. His hair, only a few thin wisps, hung limply from his scalp, which was covered with bleeding sores. His eyes—pale blue, shot through with reddish veins—fixed greedily on her, and when his lips curled back in an evil smile, she could see his rotting teeth, worn nearly away, crumbling from his gums.

He reached for her, clawlike fingers ending in jagged, torn nails, touching the skin of her face.

"No!" The word choked in her throat. With a valiant effort she tried to jerk away from the specter's touch, tried to wrest herself free from the constricting vines.

It was the effort of that final struggle before the man grasped her that finally woke Jenny, and now she did cry out, her voice a strangled scream as the last vestiges of the dream still held her in their grip.

Her eyes opened and she tried to sit up, but the thick straps that bound her to the bed held fast, and at last, her eyes filling with tears, she gave up.

She had no idea what time it was, nor how long she'd been here.

There were no windows in the room, nor was it ever dark. Always, when she woke up from the horrible nightmares that seized her whenever she fell asleep, the lights were on.

She wasn't alone in the room. It was filled with cribs, four of which had babies in them. If she turned her head, she could see one of them, and now, as the dream released her from its terrifying grip, she gazed over at the tiny form.

The baby was also awake, looking back at her, its small eyes fixed on her as if it knew how frightened she was.

"It's all right, baby," Jenny whispered softly, the sound of her own voice comforting her, if only slightly. "It was just a dream, and my mommy says dreams can't hurt you."

Her mommy.

Why didn't her mommy come for her?

Over and over she'd begged Dr. Phillips to let her see her parents, but he always told her the same thing. "When you're better. You don't want to make your mommy and daddy sick, too, do you?"

She heard a door open, and turned her head the other way.

Sometimes it was the woman who came in, the silent woman who never said a word, no matter how much Jenny begged.

But this time it was Dr. Phillips, and when he came over to the bed to look down at her, smiling, she started crying.

"I had the dream again," she said. "The man—the old man who looks like he's dead."

"It was just a bad dream, Jenny. You mustn't let it scare you," she heard the doctor tell her.

"But it *does* scare me," Jenny wailed. "I want my mother. Why can't I have my mother?"

"Because you're sick," Phillips explained. "And that's why I'm here. To take care of you. Haven't I always taken care of you?"

Jenny hesitated, but finally nodded. She'd known Dr. Phillips as long as she could remember, and he'd never hurt her, not really. Sometimes, when he gave her shots, it stung a little, but after he took the needle out of her arm, he always gave her a lollipop and she always felt better.

Except this time she kept feeling worse every time she woke up.

It was a funny kind of feeling. Every time she went to sleep, she hoped she'd feel better when she woke up, but she didn't. She always woke up feeling empty, as if something inside of her was slowly draining out. She felt all cold inside, and when she thought about her mother and father, and even Michael, something was different.

She still wished they'd come and see her, and take her away from this place, but each time she woke up, the ache inside her when she thought about them didn't hurt as much.

Instead, that strange icy lump inside seemed to get a little bit bigger each day, numbing her.

Jenny silently wondered if she was dying, and if she was, what being dead would be like. But she was afraid she already knew—it would be like being in the dream again, with the man coming after her, reaching for her, wanting something from her.

But if she was dead, she wouldn't wake up from the dream, and it would just go on and on and on.

The thought made her gasp, and Dr. Phillips frowned down at her, his eyes leaving the bottle that hung on the rack above her, dripping clear liquid that she had been told was food into a tube that went into her arm.

There was another tube, coming from a big needle that was in her chest, held in place with a piece of tape. That needle hurt, and the tape itched, but she couldn't scratch it because of the straps that bound her to the bed, which were only undone when she had to go to the bathroom.

"Are you all right? Does something hurt?" Dr. Phillips asked.

Jenny shook her head. "What are you doing?"

"I'm just adding something to your food."

"What?"

Phillips smiled at her. "Something to make you sleep," he told her. "Haven't you been telling Lavinia that you can't sleep?"

Lavinia. That was the name of the woman who came to take her to the bathroom, and change the babies' diapers, and sat with her sometimes, even holding her hand, though she never said a word. "I don't want to sleep," she complained. "If I go to sleep, the dream will come back."

"No, it won't," Dr. Phillips promised. "I'm putting something in your food to make it go away, and when you go to sleep, it won't be there at all."

Jenny looked up at him, her eyes wide with apprehension. "Promise?"

"Promise," Phillips repeated. He finished attaching the morphine vial to the IV, and turned the valve that switched the feeder tube from the glucose solution to the narcotic. "Go to sleep, Jenny," he said. "Just let yourself drift away."

He stayed with her, waiting for the narcotic to take effect. Only when she had fallen once more into a deathlike coma did he unstrap her bonds and carefully remove the needles that had been inserted in her body. Finally he picked her up, carrying her out of the room, then up the stairs to the main floor of his isolated house. He stepped out into the darkness, glancing to the east, but there was no sign yet of the rising sun.

It had been three days since he'd brought Jenny here. Each day he'd brought her up from the subterranean chambers before dawn and taken her back to Villejeune, where she'd lain all day in her coffin, deep in a narcotic-induced coma, her life apparently over. And each night, after dark, he'd taken her back to the laboratory beneath his house, bringing her out of the deathlike sleep.

Each day, he'd drained a little more of the priceless fluid from her thymus.

Stolen her youth, to prolong his own.

Stolen her soul to stave off his own mortality.

But this would be the last time he would take her into Ville-jeune, for today was a very special day for Jenny Sheffield.

Today was the day of her funeral.

═══

Just a few more minutes, Barbara told herself. Just a few more minutes, and then I'll be alone with Craig and Michael, and I can let go.

She was sitting in the small darkened alcove to the right of the altar in the chapel of the Childress Funeral Home. Though a gauzy curtain separated her and her husband and son from the rest of the people who had come to Jenny's funeral, she could see their faces clearly enough, see the confusion they were feeling as they listened to the eulogy for the little girl whose body lay in the coffin in front of the altar.

A funeral for a child.

It was wrong—children don't have funerals; they have parties. Birthday parties, and graduation parties, and parties after proms, and finally wedding parties.

But not funerals.

What would they say to her when it was finally over and they had to take her hand and try to soothe the pain she was feeling? With an aged parent, especially one who had been ill, it was simple enough.

"It's a blessing, Barbara."

"I know it's hard, Barbara, but at least your mother's pain is over."

"It's better this way, Barbara."

She'd heard it all, first at her father's funeral ten years ago, and then at her mother's two years later.

But there was no blessing in losing your six-year-old daughter.

Jenny had had no pain, rarely suffered so much as a day in her life.

And she hadn't wanted to die.

Barbara had tried not to think about it during the last three days, tried to keep her mind from focusing on her little girl, slipping on the muddy edge of the canal, tumbling into the water and then struggling to get out.

Struggling, and calling, with no one to hear her or to help her.

Her hands, resting tensely in her lap, clenched the handkerchief that was soaked through from her tears, and she resolutely pushed the image out of her mind.

It won't change anything, she told herself. It won't bring her back.

She forced herself to gaze through the filmy curtain once again, but found herself unable to look at Jenny's coffin. Instead, she scanned the faces of her friends and neighbors—people she had known for years—and wondered yet again what they would say to her after this ordeal was over.

Would they—*could* they—find any words of comfort?

Suddenly the organ began to play, and the gathering of mourners rose to its feet as the first strains of Jenny's favorite hymn began to sound.

"Away in a Manger."

As Barbara, too, rose shakily to her feet, she could almost hear Jenny's piping voice as she sang in the Christmas pageant last year, looking like a tiny angel in the costume Barbara had spent three days working on.

The costume she was being buried in today.

Barbara tried to imagine her entering into heaven, dressed as the angel she had already become.

She raised the handkerchief to her eyes, dabbing once more at the tears she was powerless to control.

The last chords of the hymn died away, the final prayer was softly uttered by the minister who had christened Jenny only six short years ago, and then the service was over. The curtain was raised, and Barbara felt Craig's hand on her arm, steadying her as he led her toward the altar to look at her daughter's face for the last time.

Sleeping, she thought as she gazed into Jenny's gentle countenance a moment later.

She looks as though she's sleeping.

As Craig's grip tightened on her elbow, she turned away and let him guide her up the aisle and out of the chapel.

———

Michael paused in front of his sister's coffin, his eyes searching her face for some sign of life. And yet he'd seen her each day as she'd lain in the viewing room, and each day she'd looked the same.

Her eyes closed, her face expressionless.

At last he reached down to touch her, resting his hand on her own much smaller ones, which were folded on her breast, holding a flower.

He squeezed her hands gently and was about to withdraw his fingers from her when he thought he felt a movement.

He froze, his hand remaining where it was, waiting for it to come again.

But no.

He'd only imagined it.

And yet as he, too, turned away from the coffin, he still couldn't bring himself to believe that Jenny was really gone, that he'd never see her again.

Something inside him, something he didn't quite understand, told him that she was still alive, that she wasn't dead at all, that she was still a part of his life.

"I feel the same way," his father had told him last night when he'd finally confessed the strange feeling he had. "We all feel like that. It's so hard to accept the finality of death, especially with someone like Jenny. I still expect her to come running in, climb into my lap, and plant one of those wet kisses on my cheek. Sometimes I wake up in the night and think I hear her crying. It's part of mourning, Michael. I know it all seems impossible, but it's happened. We have to accept it."

But for Michael it was different. Each morning, when he woke up, the feeling that Jenny was alive was stronger.

It was as if she was reaching out to him, calling to him, crying out for him to help her.

He moved down the aisle, searching the crowd for Kelly Anderson, and finally spotted her sitting with her parents and grandfather. As their eyes met, she nodded at him, not in greeting, but as if they shared some unspoken secret.

He understood.

She had the same feeling he had.

She had it, and recognized it in him.

═══

Barbara watched in silence as Jenny's coffin was placed in the crypt, a cold chill passing over her as the door closed and her daughter's body was sealed into the stone chamber. Almost involuntarily, her eyes shifted to the crypt next to Jenny's, and she read the inscription on its door.

SHARON SHEFFIELD

JULY 26, 1975

TAKEN HOME BY THE LORD THE SAME DAY

For Sharon, there had been no funeral. Her tiny body had simply been taken from the hospital to Childress's, then interred here.

On the first Sunday that Barbara had felt well enough, there had been a prayer said for her at church.

And that was all.

She'd never seen her, never once held that first little girl in her arms.

Suddenly she sensed a movement behind her, and turned to see Amelie Coulton pushing her way through the small gathering in the cemetery. Her lifeless blond hair, unwashed, hung limply around her face, and she was clad in a shapeless dress whose color had long ago faded into a mottled off-white.

But it was Amelie's eyes that riveted Barbara's attention, for they burned feverishly with an inner light that reached out to Barbara, seizing her.

"She ain't dead!" Amelie said, her voice quavering. "She ain't dead any more'n my own little baby is!"

Barbara's heart lurched as the words struck her. What was Amelie saying? She'd *seen* Jenny.

Not Jenny.

Sharon!

Was she talking about Sharon?

"Ask Clarey Lambert!" Amelie went on. "She knows! She knows it all!"

Suddenly two men appeared at Amelie's side, taking her arms. Amelie tried to shake them off, but they held her tight, keeping her from coming any closer to Barbara.

"I ain't lyin'," Amelie went on, her voice breaking now. "You got to believe me, Miz Sheffield. You was nice to me—I wouldn't lie to you!"

Barbara said nothing for a moment, her mind swimming.

"It's all right, Barbara," she heard someone saying. "We'll get her out—"

"No," Barbara said, her voice suddenly coming back to her. "Let her go. Please. She's all right."

The men hesitated, but finally released Amelie, who stayed where she was for a second, then came forward to put her hand gently on Barbara's arm. "I ain't wrong," she said. "If'n your baby'd died, you'd know. A mama knows them things." She seemed about to say something else, but then apparently changed her mind. Turning away, she disappeared through the crowd as quickly as she'd come.

But her words stuck in Barbara's mind, echoing there, festering.

Could it be true?

No!

But as the graveside service finally came to an end a few minutes later, Barbara's eyes fell on Kelly Anderson.

Kelly, who looked so much like her niece Tisha.

Kelly, who was the same age Sharon would have been had she lived.

Kelly, who was adopted.

Kelly was approaching her now, her eyes serious, her face pale beneath the simple makeup she was wearing.

"I'm so sorry, Mrs. Sheffield," she said. "I—I don't know what—"

Barbara put her arms around the girl and pulled her close. "You don't have to say anything, Kelly," she whispered. "I'm just so glad you're here. Sometimes, when I look at you, I can almost imagine I haven't lost both my little girls. I can almost believe that maybe Sharon didn't die at all, and grew up to be you." She felt Kelly stiffen in her arms, and immediately regretted her words. "I'm sorry," she said, releasing Kelly from the embrace and dabbing at her suddenly tear-filled eyes. "I had no right to say that. I—"

But before she could go on, Kelly stopped her. "It's all right, Mrs. Sheffield," she said so softly that Barbara could barely make out the words. "If I ever find out who my real mother is, I wish it could turn out to be you."

Their eyes met for a moment, neither of them speaking. Finally Kelly turned away, but as she rejoined her parents and grandfather, Barbara kept watching her.

Who is she? she thought. Where did she come from?

Suddenly, with an intensity she'd rarely felt before, she knew she had to find out.

═══

Kelly and Michael were sitting on the dock behind the Sheffield house. Above them, on the lawn, they could hear the buzz of conversation, as people talked quietly among themselves. The reception had been going on for an hour, and people were finally beginning to drift away, but Michael was certain that some of them—his parents' closest friends—would stay on into the evening, unwilling to leave his mother alone.

"I don't know why they don't just go away," he said, glancing over his shoulder. "It's not like they can do anything."

"I know," Kelly agreed. "I guess it's just what people do at funerals." She was silent for a moment, and when she spoke again, she didn't look at Michael. "Do you think Jenny's really dead?"

Michael stiffened, knowing instantly what she was talking about. "No. I don't know what happened. But when Judd Duval told me how he found her, I didn't believe him." He shifted position, his brows knitting into a deep frown. "I just don't *feel* like she's dead. It's really weird—but I keep feeling like she's still alive and needs me to help her."

Kelly finally looked at him. "I know. I keep getting the same feeling. Last night I dreamed about Jenny. And in the dream, I saw that old man, too. Only he was trying to get Jenny, not me."

"But—"

"We have to find out, Michael. And it's not just about Jenny, either." Michael cocked his head curiously. "I keep thinking about what Amelie said, too."

Michael's frown deepened. "She said to ask Clarey. She said that Clarey knows."

They were silent for a few minutes, and then Kelly said, "There's a way we can find out."

Michael looked at her intently. "I know. I've been thinking about it, too." He was silent for a moment, then: "Tonight?"

Kelly hesitated, then nodded.

Fred Childress picked up the large ring of keys he'd brought home with him from the mortuary that afternoon and glanced at his watch. Ten more minutes.

Midnight, Warren Phillips had told him.

Childress had known better than to argue with Phillips. He'd done that once, years ago, and though he hadn't thought much of it at the time, the next week, when he'd gone for his shot, Phillips had refused to give it to him. Two days later, when he'd gotten up in the morning and seen himself in the mirror, he'd felt a cold wave of fear he never wanted to experience again. Overnight, he'd aged at least thirty years, and when he'd called Phillips, begging for the shot, Phillips had coolly replied that the mortician didn't seem to understand the rules. "I'll give you the shot," he'd said. "But you'll never argue with me again. Is that clear?" With the reflection of his own death mocking him from the mirror, Fred Childress had quickly agreed.

Now, at a few minutes before midnight, he got into his Cadillac and drove out to Judd Duval's shack at the edge of the swamp.

Judd was sitting in front of the television, a can of beer in his hand, two empty ones sitting on the scarred table next to his chair.

"Are you drunk?" the mortician demanded.

Duval glared at him through bloodshot eyes. "Ain't you that has to watch out for them kids every night," he growled, lifting himself out of the chair and draining the beer in a single long pull. Leaving the television on, he followed Childress out to the car.

Childress said little on the way to the cemetery, nervously glancing in the mirror every few seconds, certain that unseen eyes were following every move the car made.

The deputy chuckled darkly. "What's the problem, Fred? The way you're actin', anyone'd think you'd never even been in a grave-yard before!" The chuckle turned into an ugly laugh as Childress glared at Duval, but he said nothing more until the undertaker had parked his dark blue Cadillac in the deep shadows of the dirt road that led around to the back gate of the cemetery. But before he got out of the car, Judd saw Childress glancing around yet again. "Shit, Fred, would you take it easy? There warn't another car on the road. Now let's just get this done, so's you can go on home while I do the hard part, okay? Sometimes I don't know why Phillips puts up with a chickenshit like you."

Fred Childress's temper flared. "For the same reason he puts up with an ignorant swamp rat like you," he snapped. "He needs us."

Duval's lips curled derisively. "Yeah?" he drawled. "Well, I don't know 'bout you, but I'd say we need him a hell of a lot more'n he needs us. Or are you startin' to look forward to old age?"

Childress felt a vein on his forehead begin to throb as his anger rose. "Drop it, Duval," he said. Getting out of the car, he went to the gate in the cemetery's back fence and used one of the keys from the large ring to open it.

He hesitated before he actually stepped through the gate into the graveyard, his eyes scanning the limestone mausoleums, glow-ing eerily in the pale moonlight, in which lay the dead of Ville-jeune.

"I don't like this, Judd," Fred Childress said. "I don't like this at all." He glanced around, imagining eyes watching him in the darkness. "If anyone sees us—"

"No one's gonna see us," Duval growled. "If you'd just shut

your mouth and get it over with, you could be back home in fifteen minutes."

Childress steeled himself, and at last stepped into the cemetery, moving quickly to the mausoleum in which Jenny Sheffield's body had been placed only that afternoon. He fumbled with the keys, finally inserting one into the keyhole in the crypt. Opening the door, he pulled the coffin halfway out. "Give me a hand with this, will you?"

Together, the two men pulled the casket free from the crypt and lowered it to the ground. Fred Childress opened the lid, and for a moment they both stared silently down at Jenny's lifeless face. Finally Duval lifted her from the coffin and started back toward the gate.

Fred Childress, left alone in the graveyard, reclosed the coffin and raised it back up to the crypt, sliding it inside once more.

He had just closed the door of the crypt when he heard the sound.

A crack, as if someone had stepped on a twig, crushing it underfoot.

He froze, his whole body breaking out in a sweat.

He listened, but the sound didn't come again, and finally he twisted the key in the crypt's lock and hurried back to Duval, who was waiting by the car.

"What took you so long?" the deputy demanded.

Fred Childress glanced back toward the graveyard. "I heard something."

Duval's eyes narrowed. "You sure?"

Childress nodded silently. Now it was Judd Duval who gazed out into the cemetery. "I don't—"

He cut off his own words.

He'd barely missed it; indeed, he still wasn't sure he'd seen anything at all. Just the faintest flicker of movement in the shadows. "Stay here," he whispered. "I'm gonna have a look around."

———

"He heard me," Kelly whispered, but immediately fell silent as Michael held a finger to his lips and motioned to her to follow him.

Moving quickly, he started back toward the front gate of the cemetery, slipping as silently as a cat through the deep shadows cast by the mausoleums. A few moments later he paused, and as Kelly crouched beside him, slid his head around the corner of the tomb behind which they were concealed. He saw nothing at first, but then a shadowy form stepped out onto the path fifty yards away, crossed, and disappeared again. Michael straightened up, glancing quickly around, then squatted down next to Kelly.

"We're only twenty feet from the gate. He's looking in the wrong place, so we can get out. Just follow me."

He peered around the corner once more, saw nothing, and made his move. Staying low, he darted toward the gates, then dropped down behind the wall.

"Maybe we better go home," Kelly whispered as she crouched beside him once more. But Michael shook his head.

"I want to know who it is. Come on."

He started off again, staying close to the shelter of the low wall that surrounded the graveyard until he came to the unpaved road that led around to the back. Across the dirt track was a thick stand of pines, and Michael darted into it, stopping only as the deep shadows of the trees closed around him.

"What are we going to do?" Kelly asked.

"Wait," Michael told her.

———

Judd Duval silently crisscrossed the cemetery, his eyes scanning the shadows for any sign of life. Suddenly, out of the corner of his eye, he saw a movement, but even before he could start toward it, the lithe form of a cat leaped off the roof of one of the stone buildings and disappeared into the darkness. Chuckling hollowly at his own nervousness, he went back to the car where Fred Childress was waiting.

"Nothin'," he said as he slid into the car next to the mortician.

"There was something," Childress insisted, starting the engine. "It wasn't just the sound. I could feel someone watching me."

Duval's lips curled into a mocking sneer. "Are all grave diggers scared of ghosts, or is it just you?"

Childress's prim lips tightened. He put the car in gear, but left the headlights off until they reached the main road. He paused once more, searching in both directions for any sign of another car.

Nothing.

At last he turned the headlights on and pulled out onto the pavement, pressing the accelerator. The Cadillac's powerful engine surged, and the car shot away into the darkness.

With every yard he put between himself and the cemetery, Childress felt his sense of relief grow.

Perhaps, after all, he'd heard nothing.

"Did you see who it was?" Kelly asked as the car disappeared down the road and the two of them stepped out of the shelter of the pines.

Michael nodded, his mind racing. The driver had been Fred Childress. But there was someone else in the car with him, someone he hadn't been able to see. "It was Mr. Childress," he said. "He owns the funeral home. I couldn't see the other one."

"What would they be doing out here in the middle of the night?"

"And how come they didn't turn on their lights?"

They crossed the dirt road again, and a minute later were back in the cemetery, making their way quickly along the paths that wound through the tombs, coming finally to the vault in which Jenny's coffin had been placed that afternoon. Michael stepped close to it and tried to pull the door of the crypt open, but it held fast.

Looking down, he frowned, and stepped back.

Crouching low, he studied the close-cropped grass in front of the mausoleum. Though it was barely visible in the dim moonlight, he thought he could see the faint outline of something that had pressed down upon the grass only moments ago.

A coffin.

"Look," he whispered to Kelly. "See? Look how the grass is pressed down here."

Kelly dropped down next to Michael, her eyes scanning the area in front of the sepulcher. "Here?" she breathed.

Michael's eyes followed her hand. "There was something sitting there not very long ago. Watch." Using the palm of his own hand, he pressed down on the lawn, and when he lifted his hand away, its print remained clearly visible for a moment before the grass began to straighten up again, until, like the larger impression in front of the crypt, it was barely visible. Indeed, even as they watched, both of the faint impressions disappeared in the weak light of the moon.

Kelly looked up at him. "They took her, didn't they?"

Michael nodded.

"What are we going to do?" Kelly asked as they both stood up, shivering despite the heat of the night.

The words came into Michael's mind unbidden, as if they'd been there forever, waiting for the right moment to rise up into his consciousness. "Kill them," he replied, his voice empty. "We're going to kill them all."

Abstractly, as if observing himself from afar, Michael wondered why he felt nothing as he uttered the words.

And then he remembered.

He felt nothing because he had no soul.

Long ago, right after he had been born, it had been stolen from him.

Now it was time to get it back.

Barbara Sheffield stared out the window at the silver crescent of the moon. Sleep would not come. She had lain awake for what seemed like hours, feeling the exhaustion of the day in every bone of her body, but her mind refused to let her rest.

Kelly's words echoed in her mind. *If I ever find out who my real mother is, I wish it could turn out to be you.*

Then Amelie Coulton's: *She ain't dead any more'n my own little baby is!*

But it was impossible. It *had* to be impossible! She couldn't try to replace Jenny with Kelly Anderson!

Yet the thought refused to be put aside. Barbara slipped out of bed. She went to Jenny's room first, standing in the doorway, her vision blurring with tears as she looked once more at all of Jenny's things.

Her stuffed animals, propped up on her bed the way Jenny always arranged them, were sitting against the wall so that they seemed to be staring at Barbara with their big sad eyes.

The closet door stood open, and Barbara could see the row of dresses hanging inside, and the shoes, set in neat pairs, beneath them.

Pictures covered the walls, the colorful scribblings that had always made Jenny so proud and which now made Barbara's heart melt, knowing there would be no more.

A sob catching in her throat, Barbara turned out the light and went to the kitchen, where she put on a kettle of water to make herself a cup of coffee.

When she went to the living room and pulled the family picture album out of the bottom drawer of her mother's antique sideboard, she told herself that she wanted nothing more than to look at some of the pictures of Jenny, to replace the haunting image of Jenny in her casket with one of her daughter when she'd been happy and full of life.

But a few minutes later, after she'd made her coffee and settled herself at the kitchen table, she found she couldn't look at the pictures of Jenny—the wounds were still too fresh, the pain too sharp.

She paged slowly through the album and found herself stopping each time she came to a picture of Tisha.

She found herself studying the pictures of her niece carefully, comparing the images in the album to the one in her mind of Kelly Anderson.

Their resemblance was unquestionable.

The lips were the same, full and generously curved.

The same high cheekbones and arched brows.

And yet there were differences, too.

Tisha was much pudgier than Kelly, but then, her mother had always been heavier than Barbara.

And Tisha was short, like her father.

Still . . .

No! She was imagining it all, denying her grief by making up fantasies!

She turned the pages carefully back to the beginning of the album. But before she closed its cover, her eyes fell on the first picture she'd put into the book.

It was an eight-by-ten enlargement of a picture that had been taken at the Fourth of July picnic sixteen years earlier, which she'd captioned "Last Days of Freedom—Of course I can barely walk!" She smiled at the image of herself in the last days of her pregnancy with Sharon, sitting on the picnic table, Craig beside her.

They'd looked so young then, all of them.

She began looking at the people in the picture. Some of them had changed so much that she hardly recognized them.

There was Arlette Delong, wearing the same beehive hairdo then that she still wore today. Except in the picture, Arlette's elaborate coiffure didn't have the look of desperation about it that it had taken on lately. Back then Arlette had been a pretty young woman—now, sixteen years later, her figure had thickened, and her middle-aged features had hardened from the long hours in her café. But her hair had remained the same—teased and back-combed, then sprayed solid. The only thing missing in the picture was the pencil that Arlette was now in the habit of implanting in the platinum mass.

There, too, were Billy-Joe and Myrtle Hawkins, Myrtle almost as pregnant with Buddy as Barbara had been with Sharon. Billy-Joe's handsome features had all but dissolved since then, his nose now puffy from the long years of drinking, his once-flat stomach having long ago given way to a beer belly.

Barbara frowned, her eyes coming to rest on Warren Phillips, who was standing with a group of other men under a pine tree to the left of the picnic table at which Barbara herself was sitting.

The doctor didn't seem to have changed a bit. His strong chin was as well-defined now as it was in the picture, and his dark hair, shot through with gray, was unchanged as well.

Barbara paused, thinking.

Back then she had always thought of Dr. Phillips as being much older than she, but now, sixteen years later, they seemed to be closer to the same age.

But how old was he?

She studied the picture, finally getting a magnifying glass from the kitchen drawer.

If she'd had to guess, she'd have said he was around forty-five in the picture, fifty at the oldest.

Which would make him at least sixty-one now. Maybe older.

And yet he still looked forty-five.

She began looking at some of the other men in the group around Phillips.

Carl Anderson was instantly recognizable, for he, like Phillips, hadn't changed at all in the last sixteen years.

Nor had Fred Childress, or Orrin Hatfield.

She found Judd Duval, lounging on a blanket.

He, too, looked exactly the same then as he did now.

She kept studying the picture, searching for more of the faces that seemed not to have changed in nearly two decades. She looked up as a shadow passed over the album.

Craig, his eyes worried, was looking down at her. "Honey? What is it?"

Barbara smiled wanly. "I couldn't sleep," she told him. "So I finally just gave up. Want a cup of coffee?"

Craig shook his head. "What are you looking at?"

"Pictures," Barbara replied. "I—I just wanted to look at Jenny again. But I couldn't."

Craig reached over and closed the album, then pulled her up from the chair and held her close. "Things are going to be all right, honey," he whispered into her ear. "I know it doesn't seem like the pain will ever go away right now, but it will. I promise."

Barbara let him lead her back to the bedroom, but as she tried once more to go to sleep, she knew he was wrong.

The pain of her loss was only going to get worse.

And yet, despite her grief, sleep finally came, and with sleep came dreams.

Dreams of searching for her lost daughters, who were calling out to her in the darkness.

She could hear them clearly, both Jenny and Sharon.

She followed their voices through the darkness, and at last, coming upon a circle of bright light, she found them.

They were together, smiling at her.

But when she ran to gather them in her arms and comfort them, then hold them away to look into their faces, something had changed.

Jenny—her beautiful Jenny—was the same as she had always been, smiling and laughing.

But Sharon had changed.

She wasn't Sharon at all.

She was Kelly Anderson.

———

Carl Anderson was awake that night, too, lying in bed, a book open on his lap. He heard a sound, like a door closing, frowned, then put the book aside and got out of bed. Putting on a robe, he went out into the living room, leaving the lights off.

He checked the front door, then moved on to the doors to the patio.

Everything was locked.

So was the kitchen door, and the door to the garage.

At last Carl mounted the stairs to Kelly's room and stood outside, listening. Hearing nothing, he opened the door a few inches and looked inside.

Kelly was in bed, the sheet covering her. She was lying on her side, facing the door, her eyes closed in sleep.

Carl frowned.

Was she really asleep, or had it been her door he'd heard closing?

He slipped into the room and moved closer to the bed.

Now he could hear the steady rhythm of her breathing.

"Kelly?" he whispered, reaching out to touch her.

As his fingers brushed against her skin, her eyes snapped open. "Grandpa?" she gazed up at him in the dim light and felt a chill of fear. In the dim moonlight he looked different—his eyes sunken, his face older. "I—I was asleep," she said quickly, shrinking away from his touch and doing her best to conceal the fright that had seized her.

Carl straightened up. "I thought I heard a door," he explained. "I didn't mean to frighten you."

Kelly forced a smile. "It's okay. I was just dreaming." She rolled over as if going back to sleep, and a moment later heard her grandfather leaving the room.

But even after he was gone, the memory of his eyes—the eyes of the man in her dreams—remained etched in her memory.

═══════

On the way back to his room Carl paused in the bathroom to relieve his bladder. But as he was about to switch off the light, he caught a glimpse of himself in the mirror.

His eyes had sunk into their sockets, and deep wrinkles were etched in his skin.

He gazed at his fingers and saw the beginnings of the telltale liver spots.

He thought quickly. How long had it been since his last shot? Only a few days!

Then what was wrong?

He hurried back to his room, closed the door, picked up the phone and dialed Warren Phillips's home number. On the seventh ring Phillips's answering machine came on, inviting him to leave a message at the tone.

Carl swore softly, but then began speaking. "It's Carl Anderson. I need another shot right away. Call me as soon as you get in." He thought a moment, then spoke again. "No, don't call me. It'll wake up everyone else in the house, and I can't let anyone see me until I've had my shot. I'll be there in the morning, before it gets light."

He hung up the phone and sank down onto the bed.

He looked at the clock.

One-thirty.

Four and a half hours before he could get to Phillips.

He picked up the phone again, redialing the same number. "I don't think I can wait," he said into the doctor's answering machine. "I'll call every half hour until I get hold of you."

He lay back on the bed, knowing he wouldn't sleep for the rest of the night.

23

The first faint glimmers of dawn were breaking when Carl Anderson, his hands trembling, reached for the phone one more time. He'd fallen asleep several times during the night, but his sleep had been troubled, for the degeneration taking place within his body kept waking him up.

His joints were stiffening with arthritis, and his lungs felt clogged, his breath coming in deep raling gasps. As he groped for the phone, his trembling fingers failed him and the receiver clattered to the floor. He tried to reach down and pick it up, but flashes of pain in his spine made him lie back on the pillow for a moment, a cold sweat breaking out on his forehead. He waited for the pain to pass, then reached for the cord of the dangling receiver, finally grasping it and pulling it up. At last he was able to pull the phone, too, onto the bed, and laboriously punch in Warren Phillips's number. Once more the impersonal machine answered.

"I can't wait any longer," Carl gasped. "I'm coming over."

Groaning with the effort, he raised himself into a sitting position and dropped his legs over the edge of the bed, his knees protesting painfully as he forced them to flex. At last he pushed himself up. A wave of dizziness washed over him, forcing him to reach out and steady himself against the night table. He could feel his heart beating raggedly in his chest; the simple effort of getting out of bed had all but exhausted him.

He tried to breathe deeply, but each breath shot needles of pain through him. He fought against the pain, forcing himself to walk slowly to the bathroom, where, his terror mounting, he stared at the unrecognizable image in the mirror.

An old man, far older than Carl Anderson truly was. It was as if all the years kept at bay by the shots Phillips had been giving him over the last decade and a half were now crashing back on him, overwhelming him.

His skin, leathery and slack, hung loosely around his jowls, and his beard, stubbly after the long night, was shot through with gray. The hair on his head was wispy, his scalp showing through everywhere; and his bloodshot eyes, shadowed by dark circles, squinted from their deep sockets, resisting the bright lights around the mirror.

His right hand came up, reaching out, as if by touching the vile image he could erase it.

His nails were cracked, and scabs had formed around his torn cuticles. The liver spots, barely visible only a few hours ago, now blotched his hands with the unhealthy color of old age, and his fingers were gnarled and twisted, distorted by the ravages of the decay that was consuming him.

An unintelligible croak of fear rising in his throat, Carl turned away, lurching back to his bedroom, where he pulled on the same clothes he'd worn the day before.

They bagged on his shriveling frame, the pants threatening to slide off his bony hips, the shirt hanging in deep folds from his drooping shoulders.

His eyes drifted to the pillow, all but obscured by the hair that had fallen away from his scalp during the night.

He was dying—he could feel it in the weakness that was inexorably spreading through his body.

He picked up his keys from the dresser by the door, then abandoned his bedroom, stumbling through the living room toward the kitchen and the garage beyond. As he climbed into the cab of the pickup truck, groping for the remote control that would open the garage door, he was no longer certain whether the weakness he was feeling came from the degeneration of his body or the fear of death that was overwhelming his mind.

Phillips.

He had to get to Phillips before it was too late.

The garage door behind him ground slowly upward, seeming to take forever before he could finally back the truck out into the street, but at last he was on his way. He shifted the truck into forward, moving quickly off into the brightening light of the summer morning.

═══════

Kelly stood frozen at the window long after her grandfather's pickup had disappeared around the corner.

She'd stayed awake all night, watching the telephone, waiting for the red light to blink on in the darkness, signaling that her grandfather was once more calling Dr. Phillips. Each time the telltale light had come on, she'd picked up the phone, pressing it to her ear as she heard her grandfather leaving another message.

With each call his voice had sounded weaker, until finally, on the last call only a few minutes ago, she'd barely been able to distinguish his words at all.

She was certain he was sick, and getting sicker as the night went on. For a brief moment, three hours ago, she'd wondered if she shouldn't go to him and find out what was wrong. But even before she'd left her room, she'd remembered that distinct feeling she'd had earlier that he was part of the dreadful evil that was being carried out deep in the swamp.

At last, when she'd heard him coming out of his room, she'd gone to her own door, opening it just far enough to press her eye against the crack and peer down the stairs into the foyer.

She'd gasped when she'd seen him moving through the shadows toward the kitchen, his tall figure stooped as he shuffled across the flagstone floor, his pace slow and careful, as if he was afraid of losing his balance.

Then, as he'd backed down the driveway, she'd gotten a clear look at his face, and it was that vision that had made her blood run cold.

This morning it truly was the face from her dreams; the face she'd glimpsed in the mirror sometimes, leering over her shoulder.

The hands she'd seen clenching the steering wheel of the truck were the same hands that she'd shrunk away from in her dreams, the clawlike hands that reached for her, as if intent on choking the life out of her.

But it wasn't her life those hands had been reaching for at all.

It was her youth.

That hideous being wanted the resilience of her flesh, the suppleness of her muscles and strength of her bones, the freshness of her skin, the brightness of her eyes and lushness of her hair.

Did he, and the others like him, even know what else they had stolen from her?

A cold knot of hatred filled her heart, and she knew now the feeling that Michael had known just after midnight, when he was sure his sister had been taken from her crypt.

They would find a way to take back what had been stolen from them, find a way to end the evil.

At last she turned away from the window and returned to her bed, the exhaustion of the long night finally overcoming her.

She drifted into sleep, and once more the nightmares came, but when the ancient visage appeared out of the darkness this time, it was no longer the face of a stranger.

It was the face of her grandfather.

━━━━

The sun was creeping over the horizon as Carl Anderson arrived at Warren Phillips's house, and as its first brilliant rays struck his rheumy eyes, Carl blinked, cringing away from the light as a creature of the night slinks to its den at daybreak.

He felt exposed, and imagined there were eyes everywhere, watching him, uncovering the secret he'd protected for so many years, recognizing him for the skulking thief he knew he was.

He pulled the truck around to the back of Phillips's house,

abandoning it with the key still in the ignition as he staggered to the back door, pressing the doorbell with a shaking finger.

He heard the soft chime of the bell within, echoing oddly, as if to signal him that the house was still empty.

Defeated, he sagged down onto the back steps, coughing roughly to clear his throat of the thick mucus that was coagulating there, his breath rasping as he struggled to keep his lungs filled with air.

Hearing a car, he shrank back until he recognized Warren Phillips's Buick gliding down the driveway, then hope surged within him.

Phillips, seeing him, braked the car to an abrupt halt. Then he was at the foot of the steps, helping Carl up, supporting him with one arm as he opened the back door.

"I've been calling all night," Carl rasped as Phillips helped him through the house to the library. "Where the hell—"

"I've been at the hospital," Phillips snapped. "Just take it easy."

"A shot," Carl pleaded. "I'm dying . . ."

Phillips disappeared for a moment, returning with a hypodermic syringe. Carl's eyes fixed greedily on the needle as he struggled to roll up his sleeve. But then a doubt came into his mind.

"It's not full. Why isn't it a full dose?"

Phillips swabbed Carl's arm with alcohol, and inserted the needle. "You're lucky I even have this," he said, pressing the plunger. "If it weren't for Jenny Sheffield . . ."

Carl felt the restorative fluid spread through him, reveled in the miraculous warmth that seemed to wash the pain from his body. Already, only a few seconds after the shot, his pulse was smoothing out, the irregular spasms of his heart returning once more to the strong steady beats that would keep his blood surging through his body.

The panic that had consumed him only a moment ago began to recede, and the words Phillips had just spoken slowly sank in. "Jenny Sheffield?" he repeated. "But she's—"

"Don't be stupid, Carl. She's not dead. She's in my lab. And if you're lucky, she'll keep you alive until you can find someone else."

Carl Anderson felt the panic creeping back up. "I can't do that," he muttered. "I pay. I pay a lot—"

"It doesn't matter how much you pay if I don't have anything to sell," Phillips told him. His eyes fixed darkly on the old man. "And if I were you, I'd stay out of sight for a while, Carl. You look terrible."

There was a cruel note in the doctor's voice that chilled Carl's soul. "But you said—"

Warren Phillips cut him off before he could finish. "If you want to live, you know what you have to do."

Ted Anderson came into the kitchen, stopping short when he found no one there except his wife. "Where's Dad?" he asked.

Mary shrugged. "He must have gotten up early. He wasn't here when I came down, and the truck's gone."

Frowning, Ted went to the door leading to the garage. Save for his own worn Chrysler, the garage was empty. Puzzled, he moved to the stove and poured himself a cup of coffee from the pot on the back burner. "Where the hell would he go this early?"

Mary glanced archly at her husband. "I'm afraid he didn't leave a note. Would you call Kelly?"

Ted went to the bottom of the stairs leading to Kelly's room, calling out, then went up and knocked on the door. "Kelly? Time to get up." There was a silence, then he heard his daughter's voice.

"I'll be down in a second."

Returning to the kitchen, he sat down at the table just as Mary slid a plate of bacon and eggs in front of him. A minute later, wrapped in a robe, Kelly appeared. Ted glanced up at her, then looked more closely. Kelly's face was pale and her eyes were edged with dark circles, as if she hadn't slept at all. "Honey? Are you okay?"

For a moment he wasn't sure Kelly had even heard him. She was staring off into space, lost in some world of her own. Then her expression changed, as if a veil had dropped over her eyes.

"I guess I didn't sleep very well last night," she said, her voice flat.

Mary, hearing the strange vacant note in her daughter's voice, looked worriedly at her. "Do you feel all right?"

Kelly said nothing. What would they say if she told them what had happened last night and what she'd seen this morning? What would they think if she told them that her grandfather had stolen her soul from her?

They'd think she was crazy.

And yet she wasn't crazy. She knew what had happened in the swamp, knew what Clarey Lambert had told her.

This morning, at dawn, she'd seen her grandfather, and finally understood the terrifying vision that had tormented her for as long as she could remember.

And knew that it wasn't a vision from her imagination at all.

It was a vision of the truth.

A truth she couldn't speak of to anyone except Michael Sheffield, because no one else would believe her.

"I—I'm fine," she murmured at last.

But she wasn't fine at all.

In the bright light of a perfect summer morning, when she should have been feeling good about everything, she felt only a dark terror.

A terror she realized might never leave her.

━━━━

Ted pulled the Chrysler through the gates of Villejeune Links Estates and was relieved to see his father's pickup truck parked in front of the trailer that served as a construction office. Ted was early himself this morning, and except for his father's truck, the site was still empty. He pulled the Chrysler alongside the truck, shut off the engine, and went into the trailer.

"Dad?" he called out. "Dad, it's me!"

He glanced toward the closed door of the office at the far end of the trailer, then turned the other way, toward the small kitchen where he and his father usually sat conferring with the site supervisor over Cokes, feeling more relaxed around the Formica table than they did around the desk in the office.

"Dad?" Ted called again as he stepped into the kitchen, half expecting to find his father already at the table, poring over drawings, checking specifications against lists of supplies on hand.

The kitchen was empty.

He gazed out the window, over the golf course that was in the first phases of construction.

Nothing.

He turned away from the window, moving back through the trailer toward the closed office door.

Hearing his son's heavy tread, Carl Anderson realized it had been a mistake coming here. He should have simply driven on past the site and kept going until he'd come to a motel.

He could have checked into one of those anonymous tourist courts along the highway, staying out of sight for a few hours until the shot Phillips had given him did its work.

But it was early, and the site had been deserted, and he'd decided to stop for a few minutes to leave some instructions for Ted.

And now Ted was here.

"G-Go away, Ted. I need to be alone right now."

He heard the sound of his voice, rasping, rattling in his throat like that of an old man.

"Dad?" Ted called through the door. "What is it?"

"Nothing! Will you just get the—"

The door opened and he saw Ted step in, then stop short, staring at him.

"Jesus, Dad," Ted whispered. He hardly recognized the old man as his father. Carl's strong features were all but hidden under the slack skin of his face, and his frame had taken on a stooped and shrunken look. Carl's eyes, burning deep in their sockets, were fixed on Ted, and as the younger man gazed at the ancient figure, he had the feeling he was facing the countenance of death.

"I told you not to come in here," Carl rasped.

"Dad, we've got to get you to the hospital—"

"No!" Carl barked, stepping behind the desk.

"Dad, you're sick—"

"I saw Phillips this morning. I'll be all right." The fingers of his right hand curled around the handle of the drawer, and he pulled it open. Glancing down, he saw the familiar shape of the butt of the gun he kept there. "Go away, Ted. Just leave me alone."

Ted shook his head. "I can't do that, Dad. Whatever's in those shots, it's not working."

"He's running out," Carl said without thinking.

Ted's eyes bored into him. "So they're not vitamins," he said. "What are they, Dad?"

Carl's jaw tightened. "It's something he makes himself."

"Then he'll make more," Ted said, his voice taking on a note of desperation. "Whatever it is, he can make more, can't he? Dad, what is it? What's *wrong* with you? If we don't get you to the hospital, you're going to die!"

He took a step toward his father, but stopped short when Carl's hand suddenly came up from behind the desk, holding a gun.

"I want you to leave, Ted," Carl rasped coldly. "I want you to get out of here and forget about what you've seen. I'll be gone for a few hours, and when I get back I'll be fine."

Ted shook his head in disbelief. "You're dying, Dad," he whispered.

"No, goddamn it!" Carl roared, his son's words triggering a fury in him that overcame the fear that had all but paralyzed him since he'd left Phillips's house. "I'm not dying! I'm not ever going to die!"

He raised the gun, grasping it with both hands now, pointing it at Ted. Though his hands trembled violently, he was so close to his son that he knew he couldn't miss.

Ted knew it, too. His hands came up slowly and he backed toward the door. "Take it easy, Dad," he said. "If you don't want to go to the hospital, I won't make you."

"Just leave me alone," Carl rasped. "Get out of here."

Ted had reached the doorway. A moment later Carl saw him dart out of the trailer toward his car. But instead of going to the

Chrysler, Ted jerked open the door of the truck and pulled the keys from the ignition where Carl habitually left them. Pocketing them, he got into his own car and drove away.

Carl stood where he was, his mind racing.

The men would be arriving soon, and Ted would be coming back, too.

Ted thought he'd gone crazy, and when he came back, he'd bring help.

Shoving the gun into his belt, Carl, too, left the trailer. The shot Phillips had given him was working now; his legs felt much stronger, and the pain in his joints was fading quickly.

He started away from the trailer, walking rapidly, toward the canal.

They wouldn't find him, Carl had decided. Not Ted, nor whomever he brought with him. By the time Ted got back, he would be long gone.

He came to the edge of the canal and clambered down the bank, sliding into the water, his feet coming to rest on the mud bottom.

He started across, pulling the gun from his belt as the water rose to his waist. A few seconds later he was across and scrambling up the other bank.

He would find what Phillips needed, find a child somewhere in the swamp.

If he didn't, he would die.

And Carl Anderson had no intention of dying.

24

It was a hot morning, and Kelly had momentarily wondered whether to wait until this afternoon, when Michael was done working, to go talk to him. But the image of her grandfather's sepulchral face loomed vividly in her mind. And so, after breakfast, she'd left the house for Phil Stubbs's place. She'd passed through the village, and seen Buddy Hawkins and some of his friends clustered on the sidewalk in front of Arlette's café. She'd sensed them watching her, even imagined she heard them whispering among themselves, but had ignored them. Resisting the impulse to cross the street, she'd simply walked past, saying nothing.

As she left the village behind and started along the road through the marshlands, with the sun beating down and the humidity closing around her like a suffocating shroud, Kelly found herself wishing she'd stayed within the air-conditioned walls of her grandfather's house. But then she walked through the open gates of the swamp tour's headquarters and paused for a moment, enjoying the relative cool beneath the spreading trees. In the shade of the pines and cypress, she felt better, and looked around, searching for Michael. She spotted him standing by the alligator pit, surrounded by a cluster of tourists. She moved to join the group, watching as Michael tossed a dead chicken into the enclosure.

The 'gators, already alert, closed in on the chicken, one of them snatching it out of the air even before it landed. As its great jaws snapped closed on the bird, crushing it instantly into a shapeless pulp, Kelly remembered the 'gator that had come so close to killing her in the swamp, and felt her skin crawl. As Michael tossed two more chickens to the waiting reptiles, she turned away, toward the nutria cages. A moment later Michael was beside her.

"How come you didn't call me?" he asked. "If I'd known you were coming out here, I'd have picked you up with the bike."

Kelly glanced furtively around before she spoke, and dropped her voice though no one was nearby. "It's my grandfather," she said, her voice quavering. "He—Michael, he's one of them!"

Michael stared at her. "Are you sure?"

Kelly nodded. "I was up all night long. He—He kept calling Dr. Phillips, and then he left real early this morning—" She stopped to steady herself, then continued. "I saw him, Michael. He's old. I mean, really old—like he was about to die." She shuddered, but went on. "He—He looked like the man we see in the mirror," she finished.

"Did he know you saw him?" Michael asked.

Kelly shook her head. "And I didn't tell Mom and Dad, either." She looked at Michael uncertainly. "What are we going to do?"

Before Michael could reply, Phil Stubbs stepped out of his office, his voice booming through the clearing. "Michael?" he called out. Spotting Michael and Kelly, he walked quickly over to them. "Bobby Carter just called in sick. You're going to take a tour out."

Michael's mouth dropped open. "Me? But I've never done it before."

Stubbs shrugged. "You know the swamp. All you have to do is take 'em out for a couple of hours, and tell 'em what's there." Then he smiled broadly. "And why don't you take your girlfriend along, too? But keep your mind on what you're doing," he added. "I don't need you losing track of time again, and taking these folks out in the middle of nowhere all day long. Two hours, no more! Got that?"

Michael nodded, then, with Kelly beside him, he headed down to the dock where the tour boats were moored. Two of them had already departed, but one more was still tied up, a long, narrow boat with two long benches, back to back, running down its center. Across the stern was another bench, and at the front of the boat was the helmsman's seat and the public address system. Michael surveyed the group that stood at the head of the dock, waiting for him. There were about fifteen women, in their twenties and early thirties, with a flock of children ranging from babies in carriers to ten-year-olds.

"Jeez," he whispered to Kelly as they approached the women. "This is gonna be awful." He could already imagine the barrage of questions that would come from the kids, and tried to figure out how he was going to keep any of them from falling overboard.

After he'd guided them into the boat and gotten them seated, he turned on the P.A. system and picked up the microphone. A high-pitched scream rose from the speakers and he quickly turned down the volume, then experimentally tapped the mike. Satisfied, he began to speak.

"Welcome to Phil Stubbs's world-famous swamp tour," he began. "I'm Michael Sheffield, and I'll be your guide this morning. Now, one thing I want you to remember is that the swamp is a dangerous place. We have alligators and crocodiles, and all kinds of other things, so it's important that you keep your hands inside the boat at all times." He fixed one of the older boys with what he hoped was a severe look. "And don't lean out, either," he said. "Those 'gators'll come right up out of the water and pull you overboard!" The boy's eyes widened in awe, and Michael saw several others immediately back away from the gunwales of the boat to sit back down on the bench. Winking surreptitiously at Kelly, he moved back to the stern, cast off the mooring line, then returned to the prow and cast off the bow line as well. Putting the transmission in gear, he opened the throttle a little, and the boat slipped away from the dock, moving out into the channel.

For the next hour Michael cruised slowly through the swamp, telling the tourists how it had been formed and how its ecosystem worked, describing the various trees and slowing the boat to a stop whenever he spotted something interesting.

As he'd expected, the children asked endless questions, but none of them came up with anything he couldn't answer, and soon he found himself relaxing, enjoying the tour almost as much as his customers were. He began veering away from the area the boats usually operated in, taking his group into the depths of the swamp, showing them places he'd discovered long ago, that most people rarely saw.

Coming around the end of one of the islands, they emerged from the gloom of overhanging trees into a marshy grassland, and Michael searched the area with his eyes, looking for a movement in the grasses that would betray the presence of a wild boar. At last he spotted what he was looking for, then began maneuvering the long boat through the narrow channels, his eyes constantly tracking the invisible pig as it pushed its way through the wetland. Finally he cut the engines and whispered into the microphone for everyone to remain silent.

The voices of the children died away. For nearly five minutes the group sat in the quiet of the wilderness, the only sounds drifting through the morning air the twittering of the thousands of birds that nested among the grasses and reeds.

At last there was a faint snuffling sound, and Michael pointed ahead. The grasses parted and an immense sow emerged from the foliage, her snout pressed to the ground as she rooted for food.

Behind her, imitating her movements, were six tiny piglets.

"Wow," yelled one of the boys. "Look at that! Wild pigs!"

Instantly the sow's ears pricked, her head came up, and she faced the boat. A second later she was gone, her offspring disappearing even faster than she did. "Nice going, Terry," another of the boys groaned. "Can't you ever shut up?"

As the boys began to squabble, Michael restarted the engine and headed back toward tour headquarters. If he didn't make any more side trips, he should make it right on time. Glancing back at his charges, he found himself grinning as the mothers tried to mediate the argument between the two kids. "What do you think?"

he asked Kelly, switching off the mike for a moment. "How am I doing?"

"This is neat," Kelly told him. "You're really good at it."

Then he heard a voice from the rear of the boat: "Is it true that people actually live in the swamp?"

The question came from a woman in the stern, who was holding a small boy, no more than three years old, on her lap, and had another one, even younger, lying in a carrier that sat on the seat next to her. Michael nodded and began telling them about the swamp rats and how they lived. One of the older boys waved his hand and began speaking even before Michael had acknowledged him.

"What about the zombies?" the boy asked.

Michael frowned uncertainly. "Zombies?" he asked. "I'm not sure what you mean."

The little boy gazed steadily at him. "My cousin says there's zombies in this swamp. Dead people. Except they're not really dead." As some of the little girls squealed nervously, the boy warmed to his own words. "My cousin says there's kids out here. Dead kids that go around lookin' for people to kill. He says they're like vampires, an' if they get you, they suck the blood right out of you!"

"Bobby!" the boy's mother said. "What a terrible story. I can't believe Jody told you anything like that!"

"Well, he did," Bobby insisted, his eyes fixed on Michael. "Is it true?"

Michael felt Kelly's eyes on him. He glanced over at her and saw that her face was pale. For the first time that morning he had no idea what to say. When he tried to speak, his mouth had gone dry.

Say something, he told himself. Say anything. Tell them it's just a story.

But it wasn't a story, not really. It wasn't quite the way Bobby was putting it, but—

And then, as the boat drifted slowly through the narrow channel, barely wide enough here to let it pass, one of the women let out a startled gasp.

A moment later there was another gasp, and then some of the children started screaming and pointing forward.

Michael turned.

Standing on the shore only a few yards away, a man was watching the boat.

An old man.

A man whose eyes, sunk deep into their sockets, were barely visible, but from which an evil glow seemed to emanate.

Kelly, who had turned at the same time as Michael, grasped his arm. He could see recognition on her ashen face. Yet he hadn't needed to look at Kelly to know who the man was, for he, too, had recognized him the instant he'd seen him.

The awful sunken greedy eyes.

Evil eyes, eyes he'd seen before.

Eyes he'd seen in the face in the mirror.

The boat was passing the vile figure now, and Michael remained frozen, unable either to speak or to move in the face of the nightmare image that had suddenly become reality.

In the boat the women and children closest to Carl Anderson shrank away from him, as if they, too, felt the horror that was overcoming Michael.

And then, as the boat was about to move away from him, Carl reached out, his gnarled fingers curling like the talons of a carnivorous bird, and snatched up the baby that lay in its carrier on the stern seat.

It happened so quickly that for a moment Michael wasn't sure it had happened at all.

The old man was gone, disappearing into the dense junglelike foliage as if it had swallowed him up. For one happy second Michael thought that perhaps the vile apparition hadn't existed at all, that once more it was only his mind playing tricks on him.

But the screams of the child's mother told him he was wrong.

She was standing in the stern of the boat, ready to go after the man who had stolen her child; only the hands of the women around her held her back.

"My baby," the woman screamed. "He took my baby!"

Michael reacted almost without thinking. "Stay in the boat!"

he shouted at the woman. He cut the engine and spoke quickly to Kelly. "Keep them in the boat. Whatever you do, don't let them get out, or they'll all get lost."

Without waiting for Kelly to reply, he leaped over the gunwale and dropped into the shallow water, then scrambled ashore.

"Michael!" Kelly shouted. "Michael, don't!"

But it was too late.

Michael, too, had disappeared into the swamp.

Carl Anderson felt a sharp pain in his chest, and came to a stop, his breath coming in ragged gasps. His legs felt weak, and he let himself sink to the ground, leaning back against the trunk of a pine tree. Thick shrubbery surrounded the tree, so he would have a respite now, concealed from anyone who might be pursuing him.

He clutched the baby to his chest and waited for the pain to subside, waited for his breathing to return to some semblance of normality.

Exhaustion was spreading through him, draining away the last of his energy. He wasn't certain how much longer he could go on.

But he had to go on. If he didn't, he would die.

It was the shot—the shot that should have made him feel young again. But it wasn't working this time; it hadn't been strong enough. For a while, early this morning, he had felt better, confident that by this afternoon his strength would have returned to him. But as he'd worked his way deeper into the swamp, determined to lose himself until the shot's restorative powers had rejuvenated him completely, he'd slowly begun to feel the weakness of age creeping up on him once more.

He'd panicked, knowing that he had to find a child.

Today.

Now.

A child whose youth Phillips could tap into and transfer to his own aging body.

By tomorrow it would be too late.

But where could he find a child?

If Ted hadn't taken his pickup keys, he could simply have driven up toward Orlando and found a shopping mall.

There would be children everywhere, children with inattentive mothers.

Children disappeared from shopping malls every day, and by the time the child was missed, he could have been halfway back to Villejeune.

Villejeune, and Warren Phillips.

Warren Phillips, and the eternal youth most men only dreamed of.

But Ted had found him, and only the gun had bought Carl any time at all.

The gun that was still in the belt of his pants, lending him courage despite the failing strength of his body.

It was stupid to have taken the child from the tour boat, but when he'd stumbled upon it, and seen the children who filled it— plump babies with their smooth skin and supple muscles—he'd felt a surge of cold fury.

Why should they be young when he was not?

Why should they have a whole life to look forward to, while he had nothing but memories to succor his painfully failing body?

After all, it wasn't as if Phillips killed the children.

Phillips had told him that long ago, when he'd first offered the treatment, and Carl's own granddaughter was the proof.

"It doesn't hurt them. All I need is the secretion from their thymus glands," Phillips had assured him. "After I'm done with them, they grow up perfectly normally."

Still, he should have waited, should have kept hunting through the marshlands until he found one of the swamp rats' children, a child no one cared about, a child who had no future anyway.

Instead he'd given in to his panicked rage and lifted the baby out of the boat.

Now, cradled in his arms, the baby cried, and Carl clamped his hand over its mouth, silencing its tiny voice before its screams could betray their location.

Kelly knew she had to do something. A tense silence hung over the tour boat; the women, their children gathered protectively near them, watched the swamp, searching for any sign of Michael. But it was as if the marshes had swallowed him up. For the last twenty minutes they had neither seen nor heard anything at all.

And yet, though nothing had happened, the tension in the boat was mounting every second.

In the stern, the mother of the baby sobbed quietly, while two of the other women tried to comfort her. But at last the woman looked up, her eyes fixed on Kelly, who stood in the bow of the boat, desperately trying to think of something she could do.

"Take us back," one of the other women demanded. "We have to get help!"

"I—I don't know where we are," Kelly said.

Two of the women closest to her glanced at each other. "But you must know where we are," one of them finally said, her voice betraying her fear. "You work for the tour, don't you?"

Kelly shook her head. "I don't—" But before she could finish the sentence, something stirred in her mind. A memory of being in the swamp, by herself, but not getting lost.

Not like the other night, when she'd run away from her father, anger driving her forward.

No, this was like the first night, when she'd gone into the swamp looking for the boy she'd seen from across the canal, and lost track of time.

That night, obeying Clarey Lambert's unseen guidance, she'd found her way back to where she'd begun.

Now she concentrated, summoning that guidance once more.

"I can do it," she said, her voice imbued with new confidence. "I can get us back."

She gazed down at the dashboard of the boat, reaching out to brush her fingers over the unfamiliar array of instruments, grasping the key and turning it. An alarm buzzer sounded, and for a moment Kelly hesitated, but then followed the impulses that came into her mind, and pressed a button.

The engine came to life.

As she pushed the transmission forward and the boat began to slip through the water, the woman in the stern screamed.

"No! We can't leave! He has my baby!"

The words came to Kelly's ears as if from a great distance, and she was barely aware of them, for her mind was turned inward now, following only the invisible guidance to which she now gave herself.

The boat moved slowly through the writhing maze of channels, and though they all looked alike to Kelly, she let herself be guided, turning from one channel into another with no concern as to the direction she was going or the breadth of the passages she chose.

Ahead, the channel narrowed, and behind Kelly two of the women looked nervously at each other.

"We're not going to get out," one of them said. "She doesn't have the slightest idea where we are. She's making it worse."

The other woman said nothing, for she could see Kelly's face, see her eyes staring straight ahead, never wavering, never glancing around as if looking for landmarks.

Foliage closed in around the boat, choking the channel, and what little conversation had been going on died out completely as wary eyes watched the shore, certain that at any moment the frightening figure might appear again to snatch one of the other children from the boat.

Mothers tightened their grip on their children, and the children themselves clung to their mothers.

Suddenly the prow of the boat burst out of the tangling vines and the canal spread into a broad lagoon.

Ahead, directly across the lagoon, was the dock at the tour headquarters.

The invisible hand that had held Kelly's mind released its grip, and she gasped slightly, certain she had failed, that nothing at all had happened. But then she looked around and recognized the tour headquarters only a few yards away. "I did it," she said, almost inaudibly. "I got us here!"

As Kelly clumsily maneuvered the boat up against the dock, she saw Phil Stubbs glaring at her, his face red with fury.

"What the hell's going on?" he demanded. "Where's Michael? You should have been back an hour ago!"

"He's not here," Kelly told him, her voice distant, as if she'd hardly heard the question. Stubbs stared at her, seeing for the first time the strange look in her eyes. But before he could say anything else, a babble of voices broke out.

"My baby," the woman in the stern screamed. "He took my baby!"

Stubbs stared at the woman in confusion. "What—"

"It was a man," another of the women told him. "A horrible old man. He looked crazy, and he took her baby." Her voice rose. "He just came out of the swamp and took it! The guide went after him. For God's sake, call the police!"

Stubbs froze. A man? What were they talking about? But all the women were shouting at him now, and their children too.

"Now just calm down," Stubbs finally called above the confusion. He turned to Kelly, who was gazing off into the swamp, her brows knit into a deep frown. "Tell me what happened," he said.

Kelly's head swung slowly around. Her voice held a strange, abstract quality, as if she were only vaguely aware of what she was saying. "We were going through a channel. There was a man on the shore, and as we passed him, he reached in and picked up a baby. He wanted it. He wanted a baby."

Phil Stubbs's eyes narrowed. "Who?" he demanded. "Who was it? Did you recognize him?"

Kelly hesitated, but then nodded. "It was my grandfather."

===

Michael swore out loud as his foot caught under a mangrove root, throwing him forward to sprawl in the soft mud that bordered the island. Ignoring the pain in his ankle, he scrambled back to his feet and stood still, listening.

Carl Anderson seemed to have simply disappeared. And yet, only a moment ago, just before he'd tripped, Michael was sure he'd heard the sound of a baby crying. It had only lasted a fraction of a second, then was suddenly cut off, as if someone had silenced the baby by covering its mouth.

He looked around, searching the thickets with his eyes but seeing nothing. Everywhere he looked there seemed to be only tangles of mangrove roots, and the strange cypress knees that protruded above the water's surface like dead stumps, and stands of pine trees.

And yet he could feel that Carl Anderson was close by, sense his presence somewhere so near that Michael felt as though he should be able to see him.

Clarey.

The name popped into his mind unbidden, but suddenly he could see her in his mind's eye, sitting on the porch of her shanty, her eyes gazing into the swamp but her mind reaching much farther than her eyes could see.

Closing his eyes, he silently called out to her, willing her to answer him, willing her to reach into his mind and guide him to wherever Carl Anderson might be hiding.

And slowly an image took form.

An image of a single pine tree, taller than all the rest, standing alone, and surrounded by a dense thicket of brush.

He opened his eyes and looked around.

The pine tree stood not fifty feet away, exactly as he'd just pictured it in his mind.

He started toward it, his eyes fixed on the thicket but his mind concentrating on the image that had been summoned up when he called out to Clarey Lambert.

And in that image, he could see Carl Anderson clearly, crouched in the brush, his back to the tree, clutching the baby in his arms.

He could see the slack folds of Carl's skin, see his sunken, fevered eyes, see his cracking fingernails.

He pushed his way into the brush, parting the grasses before him.

A moment later his eyes beheld the vision his mind had already seen.

Carl leaned against the tree, the baby held in his left arm as he clutched his gun in the trembling fingers of his right hand.

The gun was raised, its barrel pointing at Michael's chest.

Michael paused, staring at the reality of the vision that had plagued him for so long, but now the fear he had always felt in the presence of the ancient man was gone.

"Get away from me," Carl Anderson croaked, his voice rattling in his throat. "I'll kill you."

Michael's eyes remained fixed on the old man. "You can't kill me," he heard himself say. "You know you can't kill me. I'm already dead."

Carl Anderson gasped as he heard the words, and stared up at the teenage boy whose eyes were fixed on him with a steadiness that made his heart pound.

"No," he said, his voice taking on a pleading note now. "Leave me alone. I never hurt you. None of us ever hurt you."

"Our souls," Michael said. "You stole our souls."

Carl's eyes widened. The gun wavered in his hand as Michael came toward him. He tried to steady the revolver, tried to squeeze the trigger, but the boy's eyes seemed to hold him in their own paralyzing grip, and as Michael moved steadily closer, Carl felt the gun slipping from his fingers. "No," he muttered, clutching at the weapon as his heart began to race, pounding in his chest with a terrifyingly erratic rhythm that warned him of what was to come a split second before it happened.

As Michael reached out to him, and Carl's fear turned into blind panic, a violent stab of pain slashed through his chest, shooting down into his arms and legs. The gun dropped from his fingers as his right hand fell to the ground.

The baby rolled onto the thick carpet of pine needles as Carl's left arm went limp.

Pain tore through Carl's head then, a blinding, searing agony that rent his sanity into shattered pieces a moment before he died.

As his mind collapsed, Carl saw demons rising up out of the nether world, coming toward him with pitchforks and torches, intent on torturing his body for eternity.

And an eternity, it seemed, in those last seconds before his death, as the demons fell upon him, ripping his skin from his muscles, jabbing sharp slivers beneath his fingernails and into his joints, tearing his limbs from his body and laying open his belly to spill his intestines onto the ground.

He screamed, flailing at the creatures that beset him, but his struggles were nothing more than the twitchings of a dying man, and though the Hell into which he had plunged seemed to him to go on forever, his body soon lay still beneath the pine tree.

In the silence that followed Carl's death, Michael stared at the body with an odd detachment, as if it had nothing to do with him.

And then a voice spoke inside him.

Take back what is yours.

He crouched down next to Carl Anderson's body, then ripped open his shirt to expose the old man's sunken chest. Nothing was left of the robust figure that the man had been only yesterday, for today all the years he had stolen had come back to claim him.

His ribs, brittle and soft, crumpled as Michael touched his chest, and when the boy's fingers tore into his flesh, the desiccated tissue gave way as if it had been cooked.

Michael ripped through the old man's sternum, tearing open his chest cavity, reaching inside the man, finally feeling what he was searching for.

A tiny fragment of bloody tissue, resting just above the old man's lungs, close by his heart.

Michael ripped it loose, and then, his hands covered with blood, stuffed the withered vestige of Carl Anderson's thymus into his mouth.

He swallowed the bit of tissue, his stomach heaving as he choked, but then the spasm passed.

A strange warmth he had never felt before spread out through his body, and he remained where he was, letting the aura envelop him, letting it expand into his mind, and fill him up.

The emptiness he'd felt all his life was suddenly gone, and he felt whole.

For the first time in his life Michael began to cry.

He felt the hot tears running down his cheeks, tasted the salt of them with the tip of his tongue.

He let the tears run free, washing away the pain of sixteen years.

Only when his tears were finally exhausted did he pick up the baby, cradling it in his arms.

"It's all right," he whispered. "Nothing's going to hurt you now."

The baby began to cry, but Michael held it close, kissing it gently on the forehead, and soon its sobbing began to die away. At last, the baby calm in his arms, Michael left the thicket and went to the edge of the water.

Setting the baby gently on the ground, he washed himself clean of Carl Anderson's blood.

Finally he picked the baby up again and started making his way through the swamp toward the tour headquarters.

He was whole again, and once the baby in his arms was safe, he knew what it was he had to do.

He and Kelly, together.

26

Mary Anderson was in her bed-
room, staring at the last box that still remained unopened from the
move from Atlanta. She knew what was in them—old albums,
ledgers remaining from Ted's failed attempt to start a business
three years ago, her own report cards from grade school and high
school—all the things everyone always saved but rarely looked at.
She toyed briefly with the idea of sorting through the box, but
quickly realized that in the end she would simply repack it anyway.
She picked it up to take it out to the garage, where it would join
her father-in-law's own collection of memorabilia on the metal
storage shelves that lined the south wall. But as she passed through
the living room, the doorbell chimed softly, and she set the box
down next to the sofa. She opened the door to find Barbara Sheffield standing on the porch, an air of anxiety surrounding her that
made Mary's welcoming smile fade quickly into a worried frown.
"Barbara? What is it? What's happened?"

Barbara fleetingly wondered if she shouldn't simply turn
around and go back home. But after last night and this morning,
when the thoughts that had been growing in her mind ever since
Jenny's funeral had coalesced into a deep-seated conviction, she'd
known she had no choice.

She had to talk to Mary Anderson, had to find out the truth of Kelly's origins.

If Mary even knew.

She hadn't called first, hadn't wanted to tell Mary why she was coming. After all, how would she feel if one of her friends called her up to announce that she was Michael's real mother?

A stranger calling with such an announcement would be one thing—indeed, ever since she and Craig had adopted Michael, she'd always been prepared for the possibility that at some point her son's natural mother might appear. She would have been able to deal with that, for at least she would know that Michael had no relationship with such a person.

But this was different, for Barbara had a relationship to Kelly. What if Mary thought she was planning to lay claim to her daughter?

Still, Barbara felt she simply *had* to know, had to lay all the doubts in her mind to rest.

"I need to talk to you, Mary," she said at last. "I know it's going to sound crazy, but I've been having the most awful thoughts. I can't seem to shake the idea that Kelly might be my daughter, that maybe Sharon didn't die when she was born." Speaking the thoughts out loud for the first time, she realized how bizarre they sounded. "I know it sounds crazy," she went on, stumbling on her own words now. "It's just—well, there's so many little things—the way she looks . . . And Amelie Coulton . . . you know what she said at the funeral—" Her eyes flooded with tears and her voice turned into a choking sob. "Oh, Mary, I don't know. It's all just so awful for me. I feel like I'm coming apart, and I don't know what to do. . . ."

Mary drew Barbara into the house and closed the door, then led her into the kitchen. "It's all right, Barbara. I know how you must be feeling. It has to be horrible for you right now." She poured a cup of coffee from the pot on the stove and sat down across from Barbara. "Now tell me what I can do."

Barbara took a deep breath, struggling to control her roiling emotions, finally speaking only when she was certain her voice wouldn't fail her. "I—I thought maybe if you could tell me where Kelly came from —"

"It was an adoption agency in Atlanta," Mary told her. "Ted and I had been waiting for almost a year."

"Atlanta?" Barbara echoed hollowly.

An image of the box on the living room floor popped into Mary's mind, and she stood up. "I'll be right back." A moment later she came back into the kitchen, the box in her arms. Opening it, she began piling its contents on the table, and finally lifted out a photo album. "Look through this," she said, handing the album to Barbara. "It's full of pictures of Kelly, from the day we picked her up at the agency right up until a year or so ago." Her voice took on a wistful quality. "The last couple of years I'm afraid we didn't take many pictures. Ted's business wasn't doing well, and . . ." Her voice trailed off. "I guess the last couple of years there just wasn't much we wanted to remember."

Barbara opened the album and began flipping through the pages. The early pictures, when Kelly was an infant, meant nothing. But as Kelly grew, and her features began to develop, Barbara felt the same familiarity as she had when comparing Kelly to her niece Tisha. From the age of four on the resemblance was there. The two children, apparently unrelated, looked enough alike to have been sisters.

"I found it," Mary said a few minutes later, interrupting Barbara's reverie as she sat gazing at a picture of Kelly when she was about the same age as Jenny.

Again, she looked nothing like Jenny, who took after her father, but her resemblance to Tisha, and even more so to Barbara's own sister, was eerie. At last Barbara looked up from the page. Mary, her expression almost sorrowful, was holding out a folded sheet of heavy paper. "It's Kelly's birth certificate," she said softly. "I—well, I think it tells you what you want to know."

Barbara took the certificate, her fingers trembling, but for some reason she couldn't bring herself to look at it for a moment. Finally she unfolded it, her eyes misting over as she studied it.

It was from a hospital in Orlando that she'd never heard of.

It recorded the birth of a baby girl, born a week after Sharon had been born.

The baby had been given no first name, its identification stated impersonally as "Infant Richardson," the daughter of Irene Richardson.

Father unknown.

Barbara felt her heart sink, but as she studied the signature of the attending physician, something stirred inside her.

Philip Waring.

She'd never heard the name before.

Yet there was something familiar about the signature, something flicking around the edges of her mind.

Then it came to her, and she reached into her purse, digging through it until she found the prescription Warren Phillips had given her the morning Jenny had died.

The prescription she'd never filled.

She flattened the form out and laid it next to the birth certificate.

The scrawl of the attending obstetrician's first name matched the last name of her own doctor.

The first three letters of the obstetrician's last name matched the corresponding scribble of the first syllable of Warren Phillips's own signature.

She stared at the two signatures for a long time, telling herself it wasn't possible, that it was merely a strange coincidence, that neither of the signatures was actually even legible.

They were nothing more than doctors' scribblings.

The denials still tumbling in her mind, she spoke to Mary Anderson. "There's something wrong," she said quietly. "Mary, I think this birth certificate is a fake."

Mary Anderson's eyes clouded. "Barbara, it's the certificate we were given by the agency. Why would they—"

"Let's call the hospital, Mary," Barbara broke in. "Please?"

Ten minutes later Barbara felt a cold numbness spreading through her body.

The hospital in Orlando was real.

The birth certificate was not.

There was no record of an Irene Richardson giving birth to a child in the hospital.

No record of an Infant Richardson at all.

No Dr. Philip Waring had ever been connected with the hospital in any way.

When the phone call was over, the two women looked at each other, Mary Anderson now feeling as numbed as Barbara Sheffield. "What are we going to do?" Mary asked, suddenly fully understanding—and sharing—Barbara's obsession to find the truth of Kelly's origins.

Barbara barely heard the question, for she already knew what had to be done.

She wondered if she would be able to bear to stand in the cemetery one more time, gazing at the crypt in which her first child lay.

She wondered if she would be able to watch them open it.

But most of all, she wondered if she would be able to stand the awful reality of finding it empty.

Tim Kitteridge sighed heavily, his large hands spreading across his desk in a gesture of helplessness as he faced Ted Anderson. "I still don't see what it is you expect me to do. If your father's sick—"

"He's worse than sick," Ted exploded. "He's dying. He's dying, and he's gone off into the swamp somewhere!"

"Now, you don't know that," Kitteridge replied. "All you know is that he wasn't in his office. That's a big development out there—"

"I searched it," Ted repeated for what seemed like the fifth time. He felt his temper rising, but struggled to control it. After he'd left his father early that morning, he'd gone to Warren Phillips's house and then to the hospital.

Phillips had been in neither place, nor did anyone know where he might be. "I'll page him," Jolene Mayhew had told him, but after five minutes with no reply to the page, he'd demanded an ambulance, and gone back out to the construction site.

To find that his father was gone.

Taking the paramedics with him, he'd searched every house on the site, every possible place where his father could have been hiding. When the crew had arrived for work, he'd sent them out, too, certain that somewhere on the hundred acres of Villejeune Links Estates his father would be found.

But there had been nothing.

Nothing, until one of the men had found tracks at the edge of the canal. That was when he'd come to the police station and tried to enlist Tim Kitteridge's help. He'd told him the whole story, but even as he talked, he'd seen the skepticism in the police chief's eyes.

"Now come on, Anderson," Kitteridge had told him after he'd described how his father had looked early that morning. "Nobody ages like that overnight. And I know your father—he's strong as an ox, and works harder than most men half his age."

"And he looks half his age, too," Ted had shot back. "Phillips has been giving him some kind of shots. I don't know what they are, but I saw what happened to him a week ago. It was like watching the fountain of youth or something. He was feeling really bad, and looking terrible, and an hour later he was fine! But this morning he looked like he was dying!"

Kitteridge's eyes rolled. "If he was really dying, I find it hard to believe he took off into the swamp. And I can't start sending out search parties every time someone goes in there. Especially not for someone who's lived here all his life. If your dad wanted to take off for a while, that's his business, and there's nothing I can do about it."

Ted glared angrily at the police chief. "What about Phillips? Dad saw him this morning—he told me so himself. And now he's gone. He's not home, and he's not at the hospital. Where is he?"

Kitteridge felt his own temper rising now. "Look, Mr. Anderson," he said, his voice hard. "I don't know what you think my job is, but I can tell you it's not to go hunting for people who are minding their own business. You told me yourself that Phillips was out of whatever medicine he was giving your father. Maybe he went to get more of it. Did that ever occur to you?"

"Jesus Christ," Ted swore, making no attempt to check his anger any longer. "If whatever he was giving Dad was something he could just pick up in Orlando, why the hell would he run out? Dad says he makes it himself. Aren't you even interested in what he might be giving the people around here? It's drugs, goddamn it! And you don't seem to give a shit!"

Kitteridge rose to his feet, but just as he was about to speak, the phone on his desk jangled loudly. He snatched it up. "Yes?" he snapped into the mouthpiece. But as he listened, the angry scowl that was directed at Ted Anderson began to fade. "Okay," he said. "I'll be right out there. And I'm bringing Ted Anderson with me." He placed the receiver back on the hook. When he looked back at Ted, his impatience had turned to uncertainty. "That was Phil Stubbs," he said. "One of the tour boats just came in. There's been a kidnapping. He said an old man came out of the swamp and lifted a baby right out of the boat."

Ted said nothing, but felt a cold knot of fear forming in his stomach.

"Your daughter was there," Kitteridge went on. "She saw the whole thing, and says she knows who the man was."

"Dad," Ted breathed. "It was my father, wasn't it?"

Kitteridge nodded.

Together, the two men left the police station.

———

Barbara Sheffield barely nodded to her husband's secretary as she passed through the small front office of his two-room suite over the hardware store and walked into the large room where Craig worked. He was on the telephone as she came through the doorway, but when he saw the look on her face, he abruptly cut his conversation short, rising to his feet.

"Barbara? What's happened?"

She silently crossed the room to drop a folded sheet of heavy yellowed vellum onto his desk. He picked it up, stared at it blankly for a moment, then looked curiously at his wife. "What's this?"

When she spoke, Barbara heard the hollowness in her own voice. "Kelly Anderson's birth certificate. Except that nothing on it is true. And I'm sure Warren Phillips forged the signature." The emotions she'd been holding in check by the sheer force of her will suddenly boiled up inside her. She sank into the chair in front of Craig's desk, her eyes flooding with tears. Moving around the desk, Craig dropped down to kneel next to her, putting his arm around her.

"Honey, what's going on? What are you doing to yourself?"

Doing to myself? Barbara echoed silently. The fear she'd been feeling turned into anger, and she pulled herself free of her husband's embrace. "I'm not doing anything!" she exclaimed, her voice rising. "All I'm trying to do is find out what's been done to me! To me, and to our little girl. She's not dead, Craig! Can't you understand?"

"Barbara, honey," Craig began as he stood up again, but Barbara cut him off.

"It's Sharon," Barbara told him. "Something's wrong, Craig! Sharon's not dead! Dr. Phillips took Sharon when she was born and did something to her. Then he arranged for her to be adopted by Mary and Ted Anderson."

Craig stared at her in shock. What was she talking about? The whole idea of it was so bizarre . . .

"I know it sounds crazy, Craig," Barbara went on as if she'd read the thoughts spinning through his mind. "But just listen to me. Just give me five minutes."

She told him about the pictures she'd looked at, first in her own album, then in Mary Anderson's. But it wasn't until she told him about the phone call to the hospital in Orlando that she saw the disbelief in his eyes begin to give way to a worried frown. "You can call them yourself," she said, handing him the birth certificate once more. "In fact, I wish you would. Maybe the woman I talked to made a mistake. Maybe I'm wrong. Maybe . . ." She floundered for a moment, trying to sort through her conflicting emotions, but finally gave up, leaning tiredly back in the chair. "I don't know what I think."

Craig picked up the phone and made the call, but as he spoke to the woman in Orlando, his eyes fixed on the signature at the bottom of the birth certificate. He'd seen Warren Phillips's signature hundreds of times over the years, and he knew Barbara was right. Despite the fact that the name was different, it was still clearly only a variation on the doctor's distinctive scrawl. Even so, when the phone call was finished, he tried to think of some other meaning for the anomaly. "It doesn't mean Kelly is Sharon," he said. "It could be some kind of coincidence—"

Barbara cut him off. "I thought of that," she told him. "I've tried to think of everything. But we never saw Sharon, Craig. Neither of us. Not after she was born. Not at the funeral. We simply believed what we were told." Her voice held a note of self-condemnation that tore at Craig's heart.

"What do you want me to do?" he asked, and for the first time there was no challenge in his voice.

"We have to open the crypt," Barbara told him. "We have to find out if Sharon is really dead. If we don't, I think I'm going to go crazy. I can't stand it anymore, Craig. Ever since I met Kelly, I've had the feeling that she's Sharon. I can't explain all of it, and I know her resemblance to Tisha could just be a coincidence, but I just can't get over the feeling that she's our daughter."

Craig felt as if he was standing at the lip of a great yawning abyss, and that if he weren't very, very careful, he might slip over the edge and be swallowed up by the emptiness below. If the baby they'd both looked forward to so much, and then lost even before they'd seen it—if that baby were still alive . . .

He wasn't sure he could bring himself to finish the thought, consumed as he was by a great wave of black fury that had risen inside him and threatened to sweep all reason away from him.

"Mary," he said, turning away from the dark thoughts. "What did Mary say?"

Barbara closed her eyes for a moment, wishing there were some way of avoiding what Kelly's mother had told her. But she couldn't. "She—She says she wants to know, too. She says there's always been something about Kelly she couldn't understand, as if something inside her is missing." She hesitated, then went on. "She's always thought it was her fault, that she'd failed Kelly. But if Phillips did something to her—"

Craig grasped at the straw. "What?" he demanded. "What possible motive would Phillips have? My God, he's a *doctor*! Doctors don't steal babies from their mothers."

"There's something else," Barbara said, her voice sending a chill through Craig. She opened her purse and took a picture out of it, handing it to her husband. "Remember when that picture was taken? Just before Sharon was born?"

Craig gazed down at the picture, nodding. "I don't see—"

"Look at some of the men in that picture, Craig. Warren Phillips and Carl Anderson. Orrin Hatfield and Fred Childress. Judd Duval."

Craig's eyes scanned the picture, quickly picking out the men Barbara had named. "They haven't changed much, have they?" he said. When Barbara said nothing for several long seconds, he looked up and found her staring at him.

"They haven't changed at all, Craig. Not one of them has aged a day in the last sixteen years. And I keep thinking about that. Orrin Hatfield is the county coroner. He signed the death certificates for Sharon and for Jenny. Fred Childress buried them both. Judd Duval found Jenny in the swamp. And Carl Anderson is Kelly's grandfather."

Craig didn't want to look at the picture that was coming together in his own mind, didn't want to accept what his wife was suggesting. And yet he couldn't deny her words.

"They're doing something," Barbara said. "They're doing something with our children, and it's keeping them young. They're taking something from them, Craig. I don't understand it, and I can't prove it, but I know it's true. They stole our daughters, Craig!"

Craig felt himself slipping over into the abyss. "We don't know that," he said, his voice desperate.

"And what about Michael?" Barbara asked.

Craig looked at her numbly, but understood instantly what she was asking. He got up, went to the safe, and a moment later found what he was looking for. After studying it for a moment, a cold knot of fear forming in his stomach, he handed Michael's birth certificate to Barbara.

She felt an odd dispassion as she stared at the document, as if it merely proved what she already knew.

The same hospital.

The same signature.

"Barbara, it's all supposition—" Craig began.

"Don't you think I know that? Don't you think I hope I'm wrong? That I'm just refusing to adjust to Jenny's death? But what if she's not dead, either, Craig? What if I'm not wrong? There's only one way we can find out."

Craig said nothing for a long moment, but at last he took a deep breath and met her eyes. "All right," he said. "Let's go see what we can do."

27

Kelly looked fearfully at Tim Kitteridge. "It wasn't anybody's fault," she insisted. She'd done her best to repeat to the police chief exactly what had happened, but with her father's eyes on her, she still felt oddly guilty, as if somehow she'd let him down again.

"And you told Phil Stubbs that the man who took the baby was your grandfather?" Kitteridge asked.

Kelly's eyes flicked once more toward her father. He was watching her, his eyes boring into her. If she said the wrong thing . . . But she couldn't lie, couldn't pretend she might have been mistaken.

Because she wasn't mistaken. The man in the swamp had been her grandfather, even though he'd looked much worse than he had when she'd seen him early this morning, when he left the house. Finally she nodded. "It was him," she breathed. "He—He looked different from the way he usually does, but it was him."

Ted Anderson started to say something, but Kitteridge silenced him with a look. "How, Kelly?" he asked. "How did he look different?"

Kelly hesitated. If she told them the truth, they were going to think she was crazy. But there were other people who had seen her grandfather, and even though they didn't know who he was, they knew what he looked like. "He—He looked sick," she finally said, her voice trembling. "I mean—well, it was like he'd gotten old. I mean, really old, like he was going to die or something." She paused, anticipating her father's accusation that she was lying, but when her father said nothing, she went on. "It was really weird. I saw him this morning, when he went to work, and he looked funny then, too. But in the swamp it was worse. His hair was falling out, and his face was all covered with wrinkles. And his eyes were all sunken in."

She saw the look that passed between her father and the police chief and fell silent again. But when her father spoke, he didn't challenge her words at all.

"It's what I told you," Ted said. "There's something wrong with him, and whatever it is, it has to do with the shots Phillips has been giving him. It sounds like they've made him go nuts or something."

Kitteridge nodded curtly, his mind racing. "Whatever's wrong, the first thing is to find him and get that baby back." He pulled his portable radio from its case on his belt and snapped it on. When Marty Templar's voice crackled through the small speaker, he began issuing a series of orders. "We've got Carl Anderson in the swamp, and he's got a baby with him. We need men, and we need them armed. Anderson's got a gun, and we have to assume he's willing to use it. And Marty," he added. "The Sheffield kid's out there, too. He went after Anderson. So make sure no one shoots the wrong person, got it?" He listened for a moment, then: "We'll take off from Phil Stubbs's place. Kelly Anderson can show us where the old man made the snatch, and maybe we can track him from there." He shut off the radio, then turned back to Kelly. "Can you find your way back there?"

Kelly's tongue ran nervously over her lower lip. "I—I don't know," she finally admitted.

Kitteridge frowned. "You got all those people back here, didn't you?" he asked.

Kelly felt numb. How could she explain what had happened? How could she tell them that she hadn't known where she was going at all, but instead had been simply following unspoken instructions that seemed to come from inside her head? At last she nodded. "M-Maybe I can," she stammered. "But I'm not sure. I just sort of steered the boat, going whatever way looked right."

But Kitteridge had stopped listening, his attention already shifted to the young mother, sitting in the midst of a cluster of her friends a few yards away, her face streaked with fresh tears.

Left alone with her father, Kelly looked up at him worriedly. "Daddy, what's wrong with me?" she asked.

His daughter's voice held a pathos that twisted Ted Anderson's heart, and he gently put his arms around her. "Honey, there isn't anything wrong with you. You're a heroine—you brought all those people out of the swamp—"

Before he could finish, Kelly said, "It wasn't me, Daddy. I can't even remember doing it. It was like there was a voice in my head, telling me what to do."

Ted's arms tightened around his daughter. He wanted to tell her that everything was fine, that whatever had happened in the swamp this morning, she had been the one to bring the boat out, and that he was proud of her. But before he could say anything at all, he felt her stiffen in his arms.

"Look!" she said. "Daddy, look! It's Michael. He's got the baby!"

———

Michael, the baby held securely in his arms, stepped into the shallow channel that separated the island from the mainland and the tour headquarters.

"Wait!" someone shouted from the other side. "We'll come over in the boat!"

Michael paused, then acknowledged the call with a wave of his hand. But while he waited for the boat to come and pick him up, he wondered what he was going to tell them.

He could see the police chief in the boat, and knew there were going to be questions.

Questions he couldn't answer.

They were going to want to know where Carl Anderson was, and how he had gotten the baby away from him.

And he could tell them that.

But what could he tell them about the way Carl Anderson had died, and what he had done to the corpse?

Nothing.

His mind had been reeling ever since the moment he had felt that first flush of warmth spread through his body, first felt those hot tears stinging his eyes and running down his cheeks. From that moment everything about the world had looked different to him, and felt different, and he knew why.

Somehow, in that moment when Carl Anderson was dying, Michael had recovered his soul.

And he knew now what he had to do.

As the boat reached him and he handed the baby into the waiting arms of its mother, then let Tim Kitteridge help him into the boat as well, he said nothing.

Nor did he speak as the questions began to come at him from every direction, first from the baby's mother, then from the police chief. But at last, after the boat was docked, he told them what happened.

"I followed him, and finally I caught up to him. He had a heart attack, or something. He didn't try to hurt me, or the baby, or anything. He just ran as long as he could and then collapsed."

"Collapsed?" Kitteridge asked.

Michael nodded. "He was under a tree. A tall pine—the tallest one around. He was trying to hide in some bushes, but I could see him. And he saw me, too." Michael's voice took on a hollow quality. "He died. He just died."

Kitteridge's frown deepened. "And you just left him there?"

Michael nodded distractedly, as if he was having trouble even remembering what had happened. "I had to bring the baby back," he said. "I had to bring it back to its mother."

Though Kitteridge was certain there was more to the story than Michael had told him, he decided that any more questions could wait until later. The boy's face was pale and his eyes looked glazed. "All right," he said. "You just take it easy for a few minutes. Then maybe you can take us back to where you left him. Think you can do that?"

Michael's head moved in assent, and the police chief's attention shifted to Marty Templar, who had just arrived with four other men. But while Kitteridge talked to the deputy, Michael quietly went in search of Kelly Anderson.

He found her near the dock, looking out uncertainly at the swamp. "You okay?" he asked, standing beside her.

Kelly shook her head. "Th-They wanted me to take them back to where we were when my grandfather took the baby. But I didn't think I could." She turned to face Michael. "I don't remember how I got back."

Michael took her hand in his own. "It doesn't matter. They want me to take them to where I left your grandfather, but I'm not going to." Kelly frowned but Michael kept talking, and for the first time she noticed that he'd changed, somehow. His eyes burned with indignation. "I know what's wrong with us, Kelly," he said, his voice dropping so no one but she could hear him. "I know what's wrong with all of us, and I know how to fix it."

Ten minutes later, when Tim Kitteridge went looking for Michael, he had disappeared.

He, and Kelly Anderson as well.

═════

Clarey Lambert opened her eyes, blinking in the bright sunlight. She was sitting on the porch of her house, her body erect in the rocking chair. She felt tired from the effort it had taken her to reach out first to Kelly's mind, and then to Michael Sheffield's, but now it was over, and she could hear the soft throbbing of the outboard engine as the boat bearing the two teenagers drew near. She turned in her chair, feeling the ache of her protesting muscles, and smiled at Jonas Cox. "They be coming. You hear?"

Jonas said nothing, his eyes searching the waterways in the direction from which the low sound drifted. Only when the boat came around the end of the next island and he recognized Michael and Kelly sitting in the stern did he finally relax. When he'd first heard the boat, he'd been certain that it was the Dark Man, coming for him.

As the boat bumped against the pilings beneath the structure, Jonas reached down, taking the line that Kelly held up to him, and tied it to the railing. Then Kelly and Michael climbed up the short ladder, coming to a sudden stop when they saw Clarey's eyes fixed on them.

"The baby?" the old woman asked.

"He's all right," Michael told her. "I got him back to his mother."

"It was my grandfather who took him," Kelly said. "Why did he—"

Before she could finish her question, Clarey's voice, crackling with anger, cut her off. "Not your grandpa," the old woman declared. "Don't you never think that man was your grandpa. And it don't matter now—he be dead."

Jonas Cox's pinched face paled. "Michael killed him?" he asked, his voice trembling.

"No!" Clarey replied. "Michael didn't kill Carl Anderson. Carl Anderson died a long time ago. Only his body stayed alive." Her glittering eyes shifted away from Jonas, boring into Kelly. "You saw him—you saw him in your dreams, and in your mirror. Both of you did. But it warn't just him you saw. It was all of 'em—all the old men whose souls died but whose bodies stayed alive, sucking up the lives and the souls of the young 'uns." Clarey's gaze shifted toward Michael, and now she noticed the difference in his eyes.

The empty gaze of the children of the Circle was gone, and Michael's eyes smoldered with anger.

"It's what he wanted that baby for. Gonna take that little child to the Dark Man, so he could suck the life out of it, that's what that evil man was going to do." She smiled again, and chuckled softly. "But you didn't let him, did you? You took that baby away from him, and took your soul back, too, didn't you?"

Kelly gasped, her eyes widening as she turned to Michael. "But if you didn't kill him—"

"I didn't have to," Michael told her, knowing what she was thinking. He hesitated, seeing once more the scene at the foot of the pine tree, when Carl Anderson had watched him coming close and known what he was going to do.

Known, and been unable to stop him.

"I would have killed him, though," he said at last, his voice quiet. "If he hadn't died, I would have killed him." His eyes, glistening with tears he made no attempt to wipe away, held steadily on Kelly as he told her what had happened.

"It was something inside him," he concluded, after describing his attack on Carl Anderson's corpse. "I could feel that there was something there, something I had to find." He hesitated, then went on. "It was something that was mine, that I knew he'd taken from me. And when I found it—" His voice broke, and he couldn't tell her what he'd done.

The memory of stuffing that bloody piece of atrophied tissue into his mouth, then forcing himself to swallow it, was still too fresh in his mind.

He smiled at Kelly, feeling once more that welcome warmth within him that until a little while ago he'd never experienced, nor even missed. "I'm free now," he went on. "I know what's wrong with you. And Jonas, and all the rest of us, too. I know what he took from all of us. And I know how to make us well again."

Jonas Cox's eyes narrowed suspiciously. "Ain't no way to do nothin' to the Dark Man," he said. "Ain't nobody even knows where to find him. An' if he wants you, ain't nowheres to hide."

Michael shook his head. "It's over," he told the frightened boy. "He can't make us do anything. Maybe he never could. All he could do was frighten us. But we're all together, and we're stronger than he is."

He turned to Clarey Lambert, their eyes meeting. "Call them, Clarey. Call everyone."

Clarey turned and went back into the house, the three children following her. "I knew the time were comin'," she muttered softly, almost to herself. "Ain't nothin' bad gonna happen anymore, after tonight."

She moved to her worn chair and let herself sink into it, closing her eyes. Silence settled over the room, and then Kelly began once more to hear the strange melody inside her head. As its intangible threads began to wind around her, she turned to Michael, her eyes questioning.

"She's calling the Circle," he said. "She's calling us together for the last time."

As Kelly gave herself to the haunting strains that seemed to come out of nowhere, she felt a pang of fear.

What if she wasn't strong enough?

What if she couldn't find the will within herself to do whatever it was that Michael had done?

But she put the thoughts aside.

She would do whatever was necessary, if it would free her from the awful terror of her nightmares, and from the chilling emptiness that had always yawned within her, threatening to swallow her up as if she'd never existed at all.

28

Craig and Barbara Sheffield sat in the car, staring at the peaceful facade of the small white colonial building with green shutters that housed the Villejeune mortuary, neither of them willing to go inside, neither of them ready to face what they might find there. But at last Craig sighed, opened the door, and got out. A moment later Barbara joined him on the sidewalk. Craig gave her an encouraging squeeze. "Ready?"

Saying nothing, Barbara pulled open the front door and stepped into the unnatural hush of the funeral home's foyer. Ahead and to the left was the viewing room in which Jenny had lain only a few days ago. It was empty now, its door standing open. To the right, across from the viewing room, was a small office, and as Craig and Barbara stepped inside, Fred Childress looked up, his eyes clouding as he recognized them and saw the strained look on Barbara's face.

"Barbara? Craig? Is something wrong?"

"Yes," Craig replied coldly. "Something is very wrong. I want the keys to our mausoleum, Fred."

The undertaker's eyes widened in shock. "The maus—"

"My mausoleum. The one where my children were buried. If they were buried at all!"

Fred Childress rose to his feet, his expression indignant. "I don't know what you're implying, Craig—" he began, but once again Craig cut him off.

"Get me the keys, Fred," he said. "If you don't, I'm going to break into the crypt without them, and if I find what I think I'm going to find, you're going to be spending a very long time in jail."

Childress's mind reeled. It wasn't possible—this wasn't supposed to happen! "Craig, you know I can't open a crypt without a court order—" he began, stalling for time, trying to straighten out the confusion that muddled his mind.

"I don't have time, Fred," Craig grated. "Now make up your mind! Do you want to give me those keys, or shall I break in?"

Childress's jaw worked for a moment, but suddenly he found an answer.

Give them the keys!

Let them open the tombs, and then deny anything they might suggest. Surely, if he cooperated with them, they couldn't blame him for what they found!

Quickly, he disappeared from the office, returning a moment later with a heavy ring of keys in his hand. "This is most unusual, Craig," he insisted. "According to the law—"

"I know the law," Craig said, taking the keys from the undertaker's hand. "Come on, Barbara."

Wheeling, he strode out of the office.

As soon as he was gone, Fred Childress picked up the phone and began searching for Warren Phillips.

═══════

Barbara stood rigidly in front of the mausoleum, not really seeing the stained limestone with its ornate facade. Indeed, as she waited while Craig searched for the right key, she barely saw the tomb at all. Suddenly she felt consumed by doubts. Did she really want to know?

If the coffin was empty, what would it mean?

Not only for her, but for Kelly, too. If Warren Phillips had taken her the moment she was born, and given her to the Andersons a week later, what would it mean?

What had been done to her during that week?

And now, sixteen years later, what could be done about it?

Though the afternoon was hot, Barbara felt herself shiver. For a moment she was almost tempted to tell Craig she'd changed her mind, to tell him to stop before it was too late. But before she could speak, she heard his voice.

"I have it," he said softly.

Her eyes suddenly focused, and she saw the large key that he'd inserted in the bronze door of the crypt. His hand was still on it, but he was looking at her as if he understood the doubts that were suddenly assailing her. "Are you sure?" he asked one more time.

Barbara braced herself, then nodded. Craig turned the key in the lock. It stuck for a moment, then she heard the bolt slide back.

Craig pulled the heavy door open, the hinges screeching in sharp protest at the intrusion. For the first time in sixteen years, sunlight struck the small mahogany casket in which Sharon's tiny body had been interred.

The wood had lost its luster over the years, and as Craig pulled the casket out of the tomb and set it carefully on the ground, an awful sadness came over Barbara.

There was something about the coffin, after its years in the mausoleum, that struck her as even more final than death itself.

As Craig began to lift the lid, Barbara turned away, unable to look at whatever might be inside. Only when Craig groaned softly did she finally force herself to look.

What she saw bore no resemblance to anything human.

Instead, lying on the yellowed and rotting satin with which the coffin was lined, was the desiccated body of an alley cat.

There was little left of it—a few fragments of skin, long ago hardened into leather, and the bones, laid out with a macabre naturalness. It was as if the creature had died in its sleep, one skeletal paw folded beneath its jaw, its tail curled up its side.

The empty sockets of its eyes seemed to stare reproachfully up at her.

Barbara's stomach twisted, and she quickly looked away. "Put it back," she whispered. "For God's sake, put it back."

Craig lifted the coffin back into the tomb and closed the door, relocking it as if it had never been disturbed at all.

Then, his own heart beating hard now, he began testing keys in Jenny's crypt. A moment later he found the right one, but this time it twisted easily in the lock, and when the door swung open, there was no screech of protest from the recently oiled hinges.

He stared at the end of his youngest daughter's coffin, putting off as long as he could the moment when he would have to slide it out.

His hands trembled as he grasped the end of the box, but he pulled it out just enough to open the section of its lid that had been closed on Jenny's face only a few days ago.

He lifted it up and peered inside. Staring into the empty interior of the casket, his mind reeled, threatening to shatter into a thousand broken fragments.

"I was right, wasn't I?" Barbara whispered, seeing the anguish on her husband's face. "She's not there, is she?"

Craig swallowed hard in a futile attempt to dislodge the lump that had risen in his throat. He shook his head, unable to speak.

"Oh, God," Barbara moaned. "What's happening, Craig? What did he do to our children?"

Craig dropped the lid and turned away, leaving Jenny's coffin protruding from the open door of the tomb. Putting his arm around his wife, he led her out of the cemetery.

———

Warren Phillips glanced at his watch.

In a few more hours the last batch of thymus extract would be refined, and he would be ready to leave. Once he was gone, there would be no one left to answer the questions Tim Kitteridge would have.

Within a few days Judd Duval would be dead.

So would Orrin Hatfield.

And Fred Childress.

All of them, crumbling into dust as their bodies consumed the youth he had given them.

But he, along with his research and the few vials of the precious fluid he had left, would have simply disappeared, leaving behind him the laboratory in the basement, and the empty nursery.

He almost laughed out loud as he remembered the reassurances he'd given the undertaker when he'd called an hour ago: "Stop worrying, Fred—there's nothing they can prove! Graves get robbed all the time, and there's nothing to lead them back to us!"

Except for the birth certificates, but he hadn't told Fred about those. Fred, or anyone else. And even if the Sheffields had discovered the forgery, it would still take some time before they'd be able to convince anyone to issue a search warrant for his house.

At least until tomorrow morning, and tomorrow morning it would be too late.

The five volumes of meticulous notes he'd accumulated over the years, detailing the research and experimentation he'd done before he'd finally succeeded in isolating the single compound within the body that held off the aging process, was already carefully packed in the trunk of his car.

Five volumes of complicated research that, in retrospect, seemed so simple.

The thymus gland, that mysterious organ that was so large in an infant and shrank so steadily through puberty and adolescence, almost disappearing in adults, should have been the most obvious place for him to look when he'd started on the project forty years ago.

And yet, even after he'd become convinced that the thymus was the key to his search, it had still taken him years before he'd finally developed a method of extracting the secretion of the gland and refining it without destroying the precious hormone it contained.

The answer to that problem, too, seemed simple now, for in retrospect it appeared obvious that it would be impossible to extract life from that which was already dead.

The glands he'd taken from corpses in the morgue had proved all but useless, and it wasn't until he'd begun experimenting with live animals—mice at first, and then later, dogs and cats—that he'd finally begun to find success.

Only when he'd been quite sure of his methods had he begun experimenting on children, first using only the unwanted babies of the women of the swamp, the babies they'd neither planned for nor expected to survive.

But as the work had progressed and the technique had finally been perfected, he'd known he would need more babies, for as the children began to grow up, and as their thymuses shrank, they became less and less useful to him.

And he'd seen the differences in them, the differences he'd created by tapping into them long before they'd had a chance to develop normally.

They'd grown up to be strange, quiet children, children who never cried, but rarely laughed, either.

There was an ennui about them, as if something inside them—something almost spiritual—were lacking.

They seemed to care nothing for themselves, or for anything else, either.

And yet they seemed to have developed some special form of communication, some new sense to compensate for the loss of their youth. He didn't pretend to understand this new sense, but had nevertheless found a use for it.

He had created a cult for them, carefully nurturing it over the years, building a mystique around the children, exploiting their differences from normal children, using those differences to control them.

He'd taught them that they were special children, but special only because of the Dark Man.

The Dark Man that he'd given them almost as a god, to be respected, and obeyed. And to be provided with more children, whom they would bear themselves.

Phillips had never appeared before them without the black mask that concealed his face, never let them know who he really was.

And sixteen years ago he'd put his own son into the project, too. But his own son would be different.

His son wouldn't grow up in the swamp, wouldn't be a part of the cult.

Instead, his son would grow up in Villejeune, where Phillips could watch him, study him.

He had carefully chosen Craig and Barbara Sheffield to be the parents of his son, certain that they would be able to give the child every advantage. They would raise his son outside the swamp, away from the ignorance and superstition of its denizens.

Away from the other children like him.

So he'd taken their baby, replacing it with his own, but out of his own peculiar morality—and perhaps an instinctive sense that the Circle of children should always remain incomplete—he'd seen to it that the Sheffields' little girl didn't grow up in the swamp, either.

She would grow up in Atlanta, and though he wouldn't be able to keep as close track of her as he might have liked, still he would be able to find out what he needed to know.

Those two children, growing up in the normal world, would provide him with yet more knowledge.

But Carl Anderson had let his son bring the Sheffields' daughter back to Villejeune.

And now it was all coming apart.

The Circle, completed, was discovering the truth.

Even before Fred Childress had called him today and told him of Craig and Barbara Sheffield's visit, he'd known that it was time to leave.

But it was all right—there were other places he could go, other places he could find where there would be babies available to him. He could begin again.

But until he could find that place, he would need enough of the hormone to keep himself young, to stave off the ravages of his own mortality.

He moved into the nursery, ignoring Lavinia Carter, and took the bottle from the IV rack above the crib in which Amelie Coulton's baby lay, its eyes staring up at him, almost as if it knew what was happening to it.

Then he moved to Jenny Sheffield's bed. Jenny, too, was awake, and she shrank away from him as he approached, her eyes suspicious.

"I want to go home," she said. "I'm not sick, and I want my mother."

Phillips replaced the bottle that was attached to the tube in Jenny's chest with a new one, then looked coldly down at the little girl.

"You're not going to go home, Jenny," he said. "You're sick. You're very sick, and tonight I'm afraid you're going to die."

Leaving Jenny staring after him, her eyes wide with terror, he turned and left the room.

———

Barbara and Craig listened numbly as Ted Anderson told them what had happened. "I don't know what happened to the kids," he finished. "Kelly brought the tour boat back, and a little while later Michael showed up with the baby. And then they just disappeared. We don't know where they went, or why. No one even saw them go."

Barbara sank down onto a wooden bench on which Mary Anderson, called out to the tour headquarters an hour ago, was sitting. She saw Tim Kitteridge working his way through the crowd toward them, and tried to stand up to meet him, but couldn't.

"I'm sorry about this, Craig," he said, then turned to Barbara. "I'm sure the kids are all right," he went on. "God knows, they seem to know the swamp better than anyone else. We'll find them."

"You'd better find Warren Phillips, too," Craig broke in. "It wasn't the kidnapping that brought us out here, Tim. We were just at the cemetery, and something's very wrong around here. Neither of our daughters' bodies is in its crypt."

Kitteridge stared at him blankly. "What the hell—"

"It's Warren Phillips!" Barbara blurted, her voice ragged with the beginnings of hysteria. "He took Sharon, and he took Jenny, too! They didn't die! They never died at all! He's doing something with children! That's why Carl took that poor baby!"

The color drained out of Mary Anderson's face. "You mean Kelly—"

Barbara nodded. "It's the only thing that makes sense. Michael's birth certificate was forged, too. For some reason, Warren Phillips is taking babies, and he's been doing it for years!" Her pent-up emotions spilling over, she collapsed against Mary Anderson. "What are we going to do?" she sobbed. "What has he done to them?"

Kitteridge, still uncertain about what Barbara meant, turned to Craig. "Can you tell me what this is all about?"

As calmly as he could, Craig tried to explain to the police chief what first Barbara, and then the two of them, had discovered that morning. "We don't have any idea what it's all about," he finished. "But we know that there seem to be a lot of men around here who don't look nearly as old as they are. I'm talking about men who don't seem to have aged a day in the last fifteen or twenty years." He ticked off half a dozen names. When he came to Carl Anderson's, Kitteridge suddenly stopped him.

"Carl had changed this morning," he said. "According to Ted, he'd gotten old overnight. I mean, really old. When Ted saw him this morning, he looked like he was ready to die."

Suddenly, for the first time in weeks, he remembered George Coulton. George Coulton, whose body—if it was his body—even Amelie had been unable to identify.

He warn't that old, she had said. *He warn't much older'n me.*

But the body—the body he was certain in his own mind *was* George Coulton—had looked at least eighty, maybe even older.

"What the hell is going on around here?" he said almost under his breath. "It sounds like Phillips must have found the fountain of youth or something."

In Craig Sheffield's mind it all came together. "No," he said. "It's worse. He's found out how to take the youth away from our children and sell it to his friends. That's what he needs the babies for. To take something out of them and use it himself." Suddenly he remembered one other name, a name he'd left off the list he'd just recited to Tim Kitteridge.

"Where's Judd Duval?"

Kitteridge looked at him blankly. "He's in the swamp," he said. "He's looking for Carl Anderson and the kids."

Craig was silent for a moment. Then, his voice hollow, he said, "You'd better hope he doesn't find them."

As dusk began to settle over the swamp, Judd Duval felt the first icy fingers of fear brush against him, making the hairs on the back of his neck rise up and his skin crawl as if tiny insects were creeping into his pores. He'd been in the swamp most of the afternoon, and as the day had worn on, an intangible sense of impending danger had come over him. Part of it, he knew, was simply the swamp itself. Despite having lived in it all his life, his fear of it seemed to grow steadily, and today he felt its thousands of eyes watching him from every direction.

Yet no matter where he looked, he saw nothing.

Nothing except the moss-laden trees, the twisting vines, the black impenetrable water.

And the creatures.

Water moccasins slithered silently through the waterways, leaving only the faintest ripples behind them, and the ever-present alligators and crocodiles basked in the mud, their cold, glittering eyes seeming to fix hungrily on him as he passed.

An hour ago he'd wound his way through the swamp rats' scattered settlement, and found a difference there, too.

The houses had seemed deserted, with no women sitting on their porches, no children playing at their feet.

He'd seen no men mending their fishnets or patching their boats.

Yet he'd sensed their presence inside the houses, felt them watching him.

It was as if they knew something, were hiding from some unseen danger that, though invisible, lay like a palpable force over the wetlands this afternoon.

Now, as the light began to fade, Judd found himself staring at a small island that loomed ahead of him. A single dying pine tree rose up out of a thicket of undergrowth, its branches silhouetted against the reddening sky like beckoning arms. Judd slowed his boat, letting it drift forward on the slow-moving current until the prow scraped against the bottom.

Judd's eyes left the tree, scanning the soft land along the shore line.

Reeds were broken, and footprints showed clearly in the mud.

Footprints that led toward the thicket around the soaring pine.

His heartbeat quickening, his sense of dread gathering around him like the cloak of darkness that was falling over the swamp, Judd got out of the boat and followed the tracks.

He came to the tangle of brush around the pine tree and paused, his skin prickling. Every nerve fiber within him sensed that something vile was hidden within those bushes.

A memory flashed into his mind, an image of the body in the swamp, to which Amelie Coulton had guided him.

He pushed the memory aside and thrust himself into the dense foliage, forcing the branches aside.

And saw Carl Anderson's body, stretched out on its back, already crawling with insects. A vulture, perched on Carl's face, one of his eyeballs clutched in its beak, screamed with indignation at the interruption of its feast, then leaped upward, its wings beating as it scrambled into the sky.

Judd stared at the carnage that had been Carl Anderson's chest, torn open, congealing blood filling the cavity with a reddish brown ooze.

He gazed at the ruin of Carl's face, the eyes torn from their now empty sockets, only a few remaining scraps of skin still clinging to the bones of the old man's skull.

Knowing now the truth of the danger he sensed, Judd backed away, then turned and fled to the safety of his boat. Starting the engine, he pulled away from the island, the image of the defiled corpse still fresh in his mind.

He turned the boat homeward, intent only on reaching his cabin, where, perhaps, he could lock the doors and windows against the terrible fear that was building within him. But even as he left the island where Carl Anderson lay, his panic began to peak, for moving through the gathering darkness, there were boats.

Not boats filled with the other men who had come out with him to search for Carl Anderson's body.

Boats filled with children.

Strange, silent children, their eyes staring straight ahead, as if they were following some invisible beacon that only they could see.

As they passed him, Judd Duval's heart began to pound, and an icy knot of pure terror took form in his belly, spreading slowly outward, threatening to paralyze him.

Only when the last of the boats had finally passed did he start the engine of his own skiff and turn the other way, intent only on getting away from those mute, menacing children with their empty eyes.

———

Barbara Sheffield felt her frustration reaching the breaking point. All afternoon she had tried to convince Tim Kitteridge that he should be searching Warren Phillips's office—his house—any-place where they might be able to find proof of what she was cer-tain he had done.

But the chief had been adamant. "I can't do it, Mrs. Sheffield," he'd told her only half an hour ago, with a patronizing tone of long-suffering forbearance in his voice that had made Barbara want to slap him. "Right now I have other things to worry about. According to your own son, there's a body somewhere in the swamp, and now we've got those two kids missing as well. When we've taken care of that, I'll start looking into Warren Phillips."

What he hadn't told her was that he also had nothing with which to justify a search of Warren Phillips's premises. Until he'd had an expert study the birth certificates that Barbara and Craig Sheffield claimed were forged—and who might give him some evidence that Phillips had been the forger—he couldn't even go to a judge for a search warrant. And despite the pleas of the Sheffields, he wasn't about to commit himself to an illegal search of anything. That, he was certain, would leave him defending himself against a lawsuit for the rest of his career.

But when Carl Anderson's body was found, it might be a different story. For if Carl looked as Kelly and Michael—and even Carl's own son—said he did, Kitteridge would have sufficient reason to talk to Phillips about what condition he might have been treating Carl for, and what drugs he had administered. But until the body was found, he had only secondhand impressions of Carl's condition.

"Does he really expect us just to wait here?" Barbara demanded of Craig as night began to gather over the swamp.

Craig, no less frustrated than his wife, sighed heavily. "I wish I could tell you there's something else we can do, but he's right. What we think we know just doesn't matter, honey. Not to the law. He's only protecting himself, and if it weren't our own children involved, I'd have to agree with him. Two empty crypts and a couple of birth certificates we don't think are real just isn't enough. But when Carl Anderson's body turns up—"

"*If* it turns up!" Barbara interrupted him, her voice quavering. "And what about Michael and Kelly? Where would they have gone? And why?"

Craig Sheffield could only shrug helplessly. But if another hour passed and the searchers had still turned up nothing, then despite the objections of Tim Kitteridge, he and Ted Anderson intended to join the search.

Not that they had much hope of finding anything—the memory of his last search of the swamp was still all too fresh for him to delude himself about that—but at least he would be doing something.

And doing something, at this point, would be better than waiting.

Waiting and wondering.

Michael rose from the sagging sofa and went to the door.

Though it was dark out now, he couldn't remember the sunset at all. Indeed, the afternoon seemed to have disappeared, passing without a trace, as Clarey's silent song had filled his mind.

But this time—unlike those days and nights in the swamp when he'd lost track of time, and been left with nothing more than empty gaps of hours gone from his life—he knew what had happened.

The memories were sharp and clear.

Once more he'd seen the man who until today had come to him only in his dreams, or haunted him in the mirror as he gazed at his own image.

But now he understood that it was not just one man he'd seen, but many.

Every man who had partaken of his youth had been in those dreams, but the visions he had seen of them since he was a child were as they truly were, stripped of their masks of stolen youth.

Old men, ravaged not only by time, but by the evil that had consumed them, preserving their bodies even as it rotted their souls.

This afternoon he had seen them again, and this time he'd seen them for what they were, recognized clearly the corruption within them.

But today he felt no fear of them. Indeed, he felt their own fear, sensed their terror, saw them cowering away from him, knowing he was there, knowing what he intended to do.

And knowing they had nothing left of their own with which to defend themselves.

In each of them he had recognized tiny fragments of his own

being, fragments that had reposed within them for years, waiting for him to claim them. And now the time was at hand.

Turning away from the darkness outside, Michael went back into Clarey's house.

The old woman's eyes opened. It was fully dark now, and she lifted herself out of her chair, feeling once more the stiffness of her years. With trembling fingers she struck a match and lit the wick of the oil lamp on the table. A soft glow of light diffused the darkness of the room, and Jonas Cox, dozing on the sofa next to Kelly Anderson, stirred at the sudden light. Clarey went to the stove, opening the door to poke at the embers glowing within, and added a couple of sticks of wood from the pile on the floor next to the stove, then put a kettle of water on the burner. As the water heated, and she added coffee grounds to the kettle, she turned to the three teenagers, who were watching her uncertainly.

Kelly still sat on the sofa, her face pale even in the warm lamp-light, her eyes expressionless.

Next to her was Jonas Cox, fully awake now, his body as tense as a ferret's, ready to dart away at the first hint of danger.

Michael was near the door, and as Clarey's ancient eyes fixed on him, she could see the difference in him, the change that had taken place inside him when he'd come to her, and since then, during the long hours of her summoning of the Circle.

"They be comin' now," she said, knowing he would understand her words. "The children be comin'. They be nearby."

She went back to the stove and poured the steaming brew from the kettle into four cups, handing one of them to each of the children. As if they knew that the night ahead might be long, they drained the thick mugs of the bitter liquid and felt its heat spread through their bodies.

At last, when the kettle on the stove was empty, Clarey turned the lamp so that the wick burned low, leaving nothing more than a faint glow to soften the shadows in the corners of the room.

"It be time," she said.

She went out to the porch, then waited while first Kelly and then Jonas Cox climbed into the waiting boat. Finally Michael helped her down the ladder, and she carefully seated herself in the small skiff.

As Jonas Cox dipped the oars into the water, Michael cast loose the line and stepped into the boat. It drifted out into the quiet lagoon.

The moon began to rise as the skiff moved slowly across the water, disappearing at last into the twisting channels, joining the flotilla that was already silently converging on the small island on which stood an altar in the center of a clearing.

———

Clarey Lambert watched the candles on the altar. They burned bright, their flames steady in the stillness of the night. She was alone now, the Circle of children departed, following Michael as he led them through the darkness.

She knew where they were going and what they were going to do, but she chose not to think about it. Rather, she preferred to sit by herself, close to the glowing embers of the bonfire, feeling its warmth penetrate the chill in her ancient bones in a way that the heat from the sun never could.

Tonight, she knew, was the night she would die.

But not yet.

Not until the last of the candles went out, not until the eyes of the dolls on the altar flooded with tears and she knew that all the children were whole again.

Only then would she let go of the life within her, the life she had clung to with a will that defied the vows of the Dark Man, who had sworn to live forever.

Clarey Lambert would outlive him, and laugh at him when she met him beyond the grave.

Tonight was a night she had long dreamed of, long prayed for. In her dreams she had always been there to watch the Dark Man die, watch him suffer as he had made the children suffer. But tonight, when at last the time had come, she found her hatred of him draining away, replaced by a pity she didn't quite understand.

So she had stayed by herself on the island, content to tend the fire, certain in her own mind that when the time came for the Dark Man to die, she would know about it.

Just as she would know when each of the children regained his soul.

A faint sound drifted to Clarey's ears, interrupting her reverie.

Barely audible at first, it slowly rose above the steady drone of the tiny night creatures until it filled the night with a scream of pent-up rage, a rising wall of sound that swept across the swamp, finally culminating in a shriek of anguish that shook Clarey's body like a physical blow.

The end, Clarey knew, was finally beginning.

Fred Childress had left the mortuary immediately after calling Warren Phillips. He'd gone home to the empty house he'd lived alone in ever since his wife had died fifteen years ago. All afternoon he'd paced nervously around the house, every instinct in him telling him to pack a few clothes into a suitcase and drive away from Villejeune.

But he knew he couldn't, for if he left Villejeune, he would also leave Warren Phillips and the magic injections that had kept him young for nearly twenty years.

Without the injections . . .

He put the thought out of his mind, remembering the sight of George Coulton's body when he'd taken it from the morgue to inter in one of the crypts in the cemetery.

"That's you, Fred," Warren Phillips had told him. "That's you, without the shots I give you."

Fred Childress had said nothing, but for the first time he'd truly understood what would happen to him without Warren Phillips. So he wouldn't leave town. He would do as Phillips had told him, saying nothing, admitting nothing about the empty tombs in the Sheffields' mausoleum.

And it would be all right.

Warren Phillips would take care of him—him, and Orrin Hatfield, and Judd Duval, all of them—just as he had for nearly two
decades.

But as night began to fall, he'd grown increasingly nervous. His
skin had begun to crawl, as if thousands of ants were creeping over
his body, and he'd begun to imagine that he heard sounds outside
in the night.

Sounds of children, coming out of the darkness, creeping up
from the depths of the swamp, surrounding his house.

Watching him through his uncurtained windows.

He scurried around the house, turning off all the lights, and
then sat in the darkness, telling himself that he was only imagining
the demons that filled the night.

And then he heard the howling outside the door.

He froze, fear drying his mouth and clutching at his belly.

The howl came again, rising out of the marshes, reaching out
to him, and Fred Childress, unable to resist the keening in the
night, moved toward the door.

Against his will, he opened it.

He saw nothing for a split second, but then there was movement
in the darkness, shadows beginning to move out of the pine trees.

Fred Childress's heart began to pound once more as he saw the
children emerge from the trees.

There were five of them, two of whom Fred recognized.

Quint and Tammy-Jo Millard, their hands intertwined, stopped
at the bottom of the steps to his porch, gazing up at him.

Their empty eyes glittered coldly in the moonlight.

As the other three children joined them, and Fred Childress's
fear blossomed into panic, he felt a white-hot surge of adrenaline
race through him.

For he knew what they wanted from him.

They wanted what was theirs.

They wanted the youth he'd taken from them.

Tonight, they intended to have it.

Fred Childress's fear grew into abject terror as he felt the
shadow of death begin to pass over his soul.

He felt them reaching out to him with their minds, boring into him, as if examining every corner of his being. And then grasping something deep within him.

Grasping it, and tearing it loose.

Fred screamed as a searing pain passed through his chest. The agony grew, as if a hot knife had been plunged into him, and he could feel its heat radiating through his body, slowly destroying him.

He raised his hands to his face and felt a rough scaliness on the folds of his skin.

The folds that had not been there only a few seconds ago, before he'd opened the door to face the children.

The children moved closer, and though Fred Childress tried to back away, tried to retreat into the shelter of his house, his body refused to obey his mind.

He felt the hands of the children on him now, pulling him off his porch, clutching at him, tearing at him.

They lifted him up, his quickly weakening body no longer able to resist at all, and carried him off into the night.

They came at last to the edge of the swamp, where they hurled the dying man to the ground.

Quint Millard threw himself on the twitching ruin of the undertaker, his strong hands tearing at the old man's chest, ripping it open to seize the shrunken vestige of a gland that was all but lost within the desiccating tissues of Childress's lungs.

Ripping a fragment of it away, Quint passed the small mass of tissue to the waiting hands of the other children.

As Fred Childress's body finally died, the five children felt an unfamiliar warmth pass into their bodies.

And felt tears form in their eyes.

Tammy-Jo Millard, her eyes glistening, put her arms around Quint. "I'm scared," she whispered. "I ain't never been so scared in my life. I feel like maybe I be dyin'!"

Quint held his wife close. "Not dyin'," he whispered. "Not dyin' at all. We're alive. We're alive, and we're free."

On the island where Clarey Lambert waited, five of the candles on the altar were suddenly snuffed out, though not a breath of air had moved in the night.

And the eyes of five of the dolls overflowed with tears.

"Nothing," Marty Templar said as he stepped out of the boat into the knot of people clustered on the dock at the tour headquarters. "All I could find was a bunch of swamp rats, and you know how they are—they'd as soon spit at you as give you the time of day."

Tim Kitteridge nodded grimly, wondering why the swamp rats clung so tenaciously to their own ignorance. But if they wouldn't talk, there wasn't anything he could do about it. "What about Judd Duval?" he asked. "Did you see him?"

Templar shook his head. "Not a trace. I even swung by his house a while ago, but no one's there. You ask me, we've got one more person to start lookin' for."

A muted howl erupted out of the darkness, then began to build into a chorus of fury that chilled Kitteridge's blood. The hair on the back of his neck rising, he spoke to Marty Templar, though his eyes searched the night for the source of the baleful din. "Jesus," he whispered. "What the hell is that?"

Templar said nothing, his own skin prickling with goose bumps.

"Hounds," Ted Anderson breathed. "It sounds like the hounds of Hell, baying."

As quickly as it had come, the clamor died away, and for a moment there was a deathly silence over the wilderness.

Then another scream rose, this one driven by pain and agony, cutting through the night like a ripping blade.

As the screams built, the swamp came alive with the wingbeats of birds bursting out of the trees into the air and insects swarming up from the water's surface.

The water itself began to roil as the basking alligators and crocodiles caught the first faint scent of blood spreading through the channels and drifting on the wind. Coming fully awake, they slid off the muddy banks, their tails lashing furiously as they raced toward the source of the pungent aroma.

More screams filled the night.

"Dear God," Barbara Sheffield breathed. "What is it? What's happening out there?"

But there was no answer as everyone on the dock listened to the still-mounting cries of anguish.

———

Judd Duval no longer knew where he was nor what time it was, for since darkness had gathered around him and he'd fled toward the shelter of his cabin, something had happened to him.

Something he didn't understand.

His mind had played tricks on him.

He'd moved through the waterways, certain that just around the next bend he would find his shack and refuge from the fear that was engulfing him.

Yet as he rounded each familiar landmark, the swamp seemed to change before his very eyes, and instead of seeing the shelter of his house, he saw only another of the children—the empty-eyed, silently staring children of the swamp—gazing steadily at him.

Watching him, as if they were expecting him.

At first, each time he saw one of them he brought his boat to a stop, staring back at the child, challenging it.

But each time the child—never blinking—moved toward him, and Judd's nerve broke. Gunning his engine, he steered into one of the narrow channels, heedless of where he was going, determined only to get away from those dead, hypnotic eyes.

At last, though, he came to his cabin, and the fear began to ebb out of him as he hurried toward the safety of his home. But as he drew closer, he felt the children's presence yet again, felt their cold eyes reaching out to him, felt his skin crawling with their unseen gaze.

Then the howling began, the eerie baying that shattered what was left of his courage. The sound seemed to come from everywhere, and now, as his eyes searched the darkness, he could see them once more.

Everywhere he turned, the wailing furies stood.

He froze, watching the children, his eyes darting from one of them to another, panic growing inside him like a wild beast, gnawing at him, sapping his strength.

Then, coming toward him out of the darkness, he recognized Jonas Cox. The boy's face seemed to hang in front of Judd, staring at him, looming just beyond his reach.

But Jonas's eyes had changed. Their empty gaze had taken on a glowing fury, and they bored into him, accusing him, condemning him.

Judd tried to look away, but it made no difference where he turned; Jonas seemed to be everywhere, surrounding him.

Finally Judd closed his eyes, determined to face the vision no more, but Jonas's image stayed with him.

And then, as Judd's skin crawled with an icy chill of terror, Jonas reached out to him, touching him.

Judd tried to shrink away from the boy's touch, but Jonas's fingers somehow reached inside him, penetrating him, twisting and turning within him, as if searching for something.

And finally, in the center of his chest, he felt a burst of blinding pain, a pain that shot outward, paralyzing him, then twisting his muscles into knots that threatened to snap every bone in his body.

A moment later he felt the rest of the children falling upon him, tearing at him, and his mind began to close down so that all he was aware of was the pain, an agony that crept into every cell of his body.

He felt as if he were being tortured with millions of tiny needles, each of them twisting within him, jabbing at him, destroying him.

He could feel his body beginning to decay as his cells began to die.

An image of Carl Anderson came into his mind—his chest torn open, a vulture perched upon his skull as it plucked his eyes from their sockets.

As he felt the same thing happening to himself, as he under-

stood with a terrible clarity the reason for his death, the last of his
will to resist crumbled within him.

The six children led by Jonas Cox pulled Judd Duval's body
from his boat and began tearing it to pieces, dropping fragments of
it into the water, to be devoured by the gathering alligators and
crocodiles. Their cries of rage began to die away as they tore their
souls from Judd Duval's dying corpse, and as tears began to fill
their eyes, they backed away, numbed by what they had done.

And yet, for the first time in their lives, they felt whole.

———

On the island where Clarey Lambert waited, six more candles
blinked out, and six more of the dolls began to weep. . . .

31

Warren Phillips had been working steadily, reducing the last of the fluid he'd extracted from the thymus glands of the four children in the nursery into the life-giving element that would keep his body alive and vital.

With the three small vials he was now placing into his medical bag, he would be safe for several weeks, weeks he would use to find a place to continue his work, a place where he was unknown.

Yes, the future was bright, for everywhere in the world he would find people willing to pay anything for the magic he had discovered in newborn children.

And there were places, he knew, where babies were cheap, where children were born every day who could be bought for a few dollars.

A few dollars, without questions of the purchaser or his motives.

Next time he wouldn't bother to keep the children alive.

Next time he would simply milk them for a year or two and then destroy them. That, at least, was something he'd learned here in Villejeune. If he left them alive, they had to be dealt with.

But after tonight, after he was gone, it would no longer be his problem to deal with.

Dispassionately, he thought about those children, wondered

what might happen to them when he was gone and they no longer had the Dark Man as a center for their empty lives.

He suspected their minds might begin to shatter, as Kelly Anderson's had only a month ago. And if they did—

He froze as a feral howl of rage echoed through the subterranean chambers carved out of the limestone beneath his house.

As a second howl rose, he hurried from the laboratory, to the foot of the stairs leading upward.

There, Lavinia Carter, her face ashen and her body trembling with fear, gazed upward. Phillips shoved her out of the way. "The children in the nursery," he snapped. "Get rid of them!"

Without waiting to see if his order would be obeyed, Phillips mounted the stairs, pausing in the dimly lit entry hall. Outside, the night was filled with what sounded like the howling of wolves. Phillips knew it was not.

It was the children.

The children who belonged to him.

Black fury rose within him. *He* controlled them; *he* commanded them!

Consumed with rage, Warren Phillips threw open the front door of his house.

The scene before him made his blood run cold.

The children stood in a semicircle, their hands intertwined, their empty eyes fixed on him.

In the center of the semicircle, alone, stood Michael Sheffield.

His son.

The deathly howling of the children slowly died away as they saw the Dark Man standing before them.

But tonight he wore no mask, and they saw him clearly.

They began to move, edging forward, the fear he had always seen in their faces suddenly gone, replaced with something else.

Hunger.

Hunger, and hatred.

The semicircle spread outward, leaving him with no retreat but the house itself. But when Phillips glanced over his shoulder, he saw more of the silently menacing children, crowded into the foyer of his house, cutting him off from any possible escape. They moved forward, forcing him out into the darkness of the night, then joined hands with the others. The Circle was complete.

In its center, frozen with terror, stood Warren Phillips.

The Dark Man.

Michael Sheffield moved toward Phillips, pausing in front of him.

The eyes of the father and the son met.

"We want only what is ours," Michael said quietly.

As an all-consuming fear filled Warren Phillips, Michael Sheffield drew a knife from his belt.

He raised it high, its polished blade glinting brightly in the moonlight.

Then, just as the knife began to descend toward the Dark Man's throat, Michael stopped.

The knife hovered a few inches from the Dark Man's neck.

"Do it," Phillips said, the words rasping in his throat as his numbed mind slowly realized why Michael had stopped.

The fear—the all-consuming fear that had seized him only a few minutes ago—had drained his body of the hormones that had kept him alive so long.

Already he could feel the creeping aches in his joints, the congestion in his lungs.

As he realized what was happening to him, the fear rose up in him again, speeding his metabolism, accelerating the decay that was raging through his body.

He was dying from within, and he knew how painful it would be, for he had long ago determined that the last of the artificially supported organs to fail would be the heart, and the lungs.

And the brain.

As his skeleton turned brittle and began to collapse, he would be aware of what was happening to him.

As his liver and kidneys began to fail, and poisons began to rage through his body, he would feel excruciating agonies, agonies even the strongest of drugs would be unable to alleviate.

If he were lucky, he would go into shock, his brain refusing to accept the pain his body was feeling.

If he were unlucky . . .

"Please," he begged. "Don't let it happen this way. Kill me. Kill me now."

But Michael Sheffield turned away, and in the silence of the night he, and Kelly, and all the rest of his children, watched as the Dark Man began to die.

As his flesh began to putrefy, and his face collapsed into the grotesque visage of death that had haunted Kelly for so long, a glowing warmth began to spread through her body.

As he collapsed to the ground, writhing in the final agonies of death, Kelly's eyes, dry since the first few days of her life, moistened, at last overflowing.

Bursting with renewed life, Kelly Anderson joyfully let her tears flow.

———

Amelie Coulton crept out onto the porch of her shack. The moon was high, and the swamp was illuminated with a faint silvery light that made the water glint and the shadows dance like black dervishes that might swallow you up if you brushed too close to them.

But tonight Amelie felt no fear of the shadows, for there was something different about this night. It wasn't like the other nights, the nights when everyone in the swamp sensed danger in the air and stayed indoors, unwilling to venture out into the waterways, certain that some evil they didn't quite understand lurked in the shadows, waiting for them.

Those were the Dark Man's nights, the nights when the black-clad being was in the swamp, working his magic on the children who served him.

But tonight she hadn't sensed his presence at all, even when she'd looked out her window and seen boats slip silently by her shack, boats rowed by the Dark Man's children, making their way through the darkness toward some unknown place.

Then had come the howlings that had rent the night over and over again, rising up first from one place, and then from another.

The screams of demons were what they had sounded like to

Amelie, but for some reason she didn't understand, the sounds that should have chilled her blood had comforted her instead.

The Devil, that's who Amelie had been taught the Dark Man was. Even now, in the silence that followed the unearthly howls that had finally died completely away, she could hear her mother's voice: "He be out there, Amelie. He takes them when they's babies, and he changes 'em. You stay inside, hear? You go out on his night, and he be takin' you, too!"

But Amelie didn't believe in the Dark Man anymore, for in her own mind she knew he wasn't the Devil at all.

He was Dr. Phillips.

And the night she'd listened to old Clarey Lambert talking to Kelly Anderson and Michael Sheffield, she'd known what had happened to her baby.

Dr. Phillips had taken him, hiding him, to do to him what he'd done to the other children.

But tonight, as darkness gathered and the children began to move, Amelie somehow knew what they were going to do.

And so she waited in the silence, until, in the distance, she heard the soft putting of an outboard motor.

Her body tensed and her eyes strained in the darkness as a boat emerged from a narrow channel.

Her heart began to pound as the boat bumped gently into the rotting pilings that supported her house and Michael Sheffield stood up.

From Lavinia Carter's arms he took a tiny baby boy, wrapped in a blue blanket, and held it up to Amelie.

"We brought him home," Michael said as Amelie took her son from him.

Amelie's eyes flooded with tears. "An' he be all right?" she asked, her voice choked.

From her place on the center bench of the boat, where she sat next to her sister Kelly, whose arm was wrapped protectively around her, Jenny Sheffield answered her. "He's fine," she said. "He's a good baby. He never cried at all until tonight."

Amelie's breath caught, and then her eyes shifted to Lavinia Carter. "It's you who's been lookin' after him?"

Lavinia nodded silently, her face reflecting all the misery she was feeling over what she had done for the Dark Man.

Amelie hesitated, then spoke again. "Then mebbe you better stay with me," she said. "It be lonely out here, an' I don't hardly know what I'm s'posed to do with him."

Lavinia's face lit up in the moonlight, and she reached up to take Amelie's extended hand. A moment later, as the boat started away from Amelie Coulton's tiny cabin, her lips moved, forming words she would never be able to utter.

"Thank you . . ."

Michael and Kelly, whose arm still held her little sister close, waved wordlessly to her as they drifted away into the night.

Barbara Sheffield stood silently on the dock, Craig's arm around her. A few feet away Mary and Ted Anderson clung together, too.

Both couples waited in the strange silence that had fallen over the swamp.

They were alone now, for Tim Kitteridge and all the others who had been at the tour headquarters had left half an hour ago, searching for the source of the unearthly screams that had struck terror into each of their souls.

They knew neither for what they were looking nor where they might find it. But they were certain that whatever it was, it was something none of them was going to want to face.

Some evil, they knew, had met its end in the swamp that night.

The Andersons and the Sheffields, though, had refused to go.

"They'll come back," Barbara had said, speaking for all of them. "I know our children will come back here, and we're going to be here waiting for them."

And so the others had left, and they had remained, and the waiting had begun.

Now, at last, they heard the sound of a boat approaching, and their breathing all but stopped as they waited for it to appear.

It was nothing more than a shadow at first, moving across the lagoon, a dark form all but invisible in the night.

It began to take shape, emerging finally from the darkness into the bright light of the moon, and they instantly recognized the three people in it.

Their children.

But changed, somehow, for as the boat drew near, all four parents could feel the difference.

Somehow, in a way they weren't certain they would ever understand, Kelly and Michael were not the same as they had been this morning.

It was as if they, like the boat in which they rode, had just emerged from a lifetime of darkness.

As they gathered their children into their arms, Mary Anderson and Barbara Sheffield heard their children cry for the first time.

And their children's tears filled their souls with joy.

EPILOGUE

On the island at the far edge of the swamp, the last candles on the altar flickered out, the last of the dolls began to weep.

Clarey Lambert watched them for a moment, a soft smile lighting up the weathered planes of her face. And then, as the moon reached its zenith and the night began to wane, Clarey laid her body on the ground and let herself rest.

At last, after all the years of struggle, she closed her eyes for the last time and surrendered herself to the welcome darkness.